GW00382847

A Feast of Stories

CLARE FRANCIS is the author of six internationally bestselling novels, *Night Sky, Red Crystal, Wolf Winter, Requiem, Deceit* and *Betrayal*. Before these, she wrote three non-fiction books about her voyages across the oceans of the world, *Come Hell or High Water, Come Wind or Weather*, and *The Commanding Sea*. She first had M.E. as a teenager and then recovered until 1985 when she became ill again. She was actively involved in setting up Action for M.E. and was their President from 1988 to 1995.

ONDINE UPTON worked in publishing before developing M.E. seven years ago. Over the last three years, she has gradually recovered and celebrated this by travelling solo through South America for a year, where she had the idea for this book. Now thirty-five, she works part-time in charity marketing. She lives in London with her partner, James Park, and looks forward to a future in which M.E. plays a smaller role in her life.

ACTION FOR M.E. is national charity with over eight thousand members. It provides information and support services to people with M.E. (Myalgic Encephalomyelitis) as well as to their families and friends. It campaigns for a change in attitude towards this debilitating illness and funds urgently needed research into its causes and possible treatments. With an estimated hundred and fifty thousand people suffering from M.E. in the U.K., of which twenty-four thousand are children, the need for funds and support is greater than ever.

Action for M.E.
PO Box 1302
Wells
Somerset BA5 2WE
Tel. 01749 670799

A Feast of Stories

EDITED BY

CLARE FRANCIS

AND

ONDINE UPTON

MACMILLAN

First published 1996 by Macmillan

and simultaneously by Pan Books
imprints of Macmillan General Books
25 Eccleston Place
London SW1W 9NF
and Basingstoke

Associated companies throughout the world

ISBN 0 333 65340 8

1 3 5 7 9 8 6 4 2

A CIP catalogue record for this book is available from
the British Library

Phototypeset by Intype London Ltd
Printed by Mackays of Chatham PLC, Chatham, Kent

*For everyone who has M.E. and
those who care for them*

Acknowledgements

The first, and biggest, thank you must go to all the authors who have so generously given us their favourite stories. This is their book and their support has been wonderful.

We would also like to thank: Paddy Masefield and Luke Merchant for generously allowing us to include their account of what it is really like to have M.E.; Jo Odgers, our assistant editor, for charming agents, chasing text and liaising with publishers; Nicky Maitlis, for her advice and help; and Suzanne Baboneau and Ian Chapman at Macmillan, who enthusiastically backed the project from the beginning.

I should like to include a personal thank you to everyone who has helped me while I have had M.E., to all my friends and family, but most especially to my partner, James Park, for being so understanding and long-suffering, ready with a shoulder to cry on or to rage against in the bleakest moments, and for sharing my triumphs as I gradually got better. (Ondine.)

As well as the authors, we would like to thank their agents and publishers who have made this collection possible. Copyright acknowledgements for each story are included at the end of this book.

Contents

CONTENTS

CONTENTS

Introduction

Having lost some popularity to the novel over the last few decades, the short story is enjoying a welcome renaissance. And what better celebration of this colourful and energetic form could there be than a collection of stories by twenty-eight of Britain's most widely read authors? Stories, moreover, chosen by the authors themselves, making this an anthology of favourites in every sense of the word. Such a collection is a rarity. It has been made possible only by the great generosity of the authors, both in agreeing to provide the stories and in donating their royalties to Action for M.E.

Every good cause is a deserving one, of course, but sometimes a cause is so seriously underfunded that it merits special consideration, and this is the case with M.E.

Ten years ago few people had heard of M.E. (its full name is myalgic encephalomyelitis – not the most pronounceable of names – though it is also known, not entirely appropriately, as post viral fatigue syndrome). To all intents and purposes it used to be a non-disease, denied either medical or state recognition; and its victims, already struggling with a devastating and debilitating illness, had to endure widespread misdiagnosis and misunderstanding, aggravated by a total absence of information and support.

Unbelievable though it seems now, many were accused of malingering or being unable to cope with life, and told to pull themselves together. For people who had to struggle even to climb the stairs, who had been forced to give up work and social life, who could no longer walk their children to school, such suggestions added much unnecessary insult to injury.

Nowadays almost everyone has heard of M.E.: indeed, there are few people who don't have a friend or relative who suffers from the illness. It is thought that at least a hundred and fifty thousand people in the UK have M.E. (a figure which is likely to prove a significant underestimate). Sufferers come from every walk of life, and all age groups. Twenty-six thousand are children.

People are surprised to hear that children get M.E. One of the many misconceptions about the disease is that it only affects adults. Another, that it only attacks people who are 'overachievers' or who have subjected themselves to undue stress. But you only have to see a previously healthy and contented child who has been struck down by M.E. to realize how misplaced these ideas are. Not only do children from the age of five upwards get M.E., but it strikes them at random, irrespective of background or medical history. For children, M.E. is an especially cruel ordeal: not only are they robbed of schooling and friendships during the most formative years of their lives, but frequently the illness takes a powerful emotional toll. Given early diagnosis and proper advice, children have a better than average chance of recovery; without them, they may be ill for many more years. Some never recover and will have M.E. for life.

It is not generally realized that M.E. can result in

permanent disablement. While some sufferers manage to resume a much modified lifestyle after a long period of convalescence and adjustment – it may be anything from two to ten years – a proportion remain seriously affected for the rest of their lives, often wheelchair- or bed-bound, and are forced to rely on the help of family and carers. Old, young, train drivers, teachers and farmers, housewives and accountants; there are no barriers. And this, to the eternal shame of the media, is the disease they tried to dismiss as 'Yuppie flu'.

I am one of the lucky ones. Though I had M.E. quite badly for several years, I have gradually been able to resume an almost normal life. Not a day passes that I don't count my blessings and think there but for the grace of God . . .

It is hard to explain to people quite how destructive M.E. can be, how it saps not only the mind and body, but the spirit as well. Your muscles are lead-like and painful; the slightest exertion sends you to bed for hours, yet sleep does nothing to alleviate the overwhelming fatigue; your mind wallows through a dark and thickening fog, you feel you are living behind a pane of dark impenetrable glass; you are unable to process information, let alone think in an active sense; you forget the most basic things, you repeat yourself, you are easily confused; light is hurtful to your eyes, sound to your ears; you are permanently cold, even on a hot day; you may have a continuous low-level fever; your digestion gives endless trouble, you lose weight or gain it without reason.

We are taught to fight illness – to think positive, get out and about, exercise as soon as possible – yet the more you fight M.E., the worse it gets. You realize the hard way that the normal rules do not apply. After a time you lose your joy, your ability to laugh, your optimism. You take sick leave, indefinite leave, early retirement, you ask for a year off from your studies, you ask your loved ones for yet more understanding . . . And still you have no idea when the nightmare will end.

And the nightmare is worst of all for those without diagnosis or the most basic information about their illness – still, sad to say, the majority of sufferers in this country – people who are forced to struggle on without emotional or practical support, exposed to the sort of isolation which can so easily bring despair.

Ten years ago Action for M.E. (AfM.E.) was founded by a small group of people determined to change this highly unacceptable situation. AfM.E. is now a fully fledged charity which campaigns for full recognition of M.E. by doctors, health workers and government; which raises money for support services and scientific research; and which offers a wide range of information and practical support to sufferers.

Progress is being made, but it is painfully slow. Both the UK Department of Health and the World Health Organization have recognized M.E.; yet some doctors still maintain that M.E. does not exist. Early diagnosis and informed advice can give a much improved chance of recovery; yet many sufferers are still being left without diagnosis or being misdiagnosed, leading to harmful advice and/or inappropriate treatment. Small-scale research has revealed tantalizing clues to the nature of the disease; yet a chronic shortage of funds means that the research cannot be followed up. AfM.E. has sent out tens of thousands of items of information to people with M.E.; yet without the money to advertise we are unable to reach the many thousands of sufferers who do not yet know of our existence and are therefore unaware of the range of information and support services available to them.

There is still a long way to go.

Action for M.E. is a small charity which achieves a great deal with the limited funds available to it. We hope to build it into a much larger organization, capable of meeting the needs of everyone with M.E., while funding a vigorous research programme.

This book will help us to achieve that aim.

If you want to know more about M.E. or Action for M.E., there is more information at the end of this book.

Young Zaphod Plays It Safe

BY DOUGLAS ADAMS

A large flying craft moved swiftly across the surface of an astoundingly beautiful sea. From mid-morning onwards it plied back and forth in great widening arcs, and at last attracted the attention of the local islanders, a peaceful, seafood loving people who gathered on the beach and squinted up into the blinding sun, trying to see what was there.

Any sophisticated knowledgable person, who had knocked about, seen a few things, would probably have remarked on how much the craft looked like a filing cabinet – a large and recently-burgled filing cabinet lying on its back with its drawers in the air and flying.

The islanders, whose experience was of a different kind, were instead struck by how little it looked like a lobster.

They chattered excitedly about its total lack of claws, its stiff unbendy back, and the fact that it seemed to experience the greatest difficulty staying on the ground. This last feature seemed particularly funny to them. They jumped up and down on the spot a lot to demonstrate to the stupid thing that they themselves found staying on the ground the easiest thing in the world.

But soon this entertainment began to pall for them.

After all, since it was perfectly clear to them that the thing was not a lobster, and since their world was blessed with an abundance of things that were lobsters (a good half a dozen of which were now marching succulently up the beach towards them) they saw no reason to waste any more time on the thing but decided instead to adjourn immediately for a late lobster lunch.

At that exact moment the craft stopped suddenly in mid-air then upended itself and plunged headlong into the ocean with a great crash of spray which sent them shouting into the trees.

When they re-emerged, nervously, a few minutes later, all they were able to see was a smoothly scarred circle of water and a few gulping bubbles.

That's odd, they said to each other between mouthfuls of the best lobster to be had anywhere in the Western Galaxy, that's the second time that's happened in a year.

The craft which wasn't a lobster dived direct to a depth of two hundred feet, and hung there in the heavy blueness, while vast masses of water swayed about it. High above, where the water was magically clear, a brilliant formation of fish flashed away. Below, where the light had difficulty reaching the colour of the water sank to a dark and savage blue.

Here, at two hundred feet, the sun streamed feebly. A large, silk-skinned sea-mammal rolled idly by, inspecting the craft with a kind of half interest, as if it had half expected to find something of this kind round about here, and then it slid on up and away towards the rippling light.

The craft waited here for a minute or two, taking readings, and then descended another hundred feet. At this depth it was becoming seriously dark. After a moment or two the internal lights of the craft shut down, and in the second or so that passed before the main external beams suddenly stabbed out, the only visible light came from a small hazily illuminated pink sign which read The Beeblebrox Salvage and Really Wild Stuff Corporation.

The huge beams switched downwards, catching a vast shoal of silver fish, which swivelled away in silent panic.

In the dim control room which extended in a broad bow from the craft's blunt prow, four heads were gathered round a computer display that was analysing the very, very faint and intermittent signals emanating from deep on the sea-bed.

'That's it,' said the owner of one of the heads finally.

'Can we be quite sure?' said the owner of another of the heads.

'One hundred per cent positive,' replied the owner of the first head.

'You're one hundred per cent positive that the ship which has crashed on the bottom of this ocean is the ship which you said you were one hundred per cent positive could one hundred per cent positively never crash?' said the owner of the two remaining heads. 'Hey,' he put up two of his hands, 'I'm only asking.'

The two officials from the Safety and Civil Reassurance

Administration responded to this with a very cold stare, but the man with the odd, or rather the even number of heads, missed it. He flung himself back on the pilot couch, opened a couple of beers – one for himself and the other also for himself – stuck his feet on the console and said, 'Hey, baby,' through the ultra-glass at a passing fish.

'Mr Beeblebrox—' began the shorter and less reassuring of the two officials in a low voice.

'Yup?' said Zaphod, rapping a suddenly empty can down on some of the more sensitive instruments, 'you ready to dive? Let's go.'

'Mr Beeblebrox, let us make one thing perfectly clear—'

'Yeah let's,' said Zaphod, 'How about this for a start. Why don't you just tell me what's really in this ship.'

'We have told you,' said the official. 'By-products.'

Zaphod exchanged weary glances with himself.

'By-products,' he said. 'By-products of what?'

'Processes,' said the official.

'What processes?'

'Processes that are perfectly safe.'

'Santa Zarquana Voostra!' exclaimed both of Zaphod's heads in chorus. 'So safe that you have to build a zarking fortress ship to take the by-products to the nearest black hole and tip them in! Only it doesn't get there because the pilot does a detour – is this right? – to pick up some lobster . . . ? OK, so the guy is cool, but . . . I mean own up, this is barking time, this is major lunch, this is stool approaching critical mass, this is . . . this is . . . total vocabulary failure!'

'Shut up!' his right head yelled at his left. 'We're flanging!' He got a good calming grip on the remaining beer can.

'Listen, guys,' he resumed after a moment's peace and contemplation. The two officials had said nothing. Conversation at this level was not something to which they felt they could aspire. 'I just want to know,' insisted Zaphod, 'what you're getting me into here.'

He stabbed a finger at the intermittent readings trickling over the computer screen. They meant nothing to him but he didn't like the look of them at all. They were all squiggly with lots of long numbers and things.

'It's breaking up, is that it?' he shouted. 'It's got a hold full of epsilonic radiating aorist rods or something that'll fry this whole space sector for zillions of years back and it's breaking up. Is that the story? Is that what we're going down to find? Am I going to come out of that wreck with even more heads?'

'It cannot possibly be a wreck, Mr Beeblebrox,' insisted the official. 'The ship is guaranteed to be perfectly safe. It cannot possibly break up.'

'Then why are you so keen to go and look at it?'

'We like to look at things that are perfectly safe.'

'Freeeooow!'

'Mr Beeblebrox,' said one official, patiently, 'may I remind you that you have a job to do?'

'Yeah, well maybe I don't feel so keen on doing it all of a sudden. What do you think I am, completely without any moral whatsits, what are they called, those moral things?'

'Scruples?'

'Scruples, thank you, whatsoever? Well?'

The two officials waited calmly. They coughed slightly to help pass the time.

Zaphod sighed a 'what is the world coming to' sort of sigh to absolve himself from all blame, and swung himself round in his seat.

'Ship?' he called.

'Yup?' said the ship.

'Do what I do.'

The ship thought about this for a few milliseconds and then, after double-checking all the seals on its heavy-duty bulkheads, it began slowly, inexorably, in the hazy blaze of its lights, to sink to the lowest depths.

Five hundred feet.

A thousand.

Two thousand.

Here, at a pressure of nearly seventy atmospheres, in the chilling depths where no light reaches, nature keeps its most heated imaginings. Two-foot-long nightmares loomed wildly into the bleaching light, yawned, and vanished back into the blackness.

Two and a half thousand feet.

At the dim edges of the ship's lights guilty secrets flitted by with their eyes on stalks.

Gradually the topography of the distantly approaching ocean-bed resolved with greater and greater clarity on the computer displays until at last a shape could be made out that was separate and distinct from its surroundings. It was like a huge lopsided cylindrical fortress which widened sharply halfway along its length to accommodate the heavy ultra-plating with which the crucial storage holds were clad, and which were supposed by its builders to have made this the most secure and impregnable spaceship ever built. Before launch the material structure of this section had been battered, rammed, blasted and subjected to every assault its builders knew it could withstand in order to demonstrate that it could withstand them.

The tense silence in the cockpit tightened perceptibly as it became clear that it was this section that had broken rather neatly in two.

'In fact it's perfectly safe,' said one of the officials, 'it's built so that even if the ship does break up, the storage holds cannot possibly be breached.'

Three thousand, eight hundred and twenty-five feet.

Four Hi-Presh-A SmartSuits moved slowly out of the open hatchway of the salvage craft and waded through the barrage of its lights towards the monstrous shape that loomed darkly out of the sea night. They moved with a sort of clumsy grace, near weightless though weighed on by a world of water.

With his right-hand head Zaphod peered up into the black immensities above him and for a moment his mind sang with a silent roar of horror. He glanced to his left and was relieved to see that his other head was busy watching the Brockian Ultra-Cricket broadcasts on the helmet vid without concern. Slightly behind him to his left walked the two officials from the Safety and Civil Reassurance Adminis-tration; slightly in front of him to his right walked the empty suit, carrying their implements and testing the way for them.

They passed the huge rift in the broken-backed Starship Billion Year Bunker, and played their flashlights up into it. Mangled machinery loomed between torn and twisted bulkheads, two feet thick. A family of large transparent eels lived in there now and seemed to like it.

The empty suit preceded them along the length of the ship's gigantic murky hull, trying the airlocks. The third one it tested ground open uneasily. They crowded inside it and waited for several long minutes while the pump mechanisms dealt with the hideous pressure that the ocean exerted, and slowly replaced it with an equally hideous pressure of air and inert gases. At last the inner door slid open and they were admitted to a dark outer holding area of the Starship Billion Year Bunker. Several more high-security Titan-O-Hold doors had to be passed through, each of which the officials opened with a selection of quark keys. Soon they were so deep within the heavy security fields that the Ultra-Cricket broadcasts were beginning to fade, and Zaphod had to switch to one of the rock video stations, since there was nowhere that they were not able to reach.

A final doorway slid open, and they emerged into a large sepulchral space. Zaphod played his flashlight against the opposite wall and it fell full on a wild-eyed screaming face.

Zaphod screamed a diminished fifth himself, dropped

his light and sat heavily on the floor, or rather on a body which had been lying there undisturbed for around six months and which reacted to being sat on by exploding with great violence. Zaphod wondered what to do about all this, and after a brief but hectic internal debate decided that passing out would be the very thing.

He came to a few minutes later and pretended not to know who he was, where he was or how he had got there, but was not able to convince anybody. He then pretended that his memory suddenly returned with a rush and that the shock caused him to pass out again, but he was helped unwillingly to his feet by the empty suit – which he was beginning to take a serious dislike to – and forced to come to terms with his surroundings.

They were dimly and fitfully lit and unpleasant in a number of respects, the most obvious of which was the colourful arrangement of parts of the ship's late lamented Navigation Officer over the floor, walls and ceiling, and especially over the lower half of his, Zaphod's, suit. The effect of this was so astoundingly nasty that we shall not be referring to it again at any point in this narrative – other than to record briefly the fact that it caused Zaphod to throw up inside his suit, which he therefore removed and swapped, after suitable headgear modifications, with the empty one. Unfortunately the stench of the fetid air in the ship, followed by the sight of his own suit walking around casually draped in rotting intestines was enough to make him throw up in the other suit as well, which was a problem that he and the suit would simply have to live with.

There. All done. No more nastiness.

At least, no more of that particular nastiness.

The owner of the screaming face had calmed down very slightly now and was bubbling away incoherently in a large tank of yellow liquid – an emergency suspension tank.

'It was crazy,' he babbled, 'crazy! I told him we could always try the lobster on the way back, but he was crazy. Obsessed! Do you ever get like that about lobster? Because I don't. Seems to me it's all rubbery and fiddly to eat, and not that much taste, well I mean is there? I infinitely prefer scallops, and said so. Oh Zarquon, I said so!'

Zaphod stared at this extraordinary apparition, flailing in its tank. The man was attached to all kinds of life-support tubes, and his voice was bubbling out of speakers that echoed insanely round the ship, returning as haunting echoes from deep and distant corridors.

'That was where I went wrong,' the madman yelled. 'I actually said that I preferred scallops and he said it was because I hadn't had real lobster like they did where his ancestors came from, which was here, and he'd prove it. He said it was no problem, he said the lobster here was worth a whole journey, let alone the small diversion it would take to get here, and he swore he could handle the ship in the atmosphere, but it was madness, madness!' he screamed, and paused with his eyes rolling, as if the word had rung some kind of bell in his mind. 'The ship went right out of control! I couldn't believe what we were doing and just to prove a point about lobster which is really so overrated as a food. I'm sorry to go on about lobsters so much, I'll try and stop in a minute, but they've been on my mind so much for the months I've been in this tank, can you imagine what it's like to be stuck in a ship with the same guys for months eating junk food when all one guy will talk about is lobster, and then spend six months floating by yourself in a tank thinking about it. I promise I will try and shut up about the lobsters, I really will. Lobsters, lobsters, lobsters – enough! I think I'm the only survivor. I'm the only one who managed to get to an emergency tank before we went down. I sent out the Mayday and then we hit. It's a disaster isn't it? A total disaster, and all because the guy liked lobsters. How much sense am I making? It's really hard for me to tell.'

He gazed at them beseechingly, and his mind seemed to sway slowly back down to earth like a falling leaf. He blinked and looked at them oddly like a monkey peering at a strange fish. He scrabbled curiously with his wrinkled-up fingers at the glass side of the tank. Tiny, thick yellow bubbles loosed themselves from his mouth and nose, caught briefly in his swab of hair and strayed on upwards.

'Oh Zarquon, oh heavens,' he mumbled pathetically to himself, 'I've been found. I've been rescued—'

'Well,' said one of the officials, briskly, 'you've been found at least.' He strode over to the main computer bank in the middle of the chamber and started checking quickly through the ship's main monitor circuits for damage reports.

'The aorist rod chambers are intact,' he said.

'Holy dingo's dos,' snarled Zaphod, 'there are aorist rods on board ...!'

Aorist rods were devices used in a now happily abandoned form of energy production. When the hunt for new
sources of energy had at one point got particularly frantic,
one bright young chap suddenly spotted that one place
which had never used up all its available energy was – the
past. And with the sudden rush of blood to the head that
such insights tend to induce, he invented a way of mining
it that very same night, and within a year huge tracts of the
past were being drained of all their energy and simply wasting away. Those who claimed that the past should be left
unspoilt were accused of indulging in an extremely expensive form of sentimentality. The past provided a very cheap,
plentiful and clean source of energy, there could always be
a few Natural Past Reserves set up if anyone wanted to pay
for their upkeep, and as for the claim that draining the past
impoverished the present, well, maybe it did, slightly, but
the effects were immeasurable and you really had to keep a
sense of proportion.

It was only when it was realized that the present really
was being impoverished, and that the reason for it was that
those selfish plundering wastrel bastards up in the future
were doing exactly the same thing, that everyone realized
that every single aorist rod, and the terrible secret of how
they were made would have to be utterly and for ever
destroyed. They claimed it was for the sake of their
grandparents and grandchildren, but it was of course for
the sake of their grandparents' grandchildren, and their
grandchildren's grandparents. The official from the Safety
and Civil Reassurance Administration gave a dismissive
shrug. 'They're perfectly safe,' he said. He glanced up at

Zaphod and suddenly said with uncharacteristic frankness, 'There's worse than that on board. At least,' he added, tapping at one of the computer screens, 'I hope it's on board.'

The other official rounded on him sharply. 'What the hell do you think you're saying?' he snapped.

The first shrugged again. He said, 'It doesn't matter. He can say what he likes. No one would believe him. It's why we chose to use him rather than do anything official, isn't it? The more wild the story he tells, the more it'll sound like he's some hippy adventurer making it up. He can even say that we said this and it'll make him sound like a para-noid.' He smiled pleasantly at Zaphod who was seething in a suit full of sick. 'You may accompany us,' he told him, 'if you wish.'

'You see?' said the official, examining the ultra-titanium outer seals of the aorist rod hold. 'Perfectly secure, perfectly safe.'

He said the same thing as they passed holds containing chemical weapons so powerful that a teaspoonful could fatally infect an entire planet.

He said the same thing as they passed holds containing zeta-active compounds so powerful that a teaspoonful could blow up a whole planet.

He said the same thing as they passed holds containing theta-active compounds so powerful that a teaspoonful could irradiate a whole planet.

'I'm glad I'm not a planet,' muttered Zaphod.

'You'd have nothing to fear,' assured the official from the Safety and Civil Reassurance Administration, 'planets are very safe. Provided,' he added – and paused. They were approaching the hold nearest to the point where the back of the Starship Billion Year Bunker was broken. The corridor here was twisted and deformed, and the floor was damp and sticky in patches.

'Ho hum,' he said, 'ho very much hum.'

'What's in this hold?' demanded Zaphod.

'By-products,' said the official, clamming up again.

'By-products . . .' insisted Zaphod, quietly, 'of what?'

Neither official answered. Instead, they examined the hold door very carefully and saw that its seals were twisted apart by the forces that had deformed the whole corridor. One of them touched the door lightly. It swung open to his touch. There was darkness inside, with just a couple of dim yellow lights deep within it.

'Of what?' hissed Zaphod.

The leading official turned to the other. 'There's an escape capsule,' he said, 'that the crew were to use to abandon ship before jettisoning it into the black hole,' he said. 'I think it would be good to know that it's still there.' The other official nodded and left without a word. The first official quietly beckoned Zaphod in. The large dim yellow lights glowed about twenty feet from them.

'The reason,' he said, quietly, 'why everything else in this ship is, I maintain, safe, is that no one is really crazy enough to use them. No one. At least no one that crazy would ever get near them. Anyone that mad or dangerous rings very deep alarm bells. People may be stupid but they're not that stupid.'

'By-products,' hissed Zaphod again – he had to hiss in order that his voice shouldn't be heard to tremble – 'of what?'

'Er, Designer People.'

'What?'

'The Sirius Cybernetics Corporation were awarded a huge research grant to design and produce synthetic personalities to order. The results were uniformly disastrous. All the "people" and "personalities" turned out to be amalgams of characteristics which simply could not co-exist in naturally occurring life forms. Most of them were just poor pathetic misfits, but some were deeply, deeply dangerous. Dangerous because they didn't ring alarm bells in other people. They could walk through situations the way that ghosts walk through walls, because no one spotted the danger.

'The most dangerous of all were three identical ones – they were put in this hold, to be blasted, with this ship, right out of this universe. They are not evil, in fact they are rather simple and charming. But they are the most dangerous creatures that ever lived because there is nothing they will not do if allowed, and nothing they will not be allowed to do—'

Zaphod looked at the dim yellow lights, the two dim yellow lights. As his eyes became accustomed to the light he saw that the two lights framed a third space where something was broken. Wet sticky patches gleamed dully on the floor.

Zaphod and the official walked cautiously towards the lights. At that moment, four words came crashing into the helmet headsets from the other official.

'The capsule has gone,' he said tersely.

'Trace it,' snapped Zaphod's companion. 'Find exactly where it has gone. We must know where it has gone!'

Zaphod approached the two remaining tanks. A quick glance showed him that each contained an identical floating body. He examined one more carefully. The body, that of an elderly man, was floating in a thick yellow liquid. The man was kindly-looking with lots of pleasant laugh lines round his face. His hair seemed unnaturally thick and dark for someone of his age, and his right hand seemed continually to be weaving forward and back, up and down, as if shaking hands with an endless succession of unseen ghosts. He smiled genially, babbled and burbled like a half-sleeping baby and occasionally seemed to rock very slightly with little tremors of laughter, as if he had just told himself a joke he hadn't heard before, or didn't remember properly. Waving, smiling, chortling, with little yellow bubbles beading on his lips, he seemed to inhabit a distant world of simple dreams.

Another terse message suddenly came through his helmet headset. The planet towards which the escape capsule had headed had already been identified. It was in Galactic Sector ZZ9 Plural Z Alpha.

Zaphod found a small speaker by the tank and turned it on. The man in the yellow liquid was babbling gently about a shining city on a hill.

He also heard the official from the Safety and Civil Reassurance Administration issue instructions to the effect that the missing escape capsule contained a 'Reagan' and that the planet in ZZ9 Plural Z Alpha must be made 'perfectly safe'.

Never Stop on the Motorway

BY JEFFREY ARCHER

Diana had been hoping to get away by five, so she could be at the farm in time for dinner. She tried not to show her true feelings when at four thirty-seven her deputy, Phil Haskins, presented her with a complex twelve-page document that required the signature of a director before it could be sent out to the client. Haskins didn't hesitate to remind her that they had lost two similar contracts that week.

It was always the same on a Friday. The phones would go quiet in the middle of the afternoon and then, just as she thought she could slip away, an authorization would land on her desk. One glance at this particular document and Diana knew there would be no chance of escaping before six.

The demands of being a single parent as well as a director of a small but thriving City company meant there were few moments left in any day to relax, so when it came to the one weekend in four that James and Caroline spent with her ex-husband, Diana would try to leave the office a little earlier than usual to avoid getting snarled up in the weekend traffic.

She read through the first page slowly and made a couple of emendations, aware that any mistake made hastily on a Friday night could be regretted in the weeks to come. She glanced at the clock on her desk as she signed the final page of the document. It was just flicking over to five fifty-one.

Diana gathered up her bag and walked purposefully towards the door, dropping the contract on Phil's desk without bothering to suggest that he have a good weekend. She suspected that the paperwork had been on his desk since nine o'clock that morning, but that holding it until four thirty-seven was his only means of revenge now that she had been made head of department. Once she was safely in the lift, she pressed the button for the basement car park, calculating that the delay would probably add an extra hour to her journey.

She stepped out of the lift, walked over to her Audi estate, unlocked the door and threw her bag on to the back seat. When she drove up on to the street the stream of twilight traffic was just about keeping pace with the pin-striped pedestrians who, like worker ants, were hurrying towards the nearest hole in the ground.

She flicked on the six o'clock news. The chimes of Big Ben rang out, before spokesmen from each of the three main political parties gave their views on the European election results. John Major was refusing to comment on his future. The Conservative Party's explanation for its poor showing was that only thirty-six per cent of the country had bothered to go to the polls. Diana felt guilty – she was among the sixty-four per cent who had failed to register their vote.

The newcaster moved on to say that the situation in

23

Bosnia remained desperate, and that the UN was threatening dire consequences if Radovan Karadzic and the Serbs didn't come to an agreement with the other warring parties. Diana's mind began to drift – such a threat was hardly news any longer. She suspected that if she turned on the radio in a year's time they would probably be repeating it word for word.

As her car crawled round Russell Square, she began to think about the weekend ahead. It had been over a year since John had told her that he had met another woman and wanted a divorce. She still wondered why, after seven years of marriage, she hadn't been more shocked – or at least angry – at his betrayal. Since her appointment as a director, she had to admit they had spent less and less time together. And perhaps she had become anaesthetized by the fact that a third of the married couples in Britain were now divorced or separated. Her parents had been unable to hide their disappointment, but then they had been married for forty-two years.

The divorce had been amicable enough, as John, who earned less than she did – one of their problems, perhaps – had given in to most of her demands. She had kept the flat in Putney, the Audi estate and the children, to whom John was allowed access one weekend in four. He would have picked them up from school earlier that afternoon, and, as usual, he'd return them to the flat in Putney around seven on Sunday evening.

Diana would go to almost any lengths to avoid being left on her own in Putney when they weren't around, and although she regularly grumbled about being landed with the responsibility of bringing up two children without a father, she missed them desperately the moment they were out of sight.

She hadn't taken a lover and she didn't sleep around. None of the senior staff at the office had ever gone further than asking her out to lunch. Perhaps because only three of them were unmarried – and not without reason. The one person she might have considered having a relationship with had made it abundantly clear that he only wanted to spend the night with her, not the days.

In any case, Diana had decided long ago that if she was to be taken seriously as the company's first woman director, an office affair, however casual or short-lived, could only end in tears. Men are so vain, she thought. A woman only had to make one mistake and she was immediately labelled as promiscuous. Then every other man on the premises either smirks behind your back, or treats your thigh as an extension of the arm on his chair.

Diana groaned as she came to a halt at yet another red light. In twenty minutes she hadn't covered more than a couple of miles. She opened the glove box on the passenger side and fumbled in the dark for a cassette. She found one and pressed it into the slot, hoping it would be Pavarotti, only to be greeted by the strident tones of Gloria Gaynor assuring her 'I will survive'. She smiled and thought about Daniel, as the light changed to green.

She and Daniel had read Economics at Bristol University in the early eighties, friends but never lovers. Then Daniel met Rachael, who had come up a year after them, and from that moment he had never looked at another woman. They married the day he graduated, and after they returned from their honeymoon Daniel took over the management of his father's farm in Bedfordshire. Three children had followed in quick succession, and Diana had been proud when she was asked to be godmother to Sophie, the eldest. Daniel and Rachael had now been married for twelve years, and Diana felt confident that they wouldn't be disappointing *their* parents with any suggestion of a divorce. Although they were convinced she led an exciting and fulfilling life, Diana often envied their gentle and uncomplicated existence.

She was regularly asked to spend the weekend with them in the country, but for every two or three invitations Daniel issued, she only accepted one – not because she wouldn't have liked to join them more often, but because since her divorce she had no desire to take advantage of their hospitality.

Although she enjoyed her work, it had been a bloody week. Two contracts had fallen through, James had been dropped from the school football team, and Caroline had never stopped telling her that her father didn't mind her watching television when she ought to be doing her prep.

Another traffic light changed to red.

It took Diana nearly an hour to travel the seven miles out of the city, and when she reached the first dual carriage-way, she glanced up at the A1 sign, more out of habit than to seek guidance, because she knew every yard of the road from her office to the farm. She tried to increase her speed, but it was quite impossible, as both lanes remained obsti-nately crowded.

'Damn.' She had forgotten to get them a present, even a decent bottle of claret. 'Damn,' she repeated: Daniel and Rachael always did the giving. She began to wonder if she could pick something up on the way, then remembered there was nothing but service stations between here and the farm. She couldn't turn up with yet another box of chocolates they'd never eat. When she reached the round-about that led on to the A1, she managed to push the car over fifty for the first time. She began to relax, allowing her mind to drift with the music.

There was no warning. Although she immediately slammed her foot on the brakes, it was already too late. There was a dull thump from the front bumper, and a slight shudder rocked the car.

A small black creature had shot across her path, and despite her quick reactions, she hadn't been able to avoid hitting it. Diana swung on to the hard shoulder and screeched to a halt, wondering if the animal could possibly have survived. She reversed slowly back to the spot where she thought she had hit it as the traffic roared past her.

And then she saw it, lying on the grass verge – a cat that had crossed the road for the tenth time. She stepped out of the car, and walked towards the lifeless body. Suddenly Diana felt sick. She had two cats of her own, and she knew she would never be able to tell the children what she had done. She picked up the dead animal and laid it gently in the ditch by the roadside.

'I'm so sorry,' she said, feeling a little silly. She gave it one last look before walking back to her car. Ironically, she had chosen the Audi for its safety features.

She climbed back into the car and switched on the ignition to find Gloria Gaynor was still belting out her opinion of men. She turned her off, and tried to stop thinking about the cat as she waited for a gap in the traffic large enough to allow her to ease her way back into the slow lane. She eventually succeeded, but was still unable to erase the dead cat from her mind.

Diana had accelerated up to fifty again when she suddenly became aware of a pair of headlights shining through her rear windscreen. She put up her arm and waved in her rear-view mirror, but the lights continued to dazzle her. She slowed down to allow the vehicle to pass, but the driver showed no interest in doing so. Diana began to wonder if there was something wrong with her car. Was one of her lights not working? Was the exhaust billowing smoke? Was . . .

She decided to speed up and put some distance between herself and the vehicle behind, but it remained within a few yards of her bumper. She tried to snatch a look at the driver in her rear-view mirror, but it was hard to see much in the harshness of the lights. As her eyes became more accustomed to the glare, she could make out the silhouette of a large black van bearing down on her, and what looked like a young man behind the wheel. He seemed to be waving at her.

Diana slowed down again as she approached the next roundabout, giving him every chance to overtake her on the outside lane, but once again he didn't take the opportunity, and just sat on her bumper, his headlights still undimmed. She waited for a small gap in the traffic coming from her right. When one appeared she slammed her foot on the accelerator, shot across the roundabout and sped on up the A1.

She was rid of him at last. She was just beginning to relax and to think about Sophie, who always waited up so that she could read to her, when suddenly those high-beam headlights were glaring through her rear windscreen and blinding her once again. If anything, they were even closer to her than before.

She slowed down, he slowed down. She accelerated, he accelerated. She tried to think what she could do next, and began waving frantically at passing motorists as they sped by, but they remained oblivious to her predicament. She tried to think of other ways she might alert someone, and suddenly recalled that when she had joined the board of the company they had suggested she have a car phone fitted. Diana had decided it could wait until the car went in for its next service, which should have been a fortnight ago.

She brushed her hand across her forehead and removed a film of perspiration, thought for a moment, then manoeuvred her car into the fast lane. The van swung across after her, and hovered so close to her bumper that she became fearful that if she so much as touched her brakes she might unwittingly cause an enormous pile-up.

Diana took the car up to ninety, but the van wouldn't be shaken off. She pushed her foot further down on the accelerator and touched a hundred, but it still remained less than a car's length behind.

She flicked her headlights on to high-beam, turned on her hazard lights and blasted her horn at anyone who dared to remain in her path. She could only hope that the police might see her, wave her on to the hard shoulder and book her for speeding. A fine would be infinitely preferable to a crash with a young tearaway, she thought, as the Audi estate passed a hundred and ten for the first time in its life. But the black van couldn't be shaken off.

Without warning, she swerved back into the middle lane and took her foot off the accelerator, causing the van to draw level with her, which gave her a chance to look at the driver for the first time. He was wearing a black leather jacket and pointing menacingly at her. She shook her fist at him and accelerated away, but he simply swung across behind her like an Olympic runner determined not to allow his rival to break clear.

And then she remembered, and felt sick for a second time that night. 'Oh, my God,' she shouted aloud in terror. In a flood, the details of the murder that had taken place on the same road a few months before came rushing back to her. A woman had been raped before having her throat cut with a knife with a serrated edge and dumped in a ditch. For weeks there had been signs posted on the A1 appealing to passing motorists to phone a certain number if they had any information that might assist the police with their enquiries. The signs had now disappeared, but the police were still searching for the killer. Diana began to tremble as she remembered their warning to all woman drivers: 'Never stop on the motorway.'

A few seconds later she saw a road sign she knew well. She had reached it far sooner than she had anticipated. In three miles she would have to leave the motorway for the sliproad that led to the farm. She began to pray that if she took her usual turning, the black-jacketed man would continue on up the A1 and she would finally be rid of him.

Diana decided that the time had come for her to speed him on his way. She swung back into the fast lane and once again put her foot down on the accelerator. She reached a hundred miles per hour for the second time as she sped past the two-mile sign. Her body was now covered in sweat, and the speedometer touched a hundred and ten. She checked her rear-view mirror, but he was still right behind her. She would have to pick the exact moment if she was to execute her plan successfully. With a mile to go, she began to look to her left, so as to be sure her timing would be perfect. She no longer needed to check in her mirror to know that he would still be there.

The next signpost showed three diagonal white lines, warning her that she ought to be on the inside lane if she intended to leave the motorway at the next junction. She kept the car in the outside lane at a hundred miles per hour until she spotted a large enough gap. Two white lines appeared by the roadside: Diana knew she would have only one chance to make her escape. As she passed the sign with a single white line on it she suddenly swung across the road at ninety miles per hour, causing cars in the middle and inside lanes to throw on their brakes and blast out their angry opinions. But Diana didn't care what they thought of her, because she was now travelling down the sliproad to safety, and the black van was speeding on up the A1.

She laughed out loud with relief. To her right, she could see the steady flow of traffic on the motorway. But then her laugh turned to a scream as she saw the black van cut sharply across the motorway in front of a lorry, mount the grass verge and career on to the sliproad, swinging from side to side. It nearly drove over the edge and into a ditch, but somehow managed to steady itself, ending up a few yards behind her, its lights once again glaring through her rear windscreen.

When she reached the top of the sliproad, Diana turned

left in the direction of the farm, frantically trying to work out what she should do next. The nearest town was about twelve miles away on the main road, and the farm was only seven, but five of those miles were down a winding, unlit country lane. She checked her petrol gauge. It was nearing empty, but there should still be enough in the tank for her to consider either option. There was less than a mile to go before she reached the turning, so she had only a minute in which to make up her mind.

With a hundred yards to go, she settled on the farm. Despite the unlit lane, she knew every twist and turn, and she felt confident that her pursuer wouldn't. Once she reached the farm she could be out of the car and inside the house long before he could catch her. In any case, once he saw the farmhouse, surely he would flee.

The minute was up. Diana touched the brakes and skidded into a country road illuminated only by the moon.

Diana banged the palms of her hands on the steering wheel. Had she made the wrong decision? She glanced up at her rear-view mirror. Had he given up? Of course he hadn't. The back of a Land Rover loomed up in front of her. Diana slowed down, waiting for a corner she knew well, where the road widened slightly. She held her breath, crashed into third gear, and overtook. Would a head-on collision be preferable to a cut throat? She rounded the bend and saw an empty road ahead of her. Once again she pressed her foot down, this time managing to put a clear seventy, perhaps even a hundred, yards between her and her pursuer, but this only offered her a few moments' respite. Before long the familiar headlights came bearing down on her once again.

With each bend Diana was able to gain a little time as the van continued to lurch from side to side, unfamiliar with the road, but she never managed a clear break of more than a few seconds. She checked the mileometer. From the turn-off on the main road to the farm it was just over five miles, and she must have covered about two by now. She began to watch each tenth of a mile clicking up, terrified at the thought of the van overtaking her and forcing her into the ditch. She stuck determinedly to the centre of the road.

Another mile passed, and still he clung on to her. Suddenly she saw a car coming towards her. She switched her headlights to full beam and pressed on the horn. The other car retaliated by mimicking her actions, which caused her to slow down and brush against the hedgerow as they shot past each other. She checked the mileometer once again. Only two miles to go.

Diana would slow down and then speed up at each familiar bend in the road, making sure the van was never given enough room to pull level with her. She tried to concentrate on what she should do once the farmhouse came into sight. She reckoned that the drive leading up to the house must be about half a mile long. It was full of potholes and bumps which Daniel had often explained he couldn't afford to have repaired. But at least it was only wide enough for one car.

The gate to the driveway was usually left open for her, though on the odd rare occasion Daniel had forgotten, and she'd had to get out of the car and open it for herself. She couldn't risk that tonight. If the gate was closed, she would have to travel on to the next town and stop outside the

33

Crimson Kipper, which was always crowded at this time on a Friday night, or, if she could find it, on the steps of the local police station. She checked her petrol gauge again. It was now touching red. 'Oh my God,' she said, realizing she might not have enough petrol to reach the town.

She could only pray that Daniel had remembered to leave the gate open.

She swerved out of the next bend and speeded up, but once again she managed to gain only a few yards, and she knew that within seconds he would be back in place. He was. For the next few hundred yards they remained within feet of each other, and she felt certain he must run into the back of her. She didn't once dare to touch her brakes – if they crashed in that lane, far from any help, she would have no hope of getting away from him.

She checked her mileometer. A mile to go.

'The gate must be open. It must be open,' she prayed. As she swung round the next bend, she could make out the outline of the farmhouse in the distance. She almost screamed with relief when she saw that the lights were on in the downstairs rooms.

She shouted, 'Thank God!' then remembered the gate again, and changed her plea to 'Dear God, let it be open.' She would know what needed to be done as soon as she came round the last bend. 'Let it be open, just this once,' she pleaded. 'I'll never ask for anything again, ever.' She swung round the final bend only inches ahead of the black van. 'Please, please, please.' And then she saw the gate.

It was open.

Her clothes were now drenched in sweat. She slowed down, wrenched the gearbox into second, and threw the car between the gap and into the bumpy driveway, hitting the gatepost on her right-hand side as she careered on up towards the house. The van didn't hesitate to follow her, and was still only inches behind as she straightened up. Diana kept her hand pressed down on the horn as the car bounced and lurched over the mounds and potholes.

Flocks of startled crows flapped out of overhanging branches, screeching as they shot into the air. Diana began screaming, 'Daniel! Daniel!' Two hundred yards ahead of her, the porch light went on.

Her headlights were now shining onto the front of the house, and her hand was still pressed on the horn. With a hundred yards to go, she spotted Daniel coming out of the front door, but she didn't slow down, and neither did the van behind her. With fifty yards to go she began flashing her lights at Daniel. She could now make out the puzzled, anxious expression on his face.

With thirty yards to go she threw on her brakes. The heavy estate car skidded across the gravel in front of the house, coming to a halt in the flowerbed just below the kitchen window. She heard the screech of brakes behind her. The leather-jacketed man, unfamiliar with the terrain, had been unable to react quickly enough, and as soon as his wheels touched the gravelled forecourt he began to skid out of control. A second later the van came crashing into the back of her car, slamming it against the wall of the house and shattering the glass in the kitchen window.

Diana leapt out of the car, screaming, 'Daniel! Get a gun, get a gun!' She pointed back at the van. 'That bastard's been chasing me for the last twenty miles!'

The man jumped out of the van and began limping

35

towards them. Diana ran into the house. Daniel followed and grabbed a shotgun, normally reserved for rabbits, that was leaning against the wall. He ran back outside to face the unwelcome visitor, who had come to a halt by the back of Diana's Audi.

Daniel raised the shotgun to his shoulder and stared straight at him. 'Don't move or I'll shoot,' he said calmly. And then he remembered the gun wasn't loaded. Diana ducked back out of the house, but remained several yards behind him.

'Not me! Not me!' shouted the leather-jacketed youth, as Rachael appeared in the doorway.

'What's going on?' she asked nervously.

'Ring for the police,' was all Daniel said, and his wife quickly disappeared back into the house.

Daniel advanced towards the terrified-looking young man, the gun aimed squarely at his chest.

'Not me! Not me!' he shouted again, pointing at the Audi. 'He's in the car!' He quickly turned to face Diana. 'I saw him get in when you were parked on the hard shoulder. What else could I have done? You just wouldn't pull over.'

Daniel advanced cautiously towards the rear door of the car and ordered the young man to open it slowly, while he kept the gun aimed at his chest.

The youth opened the door, and quickly took a pace backwards. The three of them stared down at a man crouched on the floor of the car. In his right hand he held a long-bladed knife with a serrated edge. Daniel swung the barrel of the gun down to point at him, but said nothing.

The sound of a police siren could just be heard in the distance.

Odd Attachment

BY IAIN M. BANKS

Depressed and dejected, his unrequited love like a stony weight inside him, Fropome looked longingly at the sky, then shook his head slowly and stared disconsolately down at the meadow in front of him.

A nearby grazer cub, eating its way across the grassy plain with the rest of the herd, started cuffing one of its siblings. Normally their master would have watched the pretended fight with some amusement, but today he responded with a low creaking noise which ought to have warned the hot-blooded little animals. One of the tumbling cubs looked up briefly at Fropome, but then resumed the tussle. Fropome flicked out a vine-limb, slapping the two cubs across their rumps. They squealed, untangled, and stumbled mewling and yelping to their mothers on the outskirts of the herd.

Fropome watched them go, then – with a rustling noise very like a sigh – returned to looking at the bright orange sky. He forgot about the grazers and the prairie and thought again about his love.

His lady-love, his darling, the One for whom he would gladly climb any hillock, wade any lakelet; all that sort of thing. His love; his cruel, cold, heartless, uncaring love.

He felt crushed, dried-up inside whenever he thought

of her. She seemed so unfeeling, so unconcerned. How could she be so dismissive? Even if she didn't love him in return, you'd have thought at least she'd be flattered to have somebody express their undying love for her. Was he so unattractive? Did she actually feel insulted that he worshipped her? If she did, why did she ignore him? If his attentions were unwelcome, why didn't she say so?

But she said nothing. She acted as though all he'd said, everything he'd tried to express to her was just some embarrassing slip, a gaffe best ignored.

He didn't understand it. Did she think he would say such things lightly? Did she imagine he hadn't worried over what to say and how to say it, and where and when? He'd stopped eating! He hadn't slept for nights! He was starting to turn brown and curl up at the edges! Foodbirds were setting up roosts in his nestraps!

A grazer cub nuzzled his side. He picked the furry little animal up in a vine, lifted it up to his head, stared at it with his four front eyes, sprayed it with irritant and flung it whimpering into a nearby bush.

The bush shook itself and made a grumbling noise. Fropome apologized to it as the grazer cub disentangled itself and scuttled off, scratching furiously.

Fropome would rather have been alone with his melancholy, but he had to watch over the grazer herd, keeping them out of acidcloys, pitplants and digastids, sheltering them from the foodbirds' stupespittle and keeping them away from the ponderously poised boulderbeasts.

Everything was so predatory. Couldn't love be different? Fropome shook his withered foliage.

Surely she must feel *something*. They'd been friends for

seasons now; they got on well together, they found the same things amusing, they held similar opinions . . . if they were so alike in these respects, how could he feel such desperate, feverish passion for her and she feel nothing for him? Could this most basic root of the soul be so different when everything else seemed so in accord?

She *must* feel something for him. It was absurd to think she could feel nothing. She just didn't want to appear too forward. Her reticence was only caution; understandable, even commendable. She didn't want to commit herself too quickly . . . that was all. She was innocent as an unopened bud, shy as a moonbloom, modest as a leaf-wrapped heart . . .

. . . and pure as a star in the sky, Fropome thought. As pure, and as remote. He gazed at a bright, new star in the sky, trying to convince himself she might return his love.

The star moved.

Fropome watched it.

The star twinkled, moved slowly across the sky, gradually brightening. Fropome made a wish on it: *Be an omen, be the sign that she loves me!* Perhaps it was a lucky star. He'd never been superstitious before, but love had strange effects on the vegetable heart.

If only he could be sure of her, he thought, gazing at the slowly falling star. He wasn't impatient; he would gladly wait for ever if he only knew she cared. It was the uncertainty that tormented him and left his hopes and fears toing-and-froing in such an agonizing way.

He looked almost affectionately at the grazers as they plodded their way around him, looking for a nice patch of uneaten grass or a yukscrub to defecate into.

Poor, simple creatures. And yet lucky, in a way; their life revolved around eating and sleeping, with no room in their low-browed little heads for anguish, no space in their furry chests for a ruptured capillary system.

Ah, what it must be, to have a simple, muscle heart!

He looked back to the sky. The evening stars seemed cool and calm, like dispassionate eyes, watching him. All except the falling star he'd wished on earlier.

He reflected briefly on the wisdom of wishing on such a transitory thing as a falling star . . . even one falling as slowly as this one seemed to be.

Oh, such disturbing, bud-like emotions! Such sapling gullibility and nervousness! Such cuttingish confusion and uncertainty!

The star still fell. It became brighter and brighter in the evening sky, lowering slowly and changing colour too; from sun-white to moon-yellow to sky-orange to sunset-red. Fropome could hear its noise now; a dull roaring, like a strong wind disturbing short-tempered tree tops. The falling red star was no longer a single point of light; it had taken on a shape now, like a big seed pod.

It occurred to Fropome that this might indeed be a sign. Whatever it was had come from the stars, after all, and weren't stars the seeds of the Ancestors, shot so high they left the Earth and rooted in the celestial spheres of cold fire, all-seeing and all-knowing? Maybe the old stories were true after all, and the gods had come to tell him something momentous. A thrill of excitement rose within him. His limbs shook and his leaves beaded with moisture.

The pod was close now. It dipped and seemed to hesitate in the dark-orange sky. The pod's colour continued to deepen all the time, and Fropome realized it was *hot*; he could feel its warmth even from half a dozen reaches away.

It was an ellipsoid, a little smaller than he was. It flexed glittering roots from its bottom end, and glided through the air to land on the meadow with a sort of tentative deliberation, a couple of reaches away.

Fropome watched, thoroughly entranced. He didn't dare move. This might be important. A sign.

Everything was still; him, the grumbling bushes, the whispering grass, even the grazers looked puzzled.

The pod moved. Part of its casing fell back inside itself, producing a hole in the smooth exterior.

And something came out.

It was small and silver, and it walked on what might have been hind legs, or a pair of over-developed roots. It crossed to one of the grazers and started making noises at it. The grazer was so surprised it fell over. It lay staring up at the strange silver creature, blinking. Cubs ran, terrified, for their mothers. Other grazers looked at each other, or at Fropome, who still wasn't sure what to do.

The silver seedlet moved to another grazer and made noises at it. Confused, the grazer broke wind. The seedlet went to the animal's rear end and started speaking loudly there.

Fropome clapped a couple of vines together to request respectfully the silver creature's attention, and made to spread the same two leaf-palms on the ground before the seedlet, in a gesture of supplication.

The creature leapt back, detached a bit of its middle with one of its stubby upper limbs, and pointed it at Fropome's vines. There was a flash of light and Fropome felt pain as his leaf-palms crisped and smoked. Instinctively, he lashed out at the creature, knocking it to the ground. The detached bit flew away across the meadow and hit a grazer cub on the flank.

Fropome was shocked, then angry. He held the struggling creature down with one undamaged vine while he inspected his injuries. The leaves would probably fall off and take days to re-grow. He used another limb to grasp the silver seedlet and bring it up to his eye cluster. He shook it, then up-ended it and stuck its top down at the leaves it had burned, and shook it again.

He brought it back up to inspect it more closely.

Damn funny thing to have come out of a seed pod, he thought, twisting the object this way and that. It looked a little like a grazer except it was thinner and silvery and the head was just a smooth reflective sphere. Fropome could not work out how it stayed upright. The over-large top made it look especially unbalanced. Possibly it wasn't meant to totter around for long; those pointed leg-like parts were probably roots. The thing wriggled in his grasp.

He tore off a little of the silvery outer bark and tasted it in a nestrap. He spat it out again. Not animal or vegetable; more like mineral. Very odd.

Root-pink tendrils squirmed at the end of the stubby upper limb, where Fropome had torn the outer covering off. Fropome looked at them, and wondered.

He took hold of one of the little pink filaments and pulled.

It came off with a faint 'pop'. Another, muffled-sounding noise came from the silvery top of the creature.

She loves me . . .

Fropome pulled off another tendril. Pop. Sap the colour of the setting sun dribbled out.

She loves me not . . .

Pop pop pop. He completed that set of tendrils:

She loves me . . .

Excited, Fropome pulled the covering off the end of the other upper limb. More tendrils.

. . . She loves me not.

A grazer cub came up and pulled at one of Fropome's lower branches. In its mouth it held the silvery creature's burner device, which had hit it on the flank. Fropome ignored it.

She loves me . . .

The grazer cub gave up pulling at Fropome's branch. It squatted down on the meadow, dropping the burner on the grass and prodding inquisitively at it with one paw.

The silvery seedlet was wriggling enthusiastically in Fropome's grip, thin red sap spraying everywhere.

Fropome completed the tendrils on the second upper limb.

Pop. She loves me not.

Oh no!

The grazer cub licked the burner, tapped it with its paw. One of the other cubs saw it playing with the bright toy and started ambling over towards it.

On a hunch, Fropome tore the covering off the blunt roots at the base of the creature. Ah ha!

She loves me . . .

The grazer cub at Fropome's side got bored with the shiny bauble; it was about to abandon the thing where it lay when it saw its sibling approaching, looking inquisitive.

The first cub growled and started trying to pick the burner up with its mouth.

Pop . . . She loves me not!

Ah! Death! Shall my pollen never dust her perfectly formed ovaries? Oh, wicked, balanced, so blandly symmetrical *even* universe!

In his rage, Fropome ripped the silvery covering right off the lower half of the leaking, weakly struggling seedlet.

Oh unfair life! Oh treacherous stars!

The growling grazer cub hefted the burner device into its mouth.

Something clicked. The cub's head exploded.

Fropome didn't pay too much attention. He was staring intently at the bark-stripped creature he held.

. . . wait a moment . . . there *was* something left. Up there, just where the roots met . . .

Thank heavens; the thing was odd after all!

Oh happy day!

(pop)

She loves me!

A Likely Thing!

BY CHARLOTTE BINGHAM

Bobbie's mother, Mrs Charles, had said that quite often . . .
'a likely thing', and as she said it she would raise her eyes
to heaven and roll them around in an exaggerated manner,
which always made Bobbie glad that her mother had given
up acting in favour of running a theatrical boarding house.

Just why this old-fashioned expression had come into
Bobbie Charles's mind was because she was quite sure that
the woman seated opposite at lunch would like to be saying
it too. 'Still married? A likely thing.' She settled instead for
saying 'You *are* still married? I mean, an actress and a man
like your husband, a famous old military family. Where did
you meet? You must have had nothing in common, surely?'

Bobbie stared at her plate, trying not to let her anger at
the woman's rudeness show in her eyes.

The restaurant was hot and oppressive after the cool of
the country which she had just left, but at least her plate
was blue and white like the picnic china she and Punch still
used, like the small patches of sky that she had glimpsed
from the train that morning. Thank heaven for colour, she
thought, thank heaven for blue eyes and blue sky, and shirts
of a faded blue, and thank heaven for pink, the pink stain
blackberries left on fingertips, and for the green of the
leaves of the beech trees that bordered their fields. The

thought came to her, 'too terrible if all nature was black and white like this woman's mind'.

'We met just after the war,' Bobbie began, but then stopped.

Kintlebury was small, even then, but not so small that it didn't have its own theatre company. Each week they gave a different play, and each week Bobbie and her mother were given seats in the third row of the stalls. Friday nights, it always had to be a Friday. 'Give them time to get into the piece and remember the words, dear,' Bobbie's mother would say.

Bobbie's mother, Mrs Charles, was a stout woman. She often had trouble with her corsets, and said so. They killed her, actually. Well, that's what she used to tell theatrical lodgers if they asked after her health. Bobbie found this embarrassing, but the actors for whom her mother provided such excellent lodgings were not in the least embarrassed. They would nod sympathetically while waiting for their dried egg and lightly margarined toast for, although the war was over, the rationing and war-time conditions had been for nothing, so dried was the egg still, so snooky the snook.

But mother could do wonders with the boarding-house fare.

'Your illustrious mother can make dried egg seem like pre-war buttered,' Mr Jeffrey Hutchins announced to Bobbie in adoring tones that morning as, Bobbie, having climbed the stairs while reciting '*The quality of mercy is not* strain'd; It droppeth as the gentle rain from heaven,' reached his room bearing his breakfast on a wooden tray.

Mr Hutchins had finished Shakespeare's famous lines off with her as she pushed open his door with her backside.

'*Upon the place beneath: It is twice bless'd: It blesseth him that gives and him that takes: Tis mightiest in the mightiest.*' Bobbie put down the tray quite thankfully across his bed-clothed knees as they finished together.

'*And earthly power doth then show likest God's, when mercy seasons justice. Therefore . . . though justice be thy plea, consider this— That in the course of justice none of us should see salvation: we do pray for mercy; and that same prayer doth teach us all to render the deeds of mercy.*'

'Ah, dear me, Bobbie darling, how that takes me back,' he sighed. 'I played the role of Portia when I first joined the Basil Hudson Players at the Majesty, Solness, over thirty years ago.

'And what splendour I was!' he said. 'Utterly, utterly splendid – of course I was billed as *Alexandra Hutchins*. My, but this is dee-lishus. Your mother is a genius of the post-war stove.'

Bobbie watched in silent admiration as the former 'Alexandra Hutchins' put up such an acting feat of enjoying his breakfast that, despite herself, she found her mouth watering.

'Now, Bobbie, heart of oak, we have to face facts. You are beautiful, you are nearly sixteen, it's time you joined the profession! I shall procure for you a non-speaking part next week,' Bobbie's self-appointed patron announced and kissed the tips of her fingers, in reply to which Bobbie sank into her best ballet curtsey.

The part was that of a Chinese rickshaw boy but, as far as Bobbie was concerned, it could have been Cleopatra herself, and her cue the very sound of triumphal Paradise.

'I'm not going to school any more,' Bobbie told her mother the following week.

'What are they doing this week, then?' asked Mrs Charles.

'*The Goose and the Gander* – I have a small speaking part.'

'What do they want to put *that* on for? It was such a flop in the West End – much better to have done a nice piece of Anouilh,' Mrs Charles continued, seemingly less than interested in any further discussion about her daughter's education. 'Much better to have put on a nice bit of Anouilh,' she repeated, as if the celebrated French playwright was a juicy steak. 'You must go to school though, Bobs, really you must.'

'Mr Hutchins says I will receive a better education at the hands of William Shakespeare and Oscar Wilde and George Bernard Shaw.'

'Bernard Shaw thinks Stalin's a saint, that's how much *he* knows.'

'Bobbie, darling, do not fret about ess-cee-aitch-oh-oh-ell. I know the local beak so no problem there, poppatine,' said Mr Hutchins, flowing into the kitchen already in full make-up. 'I can take care of him – and of us,' he added throwing a parcel wrapped in newspaper at Mrs Charles. 'This girl is going to be one of our greatest actresses, Mrs Charles, mark my words.'

'Oh, you do talk such tosh, Mr Hutchins, really you

do,' Mrs Charles said weeping, due to the onion she was chopping.

'Now unwrap your gift, you ungrateful woman.'

Revealed from the ingloriously wrapped parcel was a perfectly glorious piece of steak. They all stared at it, even Mr Hutchins.

'Now, do you believe me when I say I know everybody? No need for Bobbie to go to dull old school any more then, is there?'

At which he winked at Bobbie and swept out again. So that was that. Bobbie left school that day and when she became famous and was interviewed by journalists wanting to know to what she attributed her early stage success she would always reply: 'To two pounds of juicy rump steak.'

She discovered that, in dressing up and acting older for parts that needed it, Jeffrey Hutchins might be right – she might be rather beautiful. Her hair, long and dark, had never been cut from the time she was quite tiny – if only to save expense – and once it was put up in a chignon it revealed a long neck, small chin, high cheekbones and large dark grey eyes. Her feet and hands were small and exquisitely formed, or so Allan, Mr Hutchins's dresser, told her when he creamed them for her after the performance.

'Just remember, the theatre is a marsh light leading you on and on to nowhere in the end, and either side is quicksand,' he'd sometimes say, but since he had never made it as a star Bobbie felt he was prejudiced. For her the theatre was everything, and she didn't care if she was fatally trapped in its marsh light. Dancing, singing, learning new lines every week, it was all she wanted out of life.

'You're losing weight, you're too skinny, they're working you too hard, you've got salt cellars either side of that neck of yours.'

'I'm perfectly all right, Mum.'

'Well, you must be the only one who is,' sighed Mrs Charles. 'Rationing, snook, and now my fifth nasty letter from the bank manager. I'm having to take in a new lodger, so you're going to have to bunk up with Maggie Gondal.'

'*I sometimes think that spring will never come,*' said Bobbie, quoting a line from the play they were now rehearsing. 'Who?'

'The son of that magistrate Mr Hutchins is always on about.'

'But, Mum, a civilian, *here?*' Bobbie said, and just stared at her mother. 'Civilians' were what the company at the Kintlebury Theatre called non-theatricals . . . outsiders.

'His train's due at any minute – you'll go, won't you, Bobs? Mr Hutchins said you can take him on to rehearsals with you afterwards. Apparently the poor boy's got a few weeks before he goes into the Army and Mr Hutchins told his father it would do him good to see how the other half lives, so he's taken him on as a stagehand.'

The station was freezing cold and the train was so late it was going to make Bobbie late for rehearsals, so she was in no mood to be kind to their new lodger. As she said to Maggie later that night, she knew as soon as she saw Punch de Lacy with his short hair and his school tie, white shirt and incredibly pukka suit, that he was never going to fit in.

Bobbie actually found herself feeling embarrassed to walk into rehearsals with him.

'I feel sorry for him,' Maggie confided. 'I mean to say. A lad like that brought up as he has been, used to everything, the other lads are bound to take terrible advantage of him, aren't they? I mean to say. They won't be able to help themselves.'

And it seemed they couldn't either, as during the next week of rehearsals and production the newcomer met with one misfortune after another.

If Punch was meant to be 'on the book', the prompt book somehow went missing. If he was meant to be in charge of the first or second act calls, the curtain mysteriously stuck. After a couple of weeks events finally came to a head – Maggie Gondal's head, as it happened.

'Here, Miss Gondal wants you to get this from the chemist.'

It was not Maggie's usual hair colouring, nor was it her writing on the scrap of paper, but Punch, the poor fellow, wasn't to know that, as Mrs Charles observed to Maggie later. 'Not that it matters now, love,' she added staring at Maggie's newly-mauve hair. 'Just let's pray that they've got a wig at the theatre that fits until we can do something tomorrow.' Maggie cried and Mrs Charles comforted her, but no one dared say anything to Jeffrey Hutchins about the folly of taking on this la-di-dah young man for the very good reason that Jeffrey Hutchins himself seemed only too aware of it, constantly taking Punch aside and giving him what he called 'one of my finger wags'.

'He just can't do a thing right,' Bobbie sighed to Jeffrey's dresser. 'I just wish he'd go.'

'Why don't you tell him? At least you're nearer to him in age,' Allan suggested. 'It would do the company such a favour.'

Later that day Bobbie passed Punch de Lacy in the corridor after a strangely, almost dull, accident-free performance.

'Will you walk home with me?'

Punch looked at her, astonished, and coloured madly.

'Absolutely. Are you sure?'

'Why else would I ask you?' Bobbie demanded, but then she smiled because there were other people there and she knew they were sniggering at his shy, stammering, pleased reply. The air was cold, but there were stars and suddenly walking together with someone nearer her own age – he'd just told her he was nineteen to her seventeen – Bobbie felt a sense of freedom, as if up to then everybody had been able to listen in to everything she had ever thought or said but were now cut off. Besides, she had to admit it made a refreshing change to walk home with someone other than Maggie Gondal.

'You're going into the Army?' Bobbie asked after five minutes of silence.

'Yes. For my career, not just National Service.'

'Going abroad?'

'Malaya.'

'Will it be very dangerous?'

'Hardly more than working backstage at Kintlebury,' he told her with sudden humour. 'I thought Miss Gondal was going to kill me over that business with her tinting bottles.'

'If she wasn't so vain she would have seen the colour was wrong for herself . . .' Bobbie stopped and it was her turn to smile at the question in his eyes. 'Glasses, specs – she just won't wear them!'

They both laughed at this, and it wasn't long before they were seated around the kitchen table drinking their cocoa and Bobbie had quite forgotten her mission on behalf of the company: namely to suggest to Punch de Lacy that he should go back home and stay there until such time as his regiment called him up.

'I suppose what you're saying is I just don't fit in, is that it?' Punch asked her when she did finally get round to telling him, and then felt quite suicidal that she had because the hurt in his eyes was so tangible it seared right through her and made her want to cut her tongue out and throw it to the cat.

'No, no, no, of course not, no, it's just not that, it's just that you know small companies—'

'Yes, yes, of course. Like small regiments, yes? Resent outsiders. That sort of thing?'

'It's just that *you* don't seem to be having much fun.' Punch looked at her with infinite sadness.

'Oh, but you see I am. At least, I was just beginning to.'

Tears came into her eyes, but it was too late, he had left the room.

Write . . . they'd write to each other, he told her at the end of that week, but as Bobbie saw him off on the train, realizing too late that he was the tallest, handsomest young man who had ever visited Kintlebury in her short lifetime, she didn't believe him. Only his daring kiss on the cheek before springing after the train gave her hope.

But they did write, weekly, letters full of drawings and descriptions of everything except their feelings of loss. Finally, spring came and with it Bobbie's first leading part, not to mention an invitation from Punch to a ball.

Please God the date will not clash with a starring part! he wrote across the back, and it didn't as it happened, for Bobbie's chance for stardom had already come and been snatched with both hands.

'You're on your way now,' Mrs Charles said proudly, and yet, packed and on her way to meet Punch with an old costume from *Private Lives* altered to fit her in her suitcase, Bobbie felt as excited as she had ever done carrying her first starring role. As soon as she saw Punch waiting for *her* this time, she knew everything must be going to be perfect. He looked older and more sophisticated than she remembered him, and, later, even more handsome in his full dress uniform.

Bobbie did not need Maggie Gondal's specs to see at once how wrong she looked in her old-fashioned Gertie Lawrence-type evening dress compared to the other girls, all in their fashionable Norman Hartnell dresses.

As if her old-fashioned dress was not embarrassing enough, once the dancing started it became only too evident that Bobbie could not perform more than one circle of the ballroom floor without endangering Punch's life.

'Ballet, that's all I've ever done,' she confessed to Punch, both of them now white in the face from the strain of it all. 'Ballroom's so different for us ballerinas—'

'Take my arm,' Punch told her before she could finish speaking and, when she didn't, he took her hand himself and put it through his arm. 'There. Now stop looking as if you've forgotten all your lines and the play is about to close. I didn't ask you here just to dance; I asked you here to talk to you, so that's what I'm going to do, talk to you. Much better than dancing. Care for a walk, Miss Charles?'

'Oh, but you must want to stay and dance – you look so perfect,' Bobbie told him sadly, looking back at the waltzing dancers and the other young officers.

That was the moment when, in years to come, Bobbie realized she had truly fallen in love with him, the moment he pretended he did not care to dance. The moment that he had put her hand through his arm and she had walked with him through the great doors of the old house where the ball was being held, on the terrace.

Walking beside him in her ridiculous dress which he told her was 'So glam – I hate those New Look things the other girls are wearing', with her hand on his arm she knew, without any doubt at all, that she must be walking beside the love of her life and, inexplicably, she knew that he knew it, too.

'First of all, you must know that—' he began, before suddenly stopping. They had arrived at the edge of the lawn where old trees frowned down on the newly-mown lawn and an owl hooted.

Putting his finger to his lips, Punch walked quietly away from Bobbie, keeping his face raised towards a tree some hundred or so yards away.

Once stopped, Punch hooted gently. Now he increased the sound, and it grew and grew, until at last it was intense and he was using both his hands to make the effect and so carry the sound higher and further.

From above, seemingly from nowhere, there was a

powerful sound of wings, and within seconds of hearing it, Bobbie could feel an increase in the breeze until the owl, for that was what it was, landed on Punch's outstretched arm.

Bobbie stared at the sight of Punch and his owl. She could only just make out his smile in the moonlight and the myriad markings of the bird's feathers, but what she couldn't describe were her feelings.

'*For it has aroused a longing in me that is pain, and nothing seems worthwhile . . .*' Punch quoted after the bird had flown off again. 'That's how I felt after I first met you,' he went on turning her towards him.

'That's how I felt after you left Kintlebury,' Bobbie confessed. 'Everything seemed suddenly so thumb-marked compared to when you were there those last few days after we became friends. I couldn't believe it when you wrote to me.'

'I couldn't believe it when you replied. But I'm so out of place at your theatre. I felt so jealous of all those actors, so confident, whereas I couldn't even say good morning to you without stammering.'

'What shall we do now? I can't go back to the dancing!'

'I expect we can think of something,' said Punch, bending his head to kiss her, and, as Bobbie raised her face to him, it seemed to her that they had indeed found something a great deal more fascinating to do together than even dancing . . .

Back in the present, at the restaurant, Bobbie realized there must have been a very long silence indeed, for the woman journalist was staring at her, obviously still waiting for a reply to her first question.

'You met after the war—' she repeated in a bored tone.

Something in Bobbie's head exploded, moonlight, mown grass, the sound of dancing in the distance, the exquisite excitement of someone placing your hand through his arm for the first time; it was still there, but in the past, where it belonged. She carefully replaced her napkin on her plate and stood up.

'But why are you going?' the woman called after her.

'Because it's no good,' Bobbie called back. 'You see, if you lived to be a thousand, you would *never* understand.'

The Simple Soul

BY CATHARINE COOKSON

He looked at his wife through the bathroom mirror, and he told himself it was impossible to hate her, but he did hate her; he hated her pale and cool face, her light brown hair, her figure that had never got any fatter in twelve years of married life. He had slept with this woman every night of those twelve years, and they hadn't been parted for a day, well, perhaps a day but never a night. He had loved her, laughed at her and with her, and fought with her and against her, but never until this moment had he actually felt that he hated her.

The electric razor, making a refined buzz against his cheekbone, began to shake.

'Would you mind switching that thing off for a moment!'

This was one of his reasons for hating, this cool way she had of attacking: Would he mind switching that thing off for a moment? He switched it off so quickly that he stubbed his thumb.

Into the brittle silence her words came: 'I'm not asking you to consider the wife-end of this set-up, but it would be nice if you remembered that you have three children and but for good-morning and good-night, they haven't seen you for a week. They would like it very much if you

58

were to drive them down to the beach, that is if you have nothing else in mind.'

The electric razor went spinning across the glass shelf, skidded over the edge and descended into the bath after completing a wall of death circuit.

He leaned towards the mirror and watched his lips spitting out the words on to the cold surface: 'And what do you think the husband-end of the set-up has been doing all the week? Two hours each morning in a blasted train to town, two hours in the evening coming back, and to what? To an aloof creature getting more like something out of a fashion magazine every night. Only the models don't wear that "How could you do this to me" look.'

He swung round from the mirror and faced her. 'The trouble with you is that I play the game too clean,' he said. 'You've never had to wonder where I was, what I was up to; you've known my every move; like a damn fool I've mapped it all out for you.'

He stopped, waiting for her to come back at him, her voice cool, her words incisive. But she remained silent, her skin looking paler, almost transparent; then she did come back at him, but not in the way he expected; her voice quiet, but with a slight tremor in it, she said, 'This has been going on for more than a year now; it's got to come to an end. We'll talk about it later.' Her head drooped just the slightest, she turned towards the door; and then he had the bathroom to himself.

He bent over the bath and picked up what he was sure must be a damaged razor, and now he had the urge to throw it through the window and into the garden, perhaps to be returned by Andy and Stephen who, in the miraculous way they seemed to have with the inside of clocks, might make the electric razor function once more and shave everything within sight.

He ran his hands through his hair and went back to the mirror and stared once again at his reflection. He didn't like what he saw. Lifting his hair up like that showed the two receding patches at his temples; there were two deep grooves running from his nose downwards, past his mouth to the line of his jaw; and there was more than a suspicion of pouches under his eyes. He had never been handsome but it was agreed that for what he lacked in looks, he was compensated in other ways: he had what was called a personality. He repeated to himself; he had had! Now there seemed to be nothing left but a temper that was burning him up. But could it be wondered at? Five long days a week slogging in town, and then at the weekends, jobs lined up for him before he got out of bed on a Saturday morning and which kept him going until he dropped thankfully into it again on a Sunday night. The alternative was: we must drop over to Mother's . . . Mother lived a hundred and twenty miles away. We really must go and see Milly. Milly lived only seventy miles away, but Milly had a bore of a husband and six undisciplined brats, who could leave him with the feeling that he had just finished a rough scrum. Another time it would be: we must get Mother those bulbs in . . . her bottom patch needs digging, her fence needs mending, her garage gate is nearly off.

The requests would have been preceded with a laughing 'Come on the chain gang!' and he would have approached the odd jobs perhaps with some irritation, but only simulated wrath. Not lately, however. And now this morning at breakfast she had inferred he was expected to take the lot of them to the beach, and there, amid hordes of children, sun-boiled men and frowsy women oozing out of over-tight bathing costumes, he was expected to spend the day and, what was more, enjoy it. Well, be damned if he was going to; he'd had enough. She wanted to talk, did she? Well, so did he, but in his own good time. He was sick of being pushed around, sick of it. He tore the comb through his hair, took his shirt off the back of the door, marched out of the bathroom across the landing and into the bed-room, the very sight of which irritated him. Yet some thought, forcing its way in through reasonableness, pro-ferred quietly: there was a time when you thought this the most wonderful room in the world and Annette the best home-maker, with a sense of colour second to none. She had a way with greys and limes, with mustard, sea-green and autumn brown that made a room different from all others, that made a bedroom different.

But one couldn't live with a combination of colours; one wanted more than a house that was different.

Within three minutes he was running down the white staircase determinedly buttoning the middle button of his coat.

Patricia was at the foot of the stairs. She was eight, a tall eight and a replica of her mother. She looked at him with Annette's eyes now and said, 'You going out, Daddy?'

'Yes.' He was on his way to the front door.

'Where?'

'I don't know.'

She danced after him. 'Well how will you get there then?'

Wasn't that like her mother? He did not answer but

hurried along the front of the house to the garage where his eldest son was examining the car with the critical eye of a ten-year-old. 'Back tyre wants some air, I think.'

'I wasn't asking you what you think. Get out of the way!'

'What's up with you?'

'Don't you dare speak to me in that way!' The father and son surveyed each other. 'It's about time you were taken in hand.'

He pulled open the car door, and the next minute the car was out of the garage.

Through the mirror he could see his boy, with head bent, looking at the ground, and some part of him was upset, but it only urged on his departure.

He was out on the main road, where he remained for the next forty miles. It was when a road sign said YOU ARE NOW IN SUSSEX that he pulled on to the verge, and for the first time that day he relaxed against the seat. A better description would be slumped, he felt absolutely done in. Here, at half-past eleven on a Saturday morning, he felt that he had just finished a heavy week . . . Well, hadn't he? He *had had* a very heavy week. That is what some people didn't understand. The some people conjured up the face of Annette, and he swore under his breath.

Well, he was out on his own now, away from it all . . . and what was he going to do? He'd have lunch somewhere, have a good stiff drink, find a river and lie on its bank.

It was as he thought of a river that the name Jimmy rose to the surface of his mind as if it had been washed there by the gentle lap of the water. Jimmy. That is what he would do, he would go and see Jimmy. Jimmy lived in Sussex, didn't he? He looked around at the flowing fields as if they would answer him. Jimmy had been at him for years to pay him a visit.

Where was he? The last signpost had said Hastings twenty-eight miles. Jimmy lived outside Battle in a cottage in a wood. At one time Jimmy had talked so much about that cottage in the wood that it was all he could do to restrain himself from shouting at his colleague, 'For heaven's sake! man, shut up.' Jimmy had been a bachelor when he bought the cottage, and he had always considered him a bit soft in the head for saddling himself with it, and when three years later he got married, this seemed to prove it.

James Wheatley and he had started in the same office in Reynolds' Company when they were lads and step by step they had moved up from the office in the basement until they had to use the lift to the first floor. It wouldn't have done to have gone up the stairs not when you were young and earnest and full of your own importance. Now he was on the fifth and only one from the top, whereas Jimmy was still on the first floor; but nearly every day he saw Jimmy, for his one-time colleague had the embarrassing habit of waiting for him and escorting him either to the bus or to the tube. He was the kind of man it was impossible to snub.

The cottage in the wood, the cottage that he felt he knew, took quite a time to find. Several times he stopped the car and then traversed a number of side roads before he came to the farm. He felt he knew the farm too. The farmer's wife said, 'Oh, the Wheatleys. Oh yes. But you can't get the car down to them. Leave it over there' – she

63

pointed – 'so the cattle won't get round it, and then go through that gate and across the fields and you'll be on the cottage in no time.'

It was about fifteen minutes later when Richard saw the cottage. He was on a rise and he stood looking down on it in amazement. It was whitewashed or had been. It was tiny and from this distance it seemed to be almost buried in a tangle of undergrowth. But when he approached the front door he saw that there had been some attempt to make a garden. And he should know this garden. He had with nerve-tearing irritation listened to all Jimmy was doing in this garden, propagating rhododendrons, enlarging, through cuttings, his azalea stocks . . . he had marvellous azaleas!

The door was half open, and now wishing that he had never thought of Jimmy and his cottage, he leant forward and tapped twice. And then he only just stopped himself from letting his mouth drop into a wide gape when he saw the woman. That she was Jimmy's wife he had no doubt at all: Jimmy had described her to him time and time again. He knew all her virtues, but most of all he knew what she looked like: she was a ravishing blonde or as near it as made no odds. Her hair isn't gold, Jimmy had said, it's silver, and she hasn't blue eyes like an ordinary blonde, they're grey. The combination had sounded decidedly attractive, yet he had wondered at the time why any blonde, unless she was really dim, should throw in her lot with Jimmy . . . and now he knew. The woman's hair might have been silver many many years ago but now it was a tacky dull mess. The eyes were still grey but whatever allure they once had was now dimmed by a nest of lines, and the lines were not only congregated around the fine skin of the eyes but were also marking the upper lips like arrows converging to a central point. Years ago, too, the woman's face and figure might have caused an eyebrow to rise, now it would evoke only pity, if anything.

The woman stared at him. She did not smile but her eyes widened slightly before narrowing, and then she spoke.

'You're Dicky Morton, aren't you?'

'Yes. Yes, I am and' – he made himself smile – 'you're Mrs Wheatley?'

'Yes, I am.' It sounded defensive. 'Come in. I'll tell Jimmy, he's out in the field at the back.'

He followed into what was presumably the main room of the cottage. Disorder was not the term he would have used to describe it, but a phrase his mother had been apt to pelt at him about the condition of his own room came back to him, utter clutter. Here indeed was utter clutter. The woman, however, made no apology for it but, pointing to a chair, she said, 'Sit down and I'll call him.'

He watched her move out of the room. She seemed in no hurry. But then he got a further surprise when he heard her voice calling, 'Oo! Oo! . . . darling.'

Oo! Oo! darling, he repeated to himself while giving a small mystified shake of his head; and then it almost seemed that within the next minute Jimmy was in the room, Jimmy in his shirt sleeves and old trousers with a grin on his face that was embarrassing in its quality of genuine welcome.

'Why! Dicky, if this isn't a surprise. You've got round to it at last.' He was pumping Richard's hand up and down and, still holding it, he turned to his wife where she stood leaning against the table and explained, 'Didn't I tell you? I told you he would pop in one of these days.' And turning back to Richard, he said, 'I've no need to tell you who she is, have I?' Then straightening his back and with his hands now hanging limply down his sides, the smile slid from his face to leave it with a look of utter contentment, and his voice now matching his expression he said softly, 'By! Dicky, I'm glad to see you. Oh, I am.'

It was as if they hadn't met each other for the last twenty years whereas it was but scarcely twenty hours ago since they had parted.

'Have you the wife with you, and the children?'

'No, no. I just came for a run and found myself in Sussex and I thought, well . . . well, I'd look you up.'

'Well! well! What a pity! We'd have made a day of it.' Reaching out, he pulled his wife towards him, his arm encircling her waist as he went on, 'What have we left?' only for his face to blush and become confused with a boyish grin as he remarked with similar candour, 'There I go! talking as if I didn't know. We've got half a bottle of sherry; it's been there since my birthday. Anyway we'll finish it . . . what do you say, Flo?'

Flo. And metaphorically speaking, Richard closed his eyes on the abbreviation. He knew her name was Florence, but Flo, a worn-out blonde, blowsy. In the name of heaven! where had Jimmy picked her up? And yet it was more than likely that she had picked him up. Yes, she looked that type. Suddenly he felt a deep compassion for Jimmy, for being so gullible.

Jimmy had disappeared through the door, and while he looked at the woman and she looked at him he could still hear Jimmy talking, still exclaiming about the wonder of this visit. The amazing thing was he was genuinely pleased

THE SIMPLE SOUL

to see him, not a bit ashamed of this woman or this house . . . the dream cottage in a wood. How deeply could one delude oneself, for if anyone was suffering under a delusion Jimmy must be.

The woman startled him into stiffness by saying, 'Don't look so surprised.'

'What?'

'I said don't look so surprised.'

He smiled slightly as if he didn't know to what she was referring. 'What do you mean?'

'You know what I mean;' and she turned towards her husband as he entered the room, saying, 'I'll see to the dinner.'

'You'll do no such thing, well not for a tick, you'll have a drink first.' Here was a masterful Jimmy.

'But the chicken's on. It'll be burnt. I'll be back in a minute.'

'All right, darling, just as you say.' The voice was again meek; the real Jimmy. And now he turned to Richard and said, 'We must have known you were coming, we're having a chicken for lunch. Flo's a marvellous cook; just you wait, you're in for a treat. Well, here's to you.' He handed Richard the glass of sherry and bent forward, almost hovering over him in his pleasure. It was most embarrassing . . . the whole set-up was embarrassing. But one thing it had done, it had taken his mind from Annette, at least for the present.

The dinner had been well cooked, but ordinary, nothing startling: roast chicken, sage and onion stuffing, roast

67

potatoes and sprouts and, of all things, a rice pudding afterwards, and to cap it . . . a cup of tea. He would have liked to make his escape immediately after lunch but Jimmy made it awkward for him. First, he would have to see round the cottage. This didn't take long; then the garden. Undoubtedly Jimmy had not lied when he talked of his rhododendrons and azaleas, but the majority of them were nearly choked with bramble. Jimmy explained that it was difficult to get the gardening done in a weekend, and Flo was no hand at gardening, besides which she wasn't strong at all. This last was stated in very solemn tones. It was the only point of the whole meeting when some sort of a smile had not been on Jimmy's face. And then his wife had called from the house . . . 'They hadn't any milk!'

Jimmy explained that he collected the milk each evening on his return but on a Saturday and Sunday he went up for it in the afternoon. 'I won't ask you to come along,' he explained; 'You'd tear your suit to shreds. I take a short cut through the hedges. Anyway,' and here, he had nudged Richard, 'I want you and Flo to get acquainted, have a natter on your own.' He jerked his head proudly as if he were presenting Richard with an opportunity which should not be missed.

Richard had no desire to crawl through hedges and tear his suit, but he had less desire to sit in the frowsy room with Flo; but he *was* sitting in the frowsy room with Flo, and he knew that in a way this is what she wanted. He watched her light a cigarette, then lean back against the padded head of the couch and blow out the smoke with what he termed cheap expertness before she startled him

68

once again. 'If you try to open Jimmy's eyes in any way I'll pay you back . . . I might even go so far as to kill you.'

He was sitting bolt upright in his chair. 'I don't understand you, what do you mean?'

'Come off it.' She sounded to him as common as she looked. If she had been taking the part of a worn-out streetwalker in a play he would have termed her well-cast.

'Jimmy thinks I'm nice. Jimmy thinks I'm the goods, and I am the goods; as long as I have him I'll be the goods.'

'What has this to do with me?' His voice had a cold ring to it.

'Everything. You see I know all about you and I think I've hated you from the first week I knew Jimmy. You were too blooming good to be true. He's a child, is Jimmy: he's still playing with fairies at the bottom of the garden; he still believes in people. I think he's the only one left in this rotten world who still believes in people. You've climbed up the firm and Jimmy's been happy for you even when he's been left behind. To Jimmy you're a big brain, handsome, athletic. You're everything in *Boys' Own Weekly*. He's as blind about you as he is about me, because you're not a big brain, and you're not handsome or athletic; you've got bags under your eyes and you've got a paunch. And I'm not wrong in thinking you've got a rotten temper. Also I am not wrong in thinking that you came here today not to see him or even to find out what I was like but just to pass the time . . . right?'

'You're being insulting.'

'Well, that fits in with your picture of me, doesn't it? I mean the real picture, not the one that Jimmy has given you. You know . . .' as she leant forward, her forearms on her knees, her hands drooping between them, there was something masculine in the action, something threatening, and she went on, 'I'm fighting to hold on to something, something that you can kill. You see Jimmy every day. Even a child's eyes can be opened to the truth if it is rammed in hard enough and subtly enough. So don't do it. I'm warning you, don't do it.'

He stared at the woman. All this was fantastic, yet it was true. Every word she said was true.

He heard himself saying, 'You needn't worry, why should I open Jimmy's eyes? And can you be sure that they need to be opened? Perhaps he's just playing a game of his own.'

'Jimmy's playing no game, he's an innocent. I've been married three times before, I should know.'

Richard's chin moved down and his eyes dropped with it. He wasn't at all surprised.

Once again he was startled into straightness as she said, 'You're not at all surprised, are you?'

Meeting her on her own ground now, he said, 'I wouldn't have taken you for an innocent teenager.'

She stared at him and to his amazement her lips began to tremble and her teeth came down on the lower one in an attempt to steady it. She turned and stubbed out the cigarette, and her voice was different now as she said, 'I don't suppose I could convince you that I ever was.' And she now looked away from him as she went on, 'I was married when I was sixteen. He was a stoker and went to sea. Before I was nineteen I had lost two babies stillborn. He was drowned when I was twenty. I can only remember how relieved I was. When I was twenty-four I married again. This one was lazy; I worked for him for four years until he had to join up. He was torpedoed in 1941; in 1945 I married a refined guy; he was so refined that he could have charmed the Queen to put a signature to a cheque. You mightn't believe it but I wanted refinement, I craved for it in a way. Out of the ten years I was married to him he was a guest of Her Majesty's Prison for eight of them. We didn't see much of each other and I had to work again. I've always had to work . . .' and now her eyes were again directed fully on to Richard as she ended, 'until I met Jimmy. Jimmy is what you would term soft in the head, and so he fell for me.'

Richard looked away from her. It was uncanny how this woman read his mind. He kept his eyes lowered as she went on, 'All Jimmy wanted was to work for me, to love me, to protect me . . . he thinks I need protection. I've been married to Jimmy for four years and when he brought me to this neck of the woods I wondered to God how I was going to stand it, although I liked Jimmy then. Now I love him, and I want no place else on this earth but to remain here with him. You wouldn't be able to understand it.'

'Why shouldn't I?'

They remained looking at each other in silence now and it was strange but he found that he did understand this woman, wholly understand her. He didn't think that he'd be able to say he liked her or that he understood the reason why Jimmy wholeheartedly loved her, but he did understand her desire to be loved, to be protected. He understood it because he had lived for twelve years with Annette. He had felt like that about Annette when they were first married. Oh . . . oh, and long after. He had

wanted to be loved, fussed over and if not actually protected, made secure by love, and Annette had done that.
Annette had been warm and loving and giving, but what
had he given in return? All his life he had wanted to be
fussed over, wanted to be listened to. Annette had filled the
bill: she was always there to listen to him when he returned
from the office, and he couldn't get back quickly enough
to his audience. That is what Annette had been to him, a
loving audience.

He rose to his feet. He was hating the idea that he had
been forced to see himself through this woman's eyes. But
now that he was seeing himself he could no longer shut his
ears to the voice that said, 'It's taken you a long time to
grow up.' He was in his forties and it wasn't a nice feeling
to discover that one had just grown up; he needed no
bathroom mirror to see himself. The trouble between
Annette and him had started over a year ago when she
became a little tired of listening and when, because of the
heavy work entailed in his swift rise up those various office
floors, he had become a little tired in his loving.

All of a sudden he was overwhelmed by a feeling of
terror and through it he could hear Annette's flat
unemotional voice saying, 'We will have to talk.'

The woman too was on her feet an arm's length from
him now and the whole of her face was twitching as she
spoke. 'What's the matter? You're not going straight away?
He'd wonder . . . And you needn't look like that; there's
nothing I've done that I'm ashamed of, not really, it's only
being me looking like I do. I know how I look.'

He was staring at her, seeing the pathetic side of her,
but also seeing the largeness of the part she was playing,

and without thinking, first one hand went out to her, then the other, and then he was clasping them tightly and talking quickly, 'Don't worry, please! It isn't that . . . well, you see, you've brought me to my senses in a way. Yes, yes, I was surprised about you. No good trying to hoodwink you, because I showed it, but—'

'But you still pity Jimmy?'

'No. No, I don't. Why should I?'

She pulled her hands quickly away from his, saying, 'Ssh! Here he is. You'll not go yet?'

As he said, 'No, no, of course not,' he wanted to grab up his hat and get to the car and get home, home to Annette, but he stayed. And he proceeded to act as if he liked staying . . .

It was nearly five o'clock when they walked with him across the fields up to the farm, and before he got into his car Jimmy, placing his hand on his shoulder very like a character in an old-fashioned play, said solemnly as he gave him his correct Christian name, 'This has been the happiest day of my life, Richard.' Then casting a glance towards Flo, he added, with a smile, 'Well, almost, bar our wedding day, but Flo understands.'

Richard looked at Flo. She looked happier, more at ease, but she didn't look any younger, any better. To him she still looked a drab worn-out blonde. Yet taking her hand once more he asked humbly, 'May I bring my wife along some day to see you?'

There was a pause before she answered quietly, 'She'll be welcome.'

'Welcome! I should say she'd be welcome.' Jimmy slapped him into the car; he directed its backing with gusto,

73

and then, with one arm around Flo's shoulder, he stood waving until his friend disappeared.

Once away there was one thought in Richard's head, he must look out for a call-box. At last he found one.

As he lifted the receiver his hands trembled. A few minutes later, not being able to get through, he left the box. Perhaps she was in the garden, but even there she would have heard the bell ring. Well very likely she had taken a walk with the children.

He was in a deserted side road when the car stopped. Looking at the dial, he couldn't believe he was out of petrol, but he was. It took him a quarter of an hour to find a garage and get a can of petrol back to the car. At the garage, he had asked if he could use the phone. Again there had been no reply.

He couldn't really believe his ill luck when, only forty miles away from home, he had a puncture. And now it was almost dark. By the time he had changed the wheel he was in a state of panic: things seemed to be transpiring against him, keeping him away from his home and Annette. Before starting the car again he felt compelled to phone once more. He was in a village and the kiosk was only a few yards from him. When, for the third time there was no reply he leaned against the side of the box. It was nine o'clock. The children should have been in bed this past hour. Annette was very strict about bedtime. Anyway if they were in, Andy was capable of answering the phone. But if the children were in Annette would be in, she never left them alone. Frantically now he searched through the directory for the Beales' number. The Beales were their neighbours in the next detached house. They were at present away on holiday but Miss Carter was looking after the place and the dogs, she would be in.

Miss Carter said, 'Hello, who's that?'

He said, 'It's Richard Morton. I've had trouble with my car, Miss Carter, I wonder if you would tell my wife I've not been able to get through, there must be something wrong with the line?'

'Oh, Mr Morton, there's no one in. Well, there's no lights and I saw them all going away this afternoon. Didn't you know?'

His voice sounded rusty as he repeated, 'Away!' then asked, 'Where?'

'Well, I don't know, Mr Morton. But Mrs Morton was carrying a suitcase.'

After a pause he made himself laugh, and he answered on a loud note, 'Yes. Yes, of course, they were going for the day to her mother's. Thank you, Miss Carter. Goodbye. Goodbye.'

When he entered the car he sat quite still for some minutes before lighting a cigarette, and he remained sitting quietly until he had finished it. Then still slowly, as if he were very tired, he started up the car and drove home.

As Miss Carter had said, there were no lights on. He let himself in, walked through the hall and into the drawing room and switched on the central lights. Everything was as he knew it yet different, more beautiful, because it was no longer home. He had lost it. He sat down and lit another cigarette. He just couldn't believe it had happened. What did a man do in a case like this, get drunk and say, To hell! He couldn't get drunk and say, To hell! He could just moan inwardly, 'Oh, Annette. Oh, Annette.'

His elbows were on his knees and his hands were supporting his face when the voice came at him, and the surprise was so great he almost fell forward as his elbows slipped from his knees. Annette was standing in the doorway in her dressing-gown. Her face was whiter than he had ever seen it, her eyes larger, and there was a sadness about her that tore at him. She said, 'Do you want anything to eat?'

He said, 'The car broke down, then I got a puncture. I tried to get you three times.'

She moved slowly towards the fireplace. 'The Arnolds phoned,' she said. 'The boys wanted the children to go on the farm. They asked if they could stay over night. I took them this afternoon. I haven't been long back.'

'Annette. Annette . . . Oh, Annette.' He rushed at her and almost carried her to the couch. When her arms were about him, he was actually crying. She said, 'There, there! What is it? Oh, Richard, what is it?'

Shamefacedly, he wiped his face. Then lifting his head from her shoulder, he said, 'I love you, Annette.'

'Oh, darling!' She was shaking with relief. And now she, too, was crying. 'I was so worried; you didn't say where you were going. Oh, I've been so worried . . . Where did you go?'

'To Jimmy's . . . you know Jimmy.'

'But . . . but why to him? I . . . I thought you didn't get on. I thought he was . . . well, sort of a simple soul.'

'He is, but he's the happiest man I know. I think I went to him because I knew he was happy, and he is, absolutely . . . You see it was like this.'

He went on talking, talking, talking, and she went on

listening and stroking and patting. 'Things will be different now . . . I'll be different.' She smiled quietly into the crook of his arm. He had promised so many things, among them not to impose on her capacity as an audience. It was funny when she thought about it, for he had been talking steadily for an hour now. But what matter, their world was right once more, things were back where they were before the pattern of their marriage altered. It was right for them that she should give and he should take. That he should talk and she should listen. That pattern was right for them as the pattern was very right apparently for that simple soul and his Flo.

The Square Peg

BY JILLY COOPER

Clutching her parcels, Penny charged through the front door, skilfully avoided a workman on a ladder, but cannoned straight into the Sales Manager coming out of the Board Room with an important client. Gibbering apologies, she raced upstairs, tiptoed past the Personnel Officer's room, and eased herself stealthily into her office.

Miss Piggott, the Managing Director's senior secretary, looked at her watch in disapproval. 'It's nane minutes past three,' she said in her ultra-refined voice, 'Don't you think you're sailin' a bit close to the wind?'

'Oh gosh, Miss Piggott, I'm sorry,' said Penny, who was the Managing Director's junior secretary, 'but I saw this divine dress and then I found these shoes to match in a sale, and then in the same sale, I saw these garden scissors. I thought you might like them.'

Miss Piggott's disapproving face softened. 'That was very thoughtful of you, Penny. How much do Ay owe you?'

'Nothing, it's a present.' Penny kicked off her shoes, and collapsed into a chair, scattering parcels among the debris on her desk. 'I brought some éclairs, three in fact, in case *he* – she pointed contemptuously at the door leading off their office – 'gets back in time.'

'He's back,' said Miss Piggott. 'He's been ringing for you since two o'clock.'

Penny went pale. 'Mr McInnes is back already? My goodness, is he in a foul mood?'

'Ay've known him more accommodatin',' said Miss Piggott with a sniff.

'Oh dear,' sighed Penny, tugging a comb through her dark red curls, 'I do wish darling Mr Fraser was still here. Everything was so much nicer then.'

Mr Fraser had run the London office of Joshua McInnes Inc. with bumbling but good-natured incompetence; and immediately he had retired last autumn, old Joshua McInnes, who had been viewing the situation from across the Atlantic with increasing dismay, had sent his younger son, Jake, to sort out the muddle.

At first the London office hadn't known what had hit them. Young Jake McInnes went through every department with a tooth-comb, and for six months everyone had shivered in their shoes. Then gradually they began to realize things were running far more smoothly. Orders poured in and the factory had enough work in hand for three years.

People stopped flattening themselves against the wall whenever Jake McInnes walked down the passage. Everyone settled down – everyone except Penny, that is, for she was catastrophically inefficient.

Mr Fraser had kept her as a kind of office pet. He had found her useful at remembering birthdays and knowing which of the telephonist's grandchildren was down with the measles. Occasionally he had given her letters, which he always signed without bothering to read.

'Penny's beautiful and she keeps me young,' he had

insisted every time Miss Payne from Personnel had agitated for her dismissal. 'She makes a good cup of coffee, and she keeps the flowers in the conference room looking simply wonderful.'

But now Mr Fraser had gone, and Jake McInnes had taken his place, and everyone was laying bets on how much longer Penny could possibly last.

The day Penny had decided to make her shopping expedition, Jake McInnes had not been expected back until late afternoon.

'Hello, Mr McInnes, did you have a super time?' she asked nervously as she went into his office.

Jake McInnes looked her up and down for a minute, taking in the white silk shirt, the vestigial scarlet skirt over long brown legs. 'Sit down,' he said icily.

Jake McInnes was a powerfully built man in his late twenties, with thick, dark hair, deep-set eyes the colour of mahogany, and a very square jaw. With that nasty smile playing round his mouth, he looks more like a Sicilian bandit than an American businessman, thought Penny.

They glared at each other across the vast desk.

'It's twenty minutes after three. I thought your lunch break ran from twelve-thirty to one-thirty,' he said.

'I'm sorry,' mumbled Penny, 'but I saw this perfectly marvellous dress, and then—'

'I don't want any excuses,' he snapped. 'I've told Miss Payne to dock two hours' pay from your salary this week.' He picked up her folder. 'You must have been busy while I was away, these letters are beautifully typed.'

'Oh good,' said Penny, beaming at him.

'It's a pity,' he continued softly, 'that they bear absolutely no relation to what I dictated.'

Penny flinched as though he'd struck her.

'Don't you do shorthand?' he asked.

'Not a lot,' admitted Penny, 'but my longhand's terribly fast, so I can get the gist of things. Mr Fraser never complained,' she added defiantly.

'That doesn't surprise me,' said Jake McInnes.

For the next half-hour he went through each letter like an examination paper, until every shred of her self-confidence was ripped to pieces. Then he tore the letters up and dropped them into the wastepaper basket.

Scarlet in the face, Penny got to her feet.

'And another thing,' he added, 'next time you make reservations at a hotel, book single rooms. I don't like arriving in the middle of the night to find I'm expected to share a double bed with Mr Atwater.'

Penny went off into a peal of laughter, which she quickly stifled when she saw the expression of disapproval on his face.

'And one last thing,' he added, as she went out of the door. 'Put your shoes on when you come in here.'

'Was he fraightfully angry?' asked Miss Piggott.

'He wasn't pleased,' sighed Penny.

Valerie from the typing pool had just arrived with the tea. She took a cup into Jake McInnes's office, and returned a few seconds later with starry eyes.

'Isn't he beautiful,' she said to Penny. 'The way he looks at you. Not that I stand a chance when you think of all those sophisticated women who come and pick him up from Reception. That Mrs Ellerington last week looked just like a film star. Still, there's no harm in hoping, is there?'

'You need your head examined,' said Penny shortly.

Valerie bridled and glanced at the photograph over Penny's desk of a young man whose startlingly blond good looks were somewhat obscured by a long, moth-eaten beard.

'Oh well, since you fancy those drippy lefties with dirty fingernails, I don't suppose you would go for Mr McInnes,' she said sarcastically.

'Francis doesn't have dirty fingernails,' snapped Penny. 'And don't you dare mention him in the same breath as Jake McInnes. Francis is so gentle and sweet and unaggressive.'

'He wasn't so unaggressive when he broke that placard over the policeman's head in Trafalgar Square during that Disarmament Rally,' observed Miss Piggott.

'That's different,' said Penny scornfully. 'Francis was just showing how deeply he feels about non-violence.'

'Funny way of showing it,' said Miss Piggott, who disapproved of Francis not so much for his politics or his appearance, as for the casual way he treated Penny.

At that moment the telephone rang. Penny swooped on it. 'Hello . . . I mean Mr McInnes's office. Francis! Darling! Is it really you? How lovely to hear your voice.' She made a triumphant face at Valerie and Miss Piggott.

Half an hour later, she reluctantly put down the receiver, gave an ecstatic shudder and buried her face in her hands. 'He rang,' she said simply.

'So Ay noticed,' said Miss Piggott. 'Mr McInnes did,

82

too. He came in twice and went out looking like a thunder cloud.'

'To hell with Mr McInnes,' said Penny. 'Oh Miss Piggott, Francis still loves me. I thought he was cooling off. There's a demo on Saturday and he wants me to join him.'

Thrilled by this evidence of Francis's continuing interest, she wandered off to the typing pool to give Valerie the third éclair as a peace offering.

During the next fortnight Penny tried very hard to be more efficient, but she dropped enough bricks to build her own office block. She booked tables at the wrong restaurants, arranged meetings for the wrong days, and spilled a cup of tea over Miss Piggott's electric typewriter. She also got more and more depressed because Francis hadn't rung her, her only comfort being that he had promised to take her to the theatre the following Thursday.

Thursday dawned. Having washed her hair that morning, Penny arrived later than usual at the office. Jake McInnes sent for her immediately. 'Penny,' he said wearily.

'Oh golly, what have I done now?'

'Remember last week I wrote two letters, one to my father saying Atkinsons' were playing hard to get, but I thought we'd clinch the deal with them by the end of the month; and the other letter to Atkinsons' playing it very, very cool?'

'Yes,' said Penny. 'You signed them both.'

'And you put them into the wrong envelopes. Now get out, just get out. And I don't want to talk to Emma McBride if she rings.'

Towards the end of the morning, Penny's telephone rang.

83

'Can I speak to Jake?' said a soft, smoky voice.

Oh goodness, thought Penny, which one did he say he didn't want to talk to? 'Who's that speaking,' she said cautiously.

'It's a personal call,' murmured the voice.

Penny had a brainwave. 'How's your little dog?' she asked.

'He's fine Penny, just fine.'

It must be Mrs Ellerington, who had a peke. Penny decided to throw herself on her mercy. 'Well, Mrs Ellerington, Mr McInnes said he specially didn't want to talk to someone, but I can't remember who it was; you or Emma McBride, or it might have been Mrs Lusty. I'd ask him, but he's so mad at me this morning. You haven't fallen out with him lately, have you?'

'No, but I'm just about to.' The smoky voice had hardened. 'I think you'd bettter put me through.'

Two minutes later, Jake McInnes came out of his office. It was the first time he'd really lost his temper with Penny and it was the most terrifying thing that had ever happened to her.

'And take down that photograph of your boyfriend,' he shouted finally. 'This is an office not a film studio.'

'Well Ay never,' said Miss Piggott, as he slammed the door behind him. 'Ay've never known him flay off the handle like that before. Perhaps he is keen on that Mrs Ellerington after all!'

'I think I'd better look for another job,' said Penny listlessly, unpinning Francis's photograph.

'It might be advaisable; have a look in the newspaper,'

said Miss Piggott. She brandished a toothbrush. 'Well, Ay'm off to the dentist. Ay shan't be back.'

'Bye. Hope it doesn't hurt too much,' said Penny, who was already poring over the Situations Vacant column.

Nothing really took her fancy, until she suddenly read:

'Managing Director requires highly intelligent, hard-working secretary/personal assistant. Meticulous short-hand and typing essential. Salary £8,000 upwards for the right person. Apply Box 9873.'

The salary was almost twice what she was getting at the moment, and Penny thought of all the clothes she could buy. Her two cats could have liver every day.

The letter of application took her only a few minutes. She saw her new boss as a younger version of Mr Fraser, kindly and appreciative, just waiting for someone to bring sunshine into his life. She told him all about her troubles with Jake McInnes, and gave a much embellished version of her own career. Very pleased with herself, she sealed the letter and delivered it to the newpaper office by hand during her lunch hour.

Late that afternoon, Jake McInnes faced one of the toughest battles of his career. He lounged, outwardly relaxed, at the end of the long Board Room table. On either side of him sat the Board, all distinguished Englishmen, many years his senior. He was outlining the reforms he intended to make; reforms which, he must make them see, were desirable in themselves, and not just proof that, as his father's son, he was trying to throw his weight about in the London office of the firm.

Gradually as the meeting progressed, he felt he was winning the battle, antagonism was dwindling, and he was even getting a few laughs. He had just moved on to the subject of delivery, when Charles Atwater, the Sales Director, suddenly wondered if he was seeing things. For through the thickening cigar smoke, from the direction of the door, loped a rabbit. Hastily he put on his spectacles. Yes, it was a rabbit.

'Look,' he nudged the Director of Public Relations beside him.

'Good God,' said the Director of Public Relations, clapping his hands over his eyes, and resolving to give up heavy business lunches.

Jake McInnes looked in their direction. 'Have you anything to add, Charles?'

Mr Atwater roared with laughter and pointed to the rabbit which had reached Jake McInnes's chair.

Pandemonium broke out.

'Good God, it's a rabbit.'

'Tally ho, after it, boys.'

'Perhaps it wants a seat on the Board.'

'Is that your own hare, or is it a wig? Ho, ho, ho.'

They are like a crowd of schoolboys, thought Jake McInnes, trying hard to keep his temper.

'How did it get in here?' said Mr Atwater.

'I think I know,' said Jake McInnes, picking up the panic-stricken animal. 'If you'll excuse me a minute, gentlemen.'

He found Penny on her knees by the filing cabinet.

She looked up, cheeks red, a large smudge on her nose. 'Oh,' she said, a happy smile breaking over her face, 'you've found him. I was terrified he might have escaped into the street.'

Words failed Jake McInnes, as Penny took the rabbit from him, crooning, 'There, there, poor little love, were you frightened then?'

'Penny,' he said, 'where did you get it from?'

Penny's eyes filled with tears. 'From the market. He was the last one. The man said he'd go in the pot if no one bought him.'

A faint smile flickered across Jake McInnes's face. 'Well, you'd better go and buy him a hutch, hadn't you?'

'It's Thursday,' said Penny. 'I haven't got any money left.'

Jake McInnes took out his wallet and handed her twenty pounds. 'Go round to the pet shop now. And I want all those letters finished by the time I come out of the meeting,' he added.

Half an hour later, the rabbit was happily installed in a smart, blue hutch, nibbling at some lettuce, and Penny was busily typing when the telephone rang. It was Francis.

'Darling,' cried Penny, 'what a treat. I am going to see you later, aren't I?' (Silly to let anxiety creep into her voice.)

Francis's voice was sulky with embarrassment. 'I can't make it after all,' he said.

'Oh, why not? You promised,' wailed Penny.

Francis explained that he had this picket duty . . .

'Well, I'll come too,' said Penny.

'No, no,' said Francis much too quickly. 'It's only a small picket.'

Penny panicked. 'I don't believe you. You've found

someone else. It's that horrible blonde,' she choked. 'Oh Francis. I can't bear it.'

'Well, you'll just have to lump it,' said Francis. 'I'll give you a ring sometime.' The receiver clicked.

Penny's world seemed to be crumbling round her. In one day, she'd virtually lost her job, and had certainly lost her boyfriend. 'No one loves me,' she said. 'No one wants me, and I've got a bed-sitter, two cats and now a rabbit to support. Oh Francis!'

She ripped the letter she was typing out of her machine and put in a fresh sheet.

'Darling, darling,' she typed frenziedly. *'I'm so frightfully sorry. I didn't mean to disbelieve you, I was just so disappointed—'*

A shadow fell across the page. Penny leant quickly forward to hide what she was typing.

'What the hell are you doing?' Jake McInnes's voice was like a rifle shot. Penny burst into tears. She laid her head among the papers on her desk and sobbed. Jake McInnes did nothing, he just sat on the edge of Miss Piggott's desk, drawing on his cigar, waiting for her to stop.

'I'm so sorry,' she said eventually.

'What's the matter?' he said. 'Is it the boyfriend?'

Penny nodded dolefully. 'He's not going to take me out tonight after all. I think he's found another girl, an awful blonde with a forty-inch placard.'

Jake McInnes examined his fingernails. 'Well, as we both appear to have been stood up this evening—'

'Oh no,' said Penny in horror. 'Not you too – not Mrs Ellerington. Was she furious about that telephone call?'

'She wasn't "fraightfully accommodating" as our Miss Piggott would say.'

Penny began to giggle.

'And as I was saying,' he went on, 'as we've both got nothing better to do, I suggest we sort out this mess.' He pointed to the chaos which spread in a ten-foot radius round Penny's desk. 'Now which is your in-tray?'

'Well, those two tables over there,' said Penny, wondering what terrible skeletons were going to come tumbling out of the cupboard.

In the end, she rather enjoyed herself. Jake McInnes had obviously decided to be nice, and she found lots of things she thought she'd lost: her passport, several cleaning tickets and a bar of chocolate.

Two hours later, the tables, desks and surrounding filing cabinets were cleared and Penny was shoving paper into a sack.

'Miss Piggott will have a shock in the morning,' she said happily.

'Just try and keep it like this,' said Jake McInnes. 'Now I think we both deserve some dinner.'

'I've got stacks of food at home,' said Penny

'I know, half a packet of fish fingers in the icebox. Stop being silly, and go and fix your face.'

Penny was appalled when she took a look at herself in the mirror. Crying had devastated her make-up and there was a large smudge on her nose. Hastily she repaired the damage.

Jake McInnes took her to a very smart restaurant.

'Your usual table, Mr McInnes,' said the waiter, leading them to a discreet corner. Penny wondered how often Jake McInnes had sat there, lavishing wine and compliments on the lovely Clare Ellerington.

Jake ordered drinks, and with them the waiter brought a dish of radishes, which Penny longed to pocket for the rabbit.

'It's so lovely being hungry for a change,' she said. 'I'm so overwhelmed by Francis that I can never eat a thing when he's around. I'm afraid he has definitely gone off me. I should have realized it when he started putting second class stamps on his letters instead of first class ones.'

The waiter arrived with avocado pear for Penny and oysters for Jake. For a few minutes they ate in silence, then Penny noticed that a beautiful woman at the next table was staring at Jake. How odd, she thought, and had a good look at Jake herself, taking in the breadth of the shoulders, the strong, well-shaped hands, the thick black hair. Suddenly he glanced up and caught her staring at him.

'Well?' he demanded, just like he did in the office.

Penny blushed. 'I was just thinking that you're very attractive.'

'You shouldn't say so in such a surprised tone, it isn't very flattering.'

'Well – I mean – all the typing pool are besotted with you, but, of course, I'm immune because I'm in love with Francis. And I'm never attracted to people who bully me,' she added.

'That's blackmail,' said Jake McInnes. 'From now on, have I got to put up with your crumby typing, just so you'll like me?'

90

'Oh no,' said Penny, 'I've decided I like you anyway, after this evening – in fact I like you very much.'

He looked at her for a long time, his eyes moving over her face. 'That makes me feel as though I've just won the Nobel Peace Prize,' he said slowly.

Penny stared back at him, unable to tear her eyes away, the colour mounting in her cheeks. The waiter arriving with their second course brought them both back to earth.

'Goodness, it looks delicious,' said Penny picking up her fork.

'Mr McInnes,' she said in a small voice five minutes later, looking down at her untouched plate, 'I'm terribly sorry, but I don't think I can eat this. I can't think what's happened . . . I was so hungry, and now I'm not, and it was so expensive—'

'It's all right,' he said gently. 'It doesn't matter.' And as he smiled at her she noticed the tired lines round his eyes, as though he hadn't been getting enough sleep lately. Suddenly she felt shy of him, and in the car going home, she sat as far away as possible with the rabbit hutch between them.

He didn't attempt to kiss her, as he delivered her to the door. 'Go to bed early,' he said. 'It might get you in on time in the morning.'

Back to square one, thought Penny – but she didn't go to bed. She wandered round her room, chattering to the rabbit and the two cats, drinking cups of coffee, and determinedly thinking how very much better-looking Francis was than Jake McInnes. She didn't attempt to localize the vague happiness which was stealing over her.

*

'Hello, Miss Piggott,' Penny said dreamily next morning. 'How was the dentist?'

'Fraightful,' said Miss Piggott. 'He was drillin' away for hours. Mr McInnes wants to see you.'

'I thought he might,' said Penny, drenching herself with Miss Dior.

'Ay should watch your step if Ay were you. He seems a bit taight-lipped,' warned Miss Piggott.

Jake McInnes's face was quite expressionless when Penny went into the room. She beamed at him. 'The rabbit's very well,' she said. 'He ate lots of—'

'Sit down,' snapped Jake McInnes. 'You'd better explain this letter.' He held two pieces of paper between finger and thumb.

'Oh goodness, have I put my foot in something else?' sighed Penny.

'I think I'll read it to you,' he said silkily.

'*Dear Sir*, it begins. *In answer to your advertisement for a secretary/personal assistant, I feel I have the ideal qualifications for the job.*'

'Oh,' said Penny, interested. 'Are you getting another secretary? It will be a terrible squash with me and Miss Piggott and her.'

'It goes on,' said Jake McInnes, '*I relish hard work, and my aim in life is to find a job that I can really get my teeth into!*'

'I should hire her,' said Penny. 'She sounds jolly keen.'

'You would? Well, listen to this then. *I am meticulously accurate in every way and used to acting on my own initiative.*'

Horror crept over Penny's face. 'Oh no,' she whispered, 'it can't be.'

'Now it really begins to get interesting,' he said softly. *'My reason for leaving my present job is that the Managing Director (a wonderful man) was recently replaced by a director from the parent company in America. To be quite frank, this director is one of the most tyrannical individuals you could care to meet. He has already fired dozens of my colleagues – dear people who have given many years of service to the firm. I live in dread that I may be the next to go, as he bullies me unmercifully and makes my life a misery.'*

Penny buried her face in her hands.

He looked at her sternly. 'You could be prosecuted for writing that letter,' he said. 'It's complete libel from start to finish. A good thing I got in early, and no one else saw it.'

'I'm sorry,' muttered Penny. 'Truly I am.'

'So you should be.' Then to her amazement he threw back his head and roared with laughter. 'Used to acting on your own initiative, meticulously accurate . . . Penny, Penny—' He wiped his streaming eyes.

Tears of mortification welled up in Penny's eyes. 'How was I to know it was you lurking behind a box number? And then being so sweet to me last night, when all the time you were looking for someone else to fill my job. Of all the mean, cruel—'

'Tyrannical things to do,' said Jake McInnes, still laughing.

'I'm going,' sobbed Penny. 'I'm walking out of your hateful firm right now.'

She leapt to her feet, but before she reached the door, he caught her by the arm. 'Easy now, before you go charging out of my life, just read this memo. It came from Public Relations this morning.'

Penny looked at it suspiciously.

'*Dear Jake,*' she read. '*Thanks for your letter. Just to confirm that we can fit in your leggy red-head any time you choose to release her – particularly if she's as ravishing as you say. There's a vacancy on the copy side now, and she can do the occasional shift in reception. Best wishes, Jim Stokely.*'

Penny put the memo down on his desk. 'You arranged to have me transferred,' she said slowly.

He nodded. 'So I can get some work done during the day, and some sleep at night. I thought you might do rather well in Public Relations with that fertile imagination.'

Penny was still staring at him in bewilderment. 'Ravishing and distracting,' she said quietly. 'You're not just trying to get rid of me?'

He shook his head ruefully. 'I spent most of last night thinking about you; seeing you cuddling that rabbit, I realized you were wasted as a secretary. You ought to be living in the country looking after a house and animals and babies and one very lucky man.'

'I only wrote that letter because I was mad at you,' said Penny. 'I thought that you loathed me.'

'Loathed you! I've been hooked ever since I walked into old Fraser's office for the first time. It was in the middle of the afternoon, and you were painting your nails with the radio on, and the sun was streaming through your hair.'

He was coming towards her, and the expression on his face made Penny back away from him until she was trapped against his desk. He took her into his arms.

'Oh, we can't,' she said in confusion. 'Not here.'

'Why not?' said Jake McInnes. 'I'm the boss around here.' And he kissed her very hard.

'Oh my goodness,' said Penny, very pink and glowing. 'I don't think I do want to marry Francis after all.'

'And I don't think I can afford to have you sabotaging my public relations company either; you'd be much better going into private relations with me. We'll discuss it over lunch.'

Still with his arm round her, he leant across and pressed the intercom switch. 'Miss Piggott, I'm going to lunch, and I won't be back this afternoon. You're in sole charge of the office. Hire and fire at will.'

'But, Mr McInnes,' Miss Piggott's anguished voice echoed intercommunally over the room, 'you've got a meetin'.'

'Cancel it, I've got a meeting of my own lined up.'

He released the switch and turned his attention to Penny.

'But Mr McInnes,' said Miss Piggott, charging into the room like a herd of buffaloes, 'Ay don't think Ay can contact the people comin' to the meetin' in taime.'

She broke off suddenly as she saw Penny in Jake McInnes's arms. 'Craikey,' she said.

Mission Control:
Hannibal One

BY LEN DEIGHTON

All night I had been inside my headquarters, listening to
the wind playing demented tunes upon the army badges,
eagles and other paraphernalia that a publicity-conscious
army commander had provided to mark the progress of our
tiny expedition. I dressed myself in my heavy clothing
before venturing outside. The wind blew with renewed
violence as I emerged through the shelter's small flap. Each
gust crooned a low warning that seemed to vibrate the
whole planet before becoming the shrill complaining shriek
that penetrated to the centre of my brain. It was a feat of
willpower to think clearly. But I was the Mission Commander; unless I was able to think clearly, we might all die.

Others had been here, but only for a few hours at a time.
We were the first soldiers to come, and now it looked as if
we would be the first men to wage war here. It was a
terrible place to fight a battle: a fatal place to lose it. It was
a bleak, barren, metallic landscape like none other I had
ever seen. I looked up through the clear air, and recognized
the constellation of Pleiades, now setting. The neighbouring stars were growing dim. I remembered how as a
child I had dreamed of travelling to them.

My second-in-command was an engineer. He was a balding veteran of many years. A fierce disciplinarian with his subordinates, even I was not immune from his sarcastic jeers about youth and inexperience. Perhaps that's why one of the southerners dealing out the rations that day decided to complain directly to me.

'This clothing isn't warm enough, sir. I didn't know it would be as cold as this.'

'You're wearing the same as the others,' I said. 'You'd be no use to the army in a cocoon.'

'It's such a poor-quality material the cold wind goes right through it,' he said, examining his white tunic with finger and thumb. 'A profiteer with an army contract and friends in the Senate doesn't have to worry about how cold we feel.'

'That's all, soldier,' I told him. I wasn't going to let these 'boots' think that the informality that prevailed on these missions extended to the privilege of sedition. 'You volunteered for the trip and your application was endorsed by your CO and agreed by me. Did we all make a mistake about you, soldier?'

'No, sir,' he yelled. 'It's just that where I come from in the south,' he smiled, because his accent made the qualification unnecessary, 'we never knew temperatures like this.'

I looked at him. He was a weak-faced kid. He'd cut himself shaving, and a spider of dried blood crawled down his jawline. He was probably a good enough soldier left to do a soldier's job, but here he felt inadequate, and those were the ones who showed fear first.

'I'm not looking forward to the trip back, sir. And now the men say there will be fighting before we return.'

There had been mistakes and emergencies during the ascent. The boy needed reassurance. 'It's a routine mission. It was a thousand-to-one chance that they would have men up here, too.' It was a lie, but it seemed to do the trick for him.

'There's no doubt about them being here, then?'

'They're not local inhabitants, if that's what you mean,' I said rather brutally. I spoke too loud, I suppose. My second-in-command heard me and chortled. He looked forward to the fighting. For two decades he'd been in every war the army had fought and he knew that it was the quickest way to promotion. I kept my eyes on the youngster. 'Our mission is reconnaissance, but if they come into this area we will oppose their transit. If that means fighting, we fight.' I saw my Second nod. He turned towards us; he couldn't keep out of a conversation like this. He prodded the boy with enough force to make him wince.

'If you don't like it up here, go home,' he jeered.

The boy flushed. That summed it up, really; no one could get back alone, so there was nothing to discuss. The boy turned to go, but he gripped him by the arm.

'Listen, boot, did you wonder what those apes are doing up here? You think they came here to enjoy the view? OK. Well, if they keep to their side of that,' he pointed vaguely to the ugly outcrops of rock ahead of us, 'then no one will worry them. If they poke their dirty faces around the side of it—' He snapped his fingers in a way that left no doubt that it would be an easy fight. Perhaps that was the best way of reassuring the boy. And of reassuring them all.

I said, 'We think they are here for strategic reasons. From here they can launch an attack that would raze our cities

and decimate our women and children. They will have
machines with them . . . Well, you will see.'

'Now get going on the ration detail,' said the Second,
and followed him to be sure that it was done satisfactorily.

When they had gone, I went to stare again at the landscape. The sun's orbit brought it over the peaks behind us.
In this clear air the light was redder than I'd ever seen, and
I watched the strange terrain change from blue to pink. It
seemed odd that my wife would see this same fiery planet
and rejoice in its warmth as it brought another dawn for
our people at home. As I watched the pink light spill into
the valleys and crevasses I heard the sounds of the main
unit awakening. Even before reveille ended I could hear the
metallic clink of weapon checks. They were good men:
uncomplaining and loyal. I hoped that the events of the
day would not cause me to change my opinion of them.

There was still another wheatcake left with my breakfast.
I gobbled it hastily, knowing that I might not eat again for
some time. I removed my helmet and wiped the sweat from
my close-cropped head, hearing the sentries change with a
lot of ceremony and feet-stamping, and then finally my
second-in-command brought the parade to attention and
reported to me, 'Special Mission One: on duty, sir.'

I returned his salute with parade-ground precision.
Already the blood had drained out of the sun, and there
was no heat in it. An icy wind bit into me as I walked down
the silent ranks of soldiers. I could see from their expressions
that they longed to get their circulation moving again. I
noticed too how grimy their clothing had become in the
short time. There were no laundry facilities here, so I could
not reprimand a man for a dirty uniform. And yet such

99

things – as those who had served under me before well knew – were an important part of my theories of discipline.

'At ease, soldiers,' I shouted. They looked at me quizzically. It was an unusual form of address: soldiers are seldom called soldiers by soldiers, just as artists are never called artists by their fellow artists. I waited until the first strenuous efforts to keep warm were over and then continued. 'Soldiers, today you will make history that your children will read. Your children's children, perhaps, will remember your part in the history of our great nation. Free men will always be called upon to make sacrifices that freedom may survive. Some of my senior soldiers will remember other battles in Germany, France and North Africa, where their comrades died in order that the younger men among you could grow up in freedom. Now you in turn are asked to do the same. We will prove true to that trust in us.' It was going well, damned well. I had their attention; they had even to some extent forgotten the cold. 'You are a part of the finest, best-equipped and most scientific army that the world has ever seen. We were not sent here to fight, but we brought weapons with us because the Government knew that these people who use the word "peace" so often, who profess to bring brotherhood and prosperity to the whole world, have nothing but hatred and envy in their hearts.'

I paused, casually fingering the screaming eagles on my tunic. 'The Commander-in-Chief has asked the Senate to rush a Task Force to our support. Until they get here the eyes of the world are upon us.' These high-flown words held them rapt for a moment while I issued a rapid series of orders. 'Communications detail: report to your officer for special instructions. Special duty men: stand fast.

Kitchen detail: break camp. Advance party: formate to move north under commander's orders. All remaining personnel: on parade with weapons and entrenchment tools in five minutes. Parade: to your duties. Dis-miss!'

They broke up and doubled away faster than ever before. The urgent attention to detail would drive all anxieties from their minds. My Second ambled across to me with the insolence that a fine combat record permitted. He undid the strap of his helmet and dropped it to the ground. It angered me that he should thus treat an expensive piece of equipment while standing before me. He said, 'You think all that stuff does them any good?'

'Don't you?' I asked haughtily.

'Not a hope. But if it makes you feel better, OK.' He took out a flask and gulped a mouthful. 'They don't believe that crap any more than you do.' He offered me the flask. I was very angry, and for a moment I wanted to remind him of my seniority and have him standing rigidly to atten-tion and shouting affirmative monosyllables like a recruit. He must have read my mind, for he shook his head slowly and said, 'No, it's too late for that.'

I nodded, accepting the flask, and took a long drink. I should have done that hours before. I pulled a face as it tore a warm furrow through the cold, soft earth of my gut.

'They know,' he said.

'They know what?'

He sighed. 'They know that our mission wasn't publi-cized. A couple of Senators may know we are here, but the last thing they are going to do is send a Task Force after us. I liked that "Communications detail: report to your officer for special instructions" . . . He mimicked my accent, making the slight Neapolitan consonants that I had inherited from my father into a street-vendor's cry, all the words linked into a sing-song chant. He nodded. 'That might shore up your story for ten minutes, but those Communications boots are the biggest loudmouths in the army. That's why they go for that job. Special instructions!' He laughed. 'Special instructions—' It seemed to amuse him that I had chosen those words.

'I suppose we both expected it to be like this?' I said.

'I read the entrails,' he replied. 'I've always said that we should have kept going on those babies two decades ago. Instead, the politicians put our name on a peace treaty with them.' He paused. 'I hate those bastards.'

'There's too much to do to waste time hating half the world,' I said. 'Too much to build, to mend, to discover. We should have been working together all this time, instead of the two halves of the world rattling swords at each other.'

He spat, and swore.

'You've seen combat,' I argued. 'You've seen what a modern army can do. How can you want to fight?' I shivered. 'Aren't the elements enemy enough? We still know too little about the world we live in.'

'You should have been a doctor or a lawyer or an artist or something. By jupiter, I'll wait until you've seen these barbarians for yourself. I'll wait until you've seen what they do with our prisoners. Cruelty is part of their official policy, just as lying is. They have no religion; nothing is sacred to them. There are no standards that we have in common with these bastards. Sooner or later you'll have to face the fact that violence is the only language they understand.'

'I've seen some combat,' I said distantly. He smiled the

cold sad smile that he kept for recruits who said something especially foolish. We both knew that I had been chosen for this command because of my brilliant scholastic record, and that he was there to provide the blunter skills of the combat engineer. But the tactics of bridging rivers under fire wasn't going to help us now, any more than my theoretical science.

'Believe me, sir,' he said, 'riot control in our cities, police actions against guerrillas or some tiny satellite nation on the far side of the world is one thing, this is another. We are going to come face to face with the finest soldiers they can select. They'll have modern weapons and good leadership. I don't think we'll be able to stop them.'

I'd never heard him talk like this. I realized that his brash and belligerent manner concealed a dark despair.

'They're not supermen,' I said with a smile. 'They're just a mixture of nationalities from every corner of the world.'

'Like us?' he smiled.

'Exactly.' He was always talking about race and nationality, which made me wonder what his own origins were: German, perhaps.

The scream cut through the air like a spurt of blood. Three of our men, their uniforms mud-spattered and torn, were running as fast as Olympic champions. Behind them there was a fourth. He was holding his side as he ran, leaving a trail of red spots, each one bigger than the last. The whole unit broke formation as the three men of the advance party ran past them without even a glance at their comrades. The fourth man was level with me now, and I stepped out to stand in his path. He stopped. His eyes were

103

huge and full of tears. 'You said they were men!' he accused. 'You said we'd be fighting *men!*' His voice was shrill to the point of hysteria. His helmet was askew, but the spider of blood on his jaw told me that it was the boy I'd spoken with. I grabbed his arm but he broke away from me with a surprising force. I looked down and found that my tunic was smeared with fresh shiny blood from the youngster's wounds. I watched him as he followed the others down a steep incline, dodging between the rocky outcrops. 'Come back!' I shouted. The wind snatched my voice away. I cupped my hands round my mouth. 'Come back at once! I'll have you executed!'

It was no use. The rest of them had sniffed the scent of panic and were scrambling down the hillside too. Only a few of the hardiest old campaigners remained in the roadway looking the way the four men had come. For a moment I had hope, but then they saw the sight that the others had seen and they too gibbered with fear.

'Don't be afraid,' I said, 'don't be afraid. I've seen them before. They are large, but they are controlled by men no better than us.'

Two of my senior sergeants then prostrated themselves on the roadway, screaming a mixture of prayers and oaths that betrayed a mankind for whom witchcraft lay just under the skin of science.

Other soldiers were ripping their hands and legs on the rocks and stony ledges below me as they half-ran and half-fell towards the sheltered basin in which we had camped the previous night. 'Alive!' my soldiers were shouting. 'They are alive! They are alive!'

They would not escape. There was no escape from here.

Already some of the men who had fallen were not able to regain their feet. A thousand feet below me were men who could have got there only by throwing themselves bodily from the narrow crevasse. Wearily, I turned back to where my second-in-command was standing. He'd not moved.

'Who could have believed it?' I asked, as I stood there with the bald officer: just two of us between the invaders and the rich, lush land of Italy. 'Who could have believed that Hannibal would bring elephants over the Alps?'

A Case of Misidentity

Long as had been my acquaintance with Sherlock Holmes, I had seldom heard him refer to his early life; and the only knowledge I ever gleaned of his family history sprang from the rare visits of his famous brother, Mycroft. On such occasions, our visitor invariably addressed me with courtesy, but also (let me be honest!) with some little condescension. He was – this much I knew – by some seven years the senior in age to my great friend, and was a founder member of the Diogenes Club, that peculiar institution whose members are ever forbidden to converse with one another. Physically, Mycroft was stouter than his brother (I put the matter in as kindly a manner as possible); but the single most striking feature about him was the piercing intelligence of his eyes – greyish eyes which appeared to see beyond the range of normal mortals. Holmes himself had commented upon this last point: 'My dear Watson, you have recorded – and I am flattered by it – something of my own powers of observation and deduction. Know, however, that Mycroft has a degree of observation somewhat the equal of my own; and as for deduction, he has a brain that is unrivalled – *virtually* unrivalled – in the northern hemisphere. You may be relieved, however, to learn that he is a trifle lazy, and quite decidedly somnolent – and that his executant ability on the violin is immeasurably inferior to my own.'

(Was there, I occasionally wondered, just the hint of competitive envy between those two unprecedented intellects?)

I had just called at 221B Baker Street on a fog-laden November afternoon in 188–, after taking part in some research at St Thomas's Hospital into suppurative tonsillitis (I had earlier acquainted Holmes with the particulars). Mycroft was staying with Holmes for a few days, and as I entered that well-known sitting room I caught the tail-end of the brothers' conversation.

'Possibly, Sherlock – possibly. But it is the *detail*, is it not? Give me all the evidence and it is just possible that I could match your own analyses from my corner armchair. But to be required to rush hither and thither, to find and examine witnesses, to lie along the carpet with a lens held firmly to my failing sight . . . No! It is not my *métier*!'

During this time Holmes himself had been standing before the window, gazing down into the neutral-tinted London street. And looking over his shoulder, I could see that on the pavement opposite there stood an attractive young woman draped in a heavy fur coat. She had clearly just arrived, and every few seconds was looking up to Holmes's window in hesitant fashion, her fingers fidgeting with the buttons of her gloves. On a sudden she crossed the street, and Mrs Hudson was soon ushering in our latest client.

After handing her coat to Holmes, the young lady sat nervously on the edge of the nearest armchair, and announced herself as Miss Charlotte van Allen. Mycroft nodded briefly at the newcomer, before reverting to a monograph on polyphonic plainchant; whilst Holmes himself made observation of the lady in that abstracted yet intense manner which was wholly peculiar to him.

'Do you not find,' began Holmes, 'that with your short sight it is a little difficult to engage in so much typewriting?'

Surprise, apprehension, appreciation, showed by turns upon her face, succeeded in all by a winsome smile as she appeared to acknowledge Holmes's quite extraordinary powers.

'Perhaps you will also tell me,' continued he, 'why it is that you came from home in such a great hurry?'

For a few seconds, Miss van Allen sat shaking her head with incredulity; then, as Holmes sat staring towards the ceiling, she began her remarkable narrative.

'Yes, I did bang out of the house, because it made me very angry to see the way my father, Mr Wyndham, took the whole business – refusing even to countenance the idea of going to the police, and quite certainly ruling out any recourse to yourself, Mr Holmes! He just kept repeating – and I *do* see his point – that no real harm has been done . . . although he can have no idea of the misery I have had to endure.'

'Your father?' queried Holmes quietly. 'Perhaps you refer to your stepfather, since the names are different?'

'Yes,' she confessed, 'my stepfather. I don't know why I keep referring to him as "father" – especially since he is but five years older than myself.'

'Your mother – she is still living?'

'Oh, yes! Though I will not pretend I was over-pleased when she remarried so soon after my father's death – and then to a man almost seventeen years younger than herself. Father – my real father, that is – had a plumbing business in the Tottenham Court Road, and Mother carried on the company after he died, until she married Mr Wyndham. I think he considered such things a little beneath his new wife, especially with his being in a rather superior position as a traveller in French wines. Whatever the case, though, he made Mother sell out.'

'Did you yourself derive any income from the sale of your father's business?'

'No. But I do have a hundred pounds annual income in my own right; as well as the extra I make from my typing. If I may say so, Mr Holmes, you might be surprised how many of the local businesses – including Cook and Marchant – ask me to work for them a few hours each week. You see' (she looked at us with a shy, endearing diffidence) 'I'm quite good at *that* in life, if nothing else.'

'You must then have some profitable government stock—?' began Holmes.

She smiled again: 'New Zealand, at four and a half per cent.'

'Please forgive me, Miss van Allen, but could not a single lady get by very nicely these days on – let us say, fifty pounds per annum?'

'Oh, certainly! And I myself live comfortably on but ten shillings per week, which is only half of that amount. You see, I never touch a single penny of my inheritance. Since I live at home, I cannot bear the thought of being a burden to my parents, and we have reached an arrangement whereby Mr Wyndham himself is empowered to draw my interest each quarter for as long as I remain in that household.'

Holmes nodded. 'Why have you come to see me?' he asked bluntly.

A flush stole over Miss van Allen's face and she plucked nervously at a small handkerchief drawn from her bag as she stated her errand with earnest simplicity. 'I would give everything I have to know what has become of Mr Horatio Darvill. There! Now you have it.'

'Please, could you perhaps begin at the beginning?' encouraged Holmes gently.

'Whilst my father was alive, sir, we always received tickets for the gas-fitters' ball. And after he died, the tickets were sent to my mother. But neither Mother nor I ever thought of going, because it was made plain to us that Mr Wyndham did not approve. He believed that the class of folk invited to such gatherings was inferior; and furthermore he asserted that neither of us – without considerable extra expenditure – had anything fit to wear. But believe me, Mr Holmes, I myself had the purple plush that I had never so much as taken from the drawer!'

It was after a decent interval that Holmes observed quietly: 'But you *did* go to the ball?'

'Yes. In the finish, we both went – Mother and I – when my stepfather had been called away to France.'

'And it was there that you met Mr Horatio Darvill?'

'Yes! And – do you know? – he called the very next morning. And several times after that, whilst my stepfather was in France, we walked out together.'

'Mr Wyndham must have been annoyed once he learned what had occurred?'

Miss van Allen hung her pretty head. 'Most annoyed, I'm afraid, for it became immediately clear that he did not approve of Mr Darvill.'

'Why do you think that was so?'

'I am fairly sure he thought Mr Darvill was interested only in my inheritance.'

'Did Mr Darvill not attempt to keep seeing you – in spite of these difficulties?'

'Oh yes! I thought, though, it would be wiser for us to stop seeing each other for a while. But he did write – every single day. And always, in the mornings, I used to receive the letters myself so that no one else should know.'

'Were you engaged to this gentleman?'

'Yes! For there was no problem about his supporting me. He was a cashier in a firm in Leadenhall Street—'

'Ah! Which office was that?' I interposed, for that particular area is known to me well, and I hoped that I might perhaps be of some assistance in the current investigation. Yet the look on Holmes's face was one of some annoyance, and I sank further into my chair as the interview progressed.

'I never did know exactly which firm it was,' admitted Miss van Allen.

'But where did he live?' persisted Holmes.

'He told me that he usually slept in a flat on the firm's premises.'

'You must yourself have written to this man, to whom you had agreed to become engaged?'

She nodded. 'To the Leadenhall Street Post Office, where I left my letters poste restante. Horatio – Mr Darvill – said that if I wrote to him at his work address, he'd never get to see my envelopes first, and the young clerks there would be sure to tease him about things.'

It was at this point that I was suddenly conscious of certain stertorous noises from Mycroft's corner – a wholly reprehensible lapse into poor manners, as it appeared to me.

'What else can you tell me about Mr Darvill?' asked Holmes quickly.

'He was very shy. He always preferred to walk out with me in the evening than in the daylight. "Retiring", perhaps, is the best word to describe him – even his voice. He'd had the quinsy as a young man, and was still having treatment for it. But the disability had left him with a weak larynx, and a sort of whispering fashion of speaking. His eyesight, too, was rather feeble – just as mine is – and he always wore tinted spectacles to protect his eyes against the glare of any bright light.'

Holmes nodded his understanding; and I began to sense a note of suppressed excitement in his voice.

'What next?'

'He called at the house the very evening on which Mr Wyndham next departed for France, and he proposed that we should marry before my stepfather returned. He was convinced that this would be our only chance; and he was so dreadfully in earnest that he made me swear, with my hand upon both Testaments, that whatever happened I would always be true and faithful to him.'

'Your mother was aware of what was taking place?'

'Oh, *yes*! And she approved so much. In a strange way, she was even fonder of my fiancé than I was myself, and she agreed that our only chance was to arrange a secret marriage.'

'The wedding was to be in church?'

'Last Friday, at St Saviour's, near King's Cross; and we were to go on to a wedding breakfast afterwards at the St Pancras Hotel. Horatio called a hansom for us, and put Mother and me into it before stepping himself into a four-wheeler which happened to be in the street. Mother and I got to St Saviour's first – it was only a few minutes' distance away. But when the four-wheeler drove up and we waited for him to step out – he never did, Mr Holmes! And when the cabman got down from the box and looked inside the carriage – *it was empty.*'

'You have neither seen nor heard of Mr Darvill since?'

'Nothing,' she whispered.

'You had planned a honeymoon, I suppose?'

'We had planned,' said Miss van Allen, biting her lip and scarce managing her reply, 'a fortnight's stay at The Royal Gleneagles in Inverness, and we were to have caught the lunch-time express from King's Cross.'

'It seems to me,' said Holmes, with some feeling, 'that you have been most shamefully treated, dear lady.'

But Miss van Allen would hear nothing against her loved one, and protested spiritedly: 'Oh, no, sir! He was far too good and kind to treat me so.'

'Your own opinion, then,' said Holmes, 'is that some unforeseen accident or catastrophe has occurred?'

She nodded her agreement. 'And I think he must have had some premonition that very morning of possible danger, because he begged me then, once again, to remain true to him – whatever happened.'

113

'You have no idea what that danger may have been?'

'None.'

'How did your mother take this sudden disappearance?'

'She was naturally awfully worried at first. But then she became more and more angry; and she made me promise never to speak to her of the matter again.'

'And your stepfather?'

'He seemed – it was strange, really – rather more sympathetic than Mother. At least he was willing to discuss it.'

'And what was his opinion?'

'He agreed that some accident must have happened. As he said, Mr Darvill could have no possible interest in bringing me to the very doors of St Saviour's – and then in deserting me there. If he had borrowed money – or if some of my money had already been settled on him – then there might have been some reason behind such a cruel action. But he was absolutely independent about money, and he would never even look at a sixpence of mine if we went on a visit. Oh, Mr Holmes! It is driving me half-mad to think of—' But the rest of the sentence was lost as the young lady sobbed quietly into her handkerchief.

When she had recovered her composure, Holmes rose from his chair, promising that he would consider the baffling facts she had put before him. 'But if I could offer you one piece of advice,' he added, as he held the lady's coat for her, 'it is that you allow Mr Horatio Darvill to vanish as completely from your memory as he vanished from his wedding-carriage.'

'Then you think that I shall not see him again?'

'I fear not. But please leave things in my hands. Now! I wish you to send me a most accurate physical description of Mr Darvill, as well as any of his letters which you feel you can spare.'

'We can at least expedite things a little in those two respects,' replied she in business-like fashion, 'for I advertised for him in last Monday's *Chronicle*.' And promptly reaching into her handbag, she produced a newspaper cutting which she gave to Holmes, together with some other sheets. 'And here, too, are four of his letters which I happen to have with me. Will they be sufficient?'

Holmes looked quickly at the letters, and nodded. 'You say you never had Mr Darvill's address?'

'Never.'

'Your stepfather's place of business, please?'

'He travels for Cook and Marchant, the great Burgundy importers, of Fenchurch Street.'

'Thank you.'

After she had left Holmes sat brooding for several minutes, his fingertips still pressed together. 'An interesting case,' he observed finally. 'Did you not find it so, Watson?'

'You appeared to read a good deal which was quite invisible to me,' I confessed.

'Not invisible, Watson. Rather, let us say – unnoticed. And that in spite of my repeated attempts to impress upon you the importance of sleeves, of thumb-nails, of boot-laces, and the rest. Now, tell me, what did you immediately gather from the young woman's appearance? Describe it to me.'

Conscious of Mycroft's presence, I sought to recall my closest impressions of our recent visitor.

'Well, she had, beneath her fur, a dress of rich brown, somewhat darker than the coffee colour, with a little black plush at the neck and at the sleeves – you mentioned sleeves, Holmes? Her gloves were dove-grey in colour, and were worn through at the right forefinger. Her black boots, I was not able, from where I sat, to observe in any detail, yet I would suggest that she takes either the size four and a half or five. She wore small pendant earrings, almost certainly of imitation gold, and the small handkerchief into which the poor lady sobbed so charmingly had a neat darn in the monogrammed corner. In general, she had the air of a reasonably well-to-do young woman who has not quite escaped from the slightly vulgar inheritance of a father who was – let us be honest about it, Holmes! – a plumber.'

A snort from the chair beside which Holmes had so casually thrown Miss van Allen's fur coat served to remind us that the recumbent Mycroft had now reawakened, and that perhaps my own description had, in some respect, occasioned his disapproval. But he made no spoken comment, and soon resumed his former posture.

''Pon my word, Watson,' said Holmes, 'you are coming along splendidly – is he not, Mycroft? It is true, of course, that your description misses almost everything of real importance. But the method! You have hit upon the *method*, Watson. Let us take, for example, the plush you mention on the sleeves. Now, plush is a most wonderfully helpful material for showing traces; and the double line above the wrist, where the typewritist presses against the table, was beautifully defined. As for the short-sightedness, that was mere child's play. The dent-marks of a pince-nez at either side of the lady's nostrils – you did not observe it? Elementary, my dear Watson! And then the boots. You really *must* practise the art of being positioned where all the evidence is clearly visible. If you wish to observe nothing at all, like brother Mycroft, then you will seek out the furthest corner of a room where even the vaguest examination of the client will be obscured by the furniture, by a fur coat, by whatever. But reverting to the lady's boots, I observed that although they were very like each other in colour and style, they were in fact *odd* boots; the one on the right foot having a slightly decorated toe-cap, and the one on the left being of a comparatively plain design. Furthermore, the right one was fastened only at the three lower buttons out of the five; the left one only at the first, third, and fifth. Now the deduction we may reasonably draw from such evidence is that the young lady left home in an unconscionable hurry. You agree?'

'Amazing, Holmes!'

'As for the glove worn at the forefinger—'

'You would be better advised,' suddenly interposed the deeper voice of Mycroft, 'to concentrate upon the missing person!'

May it have been a flash of annoyance that showed itself in Holmes's eyes? If so, it was gone immediately. 'You are quite right, Mycroft! Come now, Watson, read to us the paragraph from the *Chronicle*.'

I held the printed slip to the light and began: 'Missing on the 14th November 188–. A gentleman named Mr Horatio Darvill: about 5′ 8″ in height; fairly firmly built; sallow complexion; black hair, just a little bald in the centre; bushy black side-whiskers and moustache; tinted spectacles; slight infirmity of speech. When last seen, was dressed in—'

'But I think,' interrupted Holmes, 'he may by now have changed his wedding vestments, Watson?'

'Oh, certainly, Holmes.'

There being nothing, it seemed, of further value in the newspaper description, Holmes turned his attention to the letters, passing them to me after studying them himself with minute concentration.

'Well?' he asked.

Apart from the fact that the letters had been typed, I could find in them nothing of interest, and I laid them down on the coffee-table in front of the somnolent Mycroft.

'Well?' persisted Holmes.

'I assume you refer to the fact that the letters are type-written.'

'Already you are neglecting your newly acquired knowledge of the *method*, Watson. Quite apart from the point you mention, there are three further points of immediate interest and importance. First, the letters are very short; second, apart from the vague "Leadenhall Street" super-scription, there is no precise address stated at any point; third, it is not only the body of the letter which has been typed, but the signature, too. Observe here, Watson – and here! – that neat little "Horatio Darvill" typed at the bottom of each of our four exhibits. And it will not have escaped you, I think, how conclusive that last point might be?'

'Conclusive, Holmes? In what way?'

'My dear fellow, is it possible for you not to see how strongly it bears upon our present investigations?'

'*Homo circumbendibus* – that's what you are, Sherlock!' (It was Mycroft once more.) 'Do you not appreciate that your client would prefer some positive action to any further proofs of your cerebral superiority?'

It is pleasing to report here that this attempt of Mycroft to provoke the most distinguished criminologist of the century proved largely ineffectual, and Holmes permitted himself a fraternal smile as his brother slowly bestirred his frame.

'You are right, Mycroft,' he rejoined lightly. 'And I shall immediately compose two letters: one to Messrs Cook and Marchant; the other to Mr Wyndham, asking that gentleman to meet us here at six o'clock tomorrow evening.'

Already I was aware of the easy and confident demeanour with which Holmes was tackling the singular mystery which confronted us all. But for the moment my attention was diverted by a small but most curious incident.

'It is just as well, Sherlock,' said Mycroft (who appeared now to be almost fully awakened), 'that you do not propose to write three letters.'

Seldom (let me admit it) have I seen my friend so perplexed: 'A *third* letter?'

'Indeed. But such a letter could have no certain destination, since it apparently slipped your memory to ask the young lady her present address, and the letters she entrusted to you appear, as I survey them, to be lacking their outer envelopes.'

Momentarily Holmes looked less than amused by this lighthearted intervention. 'You are more observant today than I thought, Mycroft, for the evidence of eye and ear had led me to entertain the suspicion that you were sleeping soundly during my recent conversation with Miss van Allen. But as regards her address, you are right.' And even as he

119

spoke I noted the twinkle of mischievous intelligence in his eyes. 'Yet it would not be too difficult perhaps to *deduce* the young lady's address, Mycroft? On such a foul day as this it is dangerous and ill-advised for a lady to travel the streets if she has a perfectly acceptable and comfortable alternative such as the Underground; and since it was precisely three-fourteen p.m. when Miss van Allen first appeared beneath my window, I would hazard the guess that she had caught the Metropolitan-line train which passes through Baker Street at three-twelve p.m. on its journey to Hammersmith. We may consider two further clues, also. The lady's boots, ill-assorted as they were, bore little evidence of the mud and mire of our London streets; and we may infer from this that her own home is perhaps as adjacent to an Underground station as is our own. More significant, however, is the fact, as we all observed, that Miss van Allen wore a dress of linen – a fabric which, though it is long-lasting and pleasing to wear, is one which has the disadvantage of creasing most easily. Now the skirt of the dress had been most recently ironed, and the slight creases in it must have resulted from her journey – to see me. And – I put this forward as conjecture, Mycroft – probably no more than three or four stops on the Underground had been involved. If we remember, too, the "few minutes" her wedding-carriage took from her home to St Saviour's, I think, perhaps ... perhaps—' Holmes drew a street-map towards him, and surveyed his chosen area with his magnification-glass.

'I shall plump,' he said directly, 'for Cowcross Street myself – that shabbily genteel little thoroughfare which links Farringdon Road with St John Street.'

'Very impressive!' said Mycroft, anticipating my own admiration. 'And would you place her on the north, or the south side, of that thoroughfare, Sherlock?'

But before Holmes could reply to this small pleasantry, Mrs Hudson entered with a slip of paper which she handed to Holmes. 'The young lady says she forgot to give you her address, sir, and she's written it down for you.'

Holmes glanced quickly at the address and a glint of pride gleamed in his eyes. 'The answer to your question, Mycroft, is the south side – for it is an even-numbered house, and if I remember correctly the numbering of houses in that part of London invariably begins at the east end of the street with the odd numbers on the right-hand side walking westwards.'

'And the number is perhaps in the middle or late thirties?' suggested Mycroft. 'Thirty-six, perhaps? Or more likely thirty-eight?'

Holmes himself handed over the paper to us and we read:

MISS CHARLOTTE VAN ALLEN
38, COWCROSS STREET

I was daily accustomed to exhibitions of the most extra-ordinary deductive logic employed by Sherlock Holmes, but I had begun at this point to suspect, in his brother Mycroft, the existence of some quite paranormal mental processes. It was only some half an hour later, when Holmes himself had strolled out for tobacco, that Mycroft, observing my continued astonishment, spoke quietly in my ear.

'If you keep your lips sealed, Dr Watson, I will tell you

a small secret – albeit a very simple one. The good lady's coat was thrown rather carelessly, as you noticed, over the back of a chair; and on the inside of the lining was sewn a tape with her name and address clearly printed on it. Alas, however, my eyes are now not so keen as they were in my youth, and sixes and eights, as you know, are readily susceptible of confusion.'

I have never been accused, I trust, of undue levity, but I could not help laughing heartily at this coup on Mycroft's part, and I assured him that his brother should never hear the truth of it from me.

'Sherlock?' said Mycroft, raising his mighty eyebrows. 'He saw through my little joke immediately.'

It was not until past six o'clock the following evening that I returned to Baker Street after (it is not an irrelevant matter) a day of deep interest at St Thomas's Hospital.

'Well, have you solved the mystery yet?' I asked, as I entered the sitting room.

Holmes I found curled up in his armchair, smoking his oily clay pipe, and discussing medieval madrigals with Mycroft.

'Yes, Watson, I believe—'

But hardly were the words from his mouth when we heard a heavy footfall in the passage and a sharp rap on the door.

'This will be the girl's stepfather,' said Holmes. 'He has written to say he would be here at a quarter after six. Come in!'

The man who entered was a sturdy, middle-sized fellow,

about thirty years of age, clean-shaven, sallow-skinned, with a pair of most penetrating eyes. He placed his shiny top-hat on the sideboard, and with an insinuating bow sidled down into the nearest chair.

'I am assuming,' said Holmes, 'that you are Mr James Wyndham and' (holding up a typewritten sheet) 'that this is the letter you wrote to me?'

'I am that person, sir, and the letter is mine. It was against my expressed wish, as you may know, that Miss van Allen contacted you in this matter. But she is an excitable young lady, and my wife and I will be happy to forgive her for such an impulsive action. Yet I must ask you to have nothing more to do with what is, unfortunately, a not uncommon misfortune. It is clear what took place, and I think it highly unlikely, sir, that even you will find so much as a single trace of Mr Darvill.'

'On the contrary,' replied Holmes quietly, 'I have reason to believe that I have already discovered the whereabouts of that gentleman.'

Mr Wyndham gave a violent start, and dropped his gloves. 'I am delighted to hear it,' he said in a strained voice.

'It is a most curious fact,' continued Holmes, 'that a typewriter has just as much individuality as does hand-writing. Even when completely new, no two machines are exactly alike; and as they get older, some characters wear on this side and some on that. Now in this letter of yours, Mr Wyndham, you will note that in every instance there is some slight slurring in the eye of the "e"; and a most easily detectable defect in the tail of the "t".'

'All our office correspondence,' interrupted our visitor,

'is typed on the same machine, and I can fully understand why it has become a little worn.'

'But I have four other letters here,' resumed Holmes, in a slow and menacing tone, 'which purport to come from Mr Horatio Darvill. And in each of these, also, the "e"s are slurred, and the "t"s un-tailed.'

Mr Wyndham was out of his chair instantly and had snatched up his hat: 'I can waste no more of my valuable time with such trivialities, Mr Holmes. If you can catch the man who so shamefully treated Miss van Allen, then catch him! I wish you well – and ask you to let me know the outcome. But I have no interest whatsoever in your fantastical notions.'

Already, however, Holmes had stepped across the room and turned the key in the door. 'Certainly I will tell you how I caught Mr Darvill, if you will but resume your chair.'

'What?' shouted Wyndham, his face white, his small eyes darting about him like those of a rat in a trap. Yet finally he sat down and glared aggressively around, as Holmes continued his analysis.

'It was as selfish and as heartless a trick as ever I encountered. The man married a woman much older than himself, largely for her money. In addition, he enjoyed the interest on the not inconsiderable sum of the stepdaughter's money, for as long as that daughter lived with them. The loss of such extra monies would have made a significant difference to the lifestyle adopted by the newly married pair. Now the daughter herself was an amiable, warm-hearted girl, and was possessed of considerable physical attractions; and with the added advantage of a personal income, it became clear that under normal circumstances she would not remain single for very long. So he – the man of whom I speak – decided to deny her the company and friendship of her contemporaries by keeping her at home. But she – and who shall blame her? – grew restive under such an unnatural regimen, and firmly announced her intention to attend a local ball. So what did her stepfather do? With the connivance of his wife, he conceived a cowardly plan. He disguised himself cleverly: he covered those sharp eyes with dully tinted spectacles; he masked that clean-shaven face with bushy side-whiskers; he sank that clear voice of his into the strained whisper of one suffering from the quinsy. And then, feeling himself doubly secure because of the young lady's short sight, he appeared *himself* at the ball, in the guise of one Horatio Darvill, and there he wooed the fair Miss van Allen for his own – thereafter taking further precaution of always arranging his assignations by candlelight.'

(I heard a deep groan which at the time I assumed to have come from our visitor, but which, upon reflection, I am inclined to think originated from Mycroft's corner.)

'Miss van Allen had fallen for her new beau; and no suspicion of deception ever entered her pretty head. She was flattered by the attention she was receiving, and the effect was heightened by the admiration of her mother for the man. An "engagement" was agreed, and the deception perpetuated. But the pretended journeys abroad were becoming more difficult to sustain, and things had to be brought to a head quickly, although in such a *dramatic* way as to leave a permanent impression upon the young girl's mind. Hence the vows of fidelity sworn on the Testaments; hence the dark hints repeated on the very morning of the proposed marriage that something sinister might be afoot.

125

James Wyndham, you see, wished his stepdaughter to be so morally bound to her fictitious suitor that for a decade, at least, she would sit and wilt in Cowcross Street, and continue paying her regular interest directly into the account of her guardian: the same blackguard of a guardian who had brought her to the doors of St Saviour's and then, himself, conveniently disappeared by the age-old ruse of stepping in at one side of a four-wheeler – and out at the other.'

Rising to his feet, Wyndham fought hard to control his outrage. 'I wish you to know that it is you, sir, who is violating the law of this land – and not me! As long as you keep that door locked, and thereby hold me in this room against my will, you lay yourself open—'

'The law,' interrupted Holmes, suddenly unlocking and throwing open the door, 'may not for the moment be empowered to touch you. Yet never, surely, was there a man who deserved punishment more. In fact . . . since my hunting-crop is close at hand—' Holmes took two swift strides across the room; but it was too late. We heard a wild clatter of steps down the stairs as Wyndham departed, and then had the satisfaction of watching him flee pell-mell down Baker Street.

'That cold-blooded scoundrel will end on the gallows, mark my words!' growled Holmes.

'Even now, though, I cannot follow all the steps in your reasoning, Holmes,' I remarked.

'It is this way,' replied Holmes. 'The only person who profited financially from the vanishing-trick – was the stepfather. Then, the fact that the two men, Wyndham and Darvill, were never actually seen *together*, was most suggestive. As were the tinted spectacles, the husky voice, the bushy whiskers – all of these latter, Watson, hinting strongly at disguise. Again, the typewritten signature betokened one thing only – that the man's handwriting was so familiar to Miss van Allen that she might easily recognize even a small sample of it. Isolated facts? Yes! But all of them leading to the same inevitable conclusion – as even my slumbering sibling might agree?'

But there was no sound from the Mycroft corner.

'You were able to verify your conclusion?' I asked.

Holmes nodded briskly. 'We know the firm for which Wyndham worked, and we had a full description of Darvill. I therefore eliminated from that description everything which could be the result of deliberate disguise—'

'Which means that you have *not* verified your conclusion!' Mycroft's sudden interjection caused us both to turn sharply towards him.

'There will always,' rejoined Holmes, 'be a need and a place for informed conjecture—'

'*Inspired* conjecture, Holmes,' I interposed.

'Phooey!' snorted Mycroft. 'You are talking of nothing but wild *guesswork*, Sherlock. And it is my opinion that in this case your guesswork is grotesquely askew.'

I can only report that never have I seen Holmes so taken aback; and he sat in silence as Mycroft raised his bulk from the chair and now stood beside the fireplace.

'Your deductive logic needs no plaudits from me, Sherlock, and like Dr Watson I admire your desperate hypothesis. But unless there is some firm evidence which you have thus far concealed from us . . .?'

Holmes did not break his silence.

'Well,' stated Mycroft, 'I will indulge in a little guesswork of my own, and tell you that the gentleman who just stormed out of this room is as innocent as Watson here!'

'He certainly did not *act* like an innocent man,' I protested, looking in vain to Holmes for some support, as Mycroft continued.

'The reasons you adduce for your suspicions are perfectly sound in most respects, and yet – I must speak with honesty, Sherlock! – I found myself sorely disappointed with your reading – or rather complete misreading – of the case. You are, I believe, wholly correct in your central thesis that there is no such person as Horatio Darvill.' (How the blood was tingling in my veins as Mycroft spoke these words!) 'But when the unfortunate Mr Wyndham who has just rushed one way up Baker Street rushes back down it the other with a writ for defamation of character – as I fear he will! – then you will be compelled to think, to analyse, and to act, with a little more care and circumspection.'

Holmes leaned forward, the sensitive nostrils of that aquiline nose a little distended. But still he made no comment.

'For example, Sherlock, two specific pieces of information vouchsafed to us by the attractive Miss van Allen herself have been strongly discounted, if not wholly ignored, in your analysis.' (I noticed Holmes's eyebrows rising quizzically.) 'First, the fact that Mr Wyndham was older than Miss van Allen *only by some five years*. Second, the fact that Miss van Allen is so competent and speedy a performer on the typewriter that she works, on a free-lance basis, for several firms in the vicinity of her home, including Messrs Cook and Marchant. Furthermore, you make the astonishing claim that Miss van Allen was totally deceived by the disguise of Mr Darvill. Indeed, you would have her not only blind, but semi-senile into the bargain! Now it is perfectly true that the lady's eyesight is far from perfect – *glaucopia Athenica*, would you not diagnose, Dr Watson? – but it is quite ludicrous to believe that she would fail to recognize the person with whom she was living. And it is wholly dishonest of you to assert that the assignations were always held by candlelight, since on at least two occasions, the morning after the first meeting – the *morning*, Sherlock! – and the morning of the planned wedding ceremony, Miss van Allen had ample opportunity of studying the physical features of Darvill in the broadest of daylight.'

'You seem to me to be taking an unconscionably long time in putting forward your own hypothesis,' snapped Holmes, somewhat testily.

'You are right,' admitted the other. 'Let me beat about the bush no longer! You have never felt emotion akin to love for any woman, Sherlock – not even for the Adler woman – and you are therefore deprived of the advantages of those who like myself are able to understand both the workings of the male and also the female mind. Five years her superior in age – her stepfather; *only five years*. Now one of the sadnesses of womankind is their tendency to age more quickly and less gracefully than men; and one of the truths about mankind in general is that if you put one of each sex, of roughly similar age, in reasonable proximity . . . And if one of them is the fair Miss van Allen – then you are inviting a packet of trouble. Yet such is what took place in the Wyndham ménage. Mrs Wyndham was seventeen years older than her young husband; and perhaps as time

129

went by some signs and tokens of this disproportionate difference in their ages began to manifest themselves. At the same time, it may be assumed that Wyndham himself could not help being attracted – however much at first he sought to resist the temptation – by the very winsome and vivacious young girl who was his stepdaughter. It would almost certainly have been Wyndham himself who introduced Miss van Allen to the part-time duties she undertook for Cook and Marchant – where the two of them were frequently thrown together, away from the restraints of wife and home, and with a result which it is not at all difficult to guess. Certain it is, in my own view, that Wyndham sought to transfer his affections from the mother to the daughter; and in due course it was the daughter who decided that whatever her own affections might be in the matter she must in all honour leave her mother and stepfather. Hence the great anxiety to get out to dances and parties and the like – activities which Wyndham objected to for the obvious reason that he wished to have Miss van Allen as close by himself for as long as he possibly could. Now you, Sherlock, assume that this objection arose as a result of the interest accruing from the New Zealand securities – and you are *guessing*, are you not? Is it not just possible that Wyndham has money of his own – find out, Brother! – and that what he craves for is not some petty addition to his wealth, but the love of a young woman with whom he has fallen rather hopelessly in love? You see, she took *him* in, just as she took *you* in, Sherlock – for you swallowed everything that calculating little soul reported.'

'Really, this is outrageous!' I objected – but Holmes held up his hand, and bid me hear his brother out.

'What is clear, is that at some point when Wyndham was in France – and why did you not verify those dates spent abroad? I am sure Cook and Marchant would have provided them just as quickly as it furnished the wretched man's description – as I was saying, with Wyndham in France, mother and daughter found themselves in a little tête-à-tête one evening, during the course of which a whole basketful of dirty linen was laid bare, with the daughter bitterly disillusioned about the behaviour of her stepfather, and the mother hurt and angry about her husband's infidelity. So, together, the pair of them devised a plan. Now, we both agree on one thing at least, Sherlock! There appears to be no evidence whatsoever for the independent existence of Horatio Darvill except for what we have heard from Miss van Allen's lips. Rightly, you drew our attention to the fact that the two men were never seen together. But, alas, having appreciated the *importance* of that clue, you completely misconceived its *significance*. *You* decided that there is no Darvill – because he is Wyndham. *I* have to tell you that there is no Darvill – *because he is the pure fabrication of the minds of Mrs Wyndham and her daughter.*'

Holmes was staring with some consternation at a pattern in the carpet, as Mycroft rounded off his extravagant and completely baseless conjectures.

'Letters were written – and incidentally I myself would have been far more cautious about those "e"s and "t"s: twin faults, as it happens, of my very own machine! But, as I say, letters were written – *but by Miss van Allen herself*, a wedding was arranged; a story concocted of a non-existent carriage into which there climbed a non-existent groom – and that was the end of the charade. Now, it was you,

131

Sherlock, who rightly asked the key question: *cui bono?* And you concluded that the real beneficiary was Wyndham. But exactly the contrary is the case! It was the mother and daughter who intended to be the beneficiaries, for they hoped to rid themselves of the rather wearisome Mr Wyndham – but not before he had been compelled, by moral and social pressures, to make some handsome money-settlement upon the pair of them – especially perhaps upon the young girl who, as Dr Watson here points out, could well have done with some decent earrings and a new handkerchief. And the *social* pressure I mention, Sherlock, was designed – carefully and cleverly designed – to come from *you*. A cock-and-bull story is told to you by some wide-eyed young thing, a story so bestrewn with clues at almost every point that even Lestrade – given a week or two! – would probably have come up with a diagnosis identical with your own. And why do you think she came to you, and not to Lestrade, say? Because "Mr Sherlock Holmes is the greatest investigator the world has ever known" – and his judgements are second only to the Almighty's in their infallibility. For if you, Sherlock, believed Wyndham to be guilty – then Wyndham *was* guilty in the eyes of the whole world – the whole world except for one, that is.'

'Except for two,' I added quietly.

Mycroft Holmes turned his full attention towards me for the first time, as though I had virtually been excluded from his previous audience. But I allowed him no opportunity of seeking the meaning of my words, as I addressed him forthwith.

'I asked Holmes a question when he presented his own

analysis, sir. I will ask you the same: have you in any way verified your hypothesis? And if so, how?'

'The answer, Dr Watson, to the first part of your question is, in large measure, "yes". Mr Wyndham, in fact, has quite enough money to be in no way embarrassed by the withdrawal of Miss van Allen's comparatively minor contribution. As for the second part . . .' Mycroft hesitated awhile. 'I am not sure what my brother has told you, of the various offices I hold under the British Crown—'

It was Holmes who intervened – and impatiently so. 'Yes, yes, Mycroft! Let us all concede immediately that the, shall we say, "unofficial" sources to which you are privy have completely invalidated my own reconstruction of the case. So be it! Yet I would wish, if you allow, to make one or two observations upon your own rather faithful interpretation of events? It is, of course, with full justice that you accuse me of having no first-hand knowledge of what are called "the matters of the heart". Furthermore, you rightly draw attention to the difficulties Mr Wyndham would have experienced in deceiving his stepdaughter. Yet how you underrate the power of disguise! And how, incidentally, you *over*rate the intelligence of Lestrade! Even Dr Watson, I would suggest, has a brain considerably superior—'

For not a second longer could I restrain myself. 'Gentlemen!' I cried, 'you are both – *both* of you! – most tragically wrong.'

The two brothers stared at me as though I had taken leave of my senses.

'I think you should seek to explain yourself, Watson,' said Holmes sharply.

'A man,' I began, 'was proposing to go to Scotland for a fortnight with his newly married wife, and he had drawn out one hundred pounds in cash – no less! – from the Oxford Street branch of the Royal National Bank on the eve of his wedding. The man, however, was abducted after entering a four-wheeler on the very morning of his wedding-day, was brutally assaulted, and then robbed of all his money and personal effects – thereafter being dumped, virtually for dead, in a deserted alley in Stepney. Quite by chance he was discovered later that same evening, and taken to the Whitechapel Hospital. But it was only after several days that the man slowly began to recover his senses, and some patches of his memory – and also, gentlemen, his *voice*. For, you see, it was partly because the man was suffering so badly from what we medical men term suppurative tonsillitis – the quinsy, as it is commonly known – that he was transferred to St Thomas's where, as you know, Holmes, I am at present engaged in some research on that very subject, and where my own professional opinion was sought only this morning. Whilst reading through the man's hospital notes, I could see that the only clue to his identity was a tag on an item of his underclothing carrying the initials "H.D." You can imagine my excitement—'

'Humphry Davy, perhaps,' muttered Mycroft flippantly.

'Oh no!' I replied, with a smile. 'I persisted patiently with the poor man, and finally he was able to communicate to me the name of his bank. After that, if I may say so, Holmes, it was almost child's play to verify *my* hypothesis. I visited the bank, where I learned about the withdrawal of money for the honeymoon, and the manager himself accompanied me back to St Thomas's where he was able to view the patient and to provide quite unequivocal proof as to his identity. I have to inform you, therefore, that not only does Mr Horatio Darvill exist, gentlemen; he is at this precise moment lying in a private ward on the second floor of St Thomas's Hospital!'

For some little while a silence fell upon the room. Then I saw Holmes, who these last few minutes had been standing by the window, give a little start: 'Oh, no!' he groaned. And looking over his shoulder I saw, dimly beneath the fogbeshrouded lamplight, an animated Mr Wyndham talking to a legal-looking gentleman who stood beside him.

Snatching up his cape, Holmes made hurriedly for the door. 'Please tell Mr Wyndham, if you will, Watson, that I have already written a letter to him containing a complete recantation of my earlier charges, and offering him my profound apologies. For the present, I am leaving – by the back door.'

He was gone. And when, a minute later, Mrs Hudson announced that two angry-looking gentlemen had called asking to see Mr Holmes, I noticed Mycroft seemingly asleep once more in his corner armchair, a monograph on polyphonic plainchant open on his knee, and a smile of vague amusement on his large, intelligent face.

'Show the gentlemen in, please, Mrs Hudson!' I said – in such peremptory fashion that for a moment or two that good lady stared at me, almost as if she had mistaken my voice for that of Sherlock Holmes himself.

A Kingsbridge Romance

BY KEN FOLLETT

Diana paused in the cathedral porch to look at the sun going down. Her husband came up beside her, and they stood still for a moment, in the quiet of a summer Sunday evening. The pink sunset was reflected on the wet roof of a railway train winding westward through the neat suburbs of Kingsbridge. Diana had always liked this view. She was a short, slight person, with dark hair cut in a bob, and neat features: little ears, a little nose, and sharp little teeth. She was normally full of energy, always on the move, but in this spot, with the grey majesty of the cathedral behind her and the town spread out below, she always felt calm and thoughtful. People have been watching the sunset from here for a thousand years, she reflected.

'Why the big sigh?' said her husband.

'Did I sigh?' she said, surprised. 'I was thinking about the past.'

He gestured towards the buildings that bordered the west side of the cathedral close. 'I remember the fight over your scheme to rebuild Market Street.'

'That was ten years ago,' she said. 'Just before we got married.' I was in my twenties, she thought; now I'm approaching forty. My hair was jet black. Now I have to have it dyed that colour, every four weeks. I wonder when he will realize I'm doing that?

'It was a time of big decisions,' he said. He took her shoulders and gently turned her towards himself. He was suddenly serious. 'Did we make the right decisions, Diana? Tell me the truth.'

She looked into his eyes, and hesitated.

On the day Nick Portez walked into her life, she had been sitting in her chic attic studio with absolutely nothing to do but worry.

Six months earlier she had made the first big decision of that momentous year: she quit her job with a London firm of architects and started her own practice in her home town.

It was not a success.

She had designed one house for the parents of a school friend; and after that, nothing. Today she had fired her cleaning woman, because she could no longer afford the wages. Soon she would be unable to pay the rent on the studio; and that would be the end of her dream.

Nick was a man of about her own age, twenty-eight, who had made a lot of money out of real estate in the centre of Kingsbridge, and liked everyone to know it. He wore a fashionable double-breasted suit with a blue shirt that showed up his blue eyes: he was the picture of a successful young businessman, and Diana felt a twinge of envy as he made himself comfortable on her couch and explained what he wanted.

His plan was ambitious: to demolish the whole stretch of Market Street that ran along the west side of the cathedral

137

close; and to build a hotel for the tourists who came to see the cathedral, a retail mall to replace the existing strip of ramshackle shops, and some offices and a few apartments.

Diana did not like people to smoke, but he lit up without asking, and she was so absorbed in his scheme that she was only slightly annoyed when he flicked ash into her potted geranium.

He wanted her to be the architect. She had worked on similar projects in London. He felt they would make a good team, because she was young and ambitious and he was young and impatient.

Diana tried not to show how excited she was. As it was six-thirty she closed the office and they continued their discussion at the pub across the road. She found herself enjoying his company: liked his restless energy and his confidence.

He explained that he had talked to the clergy, but they wouldn't even comment on the idea unless he could show them sketches.

Diana wondered what the clergy had to do with it.

Nick explained that the Church owned the land.

She was taken aback. 'So all this is just a pipedream!' she said angrily. 'You can't redevelop someone else's site.'

'I've done it before,' he said cockily. 'If the cathedral clergy like your drawings, I'll form a partnership with them. I'll get building permission, I'll raise a loan to finance the development, I'll handle the building contracts—'

'And who will pay me for my work?'

'If the scheme gets off the ground, you'll be the architect—'

'And if not?'

'If not, nobody gets paid.'

This was a blow, and suddenly she hated Nick Portez for raising her hopes only to dash them again. Then she reminded herself that she had no other work: this was her only chance. And she agreed to do some designs.

He also asked her to have dinner with him. She turned him down.

She might have been tempted, but she already had a date with John Borman, a young lawyer she had known since schooldays. As soon as she came back to Kingsbridge he had asked her out, and she had been seeing him regularly since then. They drove out to the country club and he ordered champagne. He was a neat, precise man, always impeccably dressed. He had regular features and receding brown hair. The nicest thing about him was that he was crazy about her. He said he had been in love with her since he was thirteen, and she believed him: she could see the desire shining in his eyes when he looked at her. There was something very appealing about a reserved man being hopelessly in love with you, she thought as he proposed a toast 'To us'.

When he kissed her good-night, holding her dainty shoulders in his big hands, he said he wanted to make love to her. She was embarrassed. They were both in their late twenties: men of that age did not expect to hold hands indefinitely. But she did not want to go to bed with him. If only you had more hair, she thought vaguely; and she said: 'No, John; not yet – I'm not ready.'

Afterwards she wondered why she had said no. He was good-looking; she liked him; he would be gentle and kind. She stood naked in her bathroom, looking at her small body and elfin face. People said she was pretty. Lots of men had fallen for her. Some had proposed marriage. She knew girls who would go to bed with men in a spirit of curiosity, to find out what they were like. That had never been her way. Now she tried imagining that John was waiting in her bed. How would she feel about that? Would she be eager to slip in beside him and take him in her arms? No: she would be shy, anxious, hesitant. She was glad she had turned him down.

Two weeks later, she was on her way to see Charles Boyd, the Dean of Kingsbridge, carrying a portfolio of drawings that she thought were the best work she had ever done.

She felt nervous as she walked through the rain to her rendezvous. The plan could not go ahead without the support of the Church, and clergymen were dismally conservative.

She stopped at the end of Market Street and ran her architect's eye over the existing buildings. Most of them had been built in the twenties and thirties, some earlier; none were very attractive and most of them looked a bit dilapidated, with leaning chimneys, sagging roofs and cracked woodwork. Unlike the pretty High Street, which had small boutiques in Victorian buildings, this street had old warehouses and disused factories with garish shop fronts. Diana could cheerfully pull the lot down.

She walked through an arched gateway into the rain-swept cathedral close. Despite the weather, she stopped to look at the church. No matter how many times she saw it, she would never get used to the soaring arches, the mellow grey stone, the perfect proportions. It was one of the masterpieces of European architecture – and no one knew who had designed it. I don't suppose my shopping mall will last as long, she thought ruefully.

All the same, she was proud of her drawings. Her buildings would be low, so that they would not obstruct the view from the cathedral porch. The car park would be underground. As well as the shopping mall there would be a covered market for the traditional stallholders who sold fruit and vegetables at the roadside. Every room in the hotel would have a view of Kingsbridge Cathedral. And she had craftily included small apartments for elderly clergymen. That should help persuade them.

There was a strong wind, and she had to hold her umbrella tightly as she walked around the church to the far side, where the deanery was. It was a rather ugly Victorian house of red brick, quite out of harmony with the church across the green. She rang the bell and held her skirt to stop it blowing up in the wind.

Nick did not know she was coming here. He was out of town until tonight. This morning, when the drawings were finished, Diana had been desperate to show them to someone; so, on impulse, she had called the dean. He had asked her to come and see him this afternoon. Nick might not like it. However, he was not paying her, so she could do what she liked.

She wondered nervously what kind of man the dean would be.

He opened the door himself. He was much younger than she had expected – about thirty, she guessed. He was immensely tall, thin and angular, with thick dark hair and soft brown eyes. He towered over Diana as he took her wet

141

raincoat. He smelled of soap and woodsmoke, and sure enough there was a log fire in his study. She looked around while he made tea. It was a rather bare, masculine room, with elderly oak furniture. There were a lot of books on the table, and she noticed titles about South Africa, disarmament and poverty. He seemed to be the idealistic type. That was bad news. She had been hoping for a worldly-wise man with a keen eye for the bottom line.

She also saw a pamphlet about gay clergy. She gave him a hard look when he came back in. He was shy and clumsy, not looking at her and spilling the tea in the saucer. She guessed he was not really used to women; but he did not seem gay. However, you never could tell. He certainly was not married: there was absolutely no feminine influence in this room – no curtains, no flowers, no ornaments. He gave her tea in a chipped mug.

She was too impatient for small talk. She took a token sip of her tea, then stood up and spread her drawings out on his table.

She took him through the scheme quickly, emphasizing the way it would enhance the cathedral's surroundings, rather than the financial benefits to the Church. When she had finished she looked at him and held her breath.

To her astonishment he was full of enthusiasm. 'This is a marvellous scheme,' he said, waving his long arms.

She could hardly believe her luck. 'You mean you're in favour of it?' she said stupidly.

'Of course! Think what we could do – for homeless people, for handicapped children, for the Church's work in the Third World – with the profit from this!'

142

Diana laughed merrily. 'I was afraid you would be a crusty old traditionalist!'

'Let me show you something.' He unlocked a drawer and pulled out an ancient map, drawn in ink on crumbling parchment, and sealed between two sheets of transparent plastic, for protection. Diana peered at it. It was a plan of Kingsbridge: she could see the cathedral, the High Street and the river. 'This is seven hundred years old.'

It must be worth a fortune, Diana thought.

The dean went on: 'Look at the west side of the church. Here, where you've put a car park, there was a stable. Next to it was the guest house, for visitors to the priory – just where you propose to build a hotel. And, of course, the medieval market was held outside the west door of the church – exactly where your shopping mall will be. So your design is perfectly traditional!'

Diana smiled happily.

She could hardly wait to tell Nick. That evening she met him for dinner. It was supposed to be a business meeting, but he had chosen an intimate bistro with candles on the tables and views over the moonlit river. She got there first. He was late. As soon as he walked in she told him triumphantly that the dean was on their side. He was surprised she had gone to the dean on her own, but he shrugged it off, gave her a congratulatory kiss, and hugged her a little longer than was necessary for mere congratulations.

He was wearing a tweed jacket in smoky shades of blue, and a shirt with a button-down collar. His fair hair was thick and straight. She could not help thinking that he was a good deal better-looking than John Borman.

'What kind of man is this dean?' he asked.

143

'Socially concerned clergyman,' she said. She realized that sounded condescending. 'But down-to-earth. I think you'll like him.'

'So long as he's on our side. Now, our next problem is City Hall. Isn't your boyfriend a council member?'

'Yes—' Nick was one of those people who knew everything, Diana thought.

'He ought to be on our side.'

Diana began to feel uncomfortable. She was already faintly guilty about being with Nick in this romantic restaurant, and thinking how attractive he was in the candlelight. On top of that it seemed disloyal to talk about using John for business reasons.

'I can't imagine the council turning us down,' she said evasively. 'The new buildings will pay much higher property taxes than the old.'

'Still, have a word with old John anyway . . . make sure he sees the advantages.'

She was determined not to give in. 'I'll think about it,' she said.

However, she did speak to 'old John' about it, the following Sunday, strolling beside the river that wound through the centre of the city, looking at the wild flowers that had sprung up on the grassy bank.

'I'll vote for you,' he said, 'even though it will mean your spending even more time with the handsome Nick Lopez.' He smiled sadly, and she felt mean. 'But there will be a lot of opposition.'

She was surprised. 'Why?'

'Your shopping mall will take business away from the

High Street. The Mayor owns half of the High Street, and his friends own the other half.'

'I never thought of that,' Diana said reflectively. 'You're very smart, John.' She felt a surge of affection for him. If he were to lie me down, right now, in the long grass, I think I would, I really would . . . but of course John would never do that kind of thing – he was far too conventional. She thought that perhaps he might kiss her. But he failed to pick up on her mood, and the moment passed.

On the evening the planning committee met, Nick was out of town, so Diana sat with the dean, Charles Boyd, in the lobby of City Hall. Diana was tense and restless. She felt as if her whole career depended on this decision. If it went her way, she was made as an architect. If it went against her, she would probably have to give up her independent practice.

Her skirt was rather short, and she felt embarrassed, sitting with a clergyman wearing a reversed collar; but soon they got into conversation and she forgot about how they looked. He talked passionately about all the causes in which he was involved. From wheelchair access in public buildings to freedom of worship in communist countries, his life was one long campaign. Diana began to feel it was wrong that her main interest in life was herself.

They had a long wait. They got coffee from a slot machine: it tasted dreadful, but Charles did not seem to mind. Diana noticed that the sleeves of his shirt were too short for his long arms, and his wrists, covered with curly black hair, stuck out comically. He looks after everyone except himself, she thought. His large, strong hands were carefully manicured, to her surprise. She found herself thinking how nice it would be to have an intelligent man friend who did not want to go to bed with her.

At last the committee men began to come out of the council chamber. Diana and the dean stood up. John appeared, his pinstripe suit rumpled, his face glum.

'What happened?' Diana said impatiently.

'Bad news, I'm afraid,' he said. 'Your application was rejected.'

Diana's heart sank. 'And all because the Mayor owns shops in the High Street,' she said bitterly.

'I'm sorry,' John said, and Diana knew he meant it, even though he had reason to be glad that her partnership with Nick had come to nothing.

The Mayor himself came out and shook hands with Charles. 'So sorry we couldn't accommodate you this time, Dean,' he said rather unctuously. 'Better luck next time.' Ignoring Diana, he went out.

Diana could hardly believe the man's nerve. 'What a hypocrite!' she said bitterly.

'How disappointing,' said the dean. 'Still, we did our best.'

Diana looked at him curiously. 'You get so angry about injustices done to others – children, disabled people, oppressed nations. How can you be so calm about this?'

He shrugged his bony shoulders. 'Human greed is normal. It's human cruelty that makes me cross.' He held out his hand to shake. 'Thank you very much for your efforts. I'm sorry they've come to nothing.'

Diana and John both said: 'Good-night.'

'See you in church!' the dean said as he walked away.

'What a nice man,' Diana said to John.

'He may be nice, but he didn't drive you home . . . so I will.'

Diana had a flat in a big old house a mile or so north of the cathedral. John obviously wanted to be invited in, but Diana felt too dispirited. As she was about to get out of the car he said: 'What are you going to do?'

'Rewrite my résumé,' she said. 'I've tried to make it on my own, and I've failed. Now I'll have to get a job.'

John said: 'There's another way, you know.'

'Don't be cryptic,' she said crossly. 'I'm not in the mood.'

'You could have your architectural practice, and financial security too . . . if we were together. You could build your business gradually, without worrying about paying the rent.'

She was surprised and touched.

He said: 'I love you, Diana. Please marry me.'

John was a careful, cautious man, the type who never did anything impulsively. He had thought long and hard about this before making his decision.

Diana heard her mother's voice. 'You're twenty-eight years old and you've turned down chances that most girls would jump at – but it won't go on for ever. If you keep saying no you'll end up alone. It's about time you realized that no man is perfect!'

Diana looked hard at John and saw true love in his eyes. It was the look that decided her. 'No, John, I won't marry you. You deserve someone who loves you just as much as you love her. You're a dear man, but I'm not in love with you. I probably should have said that to you before—' She sighed. I might as well go all the way, now,

147

she thought. She added: 'And I think we should stop seeing one another.'

He looked as if she had struck him. For a moment she was afraid he would cry. Then he got out of the car and came around to her side to open the door.

'Think it over,' he pleaded.

'No point,' she said. 'I'm sorry.' She kissed his cheek. He held her for a moment; then, feeling her stiffen, he let go immediately, like the gentleman he was.

She opened the gate and walked quickly up the garden path. She was sorry to have made John unhappy, but nevertheless she felt relieved that it was over. She heard his car pull away. As she was fumbling in her bag for her key, a figure emerged from the shadows.

Diana gasped.

A voice said: 'It's only me.'

It was Nick.

Diana relaxed. 'You scared me,' she said crossly.

'I just got back,' he said. 'What happened?'

'We lost.'

He swore. 'All that work I put in,' he said.

'What about the work I put in?' Diana said indignantly.

'Yes, yours too. Well.' He held up a bottle. 'Why don't we drown our sorrows in a bottle of champagne?'

Diana thought about it. She was painfully tense: it might be nice to unwind in the company of an attractive man. But if she let him in now he would surely make a pass at her. Would I like that? she wondered.

The answer came right away.

'No, thanks, Nick. Good-night.' She opened the door and stepped inside.

He held the door, preventing her from closing it. 'Come on,' he said. 'Relax! I'm not going to rape you.'

'I just don't feel like it,' she said.

'Don't you think you owe me?'

That made her angry. 'For what?'

'I gave you a break.'

It was outrageous. She had done weeks of work for no pay and he wanted her to be grateful! But there was no point in arguing with him. 'Good-night,' she said again.

Suddenly he grabbed her and kissed her lips.

She stood dead still for a moment. There was nothing more disgusting than being kissed when you didn't want to be, she thought. Then she stamped hard on his toe.

He let out a yelp of pain and backed off, cursing.

Diana slammed the door.

She went to her flat and switched on the kettle to make tea. She felt depressed. She had just been propositioned by two of the most eligible men in town, and she had turned them both down. She wondered whether she was too particular. Am I weird? she thought. Why is there no one in Kingsbridge whom I would like to spend the night with?

Then she realized there was.

Charles Boyd.

That's ridiculous, she thought.

But it was true. She thought of his strong hands and manicured fingers; his soft brown eyes; and the way his wrists stuck out from his shirt cuffs, making him look like a boy who has outgrown his clothes. She recalled how he smelled of soap and woodsmoke; she remembered him being shy and giving her tea in a chipped mug; she saw that bare study, with its plain floorboards and uncurtained

149

window, so much in need of something soft, like the man who lived there.

He was a passionate man, angered by cruelty yet tolerant of human frailty. He made most of the men she could think of appear shallow. Next to him, John was cloddish and Nick looked like a cheap crook.

Of course, he had never shown the least sign of being interested in her.

They had spent several hours together, in the last few weeks. She saw now that she had been happier with him than at any other time; but she had no reason to suppose that he felt the same.

She picked up the phone.

What am I doing? she thought. What am I going to say?

'Kingsbridge Deanery,' he said.

'It's Diana. I'm sorry to bother you—'

'I'm not doing anything important,' he said. His voice was pleasantly relaxed, but he sounded faintly intrigued.

Diana did not know what to say next. 'I . . . I felt we parted rather abruptly,' she said.

'My fault, I expect—'

'No, no! It was mine. But I wanted to tell you how sorry I am that it didn't work out.'

'I'm sorry, too. You did your part splendidly.'

'Thank you.'

There was a pause. Diana could not think of a single thing to say.

Charles said: 'Well, it was good of you to call.'

'Not at all,' she said automatically. 'Good-night.'

'Good-night.'

She kept the phone to her ear, but he hung up.

She felt let down. She put the phone down slowly. The kettle boiled, but she did not make tea.

I'm going to see him, she thought.

She shook her head. It would be crazy. He would be embarrassed. She would feel cheap.

She realized she was gripping the edge of the kitchen counter, holding on as if to keep herself from being dragged away by an invisible force.

I'll see him tomorrow, she thought.

But tomorrow seemed so far away.

Slowly, she released her grip on the kitchen counter. Moving carefully and deliberately, she switched off the kettle, put on her coat, picked up her keys and went out.

It was almost ten o'clock on a Monday night: the streets of Kingsbridge were dark and deserted. It took her fifteen minutes to walk to the centre of the city. She went into the cathedral close.

For a long time she stood under the walls of the great cathedral, hidden by the moon-shadow of a mighty buttress. The lights were on in the deanery. Charles was there, on his own, not doing anything important.

What was she going to say? 'I've realized you're the only man in Kingsbridge – the only man in the whole world – that I want to sleep with.'

At half-past ten she knocked on the door of the deanery.

I may regret this for the rest of my life, she thought.

The dean came to the door with his sleeves rolled up and a brush in his hand: he had been polishing his shoes, all alone in that big house at midnight. His face when he saw her was a mask of surprise – and something else.

'I wanted to see you,' Diana said.

151

'Come inside,' he said.

She stepped in and he closed the door.

She said: 'The thing is, I've fallen in love with you.'

He stared at her. 'Oh, thank God for that,' he said. Then he took her in his arms.

The shopping mall was never built. Ten years later, Market Street still consisted of warehouses and factory buildings.

However, they had been repaired and smartened up, and turned into lofts and chic offices.

'I think perhaps the city council was right,' Diana said. 'Market Street is better the way it is.'

'What about the other decisions that were made that year,' said Charles. 'Were they right, too?'

She looked up into his face. He was not as thin now as he had been then, and there was a little grey in his dark hair; but he still had the same soft brown eyes. She had changed, too: her figure was different, after two children; and she needed glasses when she worked at her drawing-board. He was still the Dean of Kingsbridge. She worked for the Church, too. The Church owned land all over the country, and it was her job to identify sites for redevelopment. She had made millions for her employer.

'I'm teasing you, Charles,' she said with a smile. 'Goodness, I must have been mad – knocking on the deanery door like that. But it was like a revelation. There I was, dithering between John Borman and Nick Cortez, and I suddenly realized I was in love with you.'

'And I with you.'

'You hid it very well. I even thought you might be gay.'

'You haven't answered my question.'

She looked away. The sun had gone down, but the sky was still ablaze. 'It's just that "Yes" isn't enough,' she said. She looked into his eyes again. 'It was the best decision I ever made, dear, and I've never regretted it for a minute.'

He smiled, and his expression told her he felt the same.

She slipped her arm through his, and they walked across the close to their home.

The Perfect Match

BY CLARE FRANCIS

I played the message again but there was no mistake. The weekend had been cancelled. A woman identifying herself as Mr Benham's secretary announced that, owing to illness in the family, Mr and Mrs Benham were having to call the event off. There was no mention of who was ill or what the matter was, but I felt it must be something serious. Serena was not someone to relinquish one of her faultlessly directed weekends without a compelling reason; indeed, in all the years since we had been at school together I could not think of anything in Serena's well-charted life that had not gone entirely to plan.

I thought of phoning to find out if there was anything I could do, but decided against it. Apart from this visit, which had become something of an annual event, I rarely saw Serena nowadays, and in the ten years since her marriage I hadn't really got to know her husband Simon at all. I knew even less of their relatives: it was unlikely I would be able to help.

In some ways I was quite relieved that the weekend was off. Each year I decided that I would give it a miss, yet for some reason I always found myself accepting. Perhaps it was the timing of the invitation – issued in the depths of February for what was invariably a glorious summer weekend – perhaps it was the idea that having shared a dormitory then a flat with Serena, I had a duty to catch up with her now and again, perhaps it was simply that Serena was a hard person to refuse; but year after year I heard myself telling her that I wouldn't dream of missing it.

Serena and Simon Benham lived at Longwood, an immaculately restored Georgian house set in two thousand acres at the prosperous end of the Meon Valley. I had always understood that the Benham money came from a chain of butchers' shops established around the turn of the century and long since converted into land, but on my last visit I had heard Serena telling another guest that the fortune came from sheep farming in Australia, so perhaps I was mistaken.

The Benhams' weekends were lavish in a steadfastly English way, with crumpets for tea and kippers that lurked in chafing dishes late into Sunday mornings. The dinners owed no allegiance to *nouvelle cuisine*, the wines were robust and, as long as one shot, fished or owned horses, the conversation was jolly and brisk.

Aware of my illiteracy in country pursuits, casting me as her most artistic friend (and by implication not, therefore, the easiest of people to place), Serena always asked me for the second weekend in July, when she and Simon took a row of seats at the local music festival. Serena referred to it as Our Festival Weekend, partly, one gathered obliquely, because she and Simon were generous patrons of the festival, partly to distinguish it from the numerous other occasions when they entertained, weekends with equally graphic titles such as The First Shoot and The Hunt Ball Weekend. I would be sorry to miss the music festival –

they'd had an excellent string quartet one year – but, it had to be admitted, less sorry to miss the dinner afterwards and the stream of gossip about people I didn't know.

When I got a call from Michael Radford I couldn't at first place him. It wasn't until he mentioned the cancelled weekend that I remembered the bluff red-faced estate agent I had met at the Benhams' the year before.

'Rather last minute, calling it off like that,' he grunted. 'Any idea what's going on?'

'Someone's ill, apparently.'

'Well, that's the official line, at any rate.'

'People do get ill.'

'The secretary seemed distinctly cagey when I spoke to her. Has all the ring of a matrimonial hiccup to me. Thing is, I've got a shooting weekend booked with them in September. Wondering whether to write it off. Wondered if you could shed any light . . .?'

'I have no more idea than you.'

'Oh. Thought you'd be the person to know.'

'Not really. I hardly ever see Serena nowadays.'

He gave up then. I think he thought I was hiding something, but if Serena's marriage was in trouble she had given no hint of it to me during our brief phone conversation the previous week. Considering the possibility now, I thought that Michael Radford was probably on the wrong track. While no marriage can ever be regarded as bulletproof, I had always thought Serena's more likely to succeed than most. She was one of the few people I knew who had been confident of what she wanted and, on meeting Simon, had been utterly satisfied of having found it.

'I'm not sure it's a good idea to be wildly in love,' she

used to tell me. 'That's when you make bad decisions. And passion – well, that's just another name for temporary insanity, isn't it?' She shook her head with distaste. 'No, I want to marry someone I like and respect and have lots in common with. Someone who wants the same things I want. Someone who's sensible and knows where he's going, and who wants the same sort of marriage as I do.'

'Can't you have all that and be wildly in love too?'

She considered this in her calm considered way. 'I don't think so,' she decided. 'It seems to me that attraction is a pretty poor guide to finding the right person. And passion – that just gets in the way of common sense, doesn't it?'

During the four years we shared a flat she never modified her requirements. With her model-girl looks, her pale blonde hair and clear blue eyes, her ingenuous smile and intriguing laugh, she had a stream of men beating a path to the flat door, but, though she fell in love a couple of times and had the occasional affair, she never wavered. Until Simon came on the scene she categorized each admirer as 'a temporary measure' or 'a non-starter'. She accepted invitations to all the places where she was likely to meet new people – parties, weekends, events – and avoided dining alone with men unless they made her laugh or she simply couldn't get out of it. Even then, she wouldn't commit herself to a dinner invitation until the last minute in case something less restricting came up.

She took great pains over her appearance: she dieted to a strict eight stone, she went twice weekly to the gym in the days when a circuit of Harvey Nichols' dress department was considered hard exercise, she haunted the almost-new shops for designer clothes, she paid the earth to go to the best crimper in town. She always looked perfect; all she lacked was her perfect man.

'I'm not asking for the moon,' she declared once. 'But I know he's out there somewhere and I'll keep looking until I find him. Do you think I'm crazy?'

'Not as long as you recognize him when you see him.'

'Oh, I'll recognize him all right,' she smiled quietly. 'After all, I know what I want.'

If some of her friends found Serena rather enigmatic, they could not accuse her of being in any way dishonest or unkind. She never led men on, never let them think they had hopes where there were none, though for some her very candour, and the sweetness and concern with which it was delivered, presented an even greater challenge, a response which thoroughly baffled Serena, for whom life was never less than straightforward.

I came to admire her resolution, even to envy it: she sailed past her twenty-fifth birthday unclouded by regret or uncertainty.

One day as we were gulping our morning coffee she remarked lightly, 'I've found him.'

'Who?'

'Him. The man I'm going to marry.'

'How do you know? Are you sure?'

'I'm sure.' She allowed herself a gleam of satisfaction.

'Everything you wanted?'

'And more.'

'How more?'

She looked embarrassed. 'Richer, actually.'

'You had a minimum in mind, then?'

She flashed me a reproachful look. 'Certainly not.'

158

She kept him to herself for a few weeks, running out of the flat as soon as the doorbell rang. Then a briefcase appeared in the hall one night and the next morning I was introduced to Simon over breakfast. He was tall and slim and impeccably dressed in a suit which, even in the throes of whatever passion he and Serena had enjoyed the night before, had not been left to crumple itself on the bedroom floor. He had the stance of an army officer, shoulders back, head erect, while his finely drawn features gave him the distinguished air of a diplomat. He had a clipped way of speaking and an abrupt manner. But it was his eyes one noticed most. They were pale and unblinking, a shield through which no gleam of emotion escaped. In the months leading up to the wedding I don't think I ever saw him laugh. Either he was an extremely reserved man, or an extremely proud one: I was never able to make up my mind which.

A few weeks after their return from honeymoon in Tuscany I was invited to Longwood for the first time. Serena declared herself idyllically happy. She had a large budget with which to redecorate the house, she adored the neighbourhood, she and Simon were quite swamped with invitations. Already their lives were running along well-ordered lines. Simon managed the estate, with its thriving arboretum and nursery, and went to town twice a week to pursue his various business interests; Serena looked after the house and sat on local charity committees. So attuned were they to each other's roles and requirements, so obviously in agreement on the way their lives would proceed, that one would think they had spent years together.

There was one small nuisance: Serena thought she might

be pregnant a whole two years ahead of schedule. The child, a boy, was born nine months after the wedding and named George after Simon's great-grandfather, the founder of the family fortune.

One year – it must have been the third festival weekend – I was sitting on the terrace when a shout of laughter made me look up. Simon was on the lawn, swinging the young George high into the air and twirling him round and round like a small fat aeroplane. It was half an hour before they tired of the game, and all the while Simon was laughing. Watching him over dinner that night, seeing the animation in his face, the suggestion of a sparkle in his eye, it seemed to me that for perhaps the first time in his life he was a happy man.

Remembering this, an awful thought came to me, that it might be young George who was ill. I phoned Longwood immediately and got through to the secretary. No, it wasn't George who was unwell, she told me; it was a relative. I didn't press her for details – I had caught the note of restraint in her voice – but asked her to tell Simon and Serena that if there was anything at all I could do then they only had to call me.

One says these things without really expecting to be taken up on them, and returning from dinner at midnight I was rather surprised to get a call from Simon Benham.

'Look, could we meet?' he asked in his stiff unreadable voice.

'Of course. When would suit you?'

'In two minutes? I'm not far away.'

It hadn't occurred to me that he would be in London. 'By all means.'

He didn't ring the bell but knocked hesitantly, as if he were in half a mind to go away again. As he came into the hall I noticed that his tie was askew and his hair, normally combed neatly back from his forehead, was flopping untidily over one eye. He looked as though he hadn't slept in days.

He accepted a Scotch and when he finally glanced at me his eyes were dark with anguish.

'I can't bring myself to go there,' he said. 'I just can't.' He took another gulp of his drink.

I waited silently.

'She's only just round the corner,' he said. 'I'd go, but I just can't.'

'Who's just around the corner?' I asked, needing to be sure.

It was an effort for him to voice her name. 'Serena.'

After a time I prompted gently, 'Has something happened?'

'That's it,' he said bleakly, 'I don't know. She was all right two days ago, then . . . I just don't know. Something happened, something got into her . . . I think she's ill. She *must* be ill. She'd never do anything like this, she'd never just drop everything and go off. It's just not *like* her . . .' His eyes glittered with sudden light, and he rubbed them violently.

'What can I do?' I asked. 'Do you want me to talk to her?'

He grasped at the idea with a mixture of desperation and relief. 'Would you?'

'I'll try – of course. It's a bit late now, but I could go first thing in the morning.'

'Could you? Oh, if you could! I just want to know if

she's all right, that's all. I can't bear not knowing if . . . I'd go myself but . . .' He struggled painfully with some thought, then, abandoning it, got abruptly to his feet. 'I must go. I'm keeping you up.' He had buttoned his voice down into the familiar flat monotone.

'Have you got somewhere to stay?' I asked.

'No, I'll go home. There's George, you see. He'll want to know where I am.'

'You'd better tell me how to find Serena, then.'

Reaching for the pad on the hall table, he scribbled an address. 'You'll call me as soon as . . .?'

'Straight away.'

With a contorted movement of his mouth, half smile, half grimace, he was gone.

I looked at the address on the pad. It was a house in the next street, and I had the awful feeling that I'd heard who was renting it.

At nine the following morning I went round and rang the bell. There was no reply and I tried again. Glancing up I saw a movement at an upper window and a moment later the door swung open to reveal a dishevelled Serena wearing a man's dressing gown.

'Oh dear,' she said, 'I think I can guess why you're here.'

She led the way downstairs into an untidy kitchen and filled a kettle. 'Simon's in a bit of a state, I suppose? Hate to upset him, poor old thing, but he'll get over it in time. He'll have to. Nothing to be done about it, you see.'

'You've left him?'

'Yes.' And, biting her lip, she gave a despairing little smile.

'Who for?'

162

'Damien Bland.'

That was what I had feared. I didn't know what to say. Damien Bland was a ex-champion skier with a reputation as a man-about-town and a proclivity for marrying girls with a healthy bank balance. So far as I could remember from the gossip columns he was on his third divorce. I had met him once many years before and thought him a shallow insincere man who relied rather too heavily on a smooth line in charm. He had the knack of fixing his gaze on you as if you were the only person he cared about in the entire world, though I suspected that, when it came to genuine affection, his strongest passion was reserved for himself.

'Oh, I know what you're thinking,' Serena declared immediately. 'But it's the first time either of us has been really truly deeply in love. I can't tell you how *amazing* it is. We can't believe it. All these years and then – *wham!* Just like that.' She laughed suddenly, as if she herself didn't entirely believe what had happened. 'I can't tell you how happy we are. We never dreamed it could be like this. We're like a couple of kids. We spend all our time hugging and kissing. And bed – I have to say I never realized it could be so marvellous!' Caught in some ecstatic memory, she gave a small shudder, then, catching my expression, added earnestly, 'Damien's had an awful time up till now, you know. I can't tell you what hell he's been through with his marriages, poor love. Quite ghastly. One of them was quite barmy, you know. Led him a total dance. Drugs – you name it. And the last – well, she was a complete nightmare, into control, wanting him at her beck and call, trying to get him to be a *farmer* in some wild corner of Somerset, for goodness' sake! I tell you – he's had a rotten time. He feels completely reborn. Well – we both do!'

'I thought you were happy with Simon.'

She gave me a delicate frown, as if I were missing the point. 'Of course I was – once. But honestly, we've been going through the motions for years. Dear old Simon – so British, so desperate to do everything by the book, so *upright*. I was beginning to feel that my life was over before it had begun – middle-aged at thirty-five. But now – well, I've finally discovered what it's like to feel alive!'

'What about George?'

She lifted a small shoulder. 'Oh, he'll come and live with us, of course. Just as soon as we're settled. We're going to buy a small place somewhere off Eaton Square – you know, a cute little mews house, something like that.'

Nothing remotely cute ever came cheap near Eaton Square and I wondered where they were planning to find the money. I couldn't believe that a man with Damien Bland's lifestyle had too much cash lying around, and if Serena thought she was going to get an expensive house out of Simon without protracted negotiations I suspected she was going to be disappointed. But by far her greatest battle, I felt certain, was going to be over George.

'You're quite sure about all this?' I asked.

'Absolutely,' she declared. 'This is the most amazing, astonishing thing that's ever happened to me. I've got to go with it, haven't I? I'd be mad to ignore it. Fate. It's simply fate.' And she gave a tiny gasp, as if in thrall to her own courage.

I couldn't bring myself to give Simon the news over the phone, not when he was alone with only George and the nanny, so as soon as I could get away I drove down to Longwood. Pouring us both a drink, I tried to break the outlines of the situation as gently as possible. I left out the more painful details – the extent of Serena's infatuation and her plans to take George to live in the little mews house in Belgravia – but Simon was a bright man; it didn't take him long to fill in the gaps.

'She'll be coming to me for money, I suppose, so that she can support that – *person*,' he said, his face ashen. 'Well, I won't make it easy for her, she'll have to go through the courts. Though at the end of the day I don't suppose I'll have much say in it, will I? Men don't win on the financial front any more, do they? Not when no one's to blame any more, not when people can just walk out . . .' He gasped, 'But when it comes to George, I'll never let him go. *Never*. Life wouldn't be worth living. I couldn't bear to be without him. And I couldn't stand the thought of him being under the same roof as that . . . *sponger*.'

He thrust his head into his hands, as if to hide some show of emotion, and it was a while before he spoke again. 'I believed in marriage, you know. Utterly. Completely. I believed you didn't end it unless things went terribly, desperately wrong, unless your partner went mad or committed murder or something. I thought that you counted yourself lucky for all the things that were right between you, that you fought for what you had, that you didn't abandon each other unless the whole damned shooting match became utterly unbearable. That's what I find so hard – there wasn't a lot wrong with our marriage! Oh, the excitement had worn off, but you expect that after a few years, don't you? You come to realize that each day is going to be pretty

165

much like the last, that there aren't going to be many surprises. But I rather liked that, in fact I loved it, and I thought Serena did too. We were content. What more does one want? I mean, what more *is* there?' He gave me a plaintive baffled look.

'You're asking someone who's never been married.'

Absorbed in his own unhappiness he hardly heard me. 'I thought that you put your desire for cheap thrills on hold. I thought that you ignored temptation because you cared for the other person and what the two of you had built up together. Because you cared for your child—' His voice cracked, he screwed up his face and, finally, painfully, he wept with tight awkward sobs.

I said what I could, but in the end there wasn't a great deal to say. I found a bit of lunch in the kitchen and watched him push it around his plate. I stayed until George was due home from school and left promising to come down again soon.

Somehow it never happened. I had a hectic week trying to read a set of proofs against a tight deadline, then Simon was busy – or found reasons to be busy – and in the end I didn't manage to have more than a quick word with him on the phone before leaving for a six-week tour of America and Australia.

On my return I intended to contact Simon as soon as I had cleared my desk, but before I could get round to it I had a call from Serena.

'Got a moment?' she asked. 'I can jump in a cab and be with you in twenty minutes.'

Not based around the corner any more then. When she

arrived I noticed how thin she looked and how brightly her lipstick stood out against the whiteness of her skin.

'Thought you'd never get back,' she said, walking past me into the living room. 'Listen, I need someone to sort things out with Simon for me.'

'Isn't that a job for the lawyers?'

'No. It needs a friend. You know our situation, you're neutral. Simon will listen to you.'

'I'm not sure—'

'The thing is, I want to know his terms for having me back.'

'Back?'

'That's right,' she said matter-of-factly. 'I've been a bit of an idiot. Well – more than just a bit, if the truth be told. Damien has no money, none at all. I thought he did – he *told* me he did. He's a frightful liar. It makes the whole thing hopeless, of course. One can't manage without money, and I can't face a battle with Simon. It could take months, years. Besides . . .' Her mouth creased with indignation. 'Damien's impossible. Used to getting his own way all the time, doing exactly what he pleases – including spending lots of money, I may say. A spoilt child. Must have been his mother. I really can't deal with him. I'm not even terribly sure I *like* him very much.'

'It's over then?'

She gave me an odd look. 'I wouldn't say that exactly. I still find him rather irresistible. Heaven in bed. But not so heavenly in the mornings, if you know what I mean. Just impossible. Totally irresponsible. Absolutely hopeless. I must have been mad.' She gave a sigh of forbearance. 'Anyway, the point is I've moved out – camping with a girlfriend in Chelsea – and I want to go back and be a good wife and have my lovely home again. And George too, of course.'

'But what about Simon? Do you still love him?'

'Love him?' She paused to consider this. 'I suppose so. I mean, I'm very fond of him. And we make a good team.'

'And that's enough?'

'Certainly. Compared to most marriages ours is pretty good.' She said it without irony.

'But surely I'm not the right person to talk to Simon,' I argued. 'Wouldn't it be best if you went and saw him yourself?'

'Too many lawyers have got in the way. Dreadful people – making everything so unpleasant. It's got to the point where Simon won't even talk to me on the phone, and he's banned me from going anywhere near Longwood. I thought if you wrote a letter for me—'

'A *letter*?'

'Well, you're a writer. And so *brilliant*.'

'Serena, I couldn't—'

'Oh, I know exactly what I want to say – every word. But it won't come out the way I want it to, it never does – I'm useless at that sort of thing. I'm bound to make a mess of it if you don't give me a hand. And then he won't realize how utterly serious I am about going back. I have the feeling I'll only get one chance, you see, and I don't trust myself not to muck it up.' She put on a lost smile. 'It would mean so much.'

I made a last feeble attempt at resistance. 'You're really serious about making a go of it?'

'Oh yes. No more madness, I assure you. I'll never leave again.'

It took two hours to draft the letter. Serena changed her mind frequently over what she wanted to say and how she wanted to say it. 'Make it more humble there,' she said, or: 'more miserable' or 'more loving'. 'Put in something about how good it was before' . . . 'Say how much I miss him.'

I wasn't very proud of the result, not because the prose wasn't up to the job – if anything, it read rather too well – but because the exercise had made me uncomfortable. It seemed to me that Serena didn't really believe half the things she was saying, that the deep repentance and undying love she was declaring did not run terribly deep. I felt I had become party to an act of insincerity, if not deceit, and one aimed at a person whom, rather against the odds, I had come to respect.

Some of my doubts must have shown on my face because Serena said, 'This is the best thing for everyone, believe me. Simon wants me back, I know he does.'

She must have sent the letter by courier soon after she left because at eight the same evening Simon called me and asked, 'Do you know anything about this letter from Serena?'

'Yes,' I admitted, heart sinking.

'You helped to write it?'

There was no point in denying it.

'I rather thought so,' he commented stiffly.

'I'm sorry. I shouldn't have interfered, but she begged me to help. She was so anxious to get it right. She was worried that she wouldn't be able to say everything she wanted to say.'

'I see.' There was a pause. 'Did she seem . . . keen? To come back, I mean.'

'Oh yes,' I said, persuading myself that on this point at least Serena had been sincere.

Another pause. 'There are conditions.'

'She can call you then, to discuss it?' I said, desperate to take a back seat in any further negotiations.

'I'd like to know whether she agrees first. There's no point unless she agrees.'

With an inner sigh, I prepared to make notes.

'First, she must never see that man again, nor speak to him on the phone,' Simon began haltingly in a dead voice. 'This must be a matter of honour, absolutely unbreakable. Second . . .' A long pause. 'While George is still at prep school she's to try and spend an hour with him every day after school – playing, walking, homework, whatever. Her undivided attention.' A shorter pause. 'Third . . . no overnight visits to London unless it's with me. I think that's it.'

'I'll contact her straight away,' I said. 'I'm sure you'll hear from her before the end of the evening.'

In fact it was almost midnight before I managed to get hold of Serena at the friend's in Chelsea.

'A bit steep,' she declared when I'd listed Simon's conditions. 'But then he was always a Victorian at heart.'

'You won't agree, then?'

'Oh no, I didn't say that. Not at all! No – tell him I accept absolutely. Tell him I'll be home tomorrow morning.'

With a sense of relief, I relayed the message to Simon, adding, 'Good luck.' Rarely had I put such meaning into those prosaic words.

I didn't call them over the next few days, and they didn't call me. Before I realized it several weeks had passed without a word. I took this as a good sign, an indication that the two of them were making a go of it. I was glad for them; and, it had to be said, glad for myself. I had not enjoyed my role as go-between.

By November I had started a new book and was working long and irregular hours. One evening at about ten there was a ring on the bell and I went down to find Simon on the doorstep.

'Is she here?' he barked, and his eyes were hard as ice.

'No.'

'Have you seen her?'

'No.'

He glared at me while he decided whether I was telling the truth, then with a sharp nod he marched off in the direction of Bland's house. I almost called out to him but, not knowing what to say, turned back and closed the door. Other people's lives were altogether too complicated for me.

Too distracted to work again that night I tried to read, but after beginning the same page three times I abandoned this as well, and went and ran a bath. I had just sunk into the water when the doorbell rang, a blip so short as to be almost furtive. Finding a wrap, I dripped my way downstairs. I barely had time to unlatch the door before Simon slipped past me into the house and leant against the wall, panting deeply, his face drained of colour. 'Oh God! Oh God!' he moaned agonizingly. 'God! Oh God!'

He was shaking, he seemed to be in shock. I gave him a brandy, sat him down and held his hand until he had calmed down a little. When he finally managed to speak, I thought the shock had affected his brain. 'He's *dead*,' he cried in anguish. '*Dead*, for Christ's sake.'

'Who's dead?'

'*Him.*'

'Damien Bland?'

His face creased into a fresh mask of horror. 'I walked in – the door was open – and he was lying there . . . on the kitchen floor . . . Blood all over the place . . . God, oh *God!*'

'You're sure he's dead?'

He nodded furiously.

'What about Serena?'

He groaned, 'That's what I don't know.'

'She wasn't there?'

'No.'

'Had she been there?'

But he had no answer to that.

'Where was she meant to be this evening?'

'At a party. A charity thing.'

'And she didn't go?'

He shook his head. 'A friend of hers called, saying she hadn't turned up, asking where she'd got to. And then I knew . . . I knew where she'd be.' His mouth tightened with jealousy and pain. 'I've known for a long time – that she was seeing him again. Small things, tiny things . . . I just knew.' He looked at me beseechingly. 'But *this*. You don't think it was Serena, do you? It couldn't have been Serena, could it? *Could* it?' And he covered his face with his hands and began to moan '*God! God!*' again.

I thrust his brandy in front of him and made him take another sip. 'Where was Serena meant to be ending the evening?' I demanded roughly. 'Where was she intending to stay the night?'

'The night?' he repeated with an effort of concentration. 'At home . . . She was coming home.'

'Have you checked to see if she's there?'

'I called half an hour ago. She wasn't there.'

'Well, let's just make sure.'

I went to the phone and dialled Longwood. After a few rings the answering machine picked up, then, just as I was about to abandon the call, Serena's voice cut in, 'Hello? Hello? Who's there?'

I hesitated for an instant then put the phone down. This wasn't the moment to try to explain why I was calling.

'She's at home,' I told Simon.

He stared at me, stunned. 'At home?'

'She just answered.'

'You're sure?'

'Call her yourself,' I suggested. 'Though it might be best to say nothing about the— About what happened round the corner.'

He went unsteadily to the phone. As I disappeared into the kitchen I heard him say incredulously, 'Darling? Is that you?'

When I came back he was staring at the phone as though he didn't entirely trust its message. 'She . . . went to the hairdresser,' he said. 'She felt unwell . . . She went to some friends nearby and lay down for a while. When she felt a bit better they put her in a taxi and she went and picked up her car and drove home. She got to Longwood at about ten.' He turned towards me, the bafflement written all over his face. 'She didn't call because she didn't want to worry me.'

I said as brightly as possible, 'There you are then – nothing to worry about.'

But he was still in a state of shock; he wasn't thinking too clearly. 'What about that guy?' he said. 'We can't just leave him lying there. It's *awful*. Surely we should tell someone?'

'I don't think that would be a very good idea,' I ventured carefully. 'In fact, I think it would be rather a mistake. The best thing would be to forget all about it. Forget you ever saw him. Forget you were ever there.'

'You think so?'

'It wouldn't help the poor man, would it? Nothing will. Whereas a call to the police might not be so good for you. Your visit to the house might be misunderstood.'

'You're right. Yes . . .' He rubbed his forehead savagely. 'Yes, of course . . .'

I was just beginning to think we were out of the woods when he gave a slight start and shot me an alarmed glance. '*Christ* . . .'

'What is it?'

'Someone saw me.'

'Saw you? Who?'

'A man parking his car. Outside Bland's place.'

'Did he actually see you come out of the house?'

'I . . .' He racked his memory. 'No . . . Well, I don't think so. But he got a good look at me. Stared at me.'

'Stared?'

'Yes, I remember him looking at me. Almost as if he

174

knew me. And I think I sort of recognized him too, though I can't remember who he is.'

We sat in silence for a while. Outside, a cat shrieked.

'There's only one thing for it,' I said, turning to meet his pale eyes. 'We'll have to say you spent the evening with me.'

'With you?'

'With me.'

'But – do you think that's really necessary?'

'Yes, I do. It's the only thing that could explain your being seen so close to Bland's house.'

He still wasn't entirely convinced. 'What reason would I give for being here? I've just told Serena that I had to come up unexpectedly on business.'

'You could say the meeting was cancelled and you decided to come here instead. Or' – I shrugged – 'you could tell her that you intended to come here all along.'

'But then she'll think—' His face was filled with an almost schoolboyish embarrassment.

'Simon, it doesn't matter what Serena thinks, not when you compare it with the alternative.'

At long last he saw sense. 'You're right. Of course you're right.'

'The important thing is never to tell a soul that you were inside Bland's house – not a soul, not even Serena.'

'But surely—'

'Not a soul.'

He nodded slowly. 'You're right. Serena would be horrified . . .'

He clambered to his feet as if to leave, but he was still far too shaky to drive safely and I made him sit down

175

again. He hadn't eaten since breakfast, so I made him some scrambled eggs and several cups of strong coffee. As he slowly came back to life, he started to talk. Tentatively at first and then with a flood of feeling he opened his heart about Serena, about the fresh efforts he had put into their marriage, about the compromises he had made, and the pain and torture of her betrayal.

'You're sure she *has* betrayed you?' I asked.

He gave me that unblinking stare of his, now as full of emotion as it had always seemed barren of it before. 'Oh yes, I'm sure.'

'What will you do?'

'Do?' he repeated sadly. 'Carry on, I suppose. There isn't much else to do, is there?'

By this time it was almost one o'clock. 'I think it's too late for you to leave,' I said. 'There won't be anyone to see you go. It'd be better if you stayed the night.'

'What do you mean?'

'Well, Serena and everyone at Longwood will be asleep, won't they? They won't be able to confirm the time you get back. And there won't be anyone in the street to see you leave here. It could make for awkward gaps in your timetable.'

'Gaps?'

'Look at it from the police's point of view – on leaving here you might well be going round the corner to Bland's place and killing him before driving home. No – better to stay here and leave in the morning when we can make sure that there are plenty of neighbours to see you go.'

He looked dazed again.

'It's the safest thing,' I reassured him.

'But Bland's already dead.'

'*We* know that, but the time of death may never be established with any accuracy. Every book on forensic medicine, every expert, will tell you that establishing time of death is a very approximate science, and that the longer a body remains undiscovered, the more approximate the estimation becomes. Safer not to risk it.'

His shoulders sagged then, as if the full weight of his predicament had hit him all over again. I put my arm round him, I murmured the usual things one falls back on in such situations, that everything would seem better in the morning, that it would all be all right in the end. Perhaps it was my tone, perhaps it was the touch of a sympathetic arm, but the next moment he twisted round and, with a sound like a sob, embraced me in a powerful hug.

I didn't fool myself as to the nature of this display of affection – gratitude and relief are powerful emotions – but at the same time it was rather nice to be hugged by Simon. He was warm and needy and passionate: I couldn't imagine how I had ever thought him proud, let alone cold. In different circumstances I might have returned his hug with an enthusiasm which was very far from sisterly. Sensing this, or perhaps wanting it, he moved to kiss me. For a moment I almost succumbed; the temptation was very strong. But at the last minute I managed to pull back and say with a smile, 'You should get some sleep.'

He gave me a look that was half invitation, half entreaty. I felt another tug of temptation – he was really very attractive – but the time and place weren't right, he was too vulnerable, too confused, and for better or worse I had always drawn the line at married men.

'Best not,' I said gently.

He accepted this with a rueful smile, a little abashed but also, I suspected, a little relieved.

I showed him to the spare room. He said he was very tired, but from the look of him the next morning I doubt he slept very much.

I waited until the couple who lived opposite emerged from their house before walking with Simon to his car and, in full view of the neighbours, giving him a clinging kiss which would leave little doubt as to the nature of our relationship.

Damien Bland's body was not discovered until late the next afternoon. According to the tabloids, which gave the murder wide and sensational coverage, he had been stabbed several times in what they described as a frenzied attack. In the long list of women Bland was said to have 'romanced' I was relieved to see that Serena's name was not mentioned.

The police were better informed, however, because three days later two CID officers knocked on my door and asked 'as a matter of routine' if I had seen Mr Simon Benham recently. I told them that I had seen him just a few days ago, on Tuesday night, when he had been with me between the hours of ten o'clock and eight the next morning. They asked me a whole series of questions: about the nature of our relationship (I told them we were having an affair); whether I was absolutely sure about the time he'd arrived; if there had been anything unusual about his appearance; whether he had been with me for the whole ten hours. So far as I could tell my answers seemed to satisfy them and, though they asked me to make a formal statement later that day, they gave the impression that it was just a formality.

After a few days the newspaper reports petered out, and I heard nothing more until the New Year when an acquaintance who knew friends of Damien Bland told me that despite interviewing hundreds of people the police were no closer to finding a suspect.

I had no contact with Simon or Serena, and I wasn't surprised when February came and went without an invitation to the festival weekend.

It was in late April that I bumped into Serena. I was making a dash into Harvey Nichols to find an outfit for yet another wedding when I saw her elegant figure browsing through the Armani suits. Before I could escape she spotted me and came over. Her greeting was cool, her smile chillier, and I was surprised when she suggested we go and have a coffee.

'How are you both?' I asked.

'Oh, fine.'

'Simon?'

'He's very well, thank you. Working all hours. Expanding the nursery business – more greenhouses, I think.' Her clear blue eyes were watching me appraisingly.

'I was sorry about Damien Bland,' I said.

'But you didn't like him.' Before I could point out that this didn't preclude one from feeling regret she added, 'You weren't the only one. As far as I can gather absolutely no one liked him. As for me – well, I'm sorry he's dead, of course I'm sorry, but at the same time—' She hesitated, as though she were deciding whether to trust me. 'Well, it was a bit of relief, actually.' Catching my eye, she gave me one of her most ingenuous looks. 'He was a terrible nuis-ance. I couldn't stop myself, you see. That was the worst thing, being unable to stop myself. However hard I tried I just couldn't keep away, couldn't break the habit. So humiliating. So *degrading*. It was driving me mad. You have no idea how ghastly it is to lose control over your life, to let someone trample over you time and time again. You feel like a piece of dirt. He was loathsome, you know. Utterly horrible. There was absolutely nothing good about him. I couldn't bear it any more. The humiliation . . . the constant fear that Simon would find out. It was making me ill.' She shivered, 'That's something at least – Simon never did find out.'

I was careful to keep all expression out of my face.

'He would have chucked me out, you know. He made that absolutely clear. I couldn't have taken that. I really couldn't. Not for something as worthless as Damien. That's what horrified me most of all – the thought of losing Simon for such *scum*.'

Not sure I was ready to hear more, I mumbled, 'But you're OK now, the two of you?'

'*Now* we are, oh yes. Now that the *problem* is out of the way.' There was a flash of ice in her eyes, a glint of dark satisfaction, and for a moment my imagination screeched into overdrive and I wondered if Serena had told the whole truth about her movements on the night Damien Bland had died.

'Though if Simon and I are OK,' she stated righteously, 'it's no thanks to you.'

Hearing the note of rehearsal in her voice, I realized that we had reached the real purpose of the coffee session.

180

'I must say, you do have a nerve,' she continued. 'Pretending to be my friend and then seducing my husband the moment my back was turned. He said you just talked that night, that nothing happened. Well, I may be trusting but I'm not stupid.' She stood up. 'A one-night stand probably means nothing to you. You probably try your luck with every married man you manage to trap in a corner. Well, some people may be able to overlook these things, but I think it's despicable.' She scooped up her coat. 'There's a word for women like you, you know, but I think it does a gross injustice to dogs.'

The Rape of Kingdom Hill

BY DICK FRANCIS

Thursday afternoon, Tricksy Wilcox scratched his armpit absent-mindedly and decided Claypits wasn't worth backing in the two-thirty. Tricksy Wilcox sprawled in the sagging armchair with a half-drunk can of beer within comforting reach and a huge colour television bringing him the blow by blow from the opening race of the three-day meeting at Kingdom Hill. Only mugs, he reflected complacently, would be putting in a nine-to-five stint in the sort of July heatwave that would have done justice to the Sahara. Sensible guys like himself sat around at home with the windows open and their shirts off, letting their beards grow while the sticky afternoon waned towards opening time.

In winter Tricksy was of the opinion that only mugs struggled to travel to work through snow and sleet, while sensible guys stayed warm in front of the television, betting on the jumpers; and in spring there was rain, and in the autumn, fog. Tricksy at thirty-four had brought unemployment to a fine art and considered the idea of a full honest day's work to be a joke. It was Tricksy's wife who went out in all weathers to her job in the supermarket, Tricksy's wife who paid the rent on the council flat and left the exact money for the milkman. Eleven years of Tricksy had left her cheerful, unresentful, and practical. She had waited without emotion through his two nine-month spells in prison and accepted that one day would find him back there. Her dad had been in and out all her childhood. She felt at home with the minor criminal mind.

Tricksy watched Claypits win the two-thirty with insulting ease and drank down his dented self-esteem with the last of the beer. Nothing he bloody touched, he thought gloomily, was any bloody good these days. He was distinctly short of the readies and had once or twice had to cut down on necessities like drink and fags. What he wanted, now, was a nice little wheeze, a nice little tickle, to con a lot of unsuspecting mugs into opening their wallets. The scarce-ticket racket, now, that had done him proud for years, until the coppers nicked him with a stack of forged duplicates in his pocket at Wimbledon. And tourists were too sly by half these days, you couldn't sell them subscriptions to non-existent porn magazines, let alone London Bridge.

He could never afterwards work out exactly what gave him the great bandwagon idea. One minute he was peacefully watching the three o'clock at Kingdom Hill, and the next he was flooded with a breathtaking, wild, and unholy glee.

He laughed aloud. He slapped his thigh. He stood up and jigged about, unable to bear the audacity of his thoughts sitting down. 'Oh Moses,' he said, gulping for air. 'Money for old rope. Kingdom Hill, here I come.'

Tricksy Wilcox was not the most intelligent of men.

Friday morning, Major Kevin Cawdor-Jones, Manager of Kingdom Hill Racecourse, took his briefcase to the routine meeting of the Executive Committee, most of whom detested each other. Owned and run by a small private company constantly engaged in board-room wars, the race-course suffered from the results of spiteful internecine decisions and never made the profit it could have done.

The appointment of Cawdor-Jones was typical of the mismanagement. Third on the list of possibles, and far less able than one and two, he had been chosen solely to side-step the bitter deadlock between the pro-one line-up and the pro-two. Kingdom Hill in consequence had acquired a mediocre administrator; and the sqabbling executives usually managed to thwart his more sensible suggestions.

As a soldier Cawdor-Jones had been impulsive, rashly courageous, and easy-going, qualities which had ensured that he had not been given the essential promotion to Colonel. As a man he was lazy and likeable, and as a manager, soft.

The Friday meeting as usual wasted little time in coming to blows.

'Massive step up of security,' repeated Bellamy positively. 'Number one priority. Starting at once. Today.'

Thin and sharp-featured, Bellamy glared aggressively round the table, and Roskin as usual with drawling voice opposed him.

'Security costs money, my dear Bellamy.'

Roskin spoke patronizingly, knowing that nothing infuriated Bellamy more. Bellamy's face darkened with fury, and the security of the racecourse, like so much else, was left to the outcome of a personal quarrel.

Bellamy insisted, 'We need bigger barriers, specialized

extra locks on all internal doors and double the number of police. Work must start at once.'

'Race crowds are not hooligans, my dear Bellamy.'

Cawdor-Jones inwardly groaned. He found it tedious enough already, on non-race days, to make his tours of inspection, and he was inclined anyway not to stick punctiliously to the safeguards that already existed. Bigger barriers between enclosures would mean he could no longer climb over or through, but would have to walk the long way round. More locks meant more keys, more time-wasting, more nuisance. And all presumably for the sake of frustrating the very few scroungers who tried to cross from a cheaper to a dearer enclosure without paying. He thought he would very much prefer the status quo.

The tempers rose around him, and the voices also. He waited resignedly for a gap. 'Er—' he said clearing his throat.

The heated pro-Bellamy faction and the sneering pro-Roskin clique both turned towards him hopefully. Cawdor-Jones was their mutual let-out; except, that was, when his solutions were genuinely constructive, when they both vetoed it because they wished they had thought of it themselves.

'A lot of extra security would mean more work for our staff,' he said diffidently. 'We might have to take on an extra man or two to cope with it . . . and after the big initial outlay there would always be maintenance . . . and . . . er . . . well, what real harm can anyone do to a racecourse?'

This weak oil stilled the waters enough for both sides to begin their retreat with their positions and opinions intact.

'You have a point about the staff,' Bellamy conceded

185

begrudgingly, knowing that two extra men would cost a great deal more than locks, and that the racecourse couldn't afford them. 'But I still maintain that tighter security is essential and very much overdue.'

Cawdor-Jones, in his easy-going way, privately disagreed. Nothing had ever happened to date. Why should anything ever happen in future?

The discussion grumbled on for half an hour, and nothing at all was done.

Friday afternoon, Tricksy Wilcox went to the races having pinched a tenner from his wife's holiday fund in the best teapot. The trip was a recce to spy out the land, and Tricksy, walking around with his greedy eyes wide open, couldn't stop himself chuckling. It did occur to him once or twice that his light-hearted single-handed approach was a waste: the big boys would have had it all planned to a second and would have set their sights high in their humourless way. But Tricksy was a loaner who avoided gang life on the grounds that it was too much like hard work; bossed around all the time, and with no pension rights into the bargain.

He downed half pints of beer at various bars and wagered smallish amounts on the tote. He looked at the horses in the parade ring and identified those jockeys whose faces he knew from television, and he attentively watched the races. At the end of the afternoon, with modest winnings keeping him solvent, he chuckled his way home.

Friday afternoon Mrs Angelisa Ludville sold two one-pound tote tickets to Tricksy Wilcox, and hundreds to other people whom she knew as little. Her mind was not on her job, but on the worrying pile of unpaid bills on her book-shelf at home. Life had treated her unkindly since her fiftieth birthday, robbing her of her looks, because of worry, and her husband, because of a blonde. Deserted, divorced and childless, she could nevertheless have adapted content-edly to life alone had it not been for the drastic drop in comfort. Natural optimism and good humour were gradu-ally draining away in the constant grinding struggle to make shortening ends meet.

Angelisa Ludville eyed longingly the money she took through her tote window. Wads of the stuff passed through her hands each working day, and only a fraction of what the public wasted on gambling would, she felt, solve all her problems handsomely. But honesty was a lifetime habit; and besides, stealing from the tote was impossible. The takings for each race were collected and checked immediately. Theft would be instantly revealed. Angelisa sighed and tried to resign herself to the imminent cutting off of her telephone.

Saturday morning, Tricksy Wilcox dressed himself carefully for the job in hand. His wife, had she not been stacking baked beans in the supermarket, would have advised against the fluorescent orange socks. Tricksy, seeing his image in the bedroom mirror only as far down as the knees, was confident that the dark suit, dim tie and bowler hat gave him the look of a proper race-going gent. He had even, without reluctance, cut two inches off his hair, and removed a flourishing moustache. Complete with outsize binocular case slung over his shoulder he smirked at his transform-

187

ation with approval and set out with a light step to catch the train to Kingdom Hill.

On the racecourse Major Kevin Cawdor-Jones made his raceday round of inspection with his usual lack of thoroughness. Slipshod holes in his management resulted also in the police contingent arriving half an hour late and understrength; and not enough racecards had been ordered from the printers.

'Not to worry,' said Cawdor-Jones, shrugging it all off easily.

Mrs Angelisa Ludville travelled to the course in the tote's own coach, along with fifty colleagues. She looked out of the window at the passing suburbs and thought gloomily about the price of electricity.

Saturday afternoon at two-thirty she was immersed in the routine of issuing tickets and taking money, concentrating on her work and feeling reasonably happy. She arranged before her the fresh batch of tickets, those for the three o'clock, the biggest race of the day. The extra-long queues would be forming soon outside, and speed and efficiency in serving the punters was not only her job, but, indeed, her pride.

At two fifty-five Cawdor-Jones was in his office next to the weighing room trying to sort out the muddle over the casual workers' pay. At two fifty-seven the telephone at his elbow rang for about the twentieth time in the past two hours and he picked up the receiver with his mind still on the disputed hourly rates due to the stickers-back of kicked-up chunks of turf.

'Cawdor-Jones,' he said automatically.

A man with an Irish accent began speaking quietly.

'What?' said Cawdor-Jones. 'Speak up can't you. There's too much noise here . . . I can't hear you.'

The man with the Irish accent repeated his message with the same soft half whisper.

'*What?*' said Cawdor-Jones. But his caller had rung off.

'Oh my God,' said Cawdor-Jones, and stretched a hand to the switch which connected him to the internal broadcasting system. He glanced urgently at the clock. Its hands clicked round to two fifty-nine, and at that moment the fourteen runners for the three o'clock were being led into the starting stalls.

'Ladies and gentlemen,' said Cawdor-Jones, his voice reverberating from every loudspeaker on the racecourse. 'We have been warned that a bomb has been planted somewhere in the stands. Would you please all leave at once and go over into the centre of the course while the police arrange a search.'

The moment of general shock lasted less than a second: then the huge race crowd streamed like a river down from the steps, up from the tunnels, out of the doors, running, pelting, elbowing towards the safety of the open spaces on the far side of the track.

Bars emptied dramatically with half-full glasses overturned and smashed in the panic. The tote queues melted instantaneously and the ticket-sellers followed them helter-skelter. The stewards vacated their high box at a dignified downhill rush and the racing press pell-melled to the exit without hanging round to alert their papers. City editors could wait half an hour. Bombs wouldn't.

The scrambling thousands deserted all the racecourse buildings within a space of two minutes. Only a very few stayed behind, and chief of these was Kevin Cawdor-Jones, who had never lacked for personal courage and now saw it as his duty as a soldier to remain at his post.

The under-strength band of policemen collected bit by bit outside the weighing room, each man hiding his natural apprehension under a reassuring front. Probably another bloody hoax, they told each other. It was always a hoax. Or nearly always. Their Officer took charge of organizing the search and told the civilian Cawdor-Jones to remove himself to safety.

'No, no,' said Cawdor-Jones, 'while you look for the bomb, I'll make quite sure that everyone's out.' He smiled a little anxiously and dived purposefully into the weighing room.

All clear there, he thought, peering rapidly round the jockeys' wash room. All clear in the judges' box, the photo-finish developing room, the kitchens, the boiler room, the tote, the offices, the stores . . . He bustled from building to building, knowing all the back rooms, the nooks and crannies where some deaf member of the staff, some drunk member of the public, might be sitting unawares.

He saw no people. He saw no bomb. He returned a little breathlessly to the open space outside the weighing room and waited for a report from the slower police.

Around the stands Tricksy Wilcox was putting the great bandwagon idea into sloppy execution. Chuckling away internally over the memory of an Irish impersonation good enough for entry to Equity, he bustled speedily from bar to bar and in and out of the other doors, filling his large empty binoculars' case with provender. It was amazing, he thought, giggling, how careless people were in a panic.

Twice, he came face to face with policemen.

'All clear in there, Officer,' he said purposefully, each time pointing back to where he had been. Each time the police gaze flickered unsuspectingly over the bowler hat, the dark suit, dim tie and took him for one of the racecourse staff.

Only the orange socks stopped him getting clean away. One policeman, watching his receding back view, frowned uncertainly at the brilliant segments between trouser-leg and shoe and started slowly after him.

'Hey—' he said.

Tricksy turned his head, saw the Law advancing, lost his nerve, and bolted. Tricksy was never the most intelligent of men.

Saturday afternoon at four o'clock, Cawdor-Jones made another announcement.

'It appears the bomb warning was just another hoax. It is now safe for everyone to return to the stands.'

The crowd streamed back in reverse and made for the bars. The barmaids returned to their posts and immediately raised hands and voices in a screeching sharp chorus of affronted horror.

'Someone's pinched all the takings!'

'The cheek of it! Taken our tips, and all!'

In the various tote buildings, the ticket-sellers stood appalled. Most of the huge intake for the biggest race of the meeting had simply vanished.

Angelisa Ludville looked with utter disbelief at her own

plundered cashbox. White, shaking, she joined the clamour of voices. 'The money's gone!'

Cawdor-Jones received report after report into a face of anxious despair. He knew no doors had been locked after the stampede to the exit. He knew no security measures whatever had been taken. The racecourse wasn't equipped to deal with such a situation. The Committee would undoubtedly blame him. Might even give him the sack.

At four-thirty he listened with astounded relief to news from the police that a man had been apprehended and was now helping to explain how his binoculars' case came to be crammed to overflowing with used treasury notes, many of them bearing a fresh watermark resulting from the use of a wet beer glass as a paperweight.

Monday morning Tricksy Wilcox appeared gloomily before a magistrate and was remanded in custody for seven days. The great bandwagon idea hadn't been so hot after all, and they would undoubtedly send him down for more than nine months, this time.

Only one thought brightened his future. The police had tried all weekend to get information out of him, and he had kept his mouth tight shut. Where, they wanted to know, had he hidden the biggest part of his loot?

Tricksy said nothing.

There had only been room in the binoculars' case for one-tenth of the stolen money. Where had he put the bulk?

Tricksy wasn't telling.

He would get off more lightly, they said, if he surrendered the rest.

Tricksy didn't believe it. He grinned sardonically and shook his head. Tricksy knew from past experience that he would have a much easier time inside as the owner of a large hidden cache. He'd be respected. Treated with proper awe. He'd have status. Nothing on earth would have persuaded him to spill the beans.

Monday morning Major Cawdor-Jones took his red face to an emergency meeting of his Executive Committee and agreed helplessly with Bellamy's sharply reiterated opinion that the racecourse security was a disgrace.

'I warned you,' Bellamy repeated for the tenth self-righteous time. 'I warned you all. We need more locks. There are some excellent slam-shut devices available for the cashboxes in the tote. I'm told that all money can be secured in five seconds. I propose that these devices be installed immediately throughout the racecourse.'

He glared belligerently round the table. Roskin kept his eyes down and merely pursed his mouth, and Kingdom Hill voted to bolt its doors now that the horse was gone.

Monday evening Angelisa Ludville poured a double gin, switched on the television and put her feet up. Beside her lay a pile of stamped and addressed envelopes, each containing one of the dreaded bills. She sighed contentedly. Never, she thought, would she forget the shock of seeing her empty till. Never would she get over the fright it had given her. Never would she forget the rush of relief when she realized that everyone had been robbed, not just herself. Because she knew perfectly well that it was one of the five-pound windows whose take she had scooped up on the scramble to the door. It would have been plain stupid to have lifted the money from her own place. She couldn't know that there would have been another, more ambitious thief. It would have been plain silly to steal from her own place. And besides, there was far more cash at the five-pound window.

Monday evening Kevin Cawdor-Jones sat in his bachelor flat thinking about the second search of Kingdom Hill. All day Sunday the police had repeated the nook-and-cranny inspection, but slowly, without fear, looking not for a bang but a bank. Cawdor-Jones had given his willing assistance, but nothing at all had been found.

'Tricksy must have had a partner,' said the Officer morosely. 'But we won't get a dicky bird out of him.'

Cawdor-Jones, unsacked from his managership, smiled gently at the memory of the past few days. Cawdor-Jones, impulsive and rashly courageous, had made the most of the opportunity Tricksy Wilcox had provided. Cawdor-Jones, whose nerve could never be doubted, had driven away on Saturday evening with the jackpot from the tote.

He leaned over the arm of his chair and fondly patted his bulging briefcase.

The Sheikh and
the Dustbin

BY GEORGE MACDONALD FRASER

When I was a young soldier, and had not yet acquired the tobacco vice (which began with scrounging cigarettes at route-march halts when everyone else lit up and I felt left out) I used to win cross-country races. This surprised me, for while I had been athletic enough at school I had never been fleet of foot; in the infants' egg-and-spoon race, and later in the hundred yards, I would come labouring in well behind the leaders, and as a rugby full-back I learned to be in the right place beforehand because I knew that no amount of running would get me there in time if I wasn't. So it was a revelation, when the Army hounded us out in the rain to run miles across soggy Derbyshire in PT kit, to discover that I could keep up a steady stride and finish comfortably ahead of the mud-splattered mob, winning 7s. 6d. in saving certificates and having the Company Sergeant-Major (who was seventeen stone, all fat, and smoked like a chimney) wheeze enthusiastically: 'Aye, happen lad'll mek a Brigade rooner! Good at all sport, are yeh, MacNeill? Play football, roogby, cricket, do yeh? Aye, right, yeh'll be left inner in t'coompany 'ockey team this art'noon, an' report to t'gym fer boxin' trainin' on Moon-

195

day. Welter-weight, are yeh – mebbe middle-weight, we'll see. Done any swimmin', 'ave yeh? 'Ow about 'igh joomp . . .?' That's the military mind, you see; if you're good at one thing, you're good at everything.

It didn't take long to convince him that I'd never held a hockey stick in my life and was a wildly unscientific boxer, but being a resourceful old warrant officer he made good use of my running ability, in a rather unusual way – and did much to advance my military education. For during those weeks of basic training I was detailed several times to escort prisoners to the military jail, the idea being that if during the journey by rail and road a prisoner somehow won free of the Redcap to whom he was handcuffed, I would run him down – what I was to do when I caught him was taken for granted. It never came to that; all our malefactors went quietly to the great grim converted factory at Sowerby Bridge which was the North Country's most feared and fearsome glasshouse and remains in my memory as one of the most horrible places I have ever seen. If my cross-country talents did nothing else, they won me a first-hand look at an old-style military nick which convinced me that, come what might, I was going to be a good little soldier.

The bleak walls and yards with their high wire-meshed gates, the lean, skull-faced guards screaming high-pitched, the crop-headed inmates doubling frantically wherever they went, our prisoner having to strip naked at high speed in the cold reception cell under the glaring eye of what looked like a homicidal maniac in khaki – all these were daunting enough, but what chilled my marrow was the sight of a single, everyday domestic object standing outside a door-way: an ordinary dustbin. Only this one had been burnished until it gleamed, literally, like silver; you could have shaved at it without difficulty. The mere thought of how it had got that way told me more about Sowerby Bridge than I wanted to know; think about it next time you put out the rubbish.

I don't suppose that military prisons are quite as stark as that in this enlightened age (where did they go, those gaunt, shrieking fanatics of staff men? Do they sit, in gentle senility and woolly slippers, watching *Coronation Street*?) but in their time they were places of dreadful repute – Stirling, and Aldershot (whose glazed roof is supposed to have inspired the name 'glasshouse'); Heliopolis, outside Cairo, where prisoners were forced to run up and down the infamous 'Hill', and Trimulghari, in India, home of the soul-destroying well drill in which wells had to be filled and emptied again and again and again. Perhaps rumour made them out worse than they were, but having been inside Sowerby Bridge, I doubt it. Reactionary old soldiers speculate wistfully on their reintroduction for modern criminals and football hooligans, forgetting that you can no more bring them back than you can bring back the world they belonged to; like conscription, they are just part of military history – for which the football hooligans can be thankful.

However, this is not a treatise on glasshouses, and if I have reflected on them it is only because they are part of the train of thought that begins whenever I remember Suleiman ibn Aziz, Lord of the Grey Mountain, who had no connection with them personally. But he was a military prisoner, and belongs in the same compartment of my memory as Sowerby Bridge, and barred windows, and Lovelace's poem to Lucasta, and 'jankers', and McAuslan and Wee Wullie labouring on the rockpile, and the time I myself spent in cells as a ranker (the sound of that metal-shod door slamming is one you don't forget in a hurry, when you've been on the wrong side of it), and all my varied thoughts and recollections about what the Army used to call 'close tack'. Detention, in other words, and if it has two symbols for me, one is that gleaming dustbin and the other is old Suleiman.

He was quite the unlikeliest, and certainly the most distinguished prisoner ever to occupy a cell in our North African barracks. I won't say he was the most eccentric, because those bare stone chambers at the back of the guard room were occasionally tenanted by the likes of McAuslan and Wee Wullie, but he was more trouble than all the battalion's delinquents put together – something, fortunately, which happened only on Hogmanay, when it was standing-room only in the cells and Sergeant McGarry's provost staff were hard pressed to accommodate all the revellers.

They were busy enough during the rest of the year, too, but not because our Jocks were rowdier than any other soldiers; if our cells were well used it was because the Colonel, unlike some commanders, refused to use the glass-house as a dumping-ground for incorrigibles. To him, a man in Heliopolis was a dead loss to the regiment, and a failure, and he would move heaven and earth to keep our worst offenders out of the Big House – especially if they had been good men at war. Wee Wullie's record of violence and drunkenness should have put him on the Hill for years – but Wullie had played the soldier when it counted, in the Western Desert, and the regiment had a long memory. As it did for the remarkable Phimister, a genuine hero of Japanese captivity who must thereafter be forgiven for spending more time on the run from the Redcaps than he did on parade. It wasn't easy, and the Colonel had to do some inspired string-pulling on occasion, but no one doubted it was worth it. A Highland regiment is a family, and settles its own differences within itself – if that sounds trite, it's true. So when Phimister went walkabouts yet again and was picked up trying to board a tramp steamer in Tunis, or Wullie overturned a police jeep and battled with its occupants, or McAuslan went absent and tried to pawn a two-inch mortar in the bazaar (so help me, it's a fact), there was no thought of shipping them to the glasshouse; they did their time in our own cells under the iron hand of McGarry, digging and carrying in sweltering heat, deprived of tobacco and alcohol, and safely locked in at night. It was genuine hard labour, they hated it, it kept them out of trouble, and as McGarry used to say:

'They come tae nae herm wi' me. What? They were never so weel aff in their lives! Wullie's sober an' McAuslan's clean, an' that's mair than ye can say when they're on the ootside. I don't gi'e them any bother – an' by God they don't gi'e me any.'

Looking at McGarry, you might have feared the worst from that last remark. All provost staff tend to resemble galley overseers, and he was rather like an outsize Ernest Borgnine playing Ivan the Mad Torturer, but the appearance was deceptive. Despite barrack-room gossip, McGarry never laid hands on a man unless he was hit first, in which case he hit back – once. (The exception was Wee Wullie, who had to be hit several times.) For the rest, McGarry got by on presence and personality; the mere sight of that huge figure at the top of the guard-room steps, thumbs hooked in the top of his kilt as he coldly surveyed the scene, was the most potent disciplinary force in the battalion.

It was into this strange guard-room world that Suleiman ibn Aziz came unexpectedly on a summer night. I was orderly officer, and had just finished the routine inspection of prisoners to make sure they were still breathing and not trying to tunnel their way out. There were two in residence: McAuslan starting fourteen days after his brief career as a mortar salesman, and Phimister as usual. I was signing the book when I noticed that one of the four vacant cells was open – and within there was an undoubted rug on the floor, a table, chair, chest-of-drawers, jug and wash-basin, and in place of the usual plank and blanket there was a pukka bed, with sheets and pillows. I thought I must be seeing things.

'Who in the world is that for?' I asked. 'Don't tell me you've got the Brigadier in close tack!'

'Nae idea, sir,' said McGarry. 'I just got word tae have a cell ready, an' then the Adjutant himsel' turns up tae see tae the furniture. It's no' a regular client, anyway.'

'Somebody from outside? He must be pretty special. But why us?'

'Strongest jyle in the province, this,' said McGarry, not without satisfaction. 'God kens what kind o' sodgers Mussolini built this barracks for, but he wasnae takin' ony chances wi' his defaulters. These walls is six feet thick. There's tae be a special sentry on the door, too.'

This was unprecedented – as was the appearance of the Colonel, Adjutant, and second-in-command at the main gate just after Last Post, when a staff car arrived bearing the Provost Marshal and a small figure in a black burnous and silver-trimmed *kafilyeh* handcuffed to a Redcap escort. He stood sullenly while the Colonel and the Provost Marshal conferred briefly, and then he was uncuffed and brought up the guard-room steps for delivery to McGarry; I had only a glimpse of a lean, lined, swarthy face with an enormous beak of a nose and a white tuft of beard, and two bright angry eyes glaring under the *kafilyeh* hood. They hustled him inside, and the Adjutant, who had been hovering like an agitated hen, beckoned me to follow to his office, where the Colonel was sounding off at the Provost Marshal:

'... and you can tell GHQ that I don't take kindly to having my barracks turned into a transit camp for itinerant bedouin. What did you say the beggar's name was?'

'Suleiman ibn Aziz, sir,' said the PM. 'Known in Algeria as the Lord of the Grey Mountain, apparently.' He hesitated, looking apologetic. 'In Morocco they call him the Black Hand of God. So I'm told, sir.'

'Never heard of him,' said the Colonel. 'How long are we supposed to keep him?'

'Just a week or two, I hope – until the French come to collect him. I know it's a nuisance, sir, but there's really nothing to worry about; he's over seventy.'

'I'm not in the least worried,' snapped the Colonel, who didn't like the PM at the best of times. 'Nor am I a damned innkeeper. Why's he so important, anyway?'

'Well, sir,' said the PM, looking impressive, 'I'm sure you've heard of Abd-el Krim ...?' The Adjutant's head came up at that famous name; like me, he knew his PC Wren. The Colonel frowned.

'Krim? The chief who led the Riff Rebellion in Algeria, back in the twenties? Gave the French Foreign Legion a hell of a dance, didn't he? Yes, I've heard of him—'

'The Red Shadow!' said the Adjutant brightly, and the Colonel gave him a withering look.

'Thank you, Michael, you can play a selection from "The Desert Song" later.' He turned back to the PM. 'I thought Krim surrendered to the French twenty years ago – what's this bird got to do with him?'

'Absolutely right, sir, Krim did surrender,' said the PM. 'But Suleiman didn't. He'd been Krim's right-hand man from the start of the Riff revolt, near the turn of the century, commanded his cavalry – he was the man who drove the Legion out of Taza in '24, overran their forts, beat up their columns, played hell all over. Real *Beau Geste* stuff,' he was going on enthusiastically, until the Colonel raised a bleak eye from scraping his pipe. 'Yes, well . . . he had something like twenty thousand Riffs behind him then, but when the French really went to town in '26 Krim packed in with most of 'em, and Suleiman was left with just a handful. Swore he'd never give up, took to the Moroccan mountains, and has been hammering away for twenty years, off and on – raiding, ambushing, causing no end of trouble. The French captured him twice, but he escaped both times.' The PM paused. 'The second time was from Devil's Island.'

There was silence, and the Colonel stopped scraping for a moment. Then he asked: 'Where did you learn all this?'

'Intelligence bumf, sir – it's all in the dossier there. Just came in this afternoon. Suleiman was picked up only two days ago, you see, by one of our long-range groups south of Yarhuna, acting on information from the French in Oran—'

'What the devil was he doing over here? We're more than a thousand miles from Morocco!'

The PM looked perplexed. 'Well, it's rather odd, actually. When he escaped from Devil's Island it was early in the war, about '41. He managed to get back across the Atlantic, God knows how – he was nearly seventy then, and he'd had a pretty rough time in captivity, I believe. Anyway, he reached Morocco, got a few followers, and started pasting the French again, until our desert war was at its height in '42, when for some reason he came east and pitched in against Rommel.' The PM spread his hands in wonder. 'Why, no one knows . . . unless he regarded the Germans as allies of the Vichy Government. When the war ended the French were still after him, and for the past year or so he's been hiding out down south, quite alone. There was no one with him in the village where our people found him.'

'And the French still want him? At this time of day?' The Colonel blew through his pipe. 'What do they intend to do with him, d'you know?'

The PM hesitated. 'Send him back to Devil's Island . . . so Cairo tell me, anyway. It seems the French regard him as a dangerous public enemy—'

'In his seventies? Without followers? After he's been on our side in the war?'

'It's up to the French, sir. We're just co-operating.' The PM shifted in his chair, avoiding the Colonel's eye. 'I ought to mention – there's a note in the dossier – that Cairo regards this as a top security matter.'

'Indeed?' The Colonel's tone was chilly. 'Then why don't they put him in Heliopolis, instead of my guard-room?'

The PM looked embarrassed. 'Well, we're convenient

203

here, of course – next to French territory. If they took him to Cairo, it would be bound to get talked about – might get into the papers, even.' He glanced round as though expecting to find reporters crouched behind his chair. 'You see, sir, the French want to keep it hush-hush – security, I imagine – and Cairo agrees. So the transfer, when it's made, is to be discreet. Without publicity.' He smiled uneasily. 'I'm sure that's understood.'

The Colonel blew smoke, considering him, and just from the angle of his pipe I knew he was in one of his rare cold rages, though I wasn't sure why. The PM knew it, too, and fidgeted. Finally the Colonel said:

'We'll look after your prisoner, Provost Marshal. And if we don't come up to GHQ Cairo's expectation as turnkeys, I suggest they do the job themselves. Convey that, would you? Anything else?'

The PM, who wasn't used to mere Colonels who raised two fingers to Cairo, got quite flustered, but all he could think of to add was that Suleiman ibn Aziz spoke Arabic and Spanish but only a little French, so if we needed an interpreter . . .

'Thank you, my Adjutant speaks fluent French,' said the Colonel, and the Adjutant, who had spent a hiking holiday in the Pyrenees before the war, tried to look like an accomplished linguist. The PM said that was splendid, and made his escape, and we waited while the Colonel smoked grimly and stared at the wall. The second-in-command remarked that this chap Suleiman sounded like an interesting chap. Enterprising, too.

'Imagine escaping from Devil's Island, at the age of

204

seventy!' The Adjutant shook his head in admiration. 'Poor old blighter!'

'You can probably save your sympathy,' said the Colonel abruptly. 'From what I've heard of the Riffs' treatment of prisoners I doubt if our guest is Saladin, exactly.' He gave a couple of impatient puffs and laid down his pipe. 'Still, I'm damned if we'll be any harsher than we must. You're orderly officer, MacNeill? See McGarry has him properly bedded down and I'll talk to him in the morning – you *do* speak French, don't you, Michael? God knows you've said so often enough.'

The Adjutant said hastily that he'd always managed to make himself understood – of course, he couldn't guarantee that an Arab would understand the Languedoc accent . . . why, in Perpignan they spoke French with a *Glasgow* accent, would you believe it, mong jew and tray bong, quite extraordinary . . . Listening to him babble, I resolved not to miss his interview with Suleiman next day. When the others had gone he began a frantic rummage for his French dictionary, muttering vaguely bon soir, mam'selle, voulez-vous avez un aperitif avec moi, bloody hell, some blighter's knocked it, and generally getting distraught.

'Never mind your aunt's plume,' I said. 'What's the old man so steamed up about?'

'I'll just have to speak very slowly, that's all.' He rumpled his fair hair, sighing. 'Eh? The Colonel? Well, he doesn't like having his guard-room turned into a political prison – especially not for the Frogs. You know how he loves *them*: "Brutes let us down in '14, and again in '40—" '

'I know that, but what's wrong with having to look after an old buddoo for a week or two?'

205

'It's politics, clot. The Frogs want to fix this old brig-
and's duff, and no doubt our politicians want to keep de
Gaulle happy, so the word goes to Cairo to co-operate, and
we lift him and hand him over – but quietly, without fuss,
so it doesn't get in the papers. See?'

'What if it does?'

'God, you're innocent. Look, the old bugger's past it,
the Frogs are just being bloody-minded, we're co-operating
like loyal allies – but d'you think Cairo wants to be *seen*
helping to give him a free ticket back to Devil's Island? So
we get the job, 'cos we're out here far beyond the notice
of journalists and radicals – anti-colonialists and so on –
who'd make a martyr of the old boy if they heard about it.
Are you receiving me?'

'Well . . . sort of . . . but he's a rebel, isn't he?'

'Certainly, fathead, and ten years ago no one would have
given a hoot about handing him over. But it's different
now. Don't you read the papers? The old enemies are
the new patriots. Gandhi's a saint these days . . . so why
shouldn't this old villain be a hero? After all, he always has
been, to some people – fighting for his independence, by
his way of it. Suppose his name was William Wallace – or
Hereward the Wake? See what I mean?'

It was new stuff to me, in 1947. Yes, I was an innocent.

'So that's why the Colonel gets wild,' said the Adjutant.
'Being used as a stooge, because Cairo hasn't got the guts
to pass this Suleiman on openly – or to tell the Frogs to
take a running jump. Which is what the Colonel would do
– partly because he can't stand 'em, but also because he's
got a soft spot for the Suleimans of this world. God knows
he fought them long enough, on the Frontier, and knows

what a shower they are, but still . . . he respects 'em . . . and this one's over the hill, anyway. That's why he's hopping mad at Cairo for giving him a dirty job, but it's a lawful command, and he's a soldier. So, incidentally, are you,' added the Adjutant severely, 'and you ought to have been in the guard-room hours ago, examining padlocks. I don't suppose *you* speak French? No, you ruddy wouldn't—'

All was well in the guard-room, and through the grille in his cell door I could see the prisoner on the bed, still wrapped in his burnous, snoring vigorously.

'By, but that's an angry yin!' said Sergeant McGarry. 'Hear him snarl when I asked if he wantit anything? I offered tae get him some chuck, but I micht as weel ha'e been talkin' tae mysel'. Who is he, sir?'

I was telling him, when the gargoyle features of Private McAuslan appeared at the grille of the neighbouring cell, a sight that made me feel I should have brought some nuts to throw through the bars.

'Hullaw rerr, sur,' said he, companionable as always. 'Who's ra auld wog next door? See him, Ah cannae get tae sleep fur him snorin'. Gaun like a biler, sure'n he is.'

'He's a reporter frae the *Tripoli Ghibli*, come tae inter-view ye an' write yer life story,' said McGarry, and suddenly snarled: 'Sharrap an' gedoon on yer cot, ye animal, or I'll flype ye!' McAuslan disappeared as by magic. I finished telling McGarry what I knew about his prisoner, and he shook his head as we stood looking through the grille.

'Black Hand o' God, eh? He's no verra handy noo, puir auld cratur. Mind you, he'll have been a hard man in his time.'

That was surely true, I thought. In the dim light I could

make out the hawk profile and the white stubble on the cropped skull where the *kafilyeh* had fallen away; he looked very frail and old now. The Lord of the Grey Mountain, who had led the great Riff *harkas* against the French invaders and fought the legendary Foreign Legion to a standstill, the drawn sword of Abd-el Krim, the last of the desert rebels . . . It was inevitable that I should find myself thinking of the glossy romance that had been shown at the garrison cinema not long ago, with its hordes of robed riders thundering over the California sandhills while Dennis Morgan sang the new words which, in the spirit of wartime, had been set to the stirring music of Romberg's Riff Song:

> *Show them that surrender isn't all!*
> *There's no barricade or prison wall*
> *Can keep a free man enslaved . . .*

It was pathetically ironic, looking in at the little old man who had been the anonymous inspiration for that verse, and had spent a lifetime fighting for the reality of its brave message, even taking part in the greater cause against Germany. The film fiction had ended in a blaze of glory; the tragic fact was asleep in a British Army cell, waiting to be shipped away to a felon's death in exile, the scourge of the desert keeping McAuslan awake with his snoring.

His interview with the Colonel next day was a literal frost, for during fifteen minutes' laboured interrogation by the Adjutant he spoke only once, and that was to say 'Non!' Seen in daylight he was a gaunt leathery ancient with a malevolent eye in a vulpine face whose only redeeming

feature was that splendid hooked nose, but he carried himself with a defiant pride that was impressive. Seated in his
cell, refusing even to notice his visitors, he might have been
just a sullen little ruffian, but he wasn't; there was a force
in the spare small body and a dignity in the lifted head;
whether he understood the Adjutant's questions about his
welfare (which sounded like a parody of *French without
Tears*, with such atrocities as 'Etait votre lit tendre . . .
suffisant douce, I mean,' which I construed as an enquiry
about the comfort of his bed) it was hard to say, since he
just stared stonily ahead while the Adjutant got pinker and
louder. That he was getting through became apparent only
with the last question, when the Colonel, who had been
getting restive, interrupted.

'Ask him, if we give him the freedom of the barracks,
will he give his word of honour not to try to escape?'

This was the Colonel sounding out his man, and it
brought the first reaction. Suleiman stiffened, stared angrily
at the Colonel, and fairly spat out 'Non!' before standing
up abruptly and turning on his heel to stalk across to the
window, thus indicating that the palaver was finished.

'Well, he can give a straight answer when he wants,' said
the Colonel. 'He doesn't lie at the first opportunity, either.
Keep his cell locked at night, McGarry, with a sentry posted,
but during the day he can sit on the verandah or in the little
garden if he likes. The more he's in open view, the easier he'll
be to watch. And he's not to be stared at – see that that's
understood by all ranks, Michael. Very well, carry on.'

So we did, and in the following days the small black-
robed figure became a familiar sight, seated under an arch
of the guard-room verandah or in the little rock-garden at

the side, the armed sentry at a tactful distance and McGarry as usual at the head of the steps. According to him Suleiman never uttered a word or showed any emotion except silent hatred of everything around him; at first he had even refused to sit outside, and only after McGarry had taken out the chair two or three times, leaving the cell door open, had he finally ventured forth, slowly, making a long survey of the parade square before seating himself. He would stay there, quite motionless, his hands folded before him, until it was time to go to his cell to pray, or the orderly brought his meals, which were prepared at an Arab eating-house down the road. He never seemed to see or hear the sights and sounds of the parade ground; there was something not canny about the stillness of the small, frail figure, his face shaded from the sun by the silver-trimmed *kafilyeh*, as though he were under a spell of immobility, waiting with a furious patience for it to be lifted.

The Provost Marshal must have got word of the freedom he was being given, for he called to protest to the Colonel about such a focus of nationalist unrest being in full view from the gate where local natives were forever passing by. What the Colonel replied is not recorded, but the PM came out crimson and sweating, to the general satisfaction.

For there was no doubt of it, in spite of his hostile silence and cold refusal even to notice us, a sort of protective admiration was growing in the battalion for the ugly little Bedouin warlord. Everyone knew his story by now, and what was in store for him, and sympathy was openly expressed for 'the wee wog', while the French were reviled for their persecution, and our own High Command for being part and party in it.

'Whit wye does the Colonel no' jist turn his back an' let him scarper?' was how Private Fletcher put it. 'So whit if he used tae pit the hems oan the Frogs? A helluva lot we owe them, an' chance it. Onywye, they say the wee fellah got tore in oan oor side in the war – is that right, sur? Becuz if it is, then it's a bluidy shame! We should be gi'in' him a medal, never mind sendin' him back tae Duvvil's Island!'

'Sooner him than me,' said Daft Bob Brown. 'Ever see that fillum, *King o' the Damned*? That wis aboot Duvvil's Island – scare the bluidy blue lights oot o' ye, so it wud.'

'We should gi'e him a pound oot the till an' say "On yer way, Cherlie," ' said Fletcher emphatically. 'That's whit Ah'd dae.'

You and the Colonel both, Fletcher, I thought. Scottish soldiers have a callous streak a mile wide, compensated by a band of pure marshmallow, and either is liable to surface unexpectedly, but if there is one thing they admire it is a fighting man, and it doesn't matter whether he's friend or foe, fellow or alien. Suleiman ibn Aziz was a wog – but he was a brave wog, who had gone his mile, and now he was old and done and alone and they were full of fury on his behalf. Barrack-room sentimentality, if you like, which overlooked the fact that he had been a fully-paid-up monster in his time; that didn't matter, he wis a good wee fellah, so he wis.

Their regard showed itself in a quite astonishing way. It was a regimental tradition for Jocks entering or leaving barracks to salute the guard-room, a relic of the days when the colours were housed there. Now – and how it began we never discovered – they started to extend the time of their salutes to cover the small figure in the burnous seated in the garden; I even saw a sergeant give his marching platoon 'Eyes left!' well in advance so that Suleiman was included, and the Regimental Sergeant-Major, who happened to be passing (and missed nothing) didn't bat an eyelid. Highland soldiers are a very strange law unto themselves.

I doubt whether Suleiman noticed, or was aware of the general sympathy. His own obvious hostility discouraged any approaches, and the only ones he got came from his fellow-prisoner McAuslan. The great janker-wallah was never one to deny his conversation to anybody unlucky enough to be within earshot, and since his defaulters' duties included sweeping the verandah and weeding the garden, Suleiman was a captive audience, so to speak; the fact that he didn't understand a word and paid not the slightest heed meant nothing to a blether of McAuslan's persistence. He held forth like the never-wearied rook while he shambled about the flower-bed destroying things and besmirching himself, and the Lord of the Grey Mountain sat through it like a robed idol, his unwinking gaze fastened on the distance. It was a pity he didn't speak Glaswegian, really, because McAuslan's small-talk was designed to comfort and advise; I paused once on a guard-room visit to listen to his monologue floating in through the barred window:

'. . . mind you, auld yin, there's this tae be said for bein' in the nick, ye get yer room an' board, an' at your time o' life the Frogs arenae gaun tae pit ye tae breakin' rocks, sure'n they're no? O'course, Ah dae ken whit it's like in a French cooler, but ach! they'll no' be hard on ye. An' ye never know, mebbe ye'll get a chance tae go ower the wa' again. They tell me ye've been ay-woll twice a'ready, is that

right? Frae Duvvil's Island? Jings, that's sumpn! Aye, but –
mah advice tae ye is, don't try it while ye're here, for any
favour, becuz that big bastard McGarry's got eyes in his
erse, an' ye widnae get by the gate. Naw, jist you wait till
ra Frogs come for ye, an' bide yer time an' scram when
their back's turned – they're no' organized at a', ra Frogs.
Weel, ye ken that yersel'. Here, but! it's a shame ye couldnae
tak' Phimister wi' ye – him that wis in the cell next door
tae me, the glaikit-lookin' fella. He's no' sae glaikit, Ah'm
tellin' ye! Goad kens how many times he's bust oot o' close
tack – he wid hiv ye oan a fast camel tae Wogland afore ra
Frogs knew whit time it wis! Jeez, whit a man! Aye, but
ye'll no' be as nippy as ye were . . . ach, but mebbe it'll no'
be sae bad, auld boy! Whitever Duvvil's Island's like, it
cannae be worse'n gettin' liftit by the Marine Division in
Gleska, no' kiddin'. See them? Buncha animals, so they are.
Did Ah no' tell ye aboot the time Ah got done, efter the
Cup Final? It wis like this, see—'

To this stream of Govan consciousness Suleiman
remained totally deaf, as he did to all the sounds around
him – until the seventh day, when the pipe band held a
practice behind the transport sheds in preparation for next
day's Retreat: at the first distant keening note his head
turned sharply, and after a moment he got up and walked
to the edge of the garden, evidently trying to catch a
glimpse of the pipers. For a full half hour he stood, his
hawk face turned towards the sound, and only when it
ended did he walk slowly back to the guard-room, apparently deep in thought. There he suddenly rounded on
McGarry, growling: 'L'Adjutant! Monsieur l'Adjutant!' The
Adjutant was summoned forthwith, and presently came to

the mess with momentous news: Suleiman ibn Aziz had demanded curtly that he be allowed to witness the band's next performance.

I have written elsewhere of the Arabs' delight in the sound of bagpipes, and how they would flock to listen whenever the band appeared in public. But Suleiman's interest was so unexpected and out of keeping with his grim aloofness that there was something like delight in the mess, and there was a big turn-out next day when the Adjutant conducted him to join the Colonel before HQ Company, where a chair had been provided for him. He went straight to it, ignoring the Colonel's greeting, and sat erect and impassive as the band swung on in full fig, the drums thundering and the pipes going full blast in 'Johnnie Cope'; they marched and counter-marched, the tartans swinging and the Drum-Major, resplendent in leopard-skin, flourishing his silver staff, through 'Highland Laddie', 'White Cockade', and 'Scotland the Brave', and he watched with never a flicker on his lined face or a movement of the fingers clasping his burnous about him. When they turned inwards for their routine of strathspey and reel he lifted his head to the quickening rhythm, and when they made their final advance to 'Cock o' the North' he leaned forward a little, but what he was making of it you couldn't tell. When the Drum-Major came forward to ask permission to march off, the Colonel turned to him with a smile and gesture of invitation, but he didn't move, and the Colonel returned the salute alone. The band marched away, and the Adjutant asked if he'd enjoyed it; Suleiman didn't reply, but sat forward, his eyes intent on the band as they passed out of sight.

'Oh, well, we did our best,' muttered the Adjutant. 'Don't suppose we could expect him to clap and stamp. At least he didn't walk out—'

Suleiman suddenly stood up. For a moment he continued to stare across the parade ground, then he turned to the Colonel, and for the first time there was a look on his face that wasn't baleful: his eyes were bright and staring fiercely, but they were sad, too, and he looked very old and tired. He spoke in a harsh, husky croak:

'La musique darray maklen! C'est la musique, ça!'

It was the first time he'd ever offered anything like conversation – whatever it meant. 'What did he say?' the Colonel demanded. 'Music of what?'

The Adjutant asked him to repeat it, but Suleiman just turned away, and when he was asked again he shook his head angrily and wouldn't answer. So the Adjutant took him back to the guard-room while the rest of us argued about what it was he'd said; he seemed to have been identifying the music, but no one could tell what 'darray maklen' meant. The first word might be 'arrêt', meaning anything from 'stop' to 'detention', but the Adjutant's dictionary contained no word remotely like 'maklen', and it wasn't until the end of dinner that the Colonel, who had been repeating the phrase and looking more like an irritated vulture by the minute, suddenly slapped the table.

'Good God! That's it, of course! Morocco! It fits absolutely. Well, I'll be damned!' He beamed round in triumph. 'The music of Harry Maclean! That's what he was saying! Talk about a voice from the past. Oh, the poor old chap! The music of Harry Maclean—'

'Who's Harry Maclean?' asked the Adjutant.

'Kaid Maclean . . . oh, long before your time. Came from Argyll, somewhere. One of the great Scotch mercenaries . . . packed in his commission in the seventies and went off to train the Sultan of Morocco's Army, led 'em against all sorts of rebels – of whom our guest in the guard-room would certainly be one: Maclean was still active when the Riffs broke loose. Amazing chap, used to dress as a tribesman (long before Lawrence), got to places no European had ever seen. Oh, yes, Suleiman would know him, all right – may have fought with *and* against him. And he remembers the music of Harry Maclean . . . you see, Maclean was a famous piper, always carried his bags with him. I heard him play at Gib., about 1920, when I was a subaltern – piped like a MacCrimmon! He was an old man then, of course – big, splendid-looking cove with a great snowy beard, looked more like a sheikh than the real thing!'* The Colonel laughed, shaking his head at the memory, and then his smile

* Sir Harry Aubrey de Vere Maclean (1848–1920), joined the Army in 1869, fought against Fenian raiders in Canada, and in 1877 entered the service of Sultan Mulai Hassan of Morocco as army instructor. In an adventurous career lasting more than thirty years 'Kaid Maclean' became something of a North African legend: he was the trusted adviser of the Sultan and his successor, campaigned against rebel tribes, survived court intrigues, journeyed throughout Morocco and visited the forbidden city of Tafilelt, and was once kidnapped (at the second attempt) and held to ransom by insurgents. Although unswervingly loyal to his employer, he was recognized as an unofficial British agent, and was created KCMG when he attended King Edward VII's Coronation as one of the Moroccan delegation. Maclean was a genial, popular leader although, as his biographer remarks, 'being of powerful physique he was able to deal summarily with insubordinate individuals'. He was an enthusiastic piper who also played the piano, guitar, and accordion. (See the *Dictionary of National Biography*.)

216

faded, and after a moment he said: 'And we've got one of his old enemies in the guard-room. An enemy who remembers his music.'

There was quiet round the table. Then the second-in-command, who seldom said much, surprised everyone by remarking: 'We ought to do something about that.'

'Like what?' asked the Colonel quickly.

'Well . . . I'm not sure. But if this fellow Suleiman did know Maclean, it would be interesting to get him talking, wouldn't it? Not that he's shown himself sociable, but after today . . . well, you never know.'

'Oh, I see.' The Colonel sounded almost disappointed. 'Yes, I suppose it would.'

'Have him into the mess, perhaps,' said the Senior Major. 'Dinner, something like that?'

'He wouldn't come,' said Bennet-Bruce.

'No harm in asking,' said the second-in-command.

'That's what you think,' said the Adjutant bitterly. 'Every time I speak to him he just glares and turns his back – I'm beginning to think I've got BO.'

'Then don't ask him,' said the Senior Major. 'Just bring him along, and once he's here, chances are we can thaw him out.'

'Ye daurnae offer him drink!' protested the MO.

'Of course not – but we can lay on Arab grub, make him feel at home . . . well, it would be a gesture,' said the second-in-command. 'Show him that we . . . well, you know . . . I don't suppose he'll get many invitations, after he leaves here.' He glanced at the Colonel, who was sitting lost in his own thoughts. 'I move we ask him to the mess. What d'you think, sir?'

217

The Colonel came back to earth. 'Certainly. Why not? Have him in tomorrow – make it a mess night.' He pushed back his chair and went out, followed by the seniors.

'Sentimental old bird, the skipper,' said Errol.

'How d'you mean?' said MacKenzie.

'Well, he's been on the wee wog's side all along – who hasn't? Now this Harry Maclean thing . . . it just makes having to turn Suleiman over to the French that much harder, doesn't it?'

'You're a perceptive chiel,' nodded the Padre.

'It doesn't make much odds,' said the Adjutant gloomily.

'It's rotten whichever way you look at it.' He glanced across at Errol who was flicking peanut shells at the Waterloo snuff-box. 'What would you do . . . if it was you?'

'If I were the Colonel – and felt as sorry for old Abou ben Adem as he does?' Errol gave his lazy smile. 'I certainly wouldn't connive at his escape – which is the thought at the back of everyone's mind, only we're too feart to say so. I might write to GHQ, citing his war service and decrepitude, and respectfully submitting that the French be told to fall out—'

'He's already done that,' said the Adjutant. 'Got a rocket for not minding his own business.'

'Well, *shabash* the Colonel sahib! But that's all, folks. He's done his best – so all we can do is give Suleiman the hollow apology of a dinner to show our hearts are in the right place, and wish him bon voyage to Devil's Island.'

'That's a lousy way to put it!' snapped MacKenzie.

'Only if you feel guilty, Kenny,' said Errol. 'I don't. He's a tough old bandit, down on his luck . . . and a damned bad man. No, I'd hand him over, with some regret, as the

Colonel will. But unlike the Colonel I won't vex myself wondering what Harry Maclean would have done.'

'That's a bit mystical,' protested the Adjutant.

'Is it? You're not Scotch, Mike. The Colonel is – so he gets daft thoughts about . . . oh, after the battle . . . kinship of old enemies . . . doing right by the shades. Damned nonsense, but it can play hell with a Highlander in the wee sma' hoors, especially if he's got a drink in him. Read between the lines of *The Golden Bough* sometime.' Errol stifled a yawn and got up. 'It was written by a teuchter, incidentally.'

'Interesting,' said the Padre. 'Well, what *would* Harry Maclean do about Suleiman?'

Errol paused at the door. 'Shoot the little bugger, I should think. He probably spent half his life trying.'

Acting on the Senior Major's advice, the Adjutant didn't invite Suleiman formally, but simply conducted him to the mess, where we had assembled in the dining room. The table was blazing with our two centuries' worth of silver, much of it loot – Nana Sahib's spoons, the dragon candle-sticks from the Opium Wars, the inlaid Ashanti shield (now a fruit-bowl), the silver-gilt punchbowl presented by Patton in Normandy, the snuff-box made from the hoof of the Scots Greys' drumhorse, the porcelain samovar given to a forgotten mercenary who had helped to stop the Turks at Vienna and whose grandson had brought it to the regiment. It was priceless and breathtaking; Suleiman could not doubt that he was being treated as a guest of honour. The Pipe-Sergeant had even bullied the Colonel into letting him compose a special air, 'The Music of Suleiman ibn Aziz' – it was impossible to stop the pipey creating new works of genius, all of which sounded like 'Bonnie Dundee' or 'Flowers of the Forest', depending on the tempo; it remained to be seen which had been plagiarized when the pipey strode forth to regale us after dinner.

Poor soul, he never got the chance. Suleiman took one look at the gleaming table, the thirty expectant tartan figures, the pipers ranged against the wall, the Colonel welcoming him to his seat – and straightway stormed out, raging and cursing in Arabic. Why, I'm still not sure; he must have known it was kindly meant, and we could only assume that he regarded all Franks as poison and any overture from them as an insult. The mess reaction was that it was a pity, but if that was how he felt, too bad. Strangely enough, it didn't diminish the sympathy for him, and it was a reluctant Adjutant who had to tell him next day (Sunday) that the French were coming earlier than expected, and he would be leaving the following Thursday. Either because he was taken aback, or was still in a passion over the dinner fiasco, Suleiman let fly a torrent of abuse in lingua franca, shook his fist in the Adjutant's face, and rounded things off by spitting violently on the floor.

Which was distressing, and hardly reasonable since he'd known he was going sooner or later, but the explanation emerged three nights after. On Monday he was still in a villainous temper, but McGarry thought he looked unusually tired, too, and he wouldn't leave his cell to sit on the verandah. On Tuesday he kept to his bed, sleeping most of the day. In the small hours of Wednesday morning he broke out.

He must have been working at the single bar of his cell window since his arrival, presumably calculating that he would have it loose by the end of the second week. The advance of the French arrival had upset his plans, and he had spent two and a half nights digging feverishly at the concrete sill – with what tool, and how he had not been detected, we never discovered. Only a chance look through the grille by the sentry discovered the bar askew, and thirty seconds later the guard were doubling out of barracks in the forlorn hope of catching a fugitive who had the choice of melting into the alleys of the city not far off, or vanishing into the Sahara which stretched for two thousand miles from our southern wall.

It was sheer blind luck that they came on him hobbling painfully along a dry ditch on the desert road; being reluctant to lay hands on an old man who was plainly on his last legs, they called on him to stop, but he just kept going, panting and stumbling, until they headed him off, when he turned at bay, lashing out, and after a furious clawing struggle he had to be carried bodily back to the guard-room, literally foaming at the mouth. Taken to a new cell, he collapsed on the floor, too exhausted to resist an examination by the MO which revealed what was already obvious – that he was an unusually hardy old man, and dead beat. Even so, an extra sentry was posted under his window.

There was no point in reporting the incident to the Provost Marshal, and for the last twenty-four hours before the French were due he was just confined to his cell, sitting hunched up on his cot, ignoring his food; having made his bid and failed he seemed resigned, with all the spirit drained out of him.

Then, late in the afternoon, he began to sing – or rather to chant, a high wailing cry not unlike the muezzin's prayer

221

call, but with a defiant note in it – the kind of thing which prompts the Highlander to remark: 'Sing me a Gaelic song, granny, and sing it through your nose.' It reminded me of something else, but I wasn't sure what until the Padre, who happened to be in our company office, cocked an ear to the distant keening sound and quoted:

' "The old wives will cry the coronach, and there will be a great clapping of hands, for I am one of the greatest chiefs of the Highlands." '

'I never knew that,' said Bennet-Bruce. 'I always thought you were a clergyman from Skye.'

'Pearls before swine,' said the Padre. 'I'm telling you what old Simon Fraser said before they took the head off him on Tower Green.' He listened, eyes half-closed. 'I wonder if our old buddoo isn't saying the same thing.'

'Why should he? No one's going to cut his head off.'

'Perhaps not,' said the Padre. 'But if that's not a coronach then I never heard one.'

Whatever it was, it didn't exactly set the feet tapping; the high wavering cry raised the hairs on my neck – and not on mine alone. The Colonel left his office early to get out of earshot, and the Adjutant, kept at his desk, was noticeably not his usual Bertie Woosterish self: he tore my head off over some routine enquiry, slammed his window shut, and gave vent to his feelings.

'Gosh, I'll be glad to get shot of him! Nothing but trouble! We didn't *ask* to be landed with him, we've tried to make things as easy for him as we can, tried to be decent – and the little bastard spits in our eye, gets the Colonel in the doghouse with Cairo, treats *me* like dirt, tries to bust out—'

'Well, you can't blame him for that, Mike.'

'. . . and generally gets right on the battalion's collective wick! Of course I don't blame him.' The Adjutant stared gloomily out of the window. 'That's the trouble. I'm all *for* him. We all are – and he doesn't even know it. He thinks we're as big a shower as the French and GHQ. He hates our guts.' He brooded at me in a pink, bothered way. 'Why shouldn't he? And why the hell should we worry if he does? You think I need a laxative, don't you?'

'I think you need some tea,' I said. But I thought he was right: Suleiman, somehow, had got in among us, and it would have been nice to think that he knew we were on his side – for all the good *that* would do him. A selfish, childish wish, probably, but understandable.

Because I wanted to be there when he left, I had arranged to be orderly officer next day, and after dinner I went to tell McGarry that the French probably wouldn't take him before noon. McGarry promised to have him ready; the few belongings that had come with him were in an unopened bundle in the office safe, and the man himself was asleep.

'Nae wonder, after the fight he pit up. No' the size o' a fish supper, but it took four o' them tae carry him in, an' him beatin' the bejeezus oot o' them. Say that for him,' McGarry nodded admiringly. 'He's game.'

Just how game we discovered next morning when the orderly took breakfast into the cell, and Suleiman came at him from behind the door like a wildcat, knocked him flying, ducked past McGarry, and was heading for the wide blue yonder when he went full tilt over McAuslan, who was scrubbing the floor. In the ensuing mêlée which involved two sentries (with McAuslan wallowing in suds imploring all concerned to keep the heid) Suleiman managed to grab a bayonet, and murder would have been done if McGarry had not weighed in, clasping both of Suleiman's skinny wrists in one enormous paw and swinging him off his feet with the other. Even then the little sheikh had fought like a madman, struggling and kicking and trying to bite until, to the amazement of McAuslan:

'. . . a' the fight seemed tae go oot o' him, an' he lets oot sich a helluva cry, an' ye know whit? He jist pit his heid on big McGarry's chest, like a wean wi' his mither, an' grat. No, he wisnae bubblin' – no' that kinda greetin', jist shakin' an' haudin' on like there wisnae a kick left in him. An' big McGarry pit him on his feet, an' says: "Come on, auld yin," an' pits him back in the cell – an' then turns on me, fur Goad's sake, an' starts bawlin' tae get the flair scrubbit an' dae Ah think Ah'm peyed tae staun' aboot wi' no' twa pun' o' me hingin' straight! Ye'd think it wis me had been tryin' tae murder hauf the Airmy an' go absent, no' the wee wog!'

All this I learned when I checked the guard-room at nine – the facts from McGarry, the colour from Our Correspondent on Jankers. Suleiman had stayed quiet in his cell.

The French arrived at eleven in the Provost Marshal's car and an escorting jeep: a major and captain in sky-blue kepis, a sous-officier in the navy tunic and red breeches of the Légion Etrangère, two privates with carbines, and a Moorish interpreter. The officers and the PM were escorted to the mess for hospitality while the rankers stayed with their vehicles; the sous-officier, a moustachioed stalwart with a gold chevron and no neck, paced up and down exchanging appraising glances with McGarry on the guard-room verandah.

There seemed to be more casual activity than usual in the vicinity that morning: several platoons were drilling on the square, various Jocks had found an excuse for moving to and from the nearer buildings, and others were being unobtrusive in the middle distance; nothing like a crowd, just a modest gathering, not large enough to excite the displeasure of RSM Macintosh as he made his magisterial way across the parade, pausing to survey the platoons who presently stopped drilling and stood easy, but did not dismiss. It was all very orderly, but in no way official; they were waiting to see Suleiman ibn Aziz go, without being too obvious about it. The windows and verandahs of the farther barrack-blocks had their share of spectators, and the Padre and MO were coming through the main gate and mounting the guard-room steps, returning the magnificent salute of the sous-officier – he was a slightly puzzled sous-officier, judging by the way he was studying the square: why so many Ecossaises about, he might well have been wondering. Was this how les Dames d'Enfer kept discipline, by example? What would Milor' Wellington have said? He shook his head and resumed pacing, and the Ecossaises regarded him bleakly from under their bonnet-brims.

'Now's the time for the English to attack,' observed the MO.

'Right enough, Lachlan,' agreed the Padre. 'The Auld Alliance is looking gey fragile.' He consulted his watch. 'Band practice shortly, I think – there, what did I say?'

From behind the band office came the warm-up notes of a piper, and then the slow measured strains of 'Lovat's

Lament', the loveliest and most stately of slow marches. The Padre nodded approval.

'Aye, that's pipey. Not bad, for a man that never set foot on Skye.'

'Who's idea's this?' I asked. 'The Colonel's?'

'Why don't you ask him?' said the MO. 'Here he is, wi' the Comédie-Française.'

The Colonel and Adjutant were emerging from the tamarisk grove that screened the mess, with the French officers and the PM. The RSM let out a splendid Guards-trained scream of 'Attain-shah!' and there was an echoing crash of heels on the square. The Padre chuckled.

'Canny Macintosh! You notice he didn't say "Parade-shun!" Because there is no parade, of course. A nice distinction.'

I followed the Colonel's party into the guard-room, the sous-officier and the Moorish interpreter bringing up the rear. Suleiman, with McGarry standing by, was sitting beside the table, very composed, the lean brown face impassive under the silver-edged *kafilyeh* – it was hard to believe that this frail, quiet little man had twice tried to break out, fighting like a wild beast and trying to stab a sentry with his own bayonet. He didn't get up, and the French Major smiled and turned to the Colonel.

'I am pleased he has caused you no inconvenience, sir.' He spoke English with barely a trace of accent.

'None whatever,' said the Colonel. 'All ready, Sarn't McGarry? Very well, sir.'

The Major nodded to the sous-officier, who strode across and snapped an order. Suleiman didn't stir, and the sous-officier repeated it in an explosive bark that was startling in its unexpected violence. But not as startling as what followed. McGarry stiffened to his full height and rasped:

'You don't talk tae the man like that, son!'

The sous-officier didn't speak the language, but he knew cold menace when he heard it, and gave back as though he'd been hit – which, in my opinion, he nearly had been. The others stared, all except the Colonel, who had tactfully turned aside to listen to something that the Adjutant wasn't saying. There was an embarrassed pause, and then Suleiman glanced up at McGarry and, with the smallest of deprecating gestures, rose to his feet. He turned his back on the sous-officier, looked McGarry full in the face, and made the quick graceful heart-lips-brow salutation of the *salaam*.

For once McGarry was taken flat aback, and then he did the only thing he could do – stamped his heel and nodded. Suleiman turned away and calmly surveyed the waiting officers; he looked for a moment at the Colonel and then said something in Arabic to the interpreter, who passed it on in French to the Major, indicating the bundle of coarse cloth on the table which contained Suleiman's belongings. The Major looked surprised, shrugged, and turned to the Colonel.

'It seems there is something he wishes to leave with you.'

He gave an order to the sous-officier, and we waited expectantly while the bundle was unwrapped. Outside the pipey could still be heard running through his repertoire; he was on to the marches now, with a kettle-drum rattling accompaniment, but you couldn't tell whether Suleiman was hearing it or not. He was standing absolutely still, his hands clasped before him, looking straight ahead at the

Colonel, but he must have been watching out of the corner of his eye, for as the sous-officier began to take out the bundle's contents – a packet of papers, a bunch of keys, a couple of enamelled boxes, a few rather fine-looking ornaments which were probably gold and silver, one or two strands of jewellery – he gave another grunt in Arabic and thrust out his hand, palm up. The sous-officier was holding a packet about a foot long, wrapped in red muslin; he passed it to the interpreter, who handed it nervously to Suleiman.

You could have heard a pin drop while the little man flicked a hand to indicate that the rest of his goods should be parcelled up again, and then stood looking down at the red packet, turning it in his hands, clasping it as though reluctant to let it go. Then his head came up and he walked across to the Colonel and held it out to him with both hands. The Colonel took it, and as he did so Suleiman suddenly clasped both his hands over the Colonel's on the package, holding the grip hard and staring fiercely into the Colonel's face. Then he let go, inclined his head gravely, and stepped back. The Colonel said 'Thank you', and Suleiman ibn Aziz walked out of the guard-room.

On the verandah he paused for a moment, looking at the Jocks in the square who were waiting to see him go. The unseen Pipe-Sergeant and the kettle-drums were waking the echoes, and I heard the Padre murmur to the MO:

'That'll be "The Music of Suleiman ibn Aziz" I daresay – it sounds just like "The Black Bear" to me, but then I haven't the pipey's imagination.'

Suleiman ibn Aziz went down the steps and into the waiting car, the French officers exchanged salutes with the Colonel and climbed in, the legionnaires piled into the jeep, the sous-officier exchanged a last stare with McGarry, the sentry on the gate presented arms as the vehicles drove through, and the Jocks on the square began to drift away.

The Colonel was holding the red muslin package. 'Right, let's have a look at it,' he said, and led the way back into the guard-room, for he knew McGarry would be as curious as the rest of us. We all stood round as he unwrapped the cloth, and when the contents lay on the table nobody spoke for quite some time. We just looked at it and let the thought sink in.

It was an Arab dagger, and not a rich or ornamental one. The sheath was cracked and discoloured, and while the blade was classically curved and shone like silver, it was pitted with age, the brass cross-hilt was scarred, the pommel had lost its inlay, and the haft was bound with wire in two places. You wouldn't have given two ackers for it on a bazaar stall – unless you had laid it across your finger and noted the perfect balance, or lowered its edge on to a piece of paper and watched it slice through of its own weight.

The Colonel fingered his moustache, gave a little cough, said 'Well,' and was silent. He picked the dagger up again, weighed it in his hand, and said at last: 'Not the most valuable of his possessions, I daresay. But certainly the most precious.'

'He must have had it a long time,' said the Adjutant. In a wondering tone he added: 'He gave it to us.'

The Colonel pushed the blade home. 'Right. Get it cleaned up and sterilized – God knows who it's been in. It can go with the mess silver.' He caught the Adjutant's doubtful frown. 'Well, why shouldn't it? If some cavalry

229

regiment can use Napoleon's brother's chamber-pot as a punchbowl, I see no reason why you shouldn't cut your cheese with a knife that's been through the Riff Rebellion.'

'Absolutely, sir!' agreed the Adjutant hastily. 'I'll see the mess sergeant looks after it right away.' Then he looked worried. 'I say, though – we ought to have given old Suleiman some cash for it – you know, bad luck not to pay for a knife. Cuts friendship, my aunt used to say.'

The Colonel paused in the doorway. 'I'm afraid his luck can't get much worse, Michael.' He frowned, considering. 'And I'm not sure that we were ever friends, exactly. Put it with the silver anyway.'

The Adventure of the
Laughing Jarvey

BY STEPHEN FRY

The following appeared in the Christmas 1987 issue of The
Listener:

The literary editor, when clearing out her office preparatory
to the move to *The Listener*'s new quarters, discovered a
bundle of papers wedged at the back of a drawer. The find
appeared to be an autograph manuscript of a previously
unpublished Sherlock Holmes story. Uncertain of its auth-
enticity, she asked Stephen Fry, a noted Sherlockian, to edit
the text and reflect on its provenance.

*Hand written on nineteenth-century foolscap the document
certainly appears to be genuine. According to Edinburgh
University's pioneering 'particle method' a quick count of
prepositions, final clauses and image clusters tells us that the
balance of probability is that the text was indeed written by
Watson. Three or four strange inconsistencies, however, which
do not become apparent until the very end of the story, throw
some doubt on this conclusion. Alert readers will detect these
anomalies and draw their own inferences. Apart from trim-*

ming back the typically profuse growth of commas and semi-colons familiar to scholars of the canon, I have left the body of the text unedited. I should be interested to hear the opinion of enthusiasts everywhere. In my view, if the story is not genuine then it ought to be.

The year 18— saw my friend Sherlock Holmes at the very height of his considerable powers. On leafing through the journals for that year my attention is caught by a number of cases; some startling, some macabre, some seemingly commonplace, but all demonstrating to a great extent Holmes's remarkable gifts of deduction. The Affair of the Stranded Macaw, for which he received the Order of the Silver Myrtle from the hands of His Majesty the King Miroslaw himself, presents several peculiar features of interest but in the more delicate of its details touches too many figures in public life to allow me to retell it here. The Tale of the Punctual Railway Clerk, while remaining one of Holmes's favourite triumphs, is perhaps of too technical a nature to be of interest to the general reader. The Case of the Copper Beeches I have chronicled elsewhere and the Story of the Tooting Schoolmaster and the Harness, while displaying as perhaps no other the extraordinary meticu-lousness and patience that characterized my friend's methods, has no place outside specialist journals.

Towards the very end of that year however, when it seemed to us that London had given up on sensation for the winter and was content to prepare itself comfortably for the festive season without throwing up those *outré* mys-teries that were as oxygen to Sherlock Holmes, there exploded upon us a case which wrenched him from the indolence and melancholy to which that great mind was prey when there was nothing to engage it and hurtled us into as extraordinary an adventure as any we had known. Although it is his oft repeated assertion that this problem tested his reasoning powers only to the smallest degree, there can be no doubt that its solution yielded to Holmes the richest fee he ever earned in the course of an illustrious career.

I remember that one evening in mid-December I was engaged in the task of decorating our bachelor lodgings with some seasonal sprigs of holly and mistletoe, enduring the while some tart criticisms from my friend.

'Really Watson,' said he, 'is it not enough that Mrs Hudson must come in laden with mince pies and indefatigable good cheer every hour of the day? Must we also deck ourselves out like a pagan temple?'

'I must say, Holmes,' I returned with some asperity, for the effort of standing upon a chair and reaching for the picture rail was taking its toll on the old Jezail bullet wound, 'I think this uncommonly poor-spirited of you! Christmas used to mean something, I remember. Do you not recall the Blue Carbuncle? *That* adventure saw you as full of Yuletide charity as any man.'

'Watson you are confusing the real facts of that affair with the gaudy version of it that you were pleased to set down before a gullible public. Pray do not start upon the course of believing your own fictions. As I remember it, the case was a matter for calm analysis.'

'Really, Holmes,' I ejaculated, 'you are most unfair!'

'You must forgive me Watson. But the infernal *dullness*

233

of it all! A spreading canker of bumbling good cheer seems to infect everybody at this time of year, even the most hardened of scoundrels, who are as likely to give money as they are to abstract it. Here is the *Evening News*. What foul murders or daring larcenies are there here to engage the interest? A woman is injured in a derailment at Lewisham, someone has stolen a statue from Charing Cross, a horse has bolted in Hoxton. I despair, Watson. Let us have an end to this sickening season of goodwill and peace, I say.'

'Holmes, I will not allow this assault on Christmas! You know perfectly well that—'

But my strictures were interrupted by a wild jangling of the bell downstairs.

'Ah,' said Holmes, 'I am spared your homily. Perhaps a mistaken address, perhaps a client. Such extravagant pealing denotes some urgency at any rate. Well, Billy?'

Our honest pageboy had entered the room, but before he had time to make any formal announcement there burst in like a tornado the most wildly agitated man I think I have ever laid eyes upon.

'Mr Sherlock Holmes? Which one of you is Mr Holmes?' gasped the unfortunate creature, looking wildly from one to the other of us.

'I am he,' said Holmes, 'and this is my friend Dr Watson. If you will be seated he will pour you a glass of brandy.'

'Thank you, a little brandy, yes indeed. That would be most . . . really Mr Holmes, you must forgive me, I am not given to . . . thank you, most kind, no seltzer I beg! Just so. Let me catch my breath . . . splendid rooms, most snug. Charming holly . . . so festive. I congratulate you. Ah! that is much better, I am obliged to you, Doctor.'

Despite the pitiable distress of the man I could not forbear to smile at this twittering and inconsequential monologue. I had seen physical pain induce such loquacity and delirium in wounded men and knew it to be a common sign of mental anxiety also.

Sherlock Holmes sat deep in his arm chair, touching together the tips of his fingers and running an expert eye over the extraordinary gentleman seated opposite him. Our visitor was dressed fashionably for the evening, but I could not set him down as a Society figure. Prosperity gleamed in the refulgent shirt and hand-made boots, for all the fresh traces of mud upon them, but too lively an intelligence shone in his piercingly blue eyes to suppose that he did not use his brain for a living. His thin face, in its rare moments of repose, seemed of a melancholy cast, but when it became animated the features fairly quivered with movement, a wiry beard wagged and jerked in time to his speech and the wild, disordered locks upon his head tossed about as if in a tempest.

'Such *very* good brandy . . . oh dear, oh dear, oh dear. Whatever am I to *do*, Mr Holmes?'

'Well, when you have caught your breath, you had better lay your problem before us,' said Holmes. 'To have come from at least as far as Gray's Inn all the way to Baker Street on such a night would take its toll on any man.'

Our visitor started visibly. 'But how on earth? Oh dear me, that is most extraordinary! I have indeed run all the way from Gray's Inn, though how you could know that is beyond me.'

'Tush, sir, it is as clear as day. That you have been running a child could tell from your breathlessness alone.

The line of the splashes upon the toes of your boots could not be caused any other way.'

'Well,' chuckled the other, momentarily diverted from the cause of his peculiar worry, 'I see *that*, but how the deuce can you read Gray's Inn in my appearance?'

'I was there this morning,' said Holmes. 'They are painting the iron railings that fence off the north side from the pavement. The palings themselves are painted black, but the tip is gilded, in your hurry you have brushed your left arm against the wet paint. See upon your sleeve, black topped with a smudge of gold. It is possible that there is another railing freshly painted in like manner somewhere in London, but it is highly unlikely.'

'Remarkable, remarkable. A capital game! What else, sir? What else?'

'I am afraid,' said Holmes, 'there is very little else to tell.'

'Ah, I am freshly changed into my evening clothes, after all. Every clue starched over, I fancy.'

'Beyond the obvious facts that you are a writer, that you suffered deprivation in your boyhood, that money is a little harder to come by for you than it once was and that you are fond of conjuring tricks, there is certainly very little to be seen,' said Holmes.

Our visitor started up. 'You know me then! This is a pretty trick to play, sir, upon my word! It is unworthy of you.'

'Be seated, I beg,' said Holmes, 'I have never set eyes upon you before. When I see a man with so pronounced an indentation upon the inside of his middle finger it is surely no great matter to assume that he is a writer?'

'A clerk! I might be a clerk!'

'In Lobb boots? I hardly think so.'

'Hum, the deprivation then?'

'Your face is lined beyond your years, but not, I perceive, by the trouble that has brought you here. That is too recent to have yet written itself across your brow. I have seen such marks only on those who grew up knowing misery and want.'

'True enough, Mr Holmes – but the money, the conjuring tricks?'

'Those fine boots were made some three or four years ago, I fancy. The excellently cut coat you are wearing dates from that time also. The sudden burst of prosperity that their purchase betokens has receded a little into the past, therefore. As for the conjuring, you will have noticed, I am sure, Watson, the small metal cone that protrudes a little from our visitor's waistcoat? Flesh-pink in colour, it is called a thumb-tip: an essential part of an illusionist's apparatus.'

'Bravo, Mr Holmes!' cried our guest, applauding with great energy. 'Miraculous!'

'Meretricious.'

'And a happy new year, my dear sir. Meretricious and a happy new year! Dear me,' said he, sinking in spirits once more, 'you quite take my mind from the purpose of this visit. Such a calamity, Mr Holmes. Such a dreadful calamity. I am beside myself!'

'I am all attention Mr—?'

'Oh! My name? Yes. Ah, Bosney, Culliford Bosney, novelist. You have heard of me perhaps?' He scanned our bookshelves eagerly.

'I am afraid, Mr Bosney, that with only a few exceptions I do not have much time for novels. Dr Watson is the literary man.'

Culliford Bosney turned his lively gaze upon me. 'Ah yes, Dr Watson – of course. I read your works with great interest. Accept the compliments of a fellow scribbler, I beg.'

'Thank you,' said I, 'I am afraid Mr Holmes does not share your good opinion of my efforts.'

'Nonsense, Watson! As exotic romances they stand in a class of their own,' said Holmes, filling his briar.

'You see what I have to contend with, Mr Bosney?' said I, with a rueful grin.

'Oh, Dr Watson!' answered he, with a pitiable return to his former woe. 'You will understand my misery when I tell you that it is lost! It is lost, and I am at my wits' end!'

'What is lost?' I asked in bewilderment.

'The manuscript, of course! It is lost and I am sure I shall lose my mind with worrying over it.'

'I think,' said Holmes, leaning back in his chair, 'that you had better favour us with all the facts of your narrative, Mr Bosney.'

'Of course, Mr Holmes. Omitting no details, however trivial they may seem, eh?'

'Quite so.'

'Well, you must know that I have been labouring now for some six weeks on the manuscript of a story. I was due today to deliver it to my publishers – it is necessary that they publish it within the week you understand, for it has a Yuletide theme. I have high hopes for this story, Mr Holmes. I will not palter with you, my last novel did not take at all well and I have been at great pains to do something which will in some way recoup my fortunes and restore the good opinion of the reading public. I have not been on the best of terms with my publishers for some time and I am hoping that this newest work will earn me enough by way of royalties to enable me to leave them and seek a more congenial firm.'

'Are they aware of this ambition?' asked Holmes.

'No, Mr Holmes, I do not believe that they are. I have great hopes of this story however. *Had* great hopes, for I am sure I shall never see it again!' The agonized novelist sprang up from his seat with a gesture of despair. 'Mr Holmes, it is useless. How can one find a needle in a haystack?'

'Given a strong enough magnet, Mr Bosney, it is an elementary task. Put me in possession of the relevant facts and who knows but that we will not be able to find just such a magnet?'

'Yes, yes. I must beg your pardon gentlemen, but I have been tried these past few hours, sorely tried. Well then, at half past four this afternoon I had finished reading the story back to myself and was satisfied that it was ready to be printed. Rather than have the manuscript collected I thought that I would deliver it myself, on my way to the theatre. I also wanted to give some last-minute instructions for the printing. I wished the book to be lavishly presented, Mr Holmes, in gilt and red. I thought that would be appropriately festive.

'I changed into evening clothes, tucked the manuscript under my arm and went out into the street to hail a cab. My street runs into Theobald's Road, Mr Holmes, just opposite Gray's Inn. There is usually no difficulty in finding a hackney carriage on that thoroughfare. To my surprise, however, there was already a hansom standing right outside my house. I called to the driver to ask if he were waiting for anybody. He seemed startled but replied that he was not. I opened the door, put the manuscript on to the seat and was on the point of climbing in, when I noticed that the seat was already occupied. Mr Holmes, I am not a fanciful man, but the sight of the figure sitting in the corner of that hansom made my blood run cold! A deathly pale countenance, with blank unseeing eyes. I shudder at the memory of him.'

'You recollect how the figure was dressed?' asked Holmes sharply.

'I do indeed, it was most striking. I recall a many-caped driving coat buttoned up to the throat, a billycock hat and a woollen scarf. There was something so incongruous about this strange apparel and those inhumanly blanched and spectral features that I could not help but step backwards with a cry. No sooner had I done so than the jarvey whipped up his horse with a shout and rattled down the street, disappearing into the mist.'

'Really?' said Holmes, rubbing his hands together. 'Most intriguing. Pray continue, Mr Bosney, I beg.'

'I must own, Mr Holmes, that I was at first relieved that the vision had fled so fast. I stood trembling upon the pavement, wondering at the meaning of so horrid a sight. Perhaps I had imagined it, perhaps I was still in the grip of the fever of imagination with which I had finished my story. But then I remembered that my manuscript was still lying on the seat of the vanished cab and I became quite mad with fright. I ran down into Theobald's Road and stared about me. There were dog-carts and broughams and hansoms by the dozen rattling in both directions. But which was my hansom, I could not tell. I have sent my servants out to the cab companies offering large rewards for the safe return of the manuscript, Mr Holmes, but so far with no success. I am at my wits' end!'

'A piquant mystery,' said Holmes, looking dreamily up at the ceiling. 'Can you describe the jarvey to me, I wonder?'

'I cannot, Mr Holmes!' groaned the other. 'I usually have an excellent memory for faces, but this man was so muffled up against the chill that I had no opportunity to read his features. I have an impression from his voice that he was a young man, but I may be wrong. Also—'

'Yes?'

'Well, it may only be my fancy, but I could swear that as the cab hurtled away from me I heard laughter. I attributed it to the medical students who have just moved in to lodgings next door to me and are rowdy at the best of times, but thinking back I am sure it came from the jarvey himself! What can that mean, Mr Holmes?'

'A laugh, you say? Now, that is really most revealing.' Holmes rose and began to pace about the room. 'You have mentioned students, Mr Bosney, what other neighbours do you have?'

'For the most part we are a quiet lot – solicitors and stockbrokers in the main. The street is handy for both the Inns of Court and the City of London. I am not on especially intimate terms with any of my neighbours, however. Colonel Harker, whose house adjoins mine, has recently returned from India and staffs his household with native servants, at whom he bellows with immoderate choler. I do not think that I have ever exchanged above two words with him. He is away in Hampshire for Christmas in any case, so I do not think he can have any bearing on the matter.'

'Well, Mr Bosney,' said Holmes, buttoning up his cape, 'I will look into this little problem for you.'

'Thank you, Mr Holmes!'

'Come, Watson, let us all take ourselves to Gray's Inn and see what we can discover.'

As the three of us were whisked through the dark London streets, Sherlock Holmes and Culliford Bosney looked out the window at the fog-wrapped streets and alleyways of the great capital, the former keenly, the latter with comical anxiety. Holmes, drawing heavily on his most pungent shag mixture, noted off the street names as we flew down the Euston Road. I have remarked before that his knowledge of London streets was profound, from the lowest and vilest alleys in the east to the broadest and most fashionable squares and avenues in the west. I was surprised to discover that Mr Bosney too was possessed of an exact acquaintance with the capital. The pair of them talked enthusiastically of their love for the great city, Bosney even contriving to surprise Holmes on occasion with some obscure fragment of history or local anecdote.

'Yes indeed, Mr Holmes!' cried he, 'London is alive, believe me. Every citizen is like a cell of the great organism, connected to every other. The meanest tapster in Lime-house and the grandest duke in Grosvenor Square are bound together and give life each to each! You think me fanciful perhaps?'

'Not at all, sir,' replied Holmes, 'my work largely depends upon that fact. What is a crime but a disease? My work is largely diagnostic: just as Watson here might see a deficiency of iron in a swollen elbow, so I might detect a suburban murder in a frayed cuff. A death in Houndsditch may leave the inhabitants of Belgravia unmoved, but they mistake the matter if they do not believe themselves involved.'

'Mr Holmes, you are a man after my own heart,' said Bosney warmly. 'And is this not the season for just such reflections?'

'As to that, Mr Bosney,' said Holmes with a wry look towards me, 'I must confess that what with the weather on the one hand and the false civilities on the other, Christmas leaves me quite cold.'

'Why then,' returned the other in some surprise, 'you are a perfect – ah, here is Gray's Inn. See how they have now put up signs warning the unwary of the fresh paint upon the palings. Good cheer, Tom!' This last remark was addressed to a young crossing-sweeper who had stepped smartly up to open the door for us as we drew up, and to whom Bosney tossed some pennies.

My heart sank as I looked at the tide of traffic roaring past us and crossing the Gray's Inn Road. How could Holmes hope to recover one lost bundle of papers in such a vast confusion of humanity?

As always when Sherlock Holmes was engaged on a case, his reflective lassitude gave way to an extraordinary vigour and his demeanour took on the keen expression of a grey-hound loosed from the slips.

'This is your street down here, I take it?' he enquired of our companion. 'John's Street, I think it is called.'

'Exactly so, I inhabit one of the houses further down, where it changes its name before joining Guildford Street,' replied Mr Bosney, scampering to keep up with Holmes as he strode down the well-lit thoroughfare. 'Here we are, allow me to invite you in for some warming negus, I beg.'

'Thank you. Later perhaps. Now the cab stood here, I perceive? Quite so. No rain has fallen this afternoon, that is good.'

Holmes whipped out his lens, dropped on to all fours and began to scramble about on the ground outside Culli-ford Bosney's house. To one so well acquainted with Sher-lock Holmes and his methods, the minuteness of the scrutiny and the animal energy with which he conducted it held no real surprises for me, but the novelist watched with frank astonishment as Holmes, with blithe disregard for the knees of his trousers, crawled in the mud of the cobbled kerbside, now scooping tiny objects into a fold of paper produced from an inside pocket, now measuring invisible marks upon the ground with a tape.

At last, Holmes rose to his feet. 'Now, Mr Bosney, this house here that adjoins yours, this belongs to the Colonel from India, or to the medical students?'

'To the students. That house there, all shut up, is Colonel Harker's.'

'As I assumed. We must make haste if we are to recover your manuscript. I think now I will go into the house.'

I followed Mr Bosney to his front door, but turned in

surprise to see Holmes proceeding down the front path of the neighbouring house.

'Why Holmes!' I cried, 'this is the house.'

'On the contrary Watson. You were a medical student once, you should be aware that *this* is the house.' So saying he pulled at the door bell. 'Read the ground, gentlemen, it is the skin of the great organism we were discussing and bears battlescars that can testify to many a strange history.' The door opened and a maid admitted Holmes into the dwelling.

'Well!' said Mr Bosney. 'Most extraordinary! What can these students have to do with the matter?'

'I think we should wait,' said I, 'Holmes very rarely makes a mistake. If he thinks that they have some connection with the mystery, then you may depend upon it that they have. Come, let us look at the ground and see if we cannot follow his reasoning.'

The pair of us spent a fruitless quarter of an hour examining the mud of the street with the aid of a lens that Bosney brought out from his house. Whatever code was printed there was too cryptic for us to decipher, however, and we were just climbing the steps of Mr Bosney's house to partake of a hot posset when the door of the students' lodgings opened and a young man shot out, clutching a hat to his head and running at breakneck speed down the street. He was followed a few moments later by Sherlock Holmes, who eyed the retreating figure with benevolent amusement.

'An elementary problem, Mr Bosney. Appropriately frivolous for the time of year. If you would be so good as to return with us to Baker Street, I think I may be able to shed a little light on the matter.'

245

'But . . . but Mr Holmes!' cried the other. 'The manuscript! You mean you have found it?'

'Unless we are very unfortunate, it should be in your hands within the hour.'

Not a word would Holmes vouchsafe us, on our homeward journey, save the observation that were all cases as simple as this one, life would soon become insupportably dull.

When we were ensconced in the comfortable warmth of 221B Baker Street, Holmes plucked a book from the shelves and left Culliford Bosney and I to complete the festive decoration of the rooms while he read. Of a sudden, Holmes closed his book with a laugh.

'Well, Watson, perhaps this will turn out to be a case for your memoirs after all. Most remarkable. I should have known, of course.'

'What should you have known, Holmes?' we cried in exasperation.

'We were remarking earlier, Mr Culliford Bosney,' said Sherlock Holmes, with an uncharacteristic twinkle, 'that all things in this great capital interconnect in surprising ways. The observers of life, such as ourselves, must place ourselves like spiders at the centre of the great web, and train ourselves to interpret every twitch upon the gossamer, every tremble of the fibre. As soon as you mentioned to me that you lived next door to medical students I registered just such a quiver on the web. Perhaps it meant something, perhaps nothing, but I filed it away just the same. Watson may remember my remarking that the only notable crime London had to offer today was the removal of a statue from

Charing Cross. You may be aware, Mr Bosney, that it is the habit of medical students to play pranks upon each other. The rivalry between the students of the two great hospitals at Charing Cross and Guy's is legendary.'

'Why, that's true!' I cried, 'I remember in my day that we—'

'Quite,' said Holmes, always impatient of interruption. 'I had therefore already set down in my mind the theft of the statue as an incident of just such festive exuberance. Your mention of medical students, Mr Bosney, while conceivably immaterial, prepared me for some connection. As soon as I came upon the scene of your meeting with the spectral hansom the true facts of the matter became clear to me. To the trained eye the tracks in the kerbside were easy enough to interpret. I saw at once that the cab had been waiting outside the *students'* house, Mr Bosney, not your own. The signs of movement and restlessness on the part of the horse also told me that no professional London jarvey had been at the reins. It had been all the driver could do to keep the horse still while the statue was loaded into the cab.'

'A statue!' Culliford Bosney clapped his hands together. 'Of course! The awful fixed stare and the ghostly pallor!'

'You were an excellent witness, Mr Bosney, but you failed to interpret your own evidence. Your senses had already told you that you beheld something inhuman, but you refused to make the logical inference.'

'Ghosts were much on my mind, Mr Holmes. I had after all just completed a fiction and was perhaps still dwelling in the world of the imagination. But what of the manuscript?'

'I called on the students, as you observed. They were

most communicative. They revealed to me that for the purposes of the jape one of their number had hired a hansom for the day and bribed the cabbie to stay away. He had purloined the statue and brought it straight to your street, Mr Bosney. There the other students came out and dressed it up. I already knew that something of the sort had taken place from the disposition of footprints outside. The students had then gone back into the house, leaving their ringleader in charge of the cab, while they changed into builders' overalls. It was their mad intention to climb Temple Bar and place the statue in a prominent position overlooking the traffic. The young gentleman who had played the part of the cabbie related to me how you had accosted him while his friends were still inside. You took him so by surprise when you hailed him, that he did not think to say that he was engaged.'

'The young hound!' exclaimed Culliford Bosney.

'He is most penitent, I assure you,' said Holmes. 'I think I may say without conceit that he was a little startled to find Sherlock Holmes on his trail.'

'A hammer to crack a nut, to be sure . . . but the manuscript, Mr Holmes?'

'Ah the manuscript! Your cabbie took advantage of the moment when you sprang back in amazement from the cab to make good his escape. He contrived to smuggle the statue into Charing Cross Hospital itself and put it into a bed where, as far as he knows, it remains still. He returned the hansom to the cab company who had hired it out to him and had reached his lodgings next door to your house not half an hour before we arrived upon the scene. He has a vague memory of seeing a bundle of papers in the back of the cab, but he paid them no attention. When I made it plain to him that the loss of that manuscript would result in the story of his adventures being made known to the dean of his hospital he rushed from the house to recover it. I think I hear his tread upon the stair now.'

Just at that moment the door opened to admit a flushed young man carrying a large bundle of papers.

'My manuscript!' cried Mr Bosney, leaping to his feet.

'Allow me to present Mr Jasper Corrigan,' said Holmes. 'This is my good friend Dr Watson, and this gentleman, whose manuscript you appear to have found, is your neighbour, the novelist.'

'Well, sir, I believe I owe you an apology,' said the medical student, holding out a hand. 'I'm sure Mr Holmes here has told you everything. Believe me when I say that I had no intention of doing you such a wrong.'

'My dear fellow,' said Mr Bosney, warmly shaking hands, 'think nothing of it! If the manuscript is complete . . . let me see . . .' He took the bundle of papers and examined them eagerly. 'Yes, it is all here. I will take it to the printers this instant. Will they be open at this time of the evening? But they have a night staff. Yes, this very instant! Mr Corrigan, I hope you will do me the honour of coming with your friends to my house tomorrow night. We shall have a party! Yes, with chestnuts and games and all manner of fun. A man should know his neighbours. It is disgraceful that I have not invited you before. Marshmallows too, and a hot punch! Please tell me you will come.'

'Sir, we should be honoured. We . . . I do not deserve such generosity.'

'Pooh! Is it not Christmas? As for you, Mr Holmes, I

am sure I do not know where to begin . . . such brilliance, such—'

'Really, Mr Bosney, you are too kind,' said Holmes, smiling a little at the author's exuberance. 'I am happy that your story is saved, but I think on reflection that you will see that it was not a testing problem. Indeed it is probable that it would have solved itself without my aid.'

'That I cannot allow,' replied Mr Bosney, 'I insist that you name your fee.'

'As to that,' said Holmes, 'I *will* ask a fee from you.'

'Name it, Mr Holmes, name it!'

'I have a fancy to own that manuscript of yours. When it returns from the printers, I wonder if you will send it to me?'

Mr Bosney blinked slightly. 'Really Mr Holmes, you do me a great honour. You told me you have no time for fiction.'

'Some fiction I have all the time in the world for, Mr Bosney, and I have an idea that I will enjoy your story. I think it is you who are doing me the honour.'

'Shake my hand, sir!' said the other. 'You are a remarkable man. A remarkable man.'

Mr Bosney was as good as his word and the manuscript arrived a week later through the post. Holmes took it up immediately and for the next two hours sat reading it. When he had finished, he looked up and I saw that there were tears in his eyes.

'Really, Watson,' he said at last. 'Couldn't we have more holly about the place? It is Christmas, you know.'

'But Holmes!' I expostulated.

'Read it, Watson,' he said passing the manuscript over to me. 'Just read it.'

I took it up and looked at the cover page. 'But . . . but . . . Holmes!'

'Quite, Watson.'

I looked at the manuscript again. On the cover page was written, 'A Christmas Carol, by Charles Culliford Boz Dickens.'

'And a merry Christmas to us all!' said Holmes.

Going Downriver

BY PHILIPPA GREGORY

10 August

I started this diary with a view to publishing it alongside my thesis. I thought I would call it something like 'Living with the People – a year with the Nloko' and that there would be a picture of me on the front with Shasta and a picture of me on the back on my own outside the hut they gave me. My diary was, in those early days, rather self-conscious – I'd accept that as a criticism.

I had in mind a woman reader: a rather bright anthropology student in her first year, say. I addressed her frankly – as an expert – and I charmed her. I showed her my commitment to understanding a native people, and the stripping away of my Western values. I showed myself in bad lights too: the meal of the maggots' eggs, and the time they took me swimming; but there is a sort of golden glow over it all. It reads, I suppose, as the account of an adventure by an adventurer who knows he will make it safely home. Behind it all was the awareness of my apartment in New York, and my hopes of publication, my ambitions in the university, and my certainty that among all those young women readers would be one – or indeed more than one – who would be so impressed by my diary (and the pictures

252

on the back and the front) – that I would be 'set up' when I got back to New York after my year in the back of beyond. This may sound crude; but in all fairness when a man has been away from home comforts for three hundred and three days he starts to be a little edgy and to long for a darkened bar, a Budweiser, and a woman with long legs sitting on a bar stool.

Not that I am celibate. Far (very far!) from it. I live in the best hut in the village, re-thatched especially for me, with Shasta: a stunningly beautiful bare-breasted Nloko woman. Her nose is too flat for Caucasian taste and her hips are broad and plump which the Nloko in their natural wisdom admire; and we do not. But she is a Princess of these peoples, which makes her choice of me rather flattering.

We went through some kind of ceremony. Unfortunately I was not at all fluent in Nlokoese and much of it was beyond me. But I think we were, in their terms, married. How I shall explain to her when I have to leave is a problem which I shall worry about when I go. One of the charming aspects of the Nloko people is that they have no sense of distance or time. They have no words to describe time beyond weather descriptions – such as sunrise, sunset, or, at the most distant future, the next rains. They cannot plan long-term. So to try to explain to Shasta that marrying me was a mistake because in a year I would leave her and never return, was quite beyond *my* command of the language, and her concept of time.

To be honest, she was very pressing, and very seductive. What with the ceremonial drink, and Shasta perfumed, oiled, and painted, I was pretty much of a goner. When I woke up and the ceremony was done I was in my hut, oiled, painted and perfumed myself, with the brown and beautiful Shasta spilled across my bed. It was too late to argue, and besides she awoke with a smile so gentle and trusting that I could not resist the temptation of holding her, and stroking her smooth brown legs and waist, and then I could not resist making love to her again.

To be fair to them, the whole ceremony – as well as everything else they do – is based on consent. No one may coerce any other person. Every decision of the community has to have the willing and verbal consent of every individual. This sounds idyllic. Actually it's incredibly time-consuming and inefficient! It's only because they have such a small community – about fifty people in this village – and because they do things by tradition that things ever get agreed and performed.

At the 'wedding' the rule of consent applied. And they did ask me, very slowly and clearly, if I consented to being her husband. And I must say, in fairness to them, that before I passed out from the drink I said 'Yeah. OK. Why not?'

I don't regret it. It could not have worked out better. Shasta's status as Princess has given me unique access to the Nloko people, who trust me and confide in me and actually come to me for advice. It has made the thesis as easy as writing this diary. I am investigating puberty and coming of age among the Nloko, and I have been besieged with their beliefs, taboos, and individual experiences. Nothing has been hidden from me. I know every secret. I could have wrapped up the thesis a couple of weeks ago. But the boat only comes upriver every four months so I have to wait until my appointed departure time – two months or so from now – fifty days to be precise, allowing ten days to travel downriver by canoe to meet the government launch.

I have not exploited Shasta, it's a relationship of feeling. I've never seen anyone light up in the way that Shasta does when I come near her. I've never had a woman wash me from head to toe for the sheer joy of touching every part of my body. I've never had a woman sit still, like a rock, for three hours just because I fell asleep one lazy afternoon with my head in her lap and she would never disturb my rest. It's heady stuff! I've even had thoughts of sending the manuscript home by the launch and staying here, and letting the career and the apartment (and even the willing female anthropology students) go hang. But to be honest I'm too ambitious, and too intelligent, to get stuck here.

It palls after a time. In the first few months I was awe-struck by their relationship with their world. They eat well and live well in this wonderfully constructed and organized village without leaving a mark on the forest around them. When you see them hunting they almost *become* trees and shrubs. When you see the children playing at the river edge they are as much a part of nature as the fish in the water and the parakeets shrieking in the trees overhead. Their whole world revolves around the hierarchy of the village in which women and the women's religion is totally dominant. This produces a wonderful serenity about the place. The women are the keepers of the wisdom and the health of the People. The men support them, respect them, obey them – and they have their own sub-culture of brotherhood and comradeship. I haven't cracked that, to be honest. But it doesn't bother me. At home I'm not really a guy's sort of guy. It's too competitive for me. I like the company of women, I like the admiration of women. The Nlokoese women treat me with a respect bordering on awe – I'm lapping it up!

I imagine I shall miss Shasta like hell. I don't think even the most liberated anthropology student will be as abandoned as Shasta is with me. She makes love as if it were some glorious ceremony which builds slowly and elegantly from one smooth sinuous movement to another. And then finally, when you can hardly bear the controlled beauty of it any more, she throws her dignity away and she is animal, a beautiful animal, in her passion.

It doesn't take a PhD to know that this kind of experience is rare. I shall break my heart without her, I know it already. I expect when I take the launch downriver I shall feel like throwing myself overboard rather than leave her. And I'm concerned for her too. I have tried to discover what happens when a wife of the Nloko is left by her husband. Shasta's beauty, her passion, her wonderful grace in everything she does will not last for long. You only have to look at her mother, pot-bellied, round-faced with twinkling sarcastic eyes to see where my lovely girl is headed. She should have married one of her own kind who would have stayed with her and grown fat and sarcastic with her. Instead of me, who has adored her, and been adored by her: a year of absolute passion, instead of a lifetime of conventional comfort. I know what I'd choose.

But I don't know what she would choose since she cannot imagine our parting. I told the whole tribe, when I arrived, that I would be leaving in a year – when the rains come again. And they all smiled and nodded reassuringly.

'Ralende', they said softly. Which means – as far as I can translate – 'of course', or 'naturally', or 'it has been ordained'. So she ought to know that I am going, even if she never mentions it and always behaves as if we will be together for ever.

I am, of course, taking sensible precautions. I use contraceptives both to protect her against pregnancy and to protect us both from diseases to which we might not be naturally immune. I would ruin my academic reputation if I left behind any major damage to the Nloko tribe. A Western disease, or a half-caste child would be professional death for me. Also, I think that Shasta could remarry if she has no child. Something one of the women said suggested that she had been married before. I asked the woman, one of Shasta's aunts, what she meant by the word I understood as – the previous husband. Shasta snapped at her, and the other women seemed appalled at some kind of lapse of taste. I said nothing more, but that night I asked Shasta if she had been married before. She laughed. 'Many, many times,' she said. 'A new husband every season of the rains, to make the rains come. And what fine sweet water you will bring me, my Prince! my Master! Do you still consent? Do you still consent? Will you be Prince Rainbringer? My lovely ghost-faced lover?' There was a lot more of that nonsense and love-talk, and then there was the dark tropical night and Shasta and I alone.

18 August

I was disturbed this morning to find that my chest of personal goods has been touched. More importantly, the supplies of contraceptives have been stolen. Theft is practically unknown among the Nloko so I am hoping that one of the children has taken them for playthings and that Shasta will get them back for me, despite her dislike of them. She complains that they are against nature – the nearest translation would be 'blasphemous'. I think she would like to conceive my child. But no, lovely seductive Shasta. No chance. Whatever your feelings we will use Western contraception, and until I get the packet back I shall sleep cautiously beside my Princess, refusing to touch her, even though she cried last night for a caress.

I have finished the final interviews for my thesis and much of it is already written. I experimented with a new introduction today, but I shall leave the conclusion until I get back to New York and feel settled enough to look back, to 'recollect in tranquillity'. They could not have helped me more. I think every day one of the boys or girls of my research sample – eleven- to fourteen-year-olds – has come to the hut door and squatted outside to be my companion for the day. Rarely has any anthropologist had the honour of being a Prince among his research group! They call me Prince Rainbringer – and I am thinking of that as a title for the diary. I have no idea how much travelogue-type books can earn, but I have a hunch that we are talking very big bucks indeed. I keep spending the imaginary royalty cheques in my head! I *must* have a big gas-guzzler car, and get a better apartment.

Indeed, as the time comes for me to leave I am longing for my homecoming. I long for a properly-cooked steak. My mouth just fills with water at the thought of donuts, coffee, chocolate, a Big Mac. I am going to pour junk food down my throat when I get home. All we have been eating here for the last few days is river fish and cassava bread, for breakfast, lunch and dinner, as preparation for the great feast to celebrate the coming of the rains.

I shall be sorry to miss it. It had taken place just before I arrived, and it will happen again just after I leave. It's obviously central to their religion, which is typical primitive Pantheism. They believe that all growing things have a spirit life, and that the seasons change as they wish. The big transition from the dry period to the rains has to be assisted with a ceremony and a major sacrifice. Shasta will be officiating. I asked her, rather frivolously, if they had a special rain dance, but she smiled and told me it was 'Sere' which means a mystery. She is particularly attractive these days, withdrawn and thoughtful. It is costing me a good deal in self-control not to make love with her, especially as I am going away so soon. I want a farewell fling. Last night she begged me to kiss her, just to kiss her and nothing else. I really thought I had better not.

28 August

It has happened. I suppose it was inevitable really. Shasta is powerfully seductive and I am a young man with normal appetites. I had some hope of being able to withdraw in time but her arms were tight around my back and her legs wrapped around my hips. It makes no major difference to me. Nothing can delay my departure and if my good luck holds, any baby she conceived last night will miscarry, or die young. As with most primitive peoples the infant mortality here is fairly high. If it survives I hope it won't be too white. I don't want the child to be uncomfortable, of course; but more than anything else I don't want some callow young researcher with no idea what it is like to be out in the field for a whole year, to come along and see a half-caste child and start the kind of gossip which would ruin my professional reputation.

I know that they have knowledge of plants which can cause abortions. I patted Shasta's flat belly and asked her to make sure there was no baby. She laughed delightedly and said 'ralende' 'it is ordained', so I suppose that is that. It's her decision so she will have to carry the can. There is certainly nothing *I* can do. The marriage and the child has been quite beyond my control and no one could expect me to sacrifice my chance of success and wealth in New York for a voodoo marriage and a half-caste baby.

She has painted her belly with a spiral concentric pattern in a deep orange dye. She looks breathtaking. The ceremony of the rains is obviously one which absorbs her to the exclusion of everything else. She still sleeps in my bed and services my every need but she has an inner restraint which I sense. Can it be that although she refuses to understand the concept of the future she does in fact know that I am going away? Very soon actually. Only another month.

23 September

I have some oilskin bags for my precious research papers and this diary and I have packed all but this book and pen carefully away. Shasta sealed them with sap from a tree rather like a rubber tree. She assures me it is waterproof. She is helping me prepare for my departure. She's in a cheerful optimistic mood. I was dreading this stage thinking she would be clinging and demanding, so I suppose I should be pleased that she sets about finding my old rucksack and packing my few clothes and souvenirs with such contentment. Actually, I can't help feeling a bit peeved.

They have set up a large oblong table on a huge wooden trestle for the ceremony of the rains and draped it with flowers and leaves. Shasta, who is now painted from her dark upswinging eyebrows to the very soles of her feet often walks around the table, humming softly to herself, for all the world like a suburban housewife checking the place mats. I ran up the little ramp to the high table and slapped her warm butt the other day and she led me away and said 'Dourane', 'Not yet', very sweetly. Since then I have treated it as the holy of holies and stayed well away.

Shasta's serenity and quiet joy seems to be reflected in everyone else. Everywhere I go I am greeted with smiles and often little gifts of flowers or fruit. I don't doubt that I'm being wished *bon voyage*, and I have taken a thousand photographs of everyone before sealing up my camera and films in waterproof packaging for the long journey downriver. They have no objection to photographs now – though I had to insist when I first arrived. But everything seems to be permitted to me now. I caught myself caressing the smooth thighs of Tharin, Shasta's younger sister: a girl just deliciously at the brink of womanhood. She smiled and let me touch her and I had the sudden heady sense of being able to do anything in the world that I want here. I took her by the hand and led her down towards the river. If she had hesitated for a moment I swear I would have stopped, but she followed me smiling, trusting like the little girl she

261

is; a little dappled doe in the flickering shadows. I am ashamed to say that I had her, and she was a virgin. I tried to make her promise to say nothing; but she was in pain and bleeding a little and she just waved me away. I only hope that there will not be two Caucasian-Nlokoese babies born to the tribe next year. I shan't go with her again. It's too risky.

My only major regret, as I pack, is not being able to record the ceremony of the rains. But to be honest, I can't bear to miss the launch. It would be another four months wasted for the benefit of recording a drunken all-week hen-party conducted in a language I can only just understand and for a religion which is incomprehensible to the Western mind. I suppose if I were a better scientist I would make the sacrifice and stay. As it is, I cannot bring myself to delay. The bright lights are calling me! I could drink a lake of beer! And I really want a woman of my own colour. Shasta's love and her passion and tenderness have been a great gift. I won't forget them. I'll probably dedicate the book to her. But right now (and this is *not* for publication!) I want a long-legged girl to talk dirty!

26 September

Something very strange and disturbing has happened. I was working at my little table in the doorway of the hut when I dropped my pen top and bent down to pick it up. I then saw, at the foot of the king-pole of the hut, a piece of cloth poking out through the trampled-down earth. I took my pen-knife and scraped around it and it seemed to be some kind of oilskin package. I was angry for a moment thinking that it was one of mine which Shasta had stolen as a souvenir, but when I opened it I found it was not my writing, and it had obviously been buried for some time. The most amazing thing is that it is a chapter of anthropological research notes and a couple of grainy photographs of Shasta with a middle-aged, rather unattractive Caucasian male.

My first thought was for my own thesis. It would be hopelessly redundant if this bastard had been here first. I couldn't understand it. I'd done a total search of all publications and I couldn't imagine that someone had published work on the Nloko which I had missed. The tribe's entire attraction for me had been that no one had lived with them before. I'd get them fresh.

He'd been working, predictably enough, on rites and ritual. There was a whole load of notes on primitive fertility rites – I've no time for that sort of thing. It seems to me to be hardly worth the paper it's written on. Who cares if they crush fruit to make the rains come, or kill fish, or cut the throats of monkeys? What difference does it make? My kind of research is immediately applicable to social science in the US. Puberty, how to manage it. What are adolescents like in a natural world? That kind of stuff. Solid research in its own right and very, very sellable.

I blundered out of the hut with the notes and snapshots in my hand and bumped into Shasta's aunt who was shelling beans at the foot of the feast table. I waved the photo under her nose and asked her – who is this man?

I was surprised by her reaction. She jerked back at once and I could see, under the painted spirals and the dark skin, that she had gone pale. She muttered something very softly and then she tried to take the photos and the papers away from me. I tugged back, and then finally I pushed her hard, so that she had to let go. She sat down with a bump and I asked her again, while I had the upper hand. 'Who is this man?'

She said that word again – previous husband. The word I had heard before. Previous husband. But she said nothing more. Neither my shouts nor, I'm ashamed to admit, a quick not-very-hard kick, got another word out of her.

I stamped back to my hut to sit on the sleeping board and think. There *had* been another anthropologist here, and he had lived in this hut, my hut. And he had probably slept with Shasta. And then he had gone. But why hadn't he published? And why hadn't he taken his research notes? I knew that I would never be parted from *my* research notes. So maybe something had happened to him, in the forest or on the river. Maybe he had gone out one day, taking a break from work, and had an accident, and now he would never publish and never make money and never sit in an attractive office at a good college with a sexy secretary to make the coffee.

I shivered. I looked out of the open door of the hut to the dancing ground in the centre of the village and the ramp and the big trestle table covered with flowers and fruit. I suddenly wanted to be safely away, with my feet up on the rail of the launch and a can of cold beer in my hand and all the well-kept secrets of the Nloko tribe, worth a fortune to me, safely in a briefcase in my cabin.

264

29 September

They are giving me a tremendous sending-off party. I am officially recognized as the father of Shasta's child and a man of great potency and a Prince in my own right. 'Prince Rainbringer.' All the women have made flower chains for my neck and I am required to strut around the village while they throw petals at me and sprinkle perfumed oil wherever I walk. I am consenting to do this to oblige Shasta. She has made it unusually clear that if I do *not* play my part then there will be no canoe to take me downriver. I feel manipulated and resentful towards her. But she is at the peak of her beauty and confidence and she does not seem to notice. If I were staying then we would have words and I would give her a timely introduction to patriarchy. But since I am going I might as well leave graciously. After all, I have not done at all badly out of this. I am taking away the work which is going to make my fortune, I have escaped infection, and although I have made her pregnant and possibly her little sister too, I seem to have got off scot-free without any payment or punishment.

They keep giving me the strong drink that I had at the wedding feast and it's going to my legs. I've had to sit down at my little table and I'm writing this while the women dance. Before my eyes they're just whirling colours. It's a most wonderful sight: exotic, barbaric. If my things were not all safely packed I'd take another photo, except I don't think I can see straight. I have a vague idea of bringing a camera crew back here and making a television film. I'd be good on television. I've got those sort of looks. That's probably a good career plan for me. A wider audience, and a bit of glamour to go with the academic work.

I'll have the lot. As soon as I can get out of here. I went to Shasta just now and asked her about the canoe and she gave me her sweetest smile and showed, by the wave of her hand, that when the sun starts going down I will set off. The boatmen prefer travelling at night, despite rapids and crocodiles and piranha fish and water snakes. Still, I'll have to trust them. Anyway, since the Princess is all dressed up in her ceremonial gear, and I am pissed out of my brain: I can't argue.

It is growing velvety slowly dark. I have danced, I have drunk. I have been kissed by a thousand women. I had two, roughly, greedily, one after another in my hut where Shasta and I used to love like angels. Everything seems to be permitted to me. I slapped the second one around a bit and found that I *adored* seeing her flinch even while I was lying on her. So I guess that's something else new that I have learned during this trip – and also not for publication! My legs have totally gone now. They have laid me on the table and heaped me with flowers. Actually all my muscles have gone, except my hands. I've never been so drunk in my life. Shasta, as some funny joke, has laid my diary on my chest. I'm still scrawling while they dance around me but now my fingers are getting numb. She leans over me, she asks me if I wish to ride down the river in the canoe? Do I Prince Rainbringer consent to go to the water? I say – 'Do I hell? Yeah, yeah, yeah. Let's skip the ceremony and go.'

*

The women danced around the table until the huge mango moon came swiftly up over the dark canopy of the forest. The man was slipping from sleep into coma when they lifted the cover from the table. The trestle was a beautifully carved canoe. The Princess helped them to lay him in the canoe and then took up her knife. She slit the spine of the diary and slashed the pages into ribbons of white which she sprinkled gently all around him. Then she leaned over him once more, and kissed his cold lips. Then she drew her knife slowly across his throat.

Singing quietly the women lifted the canoe and slid it down the bank into the river. They waded out beside it, Shasta with them. Singing, with their beads chinking quietly, they thrust the canoe out into the main channel of the river where it spun once, like a compass needle seeking direction, and then the water took it and it moved swiftly, smoothly downriver.

Shasta waded back to the bank and raised her arms out wide to the river to thank it for the gift of the man and his seed, and for their chance to make another, truly noble sacrifice for the rains. As she threw back her head and raised her voice there was a deep echoing thunder from the dark skies above her.

The rains began to fall.

They Don't Like Us

BY JAMES HERBERT

I know there'll be trouble the moment I go through the door. Some bars don't mind you – hell, cash is cash, no matter where it comes from – but others put up the shutters as soon as they see you approach.

They don't like us, see? We're not their kind. In fact, to *them* we're not even people. It makes life . . . it makes things . . . difficult. To say the least.

Anyway, this time I step into the place – shit, a rat-hole if ever there was one – and take a coupla seconds to blink out the darkness. There's cobwebs like dirty rags in the corners, the wood floor needs scrubbing, the mirrors need scraping. The dive is full of low-lives. You'da thought one more would'na made no difference. But then there's always the bigots. Christ on a Crutch, them are everywhere.

H'mn. They say the same about us.

One of my kind is over there in a corner, making like he don't see me as he brushes dirt from one part of the floor to another. He ignores me, and man, I ignore him. No bro' he, think I.

The buzz that's been going on stops awhiles, like they all waiting for me to make my move to the bar. I make that move and things start up again, tho' I can tell many an interested eye is still on me.

It's hard to walk well when you cold – cold and thirsty. I need some fire in me, and brother, this is the place, this is the place I'm gonna get it. I've taken enough of their shit.

I got money, the gov'mint gives me money. It don't like my kind, but there's too many Bleeding Hearts in the country for them in power to ignore their vote. 'Sides, we got the vote too. Every man is equal, right? Some is more so, is all.

It's a long hike to that old chipped bar counter, but I've taken longer ones. A bear scrapes back his chair and stands in front of me as I get near – you can always count on a redneck to make his feelings plain. I guess the idea is to stare me down, but hell, I don't even look. I've learned better by now. I shuffle round him.

He gives a kinda snort, hitches up his belt, and stomps out to the back room, probly to piss up the wall. Better than up me, right? Yeah, that's been done too.

So here I am, finally at that dusty old bar, thirsting so hard, man, my throat is kinda seized up. Raw like. Scorched.

It ain't easy to talk that way.

'Whu . . .' I try. I swallow, and fuck, that hurts like hell. 'Whiskey.' It's a rasp, but he knows what I mean all right.

'This ain't the place for you, boy,' the barman tells me, like it's fresh news.

I repeat the order. 'Whiskey . . . uh, please.' The more you talk, the easier it gets, but we don't get much chance for conversation, y'know?

'You harda hearin'?' the fat man, this pig of a barman, says to me.

I put the money – I've counted the 'xact amount outside,

269

and Christ, that took some time – on the bartop. 'Whiskey,' I say for the – what was it? Oh yeah, the third – for the third time.

So he reaches down for his baseball bat under the bar and brings it up for me to see. He shows it off, and to make sure I understand he says, 'See.' Then he points it at my head.

It's not the pain that matters – that don't matter at all. Nor the indignity. It's the fuckin' dent, man.

'Hey, give the zook a drink,' comes a voice from behind. I don't turn. No, I keep my eyes on that bat.

'Ain't nunna your busness, mister,' the barman says back.

I swear I hear that brush moving faster over there in the corner. My bro' is trying to dig hisself a hole.

A chair behind me scrapes the floor again. Different one this time, I'm sure of that. Footsteps approach. Someone moves round me, leans on the bartop.

'These guys got enough problems without you givin' 'em crap,' he tells the barman. He's a big one, big shoulders, big fuckin' hands. Even the bat looks uneasy.

'I gotta respect'ble jointa run,' says the barman, but it's a sorta whine. His weapon ain't gonna do much to this ol' boy.

'Yeah, you must be 'spectin' the President any minute,' says my man. I don't feel much these days, but I'm kinda warming to him. 'Now gimme a whiskey and make it another for my buddy here. I getta little upset when my throat's dry, unnerstand what I mean?'

The barman, that fat slimebag, seems to unnerstand pretty well. He puts two glasses on the counter, neither one of 'em too clean, tho' that don't bother me none, and I can tell my new friend's not fussed. The barman pours and if it woulda done any good, the look he gives me woulda killed.

'Down the hatch, zook,' the good guy says.

'Th – th – th—' says I.

'Thanks?' he asks. 'Fuck you,' he adds.

I try a nod, but my neck's stiff from too long out in the cold. Mainly my attention is on that half-full glass on the bar. I reach for it and it seems awful hard to pick up. I make it tho', oh man, I do pick it up, and my hand's shaky as I bring it to my dry old lips.

But someone smashes the glass from my paw and I watch it shatter on the wood top, that lovely liquid spilling out like treacle on brown bread. I just look at it.

The big guy turns and I know, shit I know, it's the other big one, the bear, behind me.

'They don't drink with us,' I hear his grizzly voice say.

'Ain't his fault he's like he is,' my buddy says back.

'No, but it's your fuckin' fault he's drinkin' here,' comes the reply.

A big hand – a mighty big hand, bigger'n the one resting on the bar 'side me – grabs my shoulder and hauls me round. The bear drops his hand away and looks at it like he's disgusted at what might be there. He wipes that nothingness away on the backside of his 501s. Then he smashes my face.

I don't groan, I don't hurt. It's just like – numb. No more'n that. But then I'm so cold I'm numb all over anyways. That's why I like the whiskey, see, the ol' firewater.

Well I don't know why – who can tell? – but this upsets my pal and he takes a swing at the bear. Bear don't like

271

that, but on his knees it's like he accepts it. He shakes his head, just like a stunned grizzly, and reaches for something stashed in his shirt pocket. There's a *click*, and then there's the blade.

I don't like blades, never did like 'em. Maybe they're the way I am, I forget.

My friend at the bar don't wait, he goes for the kneeling man. Then they're in a heap, rolling round the dirty floor, cussing and hollering, kicking and squealing. It don't take long – funny how these things never do – the Big Disease never did, it came fast, took what it wanted, then spread in other ways. But that's not the main topic right now. Not really, anyways.

So there comes one helluva scream and both of 'em lie still, leaving the rest of us wondering who's gonna get up. Luckily, my pal does. Only he looks at me and I can tell we're not friends anymore. Shit, he's outa there like a bat outa hell.

The bear gives a groan, but it's a tired one, you know, like his last. If I could smile, I'd do that. Instead I just gawk.

Man, he's dead, and everyone there knows it. And they don't like it much. They know what's gonna happen before too long. None of 'em want to rush, so they kinda drift out, in twos and threes, conversation pretty dull-like and their 'so-longs' a little half-hearted. Even the slimebag barman fades away.

So there's only three of us left. Me, the new corpse, and the bro' sweeping the floor. He's standing there resting on the broom, watching us from his corner, those big zook eyes white and staring outa his black face. (We all turn a nasty shade of black eventually, and no one's figured out why. Leastways, nobody's bothered to explain it to us.)

The process takes half-an-hour, mebbe forty minutes, and I got time to wait. I got all the time in the world. I just kinda stand there and look down on the dead old bear.

Could be he'd been half-dead already – some folks are, you know, like their souls have left their bodies long before the flesh is ready to give itself up – well, anyways, it don't seem like but ten minutes before he stirs, twitches a little. Another five and he's sitting up, looking round, wondering what the fuck he's doing there and feeling nothing.

It's the Big Disease, I could tell him, but he wouldn't appreciate it right now. Wouldn't understand. Part of the old brain cells go with the death, see? It's why we're stupid, some more so'n others. Ain't gonna mean nothing to him to say something in the air don't let us die no more, we just kinda rot away.

That's why people don't like us. It ain't the stink – we get sprayed regular nowadays – it's the sight of them lumps falling off us. If it weren't for the Bleeding Hearts we'd all be dumped somewhere. But then, we all got family, don't we?

So we roam, become a general nuisance, and remind people what's in store should they die before their natural time. It ain't no fun, but it beats nothing. I think.

Anyways, here's our boy, Mr Grizzly, all glassy-eyed and slack-jawed, the knife's hilt still sticking out his chest, lumbering to his feet.

'Whu . . . whisk . . . ey?' I ask, bearing no malice now he's one of us.

And he looks at me like he don't know what I mean. I

won't say it – tongue don't work too well all swollen and black – but I'd like to tell him he won't get much chance to drink with a buddy anymore. I show him the glass instead, the one the other big guy had been drinking from, and shit, ain't his skin turning dark already? This zook – you know, zombie-spook – is a classic. Like I said, mebbe he was half-dead already.

So I drink the hot stuff for him. Then I leave. And you know, he follows, like he's scared to be without me. He'll get use to wandering alone, tho'. He'll soon get to know that nobody likes you when you're dead, not even your own kind.

He won't feel it, tho'. No, he won't feel it at all.

Child's Play

BY ELIZABETH JANE HOWARD

'Walking out on her in the middle of the night! I'm not
easily shocked, but that shocks me!'

His conversation, she thought, was full of exceptions he
made to his own rules. 'They've only been married a few
weeks – it's just a tiff.'

'I dare say.' He stretched out a sunburned muscular arm,
reached for a ginger-nut and popped it whole into his
mouth. Speaking through it, he went on: 'But he's got
his own way out of it, hasn't he? It's he who's off to
Scotland, spoiling her holiday and leaving her on her own.
Poor little thing! She's only eighteen – only a child!'

'Shirley won't be on her own: she's coming down to us
just the same.'

He said nothing for a moment, swilled back the rest of
his chestnut-coloured tea, wiped his moustache with a huge,
navy handkerchief, and thrusting it back into his breeches
pocket pronounced, 'Well! It may sound funny to you, but
I don't like the idea of *my* daughter being mucked about.
It annoys me, that's all. Gets my goat.'

There was silence in the kitchen while Kate Ewbank did
not retort, 'She's my daughter too, isn't she? How do you
know she's being mucked about?' or simply, 'You don't
say!' Years of not airing them had cramped and damped her

responses into this kind of thing which she would not sink to out loud.

The stable clock struck five and Brian Ewbank got to his feet, collecting his old tweed jacket from the back of his chair. Then, stooping slightly to see himself in it, he combed his thick, wavy grey hair in front of the small mirror that hung by the sink. 'You'll be fetching her from the station, then?'

'I will.'

The Ewbanks lived in what had been the coachman's cottage near a large Victorian stable block built round three sides of a courtyard. It had been designed to serve the huge neo-Gothic house that was now a girls' boarding school set in vast, semi-derelict grounds of parkland and wooded drives. At five-thirty on summer term-time evenings he took a flock of girls, chiefly called Sarah and Caroline, on bulging, grass-fed ponies for a ride. They called him Brian behind his back, but he was really Captain Ewbank, and they held interminable conferences about whether his marriage was happy, or a tragic failure.

The moment Kate was alone, Marty, the tortoise-shell cat, slammed through the cat door with a mouse in her jaws. She tossed it under a chair, mentioned it several times in a high-pitched voice until she had forced Kate to meet her glassy, insolent gaze, and then began to crunch it up like a club sandwich. She liked Kate, in a limited way, to share her triumphs. In ten seconds the mouse was gone, she had drunk a saucer of milk and was polishing her spot-less paws. She kept herself in a gleaming state of perpetual readiness – like a fire engine.

When she had cleared the tea, Kate went up to make

the bed in Shirley's old room, in case she would rather sleep there than in the twin beds pushed together to make a double in the spare room. She also moved the jar of marigolds and pinks. She wanted Shirley to feel welcome. After that, she could not think at all what else she ought to do, and stood motionless, wondering what it could possibly be. But then, as sometimes nowadays, a moment after she had stopped physically moving and was still, despair engulfed her, as dense, as sudden and palpable as stepping into a raincloud or a fog. Senses of futility and failure fused; then the pall receded, leaving her with a feeling of weakness and mediocrity.

Percy was calling from his room, which was downstairs by the front door. Whenever she thought of him, she had to pull herself together. 'You still have your health,' she told herself. Apart from a touch of arthritis, migraines that irregularly punctured her attempts to face up to things, and these freakish sweats – hot flushes by name and as amusing to those unencumbered by them as piles or gout – she had little to complain about, whereas poor old Percy . . .

He had somehow got wind of the fact that she was going out in the car; must have heard Brian mentioning the station, although goodness knows he was deaf enough when he felt like it. By the time she got to him, he had levered himself to his feet with one hand perilously heavy on the corner of his loaded card-table. He had always borne a marked resemblance to Boris Karloff, and since his – fortunately mild – stroke now looked astonishingly like that actor in the role of Frankenstein's Monster. He'd got his speech painfully back, but he kept it to a minimum.

'I'm only going to fetch Shirley from the station, Father.'

'Shoes,' he said, his hopeful smile undimmed. 'Outdoor shoes.' He pointed with his stick to where his black shoes – as sleek and polished as a pair of police cars – were parked beneath his wardrobe. But his gesture with the stick involved further weight upon the card-table; it tipped, and its formidable coverage fell and rolled all over the floor as he lurched involuntarily on to his bed in a sitting position.

'Whoops-a-daisy,' he said, smiling again to show he was all right, and stuck one of his dreadful old feet with its Walt Disney ogre's toenails almost into her face as she knelt recovering his travelling clock, his pills, his spilled water-carafe, his spectacles, his address book that he kept up to date by crossing off his friends as they died, his saucer that he'd used for grape pips, a couple of chessmen he'd been mending and a plastic heart-shaped box in which he kept alternate rows of false teeth at night.

'Percy, dear, there isn't time: I'll be late. I won't be long.'

His lower lip trembled ponderously, like a baby's, working up to a scene; he withdrew his foot, and then, with a look so cunning that it was pathetic, shot the other one out at her.

'Oh – all *right* then,' she said, and fetched his socks.

In the tack room, Eunice, the stable-girl, was applying mascara to the double pair of false eyelashes that were her second most salient feature. Brian knew that she had heard him come in, but he also knew what he thought she liked. Coming up behind her, he put a large hand over each heavily confined breast, and squeezed them like someone tooting a horn. She squealed.

'Bry – *yern*!'

'I'll be a bit late tonight. Mind you wait.'

She did not answer, but he knew she would.

In the train from Manchester to London, Shirley decided over and over again that her marriage was a total, utter, flop. It must be, if in just over eight weeks they could have a row like that. After he had gone off ('Please yourself!') – what a filthy, *stupid*, *childish* thing to say! – she had never cried so much before in her life; in fact she couldn't believe he'd only been gone twenty minutes, as she discovered he had when she went to wash her face and happened to look at her watch. She'd cleared up the kitchen with meticulous care, wasn't going to let him put her in the wrong about a wife's mess in the flat, but she'd thrown away the sausage rolls so that he wouldn't have anything to eat when he came back – serve him right. But he hadn't *come* back. Instead, when she was frantic with waiting and wanting to tell him what she thought of him, he'd rung to say he was staying the night with friends. She'd been icy on the telephone, but the moment she'd rung off, she'd burst into tears again. Then, like a fool, she'd waited to see him in the morning, but he still didn't come back, and she'd missed the express and had to catch a slow train. It was a failure all right.

By the time she'd changed stations in London and caught the four-twenty from Charing Cross, her whole life with him had begun to seem faintly unreal. She hated the flat, she hated Manchester – she didn't know a single person there, she missed the country, she hated the housework and the awful, endless business of shopping for boring petty things, getting food ready and clearing it up. None of it had turned out at all as she had imagined. Beforehand, she'd thought of being married as candlelit dinners, friends dropping in, using all the presents, setting the table as perfectly as she did her face, moving in the television world (Douglas was a cameraman), Douglas's friends admiring her, envying him, sometimes even making him a little jealous . . . they'd bring her flowers and chocs and ask her advice about their girlfriends. None of this had happened at all. Instead, he'd come back at awful hours – never the same time – fagged out, only talking about his work and a whole lot of people she never met; when she wasn't bored, she was lonely. She missed her friends and her life at home and Dad who'd always been so decent to her . . .

As they changed into their riding clothes, Sarah Hughenden said to Caroline Polsden-Lacey, 'I tell you one thing. He's got the most super heavenly sweat.'
   'Who?'
   'Brian – stupid. He smells of smoked salmon.'
   'How do you know?'
   'I sort of fell up against him.'
   'Sarah! You really *are*!'

It took Kate nearly half an hour to get her father dressed and into the car. In spite of her telling him it was a hot day, he wore a vest, flannel shirt, thick Norfolk jacket, his Burberry and a cashmere muffler she'd given him last Christmas. He also took his pocket book of British birds in case a British bird got near enough – and stayed still long enough – for him to identify it. It was indeed hot. The wild roses were blanched by the heat; buttercups glittered in the rich grass, the chestnut trees lining the unkempt drive had leaves that were already shabby from drought, and the Herefords clumped together under them in a miasma of flies. Without glancing at him, Kate could feel the intensity with which her father was looking out of the car window; she was unhappily divided between going slowly to give him the maximum enjoyment, and not being late for Shirley, who would anyway not be pleased at his making a third in the car. It was extraordinary, she felt, how much of life consisted of having to displease somebody.

As Shirley walked down the platform, she could see her mother standing at the barrier, dressed, as usual, in a faded flowered cotton skirt, a blue tee-shirt and sandals, her dark glasses pushed up over her fringe. From the distance, she looked like a dowdy, rather arty girl. At least, Shirley thought, I've stopped her wearing trousers – she really wasn't the shape for them.

They kissed, rather awkwardly; neither was sure what degree of warmth was appropriate to the occasion. Kate said quickly.

'I'm terribly sorry, but I simply had to bring Percy.'

'Surely you didn't *have* to.'

'You know how he feels about going out in the car. How are you?' She looked at her daughter's incredibly pretty, apparently unravaged face, turning sulky now at the news about her grandfather.

'I'm all right,' stony, snubbing, walking ahead of her mother in silence to the car.

Percy was dragging a dusty fruit-drop from his overcoat pocket. He had recently taken to eating them with the cellophane wrappers still on, and enjoyed being asked why he did so, so that he could say he always ate his sweet papers. He longed to confound people by turning out always to have done something that surprised them. He popped the sweet in just as they got into the car, but when neither of them asked him, he took the sweet out again, dropped it on the floor and ground his foot on it as though it was a cigarette.

'Here's Shirley,' said Kate, pretending not to notice.

'So I see. Had a good term?'

'She hasn't been to school, Father. She's been in Manchester, with Douglas.'

He crunched his dentures and didn't answer. Kate thought he was sulking because he'd got something wrong, but really he was peeved because he hadn't embarrassed Shirley with his pretended memory lapse (he knew she wasn't at school, and who on earth was Douglas?).

'How's my father?'

'He's fine. He's taking the evening ride.'

'What's the new stable-girl like?'

'I've hardly seen her. She's called Eunice.'

'Is she attractive?'

Kate paused before replying evenly: 'Oh yes, I should think she's quite attractive.' It had recently begun to amaze her that in all these years, Shirley had never noticed anything . . .

'. . . and I'm not a child! Why should he suddenly spoil all our plans just because he wants to work on his wretched film! If he can't be bothered even to think what I might feel, why on earth did he ever want to marry me?' She was sitting cross-legged on the floor of her room, having a post-cry cigarette, and looking, Kate thought, very childish indeed.

'Perhaps he *had* to do the job?' she suggested – very gently, but not gently enough.

'Whenever I try to tell you anything, you always take the other person's side! You *always* do!'

'I didn't mean it to sound like that: I'm only trying to understand. I can't believe he simply wanted to hurt your feelings.'

'He doesn't care about my feelings. All he cares about is his bloody film unit. He never stops thinking and talking about them.'

'Could you have gone to Scotland with him?'

'He never said so. Anyway, I've told him it's not my idea of a holiday to sit about cooped up in some ghastly hotel while he's out on an oil rig or something. He told me he'd got three days' leave, and he promised to come home. He *promised* me.' She thrust her knuckles under her firm little chin and glared into space. After a minute, she said:

'The truth is, it's got to be all or nothing for me. I'm jealous of his work.' She looked at her mother with something like triumph. 'That's what it is! I expect him to put me first, and he doesn't, and it makes me jealous!'

The discovery seemed actually to relieve her. After it, she became much easier to reason with: allowed Kate to discuss with her the possibility of getting some sort of part-time job, admitted that Douglas had said something about standing in for a friend whose wife was having a baby, and even volunteered that she could be terrible when she didn't get her own way. She was of an age, Kate thought, when self-recrimination seemed to be unaccompanied by pain. 'I know I've got a hot temper!' She was simply very young for a situation into which her appearance had trapped her so early; an only and childish child, which Kate, in her turn, had to admit meant that she was to some degree spoiled, although with Brian as a father, how could she have prevented it? He had always defended her, backed her up whatever she did . . .

'Where's the most beautiful girl in the world?'

He was standing at the bottom of the staircase, and Kate, in the kitchen doorway, watched her as she stood at the top – dressed now in her old jeans and a sleeveless green angora jerkin: she posed for a moment, and then hurled herself down – hair flying, eyes shining – into his arms. He gave a great laugh, and held her at arm's length.

'Let's look at you. *Mrs* Thornton: let's have a look.'

'I'm fine, Daddy.' But Kate could hear that little touch of the gallant waif – knew that those dog-violet eyes were gazing at her father with the expression of quivering self-reliance that he would find irresistible. Was she play-acting, or was it real? Certainly their relationship was like the way fathers and daughters went on in bad films: even in these few weeks she had forgotten how much and how quickly it exasperated her.

'Mrs Thornton!' He had picked up her left hand now, and was contemplating the gold wedding ring quizzically. 'To think I should live to see the day! I tell you one thing. I'm jealous of Mr Thornton.'

'You needn't be. Oh – you smell – *nice*!'

Kate was conscious of a small, but regular, hammer thudding from somewhere inside her as she became miserably transfixed.

'And what, may I ask, does this call itself? He caressed the fluffy green jerkin that seemed to be fastened only in one place just below her breasts, so that the sides flew out to reveal the slender rib cage, tiny waist and concave upper belly.

'Really, Daddy – you are impossible! Your own daughter!' Some luxuriant head-tossing, and his hairy wrists picked from the sides of her jeans.

'How do you get your hair to shine like that!'

'My herbal rinse.' Demure now, walking towards her, ahead of him, into the kitchen.

('How dare you behave like this! – In front of your wife! Behind your husband's back!') She needed two voices to scream it, but her body felt like some roaring conduit of surging blood, with a trap-door slammed shut in the bottom of her throat. As they approached her, she began fiddling unsteadily with the strawberries in the colander before her.

'Oh – strawberries! How fabulous!' Kate recognized the

stringing-along-with-Mummy tone that so often came after what had gone before.

'Don't bother your mother now, she's busy, and I'm going to take you for a drink at the Woodman.' His hole-in-one-technique, she called that.

'Oh – great! Let's ride, Dad: we can ride through the wood and up the lane.'

A few minutes later, they were gone. There had been a few last moments of 'Sure you don't want any help?' 'Sure you don't mind?' followed by 'We'll be back at half past on the dot – promise,' and then they were off. She was left alone in silence – except for the cold tap dripping and the distant, velvety gabble of Percy's radio.

She discovered that things were taking on a dirty, speckled appearance, and she fumbled in her bag to find the orange pills encased in foil that helped to prevent migraine. Cafergot had to be crunched up to work quickly, and she washed down the cheap, stale chocolate taste with a glass of tap water. She wanted a cigarette, but that would be fatal. What she must do was to sit quite still, and relax, but that only made it more difficult to stop what she had just been thinking. After trying for a bit, it seemed reasonable – even mild – simply to dislike them, compared with what she felt about herself.

They came back to supper in high spirits with half a bottle of gin. She didn't dare have a drink, but he made Shirley and himself a couple of John Collins with a tin of grapefruit juice and soda. Supper was cold, so it didn't matter when they had it, and she did Percy's tray while they finished their drinks. Brian was in his entertaining, expansive mood; taking off the little girls he taught to ride; 'Oh –

Cuptain Ewbunk!' He was a good mimic – could do all the various off-white upper-class vowel sounds; could indicate the braces on their teeth, their stiff little pigtails below their hard velvet hats. He finished with a telling imitation of a fat and frightened girl being taught to jump. The sports mistress had many times told Kate how popular he was with the girls. And, of course, someone at the pub had thought Shirley was his girlfriend: Shirley thought that madly funny. She ate like a schoolgirl – three helpings of new potatoes and home-cooked tongue: 'It's so marvellous not cooking. I'm simply not the domesticated type, I've decided.' It wasn't until she returned from taking Percy his strawberries that she heard Brian say casually,

'There's no need for you to go back on Tuesday. Stay and help me knock some sense into that new pony. He's not safe for the children and he's not up to my weight.'

And Shirley, seeing her mother, said automatically: 'Oh – I couldn't. I'll have to go back.'

'Why not? If you stay a little extra, you might also knock some sense into that husband of yours.'

Kate said: 'Brian! Of course she must go back.'

'I don't see that. He shouldn't go flouncing off – out all night – that's no way to treat any woman – let alone your wife. Do him good to worry about her for a change.'

Kate turned to her daughter: 'Shirley, you don't really feel that you can—'

But Shirley, pouring cream on to her strawberries, said quickly: 'I was talking to Dad in the pub about it. I thought it would be interesting to know what another man thought, you know—'

'Damn right! Well, I think the sooner he learns that life

287

doesn't entirely revolve round his blasted television the better. I mean, he'd made a plan with Shirley, and he ought to have stuck to it, that's what he ought to have done. I mean, she's never going to know where she is, is she? One minute he makes a promise – the next minute he breaks it. That's no way to treat *any* girl – let alone *my* girl. Well?' Magnanimity was momentarily extended to her: 'What do you think?'

She took a long breath trying to control her anger at his outrageous attitude and said coldly, 'I think you should mind your own business.'

Before she had finished speaking, the telephone rang, and Shirley, glad of the escape, ran to answer it. A second later, she was back: 'It's Douglas. I'm going to take it upstairs. Will you put the receiver back for me?'

When she had done so, and returned to the kitchen determined to stop the irresponsible mischief he was making, Kate found him on his feet, cramming hunting flask, pipe and tobacco into his pockets; his face suffused, set sullen, avoiding her eye.

'I'm off. Forgot to fetch that liniment from the vet. The grey's been knocking herself. Forgot it earlier.'

'Don't bother to tell me a pack of—'

'Tell her not to wait up. I've promised her a ride in the morning.'

'Brian, listen to me. Don't you dare interfere any more with her marriage. It's not fair: it's very wrong.' It sounded weak as she said it, and he seized the advantage.

'*I'm* not interfering. She asked me what I thought, and I told her. That's natural, isn't it? She's only a child. And why should my opinion be any more interfering than yours? Tell me that.'

'You know perfectly well why it is. And she's no longer a child. She's a married woman.'

'I *don't* know. And I don't care. I do – not – care a bugger – what you think – about anything at all.'

He went, shutting, nearly slamming, the kitchen door behind him.

The telephone conversation seemed to be going on for ever. She supposed drearily that it must be a good sign they were talking at such length: she was sure Douglas cared. Poor boy, he was only twenty-two, had his way to make, and although he was reputed to be clever, cleverness was not particularly helpful when it came to making a marriage work – especially with someone as self-willed as Shirley. Could they, she and Brian, as parents, have stopped her marrying so young? If they had been united about it and had wanted to, she supposed they might just have – have made her wait longer, anyhow. But they were not united, and for different reasons neither of them had seen fit even to try. Brian had always thought that Shirley should have whatever she wanted, and she . . . she was ashamed of her reason – it wasn't even a reason really, just a hope, forlorn as it had turned out, that Brian would be – easier, a bit nicer to her, if Shirley simply wasn't there.

Her head felt as though someone had bruised something inside it rather badly, but she decided not to take any more of the migraine drug. When she had finished clearing supper, she noticed Shirley's cigarettes, and took one for something to do.

She heard Shirley ring off, and minutes later she strolled

into the kitchen, cool, expressionless, clearly pleased with herself.

'Where's Dad?'

'He's gone out – said don't wait up.'

'I wouldn't dream of going to bed yet. Whew! It's hot!' She sat on the corner of the table, kicked off her shoes and put her bare feet on the arm of her father's chair. Her toenails were painted a pale, pearly pink.

'Well – is everything better now?'

'Douglas? Oh – fine. He's coming down tomorrow.'

'Shirley, I am glad. How has he managed to get away?'

'Oh – some change in the shooting schedule – I didn't bother. The point is, I've won!'

Kate looked at her. 'How do you mean?'

She repeated impatiently, 'I've won! He wanted me to go back – to meet him at the flat, but I told him come down here or else.' She leaned across the table to take a cigarette.

'I took one, I hope you don't mind.'

'Feel free. Got a light?'

Kate struck a match and held it out, watching her daughter's face as she bent her head, cigarette poised in the wide Cupid's-bow mouth, heavy lashes lowered over the violet eyes, calmly intent upon her first puff.

'But he'll have to go back again on Monday night, won't he? It hardly seems worth it for such a little time.'

'He thinks it's worth it. Any case, he had no choice. Daddy was quite right. He'll think twice before he ever walks out on me again. I haven't even told him I'll go back with him for sure.'

'Shirley! You can't behave like this! You're just *playing* at being married! You can't be so—'

'I can! I can! I'm perfectly serious. He wants far more from me than I want from him. He's more turned on than I am. Let him sweat.'

There was a brutal pause, then she added with some feeling: 'I *hate* being alone. I *hate* that flat. I *loathe* being tied down. Daddy said I could stay as long as I like.'

Then, perhaps aware of some fractional discomfort from her mother's silence, she rose from the table and began looking for her shoes.

'Where's he gone to at this time of night?'

'To put some liniment on a horse.'

'In the stables?'

Kate hesitated only a moment: 'I expect in the stables.'

After she had gone, Kate remained completely still: why had she done it? But she refused to consider why – simply sat at the table and followed Shirley: down the garden path to the gate, along the drive to the archway; she might pause there to see if there was a light in the stables, but there would be no light since none was needed. Would she go on, as Kate had done that first time, long ago, because there had been an urgent telephone message? It had been autumn then, and dark, but some instinct had driven her to the stables door, undone at the latch and ajar. The horses had shifted softly in their straw; moonlight, like a shaft of lemonade, had lain across the little empty coal grate in the tack room and the place had the affectionate, sweet smell of warm horses and hay. She had stood there wondering (where could he have gone?), when, with shocking sudden-ness, and from just above her head, had come a high-pitched, explosively ugly and frightening laugh. Dead silence: she had heard her own heart beating . . . then a man's inaudible protest and heavy, sibilant, thrashing commotion. They were in the hay-loft; she had turned to see the ladder set squarely to its open trap. The laughter had begun moaning and she had fled. Since that first time, she had returned once or twice when he had hired new girls, but only enough to feed her reason, to keep her fearful hatred sane, because she had known that if there was no reason for feeling as she did, she must be mad.

She had done nothing. Shirley had been determined to go – she had simply not prevented her.

She became aware of Percy calling. He might have been calling for some time; for once she had forgotten him, and she hurried, with a feeling of shame, to his room. She had got him undressed and into bed before his supper, but had not even fetched his supper tray, let alone settled him for the night.

He gave her his gentle lop-sided smile as she came in; he had been sticking things into his scrap-book and seemed not to have noticed the time. As soon as he saw her, he began hunting through the back pages.

'You haven't eaten your strawberries!'

He gave her a reproachful look. 'Too many stones.' He was still searching in his book. 'Here! Found Douglas. Douglas and Shirley marriage.' It was the wedding picture cut out of the local paper. 'Douglas,' he explained again, in case she wasn't sure.

'Yes,' she agreed. She helped him out of bed to the lavatory, and got his pillows right for the night. His sheets seemed always to be covered with toast crumbs. She filled up his water-carafe, opened his window and put the box for his false teeth handy. When he was in bed again, she bent to kiss his cold, papery-dry forehead and he closed his eyes as though for a benediction. She picked up the supper tray and was turning to go when he suddenly thrust a screwed-up piece of paper at her, pushing it into her hand as though he was stopping up a chink.

'For you. To read.'

'All right, Father dear.' He sometimes wrote lists of what he needed: glue, fruit-drops, aspirin – that kind of thing.

'Read later.'

'Yes. I will.'

In the kitchen, Shirley stood heating something on the stove. She must have heard her mother come in, but neither turned round nor spoke.

Kate said: 'You're back.' She had begun to feel afraid.

'So it would seem.' Hostility was naked. She poured the contents of the saucepan into a mug and turned off the heat.

'Why did you let me go to the stables? You knew what was going on, didn't you? What made you do that?'

Kate tried to say something, but she was not a liar, and could not.

'I suppose you thought it would turn me against him, and make me sorry for you! Well it hasn't. I suppose you thought that as you don't enjoy screwing, you'd put me off it! It's him I'm sorry for – having to go to those lengths. I despise you – more completely than I've ever despised anyone in my life! Letting me go out there was just typical of how horrible you really are. Drab, and smug and self-righteous. Underneath it – you're just nasty. Nobody could love you – not a single person in the world!' Her hand holding the milk was shaking, but she didn't spill any – just walked out of the room, shutting the kitchen door behind her.

Kate stood, heart hammering, listening to the steps going away from her to the bedroom above. She put up her hand, to hold her face together, and the piece of screwed-up paper fell on to the table. When she smoothed it out the note, written large and quavering with a black felt pen, read: 'Thank you, my Darling, for the Lovely Outing in your Motor Car. Today.'

She read it for a long time. The message, with its drops of grateful love, made a slow, unsteady course, until eventually, in the end, it reached her.

Great Aunt Allie's Flypapers

BY P. D. JAMES

'You see, my dear Adam,' explained the Canon gently, as he walked with Chief Superintendent Dalgliesh under the Vicarage elms: 'Useful as the legacy would be to us, I wouldn't feel happy in accepting it if Great Aunt Allie came by her money in the first place by wrongful means.'

What the Canon meant was that he and his wife wouldn't be happy to inherit Great Aunt Allie's fifty thousand pounds if, sixty-seven years earlier, she had poisoned her elderly husband with arsenic in order to get it. As Great Aunt Allie had been accused and acquitted of just that charge in a 1902 trial which, for her Hampshire neighbours, had rivalled the Coronation as a public spectacle, the Canon's scruples were not altogether irrelevant. Admittedly, thought Dalgliesh, most people faced with the prospect of fifty thousand pounds would be happy to subscribe to the commonly held convention that, once an English Court has pronounced its verdict, the final truth of the matter had been established once and for all. There may possibly be a higher judicature in the next world but hardly in this. And so Hubert Boxdale would normally be happy to believe. But, faced with the prospect of an unexpected fortune, his scrupulous conscience was troubled. The gentle but obstinate voice went on:

'Apart from the moral principle of accepting tainted money, it wouldn't bring us happiness. I often think of that poor woman, driven restlessly round Europe in her search for peace, of that lonely life and unhappy death.'

Dalgliesh recalled that Great Aunt Allie had moved in a predictable pattern with her retinue of servants, current lover and general hangers-on from one luxury Riviera hotel to the next, with stays in Paris or Rome as the mood suited her. He was not sure that this orderly programme of comfort and entertainment could be described as being restlessly driven round Europe or that the old lady had been primarily in search of peace. She had died, he recalled, by falling overboard from a millionaire's yacht during a rather wild party given by him to celebrate her eighty-eighth birthday. It was perhaps not an edifying death by the Canon's standards but Dalgliesh doubted whether she had, in fact, been unhappy at the time. Great Aunt Allie (it was impossible to think of her by any other name), if she had been capable of coherent thought, would probably have pronounced it a very good way to go.

But this was hardly a point of view he could put forward comfortably to his present companion.

Canon Hubert Boxdale was Superintendent Adam Dalgliesh's godfather. Dalgliesh's father had been his Oxford contemporary and lifelong friend. He had been an admirable godfather: affectionate, uncensorious, genuinely concerned. In Dalgliesh's childhood, he had always been mindful of birthdays and imaginative about a small boy's preoccupations and desires.

Dalgliesh was very fond of him and privately thought him one of the few really good men he had known. It was only surprising that the Canon had managed to live to seventy-one in a carnivorous world in which gentleness, humility and unworldliness are hardly conducive to survival, let alone success. But his goodness had in some sense protected him. Faced with such manifest innocence, even those who exploited him, and they were not a few, extended some of the protection and compassion they might show to the slightly subnormal.

'Poor old darling,' his daily woman would say, pocketing pay for six hours when she had worked five and helping herself to a couple of eggs from his refrigerator. 'He's really not fit to be let out alone.' It had surprised the then young and slightly priggish Detective Constable Dalgliesh to realize that the Canon knew perfectly well about the hours and the eggs, but thought that Mrs Copthorne, with five children and an indolent husband, needed both more than he did. He also knew that if he started paying for five hours she would promptly work only four and extract another two eggs, and that this small and only dishonesty was somehow necessary to her self-esteem. He was good. But he was not a fool.

He and his wife were, of course, poor. But they were not unhappy, indeed it was a word impossible to associate with the Canon. The death of his two sons in the 1939 war had saddened but not destroyed him. But he had anxieties. His wife was suffering from disseminated sclerosis and was finding it increasingly hard to manage. There were comforts and appliances which she would need. He was now, belatedly, about to retire and his pension would be small. A legacy of fifty thousand pounds would enable them both to live in comfort for the rest of their lives and would also, Dalgliesh had no doubt, give them the pleasure of doing more for their various lame dogs. Really, he thought, the Canon was an almost embarrassingly deserving candidate for a modest fortune. Why couldn't the dear, silly old noodle take the cash and stop worrying? He said cunningly: 'Great Aunt Allie was found not guilty, you know, by an English jury. And it all happened nearly seventy years ago. Couldn't you bring yourself to accept their verdict?'

But the Canon's scrupulous mind was totally impervious to such sly innuendos. Dalgliesh told himself that he should have remembered what, as a small boy, he had discovered about Uncle Hubert's conscience – that it operated as a warning bell and that, unlike most people, Uncle Hubert never pretended that it hadn't sounded or that he hadn't heard it or that, having heard it, something must be wrong with the mechanism.

'Oh, I did, while she was alive. We never met, you know. I didn't wish to force myself on her. After all, she was a wealthy woman. My grandfather made a new will on his marriage and left her all he possessed. Our ways of life were very different. But I usually wrote briefly at Christmas and she sent a card in reply. I wanted to keep some contact in case, one day, she might want someone to turn to, and would remember that I am a priest.'

And why should she want that, thought Dalgliesh. To clear her conscience? Was that what the dear old boy had in mind? So he must have had some doubts from the beginning. But of course he had; Dalgliesh knew something of the story, and the general feeling of the family and friends was that Great Aunt Allie had been extremely lucky to escape the gallows.

His own father's view, expressed with reticence, reluctance and compassion, had not in essentials differed from that given by a local reporter at the time.

'How on earth did she expect to get away with it? Damned lucky to escape topping if you ask me.'

'The news of the legacy came as a complete surprise?' asked Dalgliesh.

'Indeed, yes. I only saw her once at that first and only Christmas, six weeks after her marriage when my grandfather died. We always talk of her as Great Aunt Allie but in fact, as you know, she married my grandfather. But it seemed impossible to think of her as a step-grandmother.

'There was the usual family gathering at Colebrook Croft at the time I was there with my parents and my twin sisters. I was barely four and the twins were just eight months old. I can remember nothing of my grandfather or of his wife. After the murder – if one has to use that dreadful word – my mother returned home with us children, leaving my father to cope with the police, the solicitors and the newsmen. It was a terrible time for him. I don't think I was even told that my grandfather was dead until about a year later. My old nurse, Nellie, who had been given Christmas as a holiday to visit her own family, told me that, soon after my return home. I asked her if Grandfather was now young and beautiful for always. She, poor woman, took it as a sign of infant prognostication and piety. Poor Nellie was sadly superstitious and sentimental, I'm afraid. But I knew nothing of Grandfather's death at the time and certainly can recall nothing of that Christmas visit or of my new step-grandmother. Mercifully, I was little more than a baby when the murder was done.'

'She was a music-hall artist, wasn't she?' asked Dalgliesh.

'Yes, and a very talented one. My grandfather met her when she was working with a partner in a hall in Cannes. He had gone to the South of France, with his man-servant, for his health. I understood that she extracted a gold watch from his chain and, when he claimed it, told him that he was English, had recently suffered from a stomach ailment, had two sons and a daughter, and was about to have a wonderful surprise. It was all correct except that his only daughter had died in childbirth leaving him a grand-daughter, Marguerite Goddard.'

'That was all easily guessable from Boxdale's voice and appearance,' said Dalgliesh. 'I can only suppose the surprise was the marriage?'

'It was certainly a surprise, and a most unpleasant one for the family. It is easy to deplore the snobbishness and the conventions of another age and, indeed, there was much in Edwardian England to deplore, but it was not a propitious marriage. I think of the difference in background, education and way of life, the lack of common interests. And there was the disparity of age. Grandfather had married a girl just three months younger than his own grand-daughter. I cannot wonder that the family were concerned, that they felt that the union could not, in the end, contribute to the contentment or happiness of either party.'

And that was putting it charitably, thought Dalgliesh. The marriage certainly hadn't contributed to their happiness. From the point of view of the family, it had been a disaster. He recalled hearing of an incident when the local vicar and his wife, a couple who had actually dined at Colebrook Croft on the night of the murder, first called on the bride. Apparently old Augustus Boxdale had introduced her, saying: 'Meet the prettiest little variety artiste in the business. Took a gold watch and notecase off me without any trouble. Would have had the elastic out of my pants if I hadn't watched out. Anyway, she stole my heart, didn't you, sweetheart?'

All this was accompanied by a hearty slap on the rump and a squeal of delight from the lady who had promptly demonstrated her skill by extracting the Reverend Arthur Venables's bunch of keys from his left ear.

Dalgliesh thought it tactful not to remind the Canon of this story.

'What do you wish me to do, sir?' he enquired.

'It's asking a great deal, I know, when you're so busy. But if I had your assurance that you believed in Aunt Allie's innocence, I should feel happy about accepting the bequest. I wondered if it would be possible for you to see the records of the trial. Perhaps it would give you a clue. You're so clever at this sort of thing.'

He spoke without flattery but with an innocent wonder at the strange vocations of men. Dalgliesh was, indeed, very clever at this sort of thing. A dozen or so men at present occupying security wings in HM prisons could testify to Chief Superintendent Dalgliesh's cleverness as, indeed, could a handful of others walking free whose defending counsel had been in their own way as clever as Chief Superintendent Dalgliesh. But to re-examine a case over sixty

301

years old seemed to require clairvoyance rather than cleverness. The trial judge and both learned counsels had been
dead for over fifty years. Two world wars had taken their
toll. Four reigns had passed. It was highly probable that, of
those who had slept under the roof of Colebrook Croft on
that fateful Boxing Day night of 1901, only the Canon still
survived. But the old man was troubled and had sought his
help, and Dalgliesh, with a day or two's leave due to him,
had the time to give it.

'I'll do what I can,' he promised.

The transcript of a trial which had taken place sixty-seven
years ago took time and trouble to obtain even for a Chief
Superintendent of the Metropolitan Police. It provided little
comfort for the Canon. Mr Justice Bellows had summed
up with that avuncular simplicity with which he was wont
to address juries, regarding them as a panel of well-inten-
tioned but cretinous children. And the facts could have
been comprehended by any child. Part of the summing up
set them out with lucidity:

'And so, gentlemen of the jury, we come to the night of
December 26th. Mr Augustus Boxdale, who had perhaps
indulged a little unwisely on Christmas Day, had retired to
bed in his dressing room after luncheon, suffering from a
recurrence of the slight indigestive trouble which had
afflicted him for most of his life. You will have heard that
he had taken luncheon with the members of his family and
ate nothing which they, too, did not eat. You may feel you
can acquit luncheon of anything worse than over-richness.

'Dinner was served at eight p.m. promptly, as was the

custom at Colebrook Croft. There were present at that meal Mrs Augustus Boxdale, the deceased's bride; his elder son Captain Maurice Boxdale with his wife; his younger son, the Reverend Henry Boxdale, with his wife; his grand-daughter Miss Marguerite Goddard, and two neighbours, the Reverend and Mrs Arthur Venables.

'You have heard how the accused took only the first course at dinner, which was ragout of beef, and then, at about eight-twenty, left the dining room to sit with her husband. Shortly after nine o'clock she rang for the parlour maid, Mary Huddy, and ordered a basin of gruel to be brought up to Mr Boxdale. You have heard that the deceased was fond of gruel, and indeed as prepared by Mrs Muncie, the cook, it sounds a most nourishing dish for an elderly gentleman of weak digestion.

'You have heard Mrs Muncie describe how she prepared the gruel according to Mrs Beaton's admirable recipe and in the presence of Mary Huddy in case, as she said, "The master should take a fancy to it when I'm not at hand and you have to make it". After the gruel had been prepared, Mrs Muncie tasted it with a spoon and Mary Huddy carried it upstairs to the main bedroom together with a jug of water to thin the gruel if it were too strong. As she reached the door, Mrs Boxdale came out, her hands full of stockings and underclothes. She has told you that she was on her way to the bathroom to wash them through. She asked the girl to put the basin of gruel on the washstand by the window and Mary Huddy did so in her presence. Miss Huddy has told us that, at the time she noticed the bowl of flypapers soaking in water and she knew that this solution was one used by Mrs Boxdale as a cosmetic wash. Indeed, all the women who spent that evening in the house, with the exception of Mrs Venables, have told you that they knew that it was Mrs Boxdale's practice to prepare this solution of flypapers.

'Mary Huddy and the accused left the bedroom together and you have heard the evidence of Mrs Muncie that Miss Huddy returned to the kitchen after an absence of only a few minutes. Shortly after nine o'clock, the ladies left the dining room and entered the drawing room to take coffee. At nine-fifteen p.m., Miss Goddard excused herself to the company and said that she would go to see if her grandfather needed anything. The time is established precisely because the clock struck the quarter hour as she left and Mrs Venables commented on the sweetness of its chime. You have also heard Mrs Venables' evidence and the evidence of Mrs Maurice Boxdale and Mrs Henry Boxdale that none of the ladies left the drawing room during the evening, and Mr Venables has testified that the three gentlemen remained together until Miss Goddard appeared about three-quarters of an hour after to inform them that her grandfather had become very ill and to request that the doctor be sent for immediately.

'Miss Goddard has told you that, when she entered her grandfather's room, he was just finishing his gruel and was grumbling about its taste. She got the impression that this was merely a protest at being deprived of his dinner rather than that he genuinely considered that there was something wrong with the gruel. At any rate, he finished most of it and appeared to enjoy it despite his grumbles.

'You have heard Miss Goddard describe how, after her grandfather had had as much as he wanted of the gruel, she took the bowl next door and left it on the washstand. She then returned to her grandfather's bedroom and Mr Boxdale, his wife and his granddaughter played three-handed whist for about three-quarters of an hour.

'At ten o'clock Mr Augustus Boxdale complained of feeling very ill. He suffered from griping pains in the stomach, from sickness and from looseness of the bowels. As soon as the symptoms began Miss Goddard went downstairs to let her uncles know that her grandfather was worse and to ask that Doctor Eversley should be sent for urgently. Doctor Eversley has given you his evidence. He arrived at Colebrook Croft at ten-thirty p.m. when he found his patient very distressed and weak. He treated the symptoms and gave what relief he could but Mr Augustus Boxdale died shortly before midnight.

'Gentlemen of the jury, you have heard Marguerite Goddard describe how, as her grandfather's paroxysms increased in intensity, she remembered the gruel and wondered whether it could have disagreed with him in some way. She mentioned this possibility to her elder uncle, Captain Maurice Boxdale. Captain Boxdale has told you how he handed the bowl with its residue of gruel to Doctor Eversley with the request that the doctor should lock it in a cupboard in the library, seal the lock and keep the key. You have heard how the contents of the bowl were later analysed and with what results.'

An extraordinary precaution for the gallant captain to have taken, thought Dalgliesh, and a most perspicacious young woman. Was it by chance or by design that the bowl hadn't been taken down to be washed up as soon as the old man had finished with it? Why was it, he wondered, that Marguerite Goddard hadn't rung for the parlour maid and requested her to remove it? Miss Goddard appeared the only other suspect. He wished he knew more about her.

But, except for those main protagonists, the characters in the drama did not emerge very clearly from the trial report. Why, indeed, should they? The British accusatorial system of trial is designed to answer one question: is the accused guilty beyond reasonable doubt of the crime charged? Exploration of the nuances of personality, speculation and gossip have no place in the witness-box. The two Boxdale brothers came out as very dull fellows indeed. They and their estimable, respectable sloping-bosomed wives had sat at dinner in full view of each other from eight until after nine o'clock (a substantial meal, that dinner) and had said so in the witness-box, more or less in identical words. The ladies' bosoms might have been heaving with far from estimable emotions of dislike, envy, embarrassment or resentment of the interloper. If so, they didn't tell the court.

But the two brothers and their wives were clearly innocent, even if a detective of that time could have conceived of the guilt of a gentlefolk so well respected, so eminently respectable. Even their impeccable alibis had a nice touch of social and sexual distinction. The Reverend Arthur Venables had vouched for the gentlemen, his good wife for the ladies. Besides, what motive had they? They could no longer gain financially by the old man's death. If anything, it was in their interests to keep him alive in the hope that disillusion with his marriage or a return to sanity might occur to cause him to change his will. So far Dalgliesh had learned nothing that could cause him to give the Canon the assurance for which he hoped.

It was then that he remembered Aubrey Glatt. Glatt was a wealthy amateur criminologist who had made a study of all the notable Victorian and Edwardian poison cases. He was not interested in anything earlier or later, being as obsessively wedded to his period as any serious historian, which indeed he had some claim to call himself. He lived in a Georgian house in Winchester – his affection for the Victorian and Edwardian age did not extend to its architecture – and was only three miles from Colebrook Croft. A visit to the London Library disclosed that he hadn't written a book on the case but it was improbable that he had totally neglected a crime close at hand and so in period. Dalgliesh had occasionally helped him with the technical details of police procedure. Glatt, in response to a telephone call, was happy to return the favour with the offer of afternoon tea and information.

Tea was served in his elegant drawing room by a parlour maid wearing a frilly cap with streamers. Dalgliesh wondered what wage Glatt paid her to persuade her to wear it. She looked as if she could have played a role in any of his favourite Victorian dreams and Dalgliesh had an uncomfortable thought that arsenic might be dispensed with the cucumber sandwiches. Glatt nibbled away and was expansive.

'It's interesting that you should have taken this sudden and, if I may say so, somewhat inexplicable interest in the Boxdale murder. I got out my notebook on the case only yesterday. Colebrook Croft is being demolished to make way for a new housing estate and I thought I would visit it

307

for the last time. The family, of course, haven't lived there since the 1914–18 war. Architecturally, it's completely undistinguished but one grieves to see it go. We might drive over after tea if you are agreeable.

'I never wrote my book on the case, you know. I planned a work entitled *The Colebrook Croft Mystery* or *Who Killed Augustus Boxdale?* But the answer was all too obvious.'

'No real mystery?' suggested Dalgliesh.

'Who else could it have been but Allegra Boxdale? She was born Allegra Porter, you know. Do you think her mother could have been thinking of Byron? I imagine not. There's a picture of her on page two of the notebook by the way, taken by a photographer in Cannes on her wedding day. I call it beauty and the beast.'

The old photograph had scarcely faded and Great Aunt Allie half-smiled at Dalgliesh across nearly seventy years. Her broad face with its wide mouth and rather snub nose was framed by two wings of dark hair swept high and topped, in the fashion of the day, by an immense flowered hat. The features were too coarse for real beauty but the eyes were magnificent, deep set and well spaced, and the chin round and determined. Beside this vital young Amazon poor Augustus Boxdale, clutching his bride as if for support, was but a very frail and under-sized beast. Their pose was unfortunate. She almost looked as if she were about to fling him over her shoulder.

Glatt shrugged. 'The face of a murderess? I've known less likely ones. Her Counsel suggested, of course, that the old man had poisoned his own gruel during the short time she left it on the washstand to cool while she visited the bathroom. But why should he? All the evidence suggests that he was in a state of post-nuptial euphoria, poor senile old booby. Our Augustus was in no hurry to leave this world, particularly by such an agonizing means. Besides, I doubt whether he even knew the gruel was there. He was in bed next door in his dressing room, remember.'

Dalgliesh asked: 'What about Marguerite Goddard? There's no evidence about the exact time when she entered the bedroom.'

'I thought you'd get on to that. She could have arrived while her step-grandmother was in the bathroom, poisoned the gruel, hidden herself either in the main bedroom or elsewhere until it had been taken into Augustus, then joined her grandfather and his bride as if she had just come upstairs. It's possible, I admit. But it is unlikely. She was less inconvenienced than any of the family by her grandfather's second marriage. Her mother was Augustus Boxdale's eldest child who married, very young, a wealthy patent medicine manufacturer. She died in childbirth and the husband only survived her by a year. Marguerite Goddard was an heiress. She was also most advantageously engaged to Captain the Honourable John Brize-Lacey, Marguerite Goddard, young, beautiful, in possession of the Goddard fortune, not to mention the Goddard emeralds and the eldest son of a Lord, was hardly a serious suspect. In my view Defence Counsel, that was Roland Gort Lloyd, remember, was wise to leave her strictly alone.'

'A memorable defence, I believe.'

'Magnificent. There's no doubt Allegra Boxdale owed her life to Gort Lloyd. I know that concluding speech by heart:

' "Gentlemen of the Jury, I beseech you in the sacred name of Justice to consider what you are at. It is your responsibility, and yours alone, to decide the fate of this young woman. She stands before you now, young, vibrant, glowing with health, the years stretching before her with their promise and their hopes. It is in your power to cut off all this as you might top a nettle with one swish of your cane. To condemn her to the slow torture of those last waiting weeks; to that last dreadful walk; to heap calumny on her name; to desecrate those few happy weeks of marriage with the man who loved her so greatly; and to cast her into the final darkness of an ignominious grave."

'Pause for dramatic effect. Then the crescendo in that magnificent voice. "And on what evidence, gentlemen? I ask you." Another pause. Then the thunder. "On what evidence?" '

'A powerful defence,' said Dalgliesh. 'But I wonder how it would go down with a modern judge and jury.'

'Well, it went down very effectively with that 1902 jury. Of course, the abolition of capital punishment has rather cramped the more histrionic style. I'm not sure that the reference to topping nettles was in the best of taste. But the jury got the message. They decided that, on the whole, they preferred not to have the responsibility of sending the accused to the gallows. They were out six hours reaching their verdict and it was greeted with some applause. If any of those worthy citizens had been asked to wager five pounds of their own good money on her innocence, I suspect that it would have been a different matter. Allegra Boxdale had helped him, of course. The Criminal Evidence Act, passed three years earlier, enabled him to put

310

her in the witness-box. She wasn't an actress of a kind for nothing. Somehow, she managed to persuade the jury that she had genuinely loved the old man.'

'Perhaps she had,' suggested Dalgliesh. 'I don't suppose there had been much kindness in her life. And he was kind.'

'No doubt, no doubt. But love!' Glatt was impatient. 'My dear Dalgliesh! He was a singularly ugly old man of sixty-nine. She was an attractive girl of twenty-one!'

Dalgliesh doubted whether love, that iconoclastic passion, was susceptible to this kind of simple arithmetic but he didn't argue. Glatt went on: 'The prosecution couldn't suggest any other romantic attachment. The police got in touch with her previous partner, of course. He was discovered to be a bald, undersized little man, sharp as a weasel, with a buxom wife and five children. He had moved down the coast after the partnership broke up and was now working with a new girl. He said regretfully that she was coming along nicely, thank you gentlemen, but would never be a patch on Allie and that, if Allie got her neck out of the noose and ever wanted a job, she knew where to come. It was obvious, even to the most suspicious policeman, that his interest was professional. As he said: "What was a grain or two of arsenic between friends?"'

'The Boxdales had no luck after the trial. Captain Maurice Boxdale was killed in 1916 leaving no children, and the Reverend Edward lost his wife and their twin daughters in the 1918 influenza epidemic. He survived until 1932. The boy Hubert may still be alive, but I doubt it. That family always were a sickly lot.

'My greatest achievement, incidentally, was in tracing Marguerite Goddard. I hadn't realized that she was still alive. She never married Brize-Lacey or, indeed, anyone else. He distinguished himself in the 1914–18 war, came successfully through, and eventually married an eminently suitable young woman, the sister of a brother officer. He inherited the title in 1925 and died in 1953. But Marguerite Goddard may be alive now for all I know. She may even be living in the same modest Bournemouth hotel where I found her. Not that my efforts in tracing her were rewarded. She absolutely refused to see me. That's the note that she sent out to me, by the way. Just there.'

It was meticulously pasted into the notebook in its chronological order and carefully annotated. Aubrey Glatt was a natural researcher; Dalgliesh couldn't help wondering whether this passion for accuracy might not have been more rewarding spent other than in the careful documentation of murder.

The note was written in an elegant upright hand, the strokes black and very thin but clear and unwavering.

Miss Goddard presents her compliments to Mr Aubrey Glatt. She did not murder her grandfather and has neither the time nor the inclination to gratify his curiosity by discussing the person who did.

Aubrey Glatt said: 'After that extremely disobliging note, I felt there was really no point in going on with the book.'

Glatt's passion for Edwardian England obviously extended to a wider field than its murders and they drove to Colebrook Croft high above the green Hampshire lanes in an elegant 1910 Daimler. Aubrey wore a thin tweed coat and deerstalker hat and looked, Dalgliesh thought, rather like a Sherlock Holmes, with himself as attendant Watson.

'We are only just in time, my dear Dalgliesh,' he said when they arrived. 'The engines of destruction are assembled. That ball on a chain looks like the eyeball of God, ready to strike. Let us make our number with the attendant artisans. You will have no wish to trespass, will you?'

The work of demolition had not yet begun but the inside of the house had been stripped and plundered, the great rooms echoed to their footsteps like gaunt and deserted barracks after the final retreat. They moved from room to room, Glatt mourning the forgotten glories of an age he had been born too late to enjoy; Dalgliesh with his mind on the somewhat more immediate and practical concerns.

The design of the house was simple and formalized. The first floor, on which were most of the main bedrooms, had a long corridor running the whole length of the façade. The master bedroom was at the southern end with two large windows giving a distant view of Winchester Cathedral tower. A communicating door led to a small dressing room.

The main corridor had a row of four identical large windows. The brass curtain rods and wooden rings had been removed (they were collectors' items now) but the ornate carved pelmets were still in place. Here must have hung pairs of heavy curtains giving cover to anyone who wished to slip out of view. And Dalgliesh noted with interest that one of the windows was exactly opposite the door of the main bedroom. By the time they had left Colebrook

Croft and Glatt had dropped him at Winchester Station, Dalgliesh was beginning to formulate a theory.

His next move was to trace Marguerite Goddard if she were still alive. It took him nearly a week of weary searching, a frustrating trail along the South Coast from hotel to hotel. Almost everywhere his enquiries were met with defensive hostility. It was the usual story of a very old lady who had become more demanding, arrogant and eccentric as her health and fortune waned; an unwelcome embarrassment to manager and fellow guests alike. The hotels were all modest, a few almost sordid. What, he wondered, had become of the legendary Goddard fortune?

From the last landlady he learned that Miss Goddard had become ill, really very sick indeed, and had been removed six months previously to the local district general hospital. And it was there that he found her.

The ward sister was surprisingly young, a petite, dark-haired girl with a tired face and challenging eyes.

'Miss Goddard is very ill. We've put her in one of the side wards. Are you a relative? If so, you're the first one who has bothered to call and you're lucky to be in time. When she is delirious she seems to expect a Captain Brize-Lacey to call. You're not he, are you?'

'Captain Brize-Lacey will not be calling. No, I'm not a relative. She doesn't even know me. But I would like to visit her if she's well enough and is willing to see me. Could you please give her this note.'

He couldn't force himself on a defenceless and dying woman. She still had the right to say no. He was afraid she would refuse him. And if she did, he might never learn the truth. He wrote four words on the back page of his diary, signed them, tore out the page, folded it and handed it to the Sister.

She was back very shortly.

'She'll see you. She's weak, of course, and very old but she's perfectly lucid now. Only please don't tire her.'

'I'll try not to stay too long.'

The girl laughed:

'Don't worry. She'll throw you out soon enough if she gets bored. The chaplain and the Red Cross librarian have a terrible time with her. Third floor, on the left. There's a stool to sit on under the bed. We will ring the bell at the end of visiting time.'

She bustled off, leaving him to find his own way. The corridor was very quiet. At the far end, he could glimpse through the open door of the main ward the regimented rows of beds, each with its pale blue coverlet, the bright glow of flowers on some of the tables, and the laden visitors making their way in pairs to each bedside. There was a faint buzz of welcome, a hum of conversation. But no one was visiting the side wards. Here, in the silence of the aseptic corridor, Dalgliesh could smell death.

The woman propped high against the pillows in the third room on the left no longer looked human. She lay rigidly, her long arms disposed like sticks on the coverlet. This was a skeleton clothed with a thin membrane of flesh beneath whose yellow transparency the tendons and veins were as plainly visible as an anatomist's model. She was nearly bald and the high-domed skull under its spare down of hair was as brittle and vulnerable as a child's. Only the eyes still held life, burning in their deep sockets with an animal vitality. But when she spoke her voice was distinctive and unwaver-

315

ing, evoking as her appearance never could the memory of imperious youth.

She took up his note and read aloud four words:

'It was the child. You are right, of course. The four-year-old Hubert Boxdale killed his grandfather. You signed this note Adam Dalgliesh. There was no Dalgliesh connected with the case.'

'I am a detective of the Metropolitan Police. But I'm not here in any official capacity. I have known about this case for a number of years from a dear friend. I have a natural curiosity to learn the truth. And I have formed a theory.'

'And now, like that poseur Aubrey Glatt, you want to write a book?'

'No. I shall tell no one. You have my promise.'

Her voice was ironic.

'Thank you. I am a dying woman, Mr Dalgliesh. I tell you that, not to invite your sympathy which it would be an impertinence for you to offer and which I neither want nor require, but to explain why it no longer matters to me what you say or do. But I, too, have a natural curiosity. Your note, cleverly, was intended to provoke it. I should like to know how you discovered the truth.'

Dalgliesh drew the visitors' stool from under the bed and sat down beside her. She did not look at him. The skeleton hands still holding his note did not move.

'Everyone in Colebrook Croft who could have killed Augustus Boxdale was accounted for, except the one person whom nobody considered, the small boy. He was an intelligent, articulate child. He was almost certainly left to his own devices. His nurse did not accompany the family to

Colebrook Croft and the servants who were there over Christmas had extra work and also the care of the delicate twin girls. The boy probably spent much time with his grandfather and the new bride. She, too, was lonely and disregarded. He could have trotted around with her as she went about her various activities. He could have watched her making her arsenical face wash and, when he asked, as a child will, what it was for, could have been told "to make me young and beautiful". He loved his grandfather but he must have known that the old man was neither young nor beautiful. Suppose he woke up on that Boxing Day night overfed and excited after the Christmas festivities? Suppose he went to Allegra Boxdale's room in search of comfort and companionship and saw there the basin of gruel and the arsenical mixture together on the washstand? Suppose he decided that here was something he could do for his grandfather?'

The voice from the bed said quietly:

'And suppose someone stood unnoticed in the doorway and watched him.'

'So you were behind the window curtains on the landing looking through the open door?'

'Of course. He knelt on the chair, two chubby hands clasping the bowl of poison, pouring it with infinite care into his grandfather's gruel. I watched while he replaced the linen cloth over the basin, got down from the chair, replaced it with careful art against the wall and trotted out into the corridor and back to the nursery. About three seconds later, Allegra came out of the bathroom and I watched while she carried the gruel into my grandfather. A second later I went into the main bedroom. The bowl of poison had been a little heavy for Hubert's small hands to manage and I saw that a small pool had been spilt on the polished top of the washstand. I mopped it up with my handkerchief. Then I poured some of the water from the jug into the poison bowl to bring up the level. It only took a couple of seconds and I was ready to join Allegra and my grandfather in the bedroom and sit with him while he ate his gruel.

'I watched him die without pity and without remorse. I think I hated them both equally. The grandfather who had adored, petted and indulged me all through my childhood and deteriorated into this disgusting old lecher, unable to keep his hands off this woman even when I was in the room. He had rejected me and his family, jeopardized my engagement, made our name a laughing stock in the County, and all for a woman that my grandmother wouldn't have employed as a kitchen maid. I wanted them both dead. And they were both going to die. But it would be by other hands than mine. I could deceive myself that it wasn't my doing.'

Dalgliesh asked: 'When did she find out?'

'She knew that evening. When my grandfather's agony began she went outside for the jug of water. She wanted a cool cloth for his head. It was then that she noticed that the level of water in the jug had fallen and that a small pool of liquid on the washstand had been mopped up. I should have realized that she would have seen that pool. She had been trained to register every detail. She thought at the time that Mary Huddy had spilt some of the water when

318

she set down the tray and the gruel. But who but I could have mopped it up? And why?'

'And when did she face you with the truth?'

'Not until after the trial. Allegra had magnificent courage. She knew what was at stake. But she also knew what she stood to gain. She gambled with her life for a fortune.'

And then Dalgliesh understood what had happened to the Goddard inheritance.

'So she made you pay?'

'Of course. Every penny. The Goddard fortune, the Goddard emeralds. She lived in luxury for sixty-seven years on my money. She ate and dressed on my money. When she moved with her lovers from hotel to hotel it was on my money. She paid them with my money. And if she has left anything, which I doubt, it is my money. My grandfather left very little. He had been senile and had let money run through his fingers like sand.'

'And your engagement?'

'It was broken, you could say by mutual consent. A marriage, Mr Dalgliesh, is like any other legal contract. It is most successful when both parties are convinced they have a bargain. Captain Brize-Lacey was sufficiently discouraged by the scandal of a murder in the family. He was a proud and highly conventional man. But that alone might have been accepted with the Goddard fortune and the Goddard emeralds to deodorize the bad smell. But the marriage couldn't have succeeded if he had discovered that he had married socially beneath him, into a family with a major scandal and no compensating fortune.'

Dalgliesh said: 'Once you had begun to pay you had no choice but to go on. I see that. But why did you pay? She could hardly have told her story. It would have meant involving the child.'

'Oh no! That wasn't her plan at all. She never meant to involve the child. She was a sentimental woman and she was fond of Hubert. No, she intended to accuse me of murder outright. Then, if I decided to tell the truth, how would it help me? After all, I wiped up the spilled liquid, I topped up the bowl. She had nothing to lose remember, neither life nor reputation. They couldn't try her twice. That's why she waited until after the trial. It made her secure for ever.

'But what of me? In the circles in which I moved at that time reputation was everything. She needed only to breathe the story in the ears of a few servants and I was finished. The truth can be remarkably tenacious. But it wasn't only reputation. I paid in the shadow of the gallows.'

Dalgliesh asked, 'But could she ever prove it?'

Suddenly she looked at him and gave an eerie screech of laughter. It tore at her throat until he thought the taut tendons would snap violently.

'Of course she could! You fool! Don't you understand? She took my handkerchief, the one I used to mop up the arsenic mixture. That was her profession, remember. Some time during that evening, perhaps when we were all crowding around the bed, two soft plump fingers insinuated themselves between the satin of my evening dress and my flesh and extracted that stained and damning piece of linen.'

She stretched out feebly towards the bedside locker. Dalgliesh saw what she wanted and pulled open the drawer.

There on the top was a small square of very fine linen with a border of hand-stitched lace. He took it up. In the corner was her monogram delicately embroidered. And half of the handkerchief was still stiff and stained with brown.

She said: 'She left instructions with her solicitors that this was to be returned to me after her death. She always knew where I was. But now she's dead. And I shall soon follow. You may have the handkerchief, Mr Dalgliesh. It can be of no further use to either of us now.

Dalgliesh put it in his pocket without speaking. As soon as possible he would see that it was burnt. But there was something else he had to say. 'Is there anything you would wish me to do? Is there anyone you want told, or to tell? Would you care to see a priest?'

Again there was that uncanny screech of laughter but softer now:

'There's nothing I can say to a priest. I only regret what I did because it wasn't successful. That is hardly the proper frame of mind for a good confession. But I bear her no ill will. One should be a good loser. But I've paid, Mr Dalgliesh. For sixty-seven years I've paid. And in this world, young man, the rich only pay once.'

She lay back as if suddenly exhausted. There was a silence for a moment. Then she said with sudden vigour:

'I believe your visit has done me good. I would be obliged if you'd return each afternoon for the next three days. I shan't trouble you after that.'

Dalgliesh extended his leave with some difficulty and stayed at a local inn. He saw her each afternoon. They never spoke again of the murder. And when he came punctually at two p.m. on the fourth day it was to be told that Miss

321

Goddard had died peacefully in the night with apparently no trouble to anyone. She was, as she had said, a good loser.

A week later, Dalgliesh reported to the Canon.

'I was able to see a man who has made a detailed study of the case. I have read the transcript of the trial and visited Colebrook Croft. And I have seen one other person, closely connected with the case but who is now dead. I know you will want me to respect confidence and to say no more than I need.'

The Canon murmured his quiet assurance. Dalgliesh went on quickly:

'As a result I can give you my word that the verdict was a just verdict and that not one penny of your grandfather's fortune is coming to you through anyone's wrong doing.'

He turned his face away and gazed out of the window. There was a long silence. The old man was probably giving thanks in his own way. Then Dalgliesh was aware of his godfather speaking. Something was being said about gratitude, about the time he had given up to the investigation.

'Please don't misunderstand me, Adam. But when the formalities have been completed I should like to donate something to a charity named by you, one close to your heart.'

Dalgliesh smiled. His contributions to charity were impersonal; a quarterly obligation discharged by banker's order. The Canon obviously regarded charities as so many old clothes; all were friends but some fitted better and were consequently more affectionately regarded than others.

But inspiration came:

'It's good of you to think of it, Sir. I rather liked what

I learned about Great Aunt Allie. It would be pleasant to give something in her name. Isn't there a society for the assistance of retired and indigent variety artists, conjurers and so on?'

The Canon, predictably, knew that there was and could name it.

Dalgliesh said: 'Then I think, Canon, that Great Aunt Allie would have agreed that a donation in her name would be entirely appropriate.'

'I'm So Happy For You, I Really Am'

BY KATHY LETTE

LOCATION: *a Soho Literary Club, frequented by the usual assortment of unpublished poets, failed film producers, Instant Celebrities and Chardonnay Socialists.*

INTERIOR. DAY. A MIDDLE-AGED WOMAN *sits alone at a table for two. She is one of London's high-powered television executives. Often photographed for* Tatler *and quoted on the* Guardian *Women's Page, she sports shoulder pads, a man's watch, silk lingerie and a Tory Party politician husband.*

A YOUNG WOMAN *approaches* . . .

My dear! I *knew* it was you, the *minute* you walked in. I just looked up and thought *yes*. That's *her*. That's just *got* to be Jerome's new friend. He told me on the phone that you looked, well, un*usual*. How *colourful*. You are *brave* to wear that in London, you *really* are . . . Besides, you can't see yourself from the *back*, so what does it matter, anyhow? I do so admire you younger girls. It's just so lovely the way you don't feel the need to keep up with fashion. Tea? . . . Oh, a drink? By all means. It's just that *I* try not to, you know, unless it's a *special* occasion . . . it does so age the skin.

– Waiter? One gin and tonic . . .? Yes and top up my tea will you?

So, you're in *love*. I'm so happy for you, I *really* am. Well – let me take a good look at you . . . When I heard that Jerome had delivered you from the wilds of the North . . . what? Oh Birmingham was it? Well, wherever . . . I just *had* to meet you. That's why I rang and arranged this little tête-à-tête. London can be so daunting. I always imagine that, to an *outsider* our little customs must seem as mysterious as, I don't know . . . a Japanese tea ceremony. So, I just want you to know that you can always come to *me* for advice. All of Jerome's other little friends have in the past. Oh God. Look who's heading our way . . .

ENTER *Another well-known television executive from a rival channel. She nods in their direction.*

Lucinda, dah-ling, hel-lo . . . Rupert? Oh yes. He's fine. Love the suit. Chanel? I had one just like it . . . *last* year . . . Tonight? Yes. I do hope Domingo's on form. See you at the reception . . . Oh, you *weren't*? You won't miss much. It'll be terribly tedious as usual. All bullying paparazzi oh, and the *Royals* of course . . .

For starters, stay right away from *her*. So *dull*. Don't you think that should be the only commandment? Thou shalt not bore? I loathe this place, I *really* do. But it is *the* literary club of London . . . You *are* interested in books aren't you dah-ling? Jerome always says that the only reading the working class can manage is the back of the cornflakes packet. He calls them 'Cornflake Conversationalists'. But he's very naughty. I mean, so far, you haven't even *men-*

tioned riboflavin or niacin, no, not *once . . . Anyhow*. I know it's a tiresomely trendy place and there's absolutely *no* privacy, but I thought you might like a glimpse of the cream of London society . . . What? No. By 'cream', I do *not* mean rich and thick . . . Gosh, how refreshing to know that Jerome's finally *maturing* – usually he goes for the *pretty* rather than the *witty* ones.

Oh dear . . . you haven't caught a London cough already have you? Here's some water. That's right. Take a big long drink. Château *Thames* I'm afraid. They say each glass has been through at least ten people already. Ghastly . . .

ENTER *Another Chanel-suited English woman. Having gone to Los Angeles, ostensibly to shore-up some West Coast business contacts, she has returned with the permanently startled expression of someone who has undergone plastic surgery.*

Dah-ling. Hel-lo . . . Rupert? Oh yes. He's fine. How's the little libel action going, you poor angel? Yes, gutter press. Oh and that frightful boy. Imagine selling his story . . . and to the *News of the World*. Absolutely ghastly . . . But you know that your friends believe you and that's what counts . . . Byee.

Can't bear that woman. You must have seen her in the papers. She's splashed all *over* the tabloids with her *toy-boy*. She used to be a very good agent, but *now* look at her? Did you see her face? I mean, that skin defied *gravity*. It's just so embarrassing when a woman can't act her . . . Oh God, now she's *waving* . . . Have they left yet? Good. Still it is *so* nice to see them *together again* . . . Oh yes, I *know* that wasn't her husband. I was talking about *her legs*.

Well . . . I'm so happy for you. I *really* am. I suppose Jerome has told you that I'm his oldest and closest friend. That's why I'm so keen to hear *all about you*. Now start at the very start. *I* first met him through my editor. . . . I was only a lowly hack way back then . . . what? No. No, he *didn't* tell me. What section of the paper are you working on, the Women's Page . . .? The Fin*ancial* Pages – oh well, how *int*eresting.

Any-how, 'Dah-ling,' my editor said to me, 'you and Jerome Forsyth were *meant* for each other.' Well, as you can imagine, I was *intrigued*. I arranged to interview him on some silly little story or other . . . a pictorial on dogs. That's right . . . 'up and coming young artists and their dogs.' Of course, Jerome doesn't have a dog, though, by God, he's slept with a few over the years. Has he introduced you to the dreaded Tiffany? She was last year's little number. It took me absolutely *months* to convince him what a disaster *she* was. So, *any*-how, Jerry and I met for lunch and well, the next thing I knew, it was back to his squat in Maida Vale . . . Oh, that *squat*! It was all smelly socks and women with moustaches and stale milk . . . Of course, *then* it was his idea of *luxury*. Oh, he knew nothing about *anything* in those days. Honestly, I had to start from scratch. Lots of potential, but still quite a barbarian . . . At first I thought it was just sex . . . By the way, does he still have that little fetish for clingfilm, whipped cream and rolled up copies of the *Guardian* . . .? Yes, by all means . . . My, you *are* thirsty.

Waiter . . .

But, then, silly boy, he went and fell in *love* with me didn't he? *Too* in love. And, well, I'm *married*. It was devastating for me actually. I hated to see what I was doing to him . . . I *begged* him to go out with other women. Really *begged*. I didn't want him wasting his whole life pining over me. I've never told anyone this, but I know I can tell you . . . He used to cry, truly weep, like a baby in my arms about how he could never, ever find someone to replace me. But, what could I do? . . .

What? . . . Leave Rupert? I *couldn't*. Impossible. You see, this has been the tragedy of my life. I'm married to *the* most remarkable man *in the world*. Can you imagine? Most women can't find *one* wonderful man and I ended up with *two*. And, of course a scandal of that kind would have ruined the chance of Rupert ever getting on in the Party . . . Family life is so important to Maggie. *And* to me too, of course. And well, let's face it, Jerome is not exactly the 'settling-down' type, now is he? . . .

You're *what? Moving in?* With *Jerome?* To our, *his* little flat? Oh . . . well . . . how wonderful. That's . . . I'm so happy for you, I *really* am.

Waiter? This tea is cold. Another pot.

As I said. I'm just so happy for you. I *really* am. God, you are certainly much more tolerant than I. You obviously don't mind the filthy plates all over the place and all that strange hair in the bathtub and oh! Those cockroaches! I never could break him of the habit of leaving food out. Oh and then there's the toilet seat. *Always* up. And never any loo paper . . . Ghastly. Oh, not to mention the other women . . .

What? *Monogamous? Jerome?* . . . Oh, excuse me laughing. Sorry? . . . A 'Male Feminist' . . . is that what he told you he is? My dear girl, Jerome treats women as *sequels* . . .

not equals. Honestly, I don't mean to laugh . . . but, look, it's just not in his *nature*. Jerome and I are old, *old* friends. How long have you known him? . . . Exactly. We always have been and always will be, the best and most intimate of friends. He still has my photos. I mean, the dah-ling man. I saw them the last time I was over at our, *his* flat, at Christmas. Beside his bed, in the drawer. As you know, we do still occasionally go to bed together, just for old time's sake . . . He did *tell* you about that didn't he? No? Oh well . . . I'm sure he *meant* to . . . God. There's that Booker Prize winner. I can never remember his name. Most boring book too . . .

ENTER *A young man. He clearly tries to avoid their table.*

Dah-ling . . . Rupert? Oh yes. He's fine . . . Congratu-lations. Fab-ulous book. Dazzling . . . The Pinters? Yes, on Sunday. We're being lectured to by some mar-vellous little green man from the Brazilian rain forest, I believe. See you there then. Byee.

I *hate* this place. I *really* do. Did you *hear* him? Dropping his *own name* . . . God, I *hate* being recognized. That's why I loved it so much when Jerome took me abroad on that little artist-exchange programme. The *anonymity*. So refreshing. It was like being an ordinary person again . . . *Any*-how, where was I? . . . Oh yes, I was trying to tell you why I didn't leave my husband for Jerome. The point is, that Jerry, dear as he is, is just not the type to really *commit* . . . never will, I'm afraid, that's the . . .

What? *Married*? To *Jerome*? Really . . . well . . . well . . . that is, well, it's mar-vellous news. I'm so happy for you, I

329

really am. Marriage . . . well, well, well. What are you doing *here* then? You should be at *home*, enjoying the romance before it fades. To be frank, that's another reason I chose not to leave Rupert and marry Jerry. It kept our affair so *vital*, so *alive*. Marriage does, well, *spoil* a man. You'll find that once married, his chief erogenous zone will be the second shelf of the pantry where he keeps the Mars bars. Yes, I'm afraid the only stiff thing about a *married* Englishman is his upper lip.

Waiter . . . Whisky.

God, marriage eh. But you know, meeting you today has reminded me just what a remarkable man Jerome is. In fact, that is truly one of his best qualities – the way he doesn't give a hoot about what other people think. *Courageous.* That's what he is. Because of course, his bohemian days are behind him. He's a very successful artist now. Really, one of the Establishment. And, of course, everyone expects him to be involved with a woman, well, with a woman of a *certain type* . . . I mean, it wasn't so long ago that Northerners were considered to be the dog turds on the sole of civilization. I've seen so many working-class types scraped off party invitation lists . . . Mind you, not *now*, so much. You don't see *me* checking the bottom of my shoes now do you? And you are lucky. You do seem to have lost your accent . . . *mostly*, don't you think? What? . . . Jerome said that did he? . . . Honestly . . . well . . . well . . . Yes. Yes, as a matter of fact I was born in Liverpool . . . but it was terribly fashionable in the sixties, you know.

But still, lovey, you're really going to need me to guide you through London's social minefield. What . . .? Well, of course you can look after yourself. Nobody said you

can't ... No, no, I don't doubt that you know what to
wear where ... by the way, it really is a lovely dress ... Did
you make it yourself...? No, no. I'm talking about what
to *say* where. Jerome's friends can be terribly daunting. It
can be difficult to know what to say to the Harolds and the
Antonias of this world. You see, they don't speak *English*
in this part of England. No. They speak *euphemism*. Oh,
yes, it's a completely different language. For example ...
let's see ... 'Do stay for *another* drink ... won't you?' is a
definite sign that you've outstayed your welcome. There!
You didn't know *that* did you? The way we talk must sound
positively Russian to an *outsider*, I've always thought. It's
sad, but not everyone you meet will be so *broad-minded*.
No matter how much you try, they'll never take you
seriously. You'll always be Jerome's 'little bit of fluff'. I'm
af ...

New York ... You're going to live in *New York?* Dah-
ling, living in New York is a contradiction in terms. Jerome
is an *Englishman*. He needs to be *here*, in the hub of things.
Doing his bit for civilization. We *are* still renowned for
our tolerance. Someone has to maintain all those values –
intellectual debate, the family ...

But wait! Wait! Speaking of families, yes, well ... I feel,
as a new *friend*, I should warn you that Jerome will *never*
consider them. *Children* that is. That was a tiny problem
between us. Men just don't understand a woman's *instincts*.
There's nothing sadder than the woman who's left it too
late because her husband didn't want children, don't you
think? I know it's hard to contemplate now, when you're
so young ... -*ish* ... but there will come a time when you'll

331

get a little wake-up call on the old biological alarm clock and . . .

Pregnant? Really? How far gone are . . . Well . . . that's, well, that's . . . I'm so happy for you, I *really* am. I mean, I'm so happy that you found out so *early.* It makes the little operation so much easier. I know a wonderful little man in Harley Street. *Everybody* goes there . . .

Oh, you both *want* it? . . . You both *planned* it. Really? Before you've established yourself in London, career-wise? Well, excuse me laughing . . . but I thought you were a genuine Feminist?

What? . . . But you can't *keep* the baby. You don't seem to understand . . .

CLOSE UP: *The middle-aged woman places her teacup crisply in its saucer and leans forward to scrutinize her young companion. For a fleeting moment she finds herself contemplating a trip to LA to shore up some West Coast business contacts.*

It is time, my dear, to *face facts.* What do you mean . . . *I* should? . . . I didn't intend to be quite this frank, but well, dah-ling, I just can't sit by and watch you ruin your life. That's why I always make a point of meeting Jerome's little friends. It's up to me to warn you that, well, it won't last. He's only *pretending* to love you, to spite *me.* The truth of the matter is, you are nothing more than a little inter-city souvenir. Jerome and *I* are *soul mates* . . . No. We *are.* Jerome has *always* been there for me. He *will* always be there for me. He *adores* me. *Forever. Nobody* and *nothing* can ever come between us . . .

Do calm down dear. That's a very cruel thing to say. Of

course he's always loved me. Just as I've always loved him. Dah-ling, ten years is a very long time . . . No. It is *not* a matter of having left my 'run too late'. My dear girl, you don't understand. Of course, I've had *other* lovers, but Jerome is my Grand Passion. We are made for each other. He'd be *nowhere* without me. If anything ever happened to Rupert, I have always intended to *marry* Jerome . . . Some people, *cruel* people say that I've been stringing him along for all these years . . . but Jerry knows my true situation. He knows that I only stayed with Rupert out of a blasted sense of duty. Not because of the money . . . or the status . . . or the Party . . . as I know some unkind people have . . .

Sorry? . . .

Who told you? . . .

Who?

Jerome? . . . He *knows* that Rupert's left me? . . . But who told . . .? How did . . .?

It doesn't matter who he's run off with . . . Well, yes, as a matter of fact it *is* his secretary . . . Ha, ha, ha . . . after all these years, can you imagine? I mean, you'd think that he could come up with something more original. A librarian, or a bloody Lithuanian for God's . . . I mean the Eastern bloc is so sensationally fashionable at the . . . Don't be so ridiculous. It's just the lemon in the tea. It makes my eyes water . . .

Waiter . . .

Do stay for *another* drink dear . . . won't you? . . .

Listen lovey. Save your sympathy. You'll need it for your-self, when Jerome dumps you. Because, of course, he'll come back to me . . . He will . . . He always does you know . . .

The middle-aged woman is now speaking to a retreating back. The waiter approaches.

Yes, you may clear away . . . My daughter? No. . . . *No.* She was *not* my daught . . . Could I have the bill . . . She's just a silly little girl who thinks she's in love. And well – if so, that's grand . . . I'm happy for her, I *really* am.

The Opium General

BY MICHAEL MOORCOCK

They had lived in a kind of besieged darkness for several weeks. At first she had welcomed the sense of solitude after the phone was cut off. They ignored the front door unless friends knew the secret knock. It was almost security, behind the blinds. From his ugly anxiety Charlie had calmed for a while but had soon grown morose and accusatory. There were too many creditors. The basement flat turned into a prison he was afraid to leave. When she had arrived three years ago it had seemed a treasure house; now she saw it merely as a record of his unrealized dreams: his half-read books, his comics, his toys, his synthesizers no longer stimulated him yet he refused to get rid of a single broken model Spitfire. They were tokens of his former substance, of a glorious past. When she suggested they go for a walk he said: 'Too many people know me in Notting Hill.' He meant the customers he had burned, taking money for drugs he never delivered, and the important dealers he had never paid. He tried to form a unity of his many frustrations: a general pattern, a calculated plot against him. A friend was murdered in a quarrel over sulphate at a house in Talbot Road. He decided the knife had been meant for him. 'I've made too many enemies.' This was his self-pitying phase.

She steered him as best as she could away from paranoia. She was frightened by overt instability, but had learned to feel relaxed so long as the signs were unadmitted, buried. In response to her nervousness he pulled himself together in the only way he knew: the appropriate image. He said it was time for a stiff upper lip, for holding the thin red line. She was perfectly satisfied, her sympathy for him was restored and she had been able to keep going. He became like Leslie Howard in an old war film. She tried to find somebody who could help him. This awful uncertainty stopped him doing his best. If he got clear, got a bit of money, they could start afresh. He wanted to write a novel: in Inverness, he thought, where he had worked in a hotel. Once away she could calm him down, get him to be his old self. But there remained the suspicion he might still choose madness as his escape. His friends said he habitually put himself into mental hospitals where he need feel no personal responsibility. He said, though, that it was chemical.

'Nobody's after you, Charlie, really.' She had spent hours trying to win round all the big dealers. She went to see some of them on her own. They assured her with dismissive disgust that they had written off his debts and forgotten about him but would never do business with him again. The landlord was trying to serve them with a summons for almost a year's unpaid rent and had been unnecessarily rude the last time she had appealed to him. She blamed herself. She had longed for a return of the euphoria of their first weeks together. There had been plenty of money then, or at least credit. She had deliberately shut out the voice of her own common sense. In her drugged passivity she let him convince her something concrete would come of his elaborate fantasies; she lent her own considerable manipulative powers to his, telling his bank manager of all the record companies who were after his work, of the planned tour, of the ex-agent who owed him a fortune. This lifted him briefly and he became the tall handsome red-headed insouciant she had first met. 'Partners in bullshit,' he said cheerfully. 'You should be on the stage, Ellie. You can be a star in my next road-show.' It had been his apparent good humoured carelessness in the face of trouble which made him seem so attractive to her three years ago when she left home to live here. She had not realized nobody in the music business would work with him any more, not even on sessions, because he got so loony. It was nerves, she knew, but he could be so rude to her, to everybody, and make a terrible impression. At the very last guest spot he had done, in Dingwalls, the roadies deliberately sabotaged his sound because he had been so overbearing. As Jimmy had told her gravely later: 'Ye canna afford to get up the roadies' noses, Ellie. They can make or break a set.' Jimmy Begg had been Charlie's partner in their first psychedelic group, but had split the third time Charlie got himself in the bin. It was a bad sign, Jimmy told her, when Charlie started wearing his 'army suit', as he had done to the Dingwalls gig.

Over the past two weeks Charlie had worn his uniform all the time. It seemed to make him feel better. 'Look out for snipers, Algy,' he warned her when she went shopping. He kept the shutters of the front room windows closed, lay in the bed all day and stayed up at night rolling himself cigarettes and fiddling with his little Casio synthesizer. He needed R&R, he said. When, through tiredness, she had

snapped at him not to be so silly, playing at soldiers, he
turned away from her sorrowfully: a military martyr, a
decent Englishman forced into the dirty business of war.
'This isn't any fun for any of us.' His father had been a
regular sergeant in the Royal Artillery and had always
wanted Charlie to go to Sandhurst. His parents were in
Africa now, running a Bulawayo grocery shop. He frequently addressed her as sergeant-major. Creditors became
'the enemy'; he needed more troops, reinforcements, fresh
supplies. 'What about a cup of coffee, s'a'rnt-major?' and
she would have to get up to make him one. His old friends
found the role familiar. They didn't help by playing up to
it. 'How's the general?' they would ask. He got out his
military prints, his badges, his model soldiers, his aircraft
charts. They were on every wall and surface now. He read
Biggles books and old copies of *The Eagle*.

His last phone call had been to Gordon in Camden.
'Morning to you, Field Marshal. Spot of bother at this end.
Pinned down under fire. Troops needing supplies. What
can you get to us?' Gordon, his main coke-supplier, told
him to fuck himself. 'The chap's gone over to the enemy.'
Charlie was almost crying. 'Turned yellow. Made of the
wrong bally stuff.' She pushed her long pale hair away
from her little oval face and begged him to talk normally.
'Nobody's going to take you seriously if you put on a funny
voice.'

'Can't think what you mean, old thing.' He straightened
his black beret on his cropped head. He had always been
vain but now he spent fifty per cent of his waking time in
front of the mirror. 'Don't tell me you're crackin', too.' He
rode his motorbike to Brixton and came back with cash,

claiming he had been cheated on the price. 'We're going to have transport and logistics problems for a bit, s'a'rnt-major. But we'll get by somehow, eh? Darkest before the dawn and so on.' She had just begun to warm to his courage when he gloomily added: 'But I suppose you'll go AWOL next. One simply can't get the quality of front-line chap.' All his other girlfriends had finally been unable to take him. She swore she was not the same. She made him a cup of tea and told him to go to bed and rest: her own universal remedy. It always seemed to work for her. Dimly she recognized his desperate reaching for certainties and order, yet his 'General' was slowly wearing her down. She asked her mother to come to stay with her for a couple of days. 'You should be on your own, love,' said her mother. She was discomfited by Charlie's role. 'Get yourself a little place. A job.'

Ellie spread her short fingers on the table and stared at them. She was numb all over. He had made her senses flare like a firework; now she felt spent. She looked dreadful, said her mother. She was too thin, she was wearing too much make-up and perfume. Charlie liked it, she said. 'He's not doing you any good, love. The state of you!' All this in a murmur, while Charlie napped in the next room.

'I can't let him down now.' Ellie polished her nails. 'Everybody owes him money.' But she knew she was both too frightened to leave and felt obscurely that she had given him more than his due, that he owed her for something. There was nobody else to support her; she was worn out. It was up to him. She would get him on his feet again, then he would in turn help her.

'You'd be better off at home,' said her mother doubtfully. 'Dad's a lot calmer than he used to be.' Her father hated Charlie. The peculiar thing was they were very much alike in a lot of ways. Her father looked back with nostalgia to wartime and his Tank Regiment.

She and her mother went up to Tesco's together. The Portobello Road was crowded as usual, full of black women with prams and shopping bags, Pakistani women in saris, clutching at the hands of two or three kids, old hippies in big miserable coats, Irish drunks, gypsies, a smattering of middle-class women from the other side of Ladbroke Grove. Her mother hated the street; she wanted them to move somewhere more respectable. They pushed the cart round the supermarket. 'At least you've got your basics for a bit,' she said. She was a tiny, harassed woman with a face permanently masked, an ear permanently deaf to anything but the most conventional statements. 'Bring Charlie to Worthing for a couple of weeks. It'll do you both good.' But Charlie knew, as well as anyone, that he and Ellie's dad would be at loggerheads within a day. 'Got to stay at HQ,' he said. 'Position could improve any moment.' He was trying to write new lyrics for Jimmy's band, but they kept coming out the same as those they'd done together ten years before, about war and nuclear bombs and cosmic soldiers. Her mother returned to Worthing with a set, melancholy face, her shoulders rounded by thirty years of dogged timidity. Ellie noticed her own shoulders were becoming hunched, too. She made an effort to straighten them and then heard in her mind Charlie (or was it her dad?) saying 'back straight, stomach in' and she let herself slump again. This self-defeating defiance was the only kind she dared allow herself. Her long hair (which Charlie insisted she keep) dragged her head to the ground.

That night he burned all his lyrics. 'Top Secret documents,' he called them. When she begged him to stop, saying somebody would buy them surely, he rounded on her. 'If you're so into money, why don't you go out and earn some?' She was afraid to leave him to his own devices. He might do anything while she was away. He'd have a new girlfriend in five minutes. He couldn't stand being alone. She had thought him sensitive and vulnerable when he courted her. They met in a pub near The Music Machine. He seemed so interested in her, at once charmingly bold, shy and attentive. He made her laugh. She had mothered him a bit, she supposed. She would have done anything for him. Could that have been a mistake?

'You've got to find out what you want,' said her sluttish friend Joan, who lived with an ex-biker. 'Be independent.' Joan worked at the health-food shop and was into feminism. 'Don't let any fucking feller mess you around. Be your own woman.' But Joan was bisexual and had her eye on Ellie. Her objectivity couldn't be trusted. Joan was having trouble with her old man yet she didn't seem about to split.

'I don't know who I am.' Ellie stared at the Victorian screen Charlie had bought her. It had pictures of Lancers and Guardsmen varnished brownish yellow. 'I was reading. We all define ourselves through other people, don't we?'

'Not as much as you do, dearie,' said Joan. 'What about a holiday? I'm thinking of staying at this cottage in Wales next month. We could both do with a break away from blokes.'

Ellie said she'd think about it. She now spent most of

her time in the kitchen looking out at the tiny overgrown yard. She made up lists in her mind: lists of things they could sell, lists of outfits she could buy, lists of places she would like to visit, lists of people who might be able to help Charlie. She had a list of their debts in a drawer somewhere. She considered a list of musicians and A&R men they knew. But these days all Charlie had that people wanted was dope contacts. Any nobody would let him have as much as a joint on credit any more. It was disgusting. People kept in touch because you could help them score. The minute you weren't useful, they dropped you. Charlie wouldn't let her say this, though. He said it was her fault. She turned friends against him. 'Why don't you fuck off, too? You've had everything I've got.' But when she began to pack (knowing she could not leave) he told her he needed her. She was all he had left. He was sorry for being a bastard.

'I think I'm bad luck for you.' Really she meant something else which she was too afraid to let into her consciousness. He was weak and selfish. She had stood by him through everything. But possibly he was right to blame her. She had let herself be entranced by his wit, his smiling mouth, his lean, nervous body so graceful in repose, so awkward when he tried to impress. She should have brought him down to earth sooner. She had known it was going wrong, but had believed something must turn up to save them. 'Can't we go away?' she asked him early one afternoon. The room was in semi-darkness. Sun fell on the polished pine of the table between them; a single beam from the crack in the shutters. 'What about that mate of yours in Tangier?' She picked unconsciously at the brocade chair left by his ex-wife. She felt she had retreated behind a wall which was her body, painted, shaved, perfumed: a lie of sexuality and compliance. She had lost all desire.

'And have the enemy seize the flat while we're there? You've got to remember, sergeant-major, that possession is nine-tenths of the law.' He lay in his red Windsor rocker. He wore nothing but army gear, with a big belt around his waist, a sure sign of his insecurity. He drew his reproduction Luger from its holster and checked its action with profound authority. She stared at the reddish hair on his thick wrists, at the flaking spots on his fingers which resembled the early stages of a disease. His large, flat cheekbones seemed inflamed; there were huge bags under his eyes. He was almost forty. He was fighting off mortality as ferociously as he fought off what he called 'the mundane world'. She continued in an abstracted way to feel sorry for him. She still thought, occasionally, of Leslie Howard in the trenches. 'Then couldn't we spend a few days on Vince's houseboat?'

'Vince has retreated to Shropshire. A non-pukkah wallah,' he said sardonically. He and Vince had often played Indian army officers. 'His old lady's given him murder. Shouldn't have taken her aboard. Women always let you down in a crunch.' He glanced away.

She was grateful for the flush of anger which pushed her to her feet and carried her into the kitchen. 'You ungrateful bastard. You should have kept your bloody dick in your trousers then, shouldn't you!' She became afraid, but it was not the old immediate terror of a blow, it was a sort of dull expectation of pain. She was seized with contempt for her own dreadful judgement. She sighed, waiting for him to respond in anger. She turned. He looked miserably at his

Luger and reholstered it. He stood up, plucking at his khaki creases, patting at his webbing. He straightened his beret in front of the mirror, clearing his throat. He was pale. 'What about organizing some tiffin, sergeant-major?'

'I'll go out and get the bread.' She took the Scottish pound note from the tin on the mantelpiece.

'Don't be long. The enemy could attack at any time.' For a second he looked genuinely frightened. He was spitting a little when he spoke. His hair needed washing. He was normally so fussy about his appearance but he hadn't bathed properly in days. She had not dared say anything.

She went up the basement steps. Powys Square was noisy with children playing Cowboys and Indians. They exasperated her. She was twenty-five and felt hundreds of years older than them, than Charlie, than her mum and dad. Perhaps I'm growing up, she thought as she turned into Portobello Road and stopped outside the baker's. She stared at the loaves, pretending to choose. She looked at the golden bread and inhaled the sweet warmth; she looked at her reflection in the glass. She wore her tailored skirt, silk blouse, stockings, lacy bra and panties. He usually liked her to be feminine, but sometimes preferred her as a tomboy. 'It's the poofter in me.' She wasn't sure what she should be wearing now. A uniform like his? But it would be a lie. She looked at herself again. It was all a lie. Then she turned away from the baker's and walked on, past stalls of avocados and Savoys, tomatoes and oranges, to the pawn shop where two weeks ago she had given up her last treasures. She paid individual attention to each electronic watch and every antique ring in the window and saw nothing she wanted. She crossed the road. Finch's pub was still open.

Black men lounged in the street drinking from bottles, engaged in conventional badinage; she hoped nobody would recognize her. She went down Elgin Crescent, past the newsagent where she owed money, into the cherry-and-apple-blossom of the residential streets. The blossom rose around her high heels like a sudden tide. Its colour, pink and white, almost blinded her. She breathed heavily. The scent came as if through a filter, no longer consoling. Feeling faint she sat on a low wall outside somebody's big house, her shopping bag and purse in her left hand, her right hand stroking mechanically at the rough concrete, desperate for sensation. Ordinary feeling was all she wanted. She could not imagine where it had gone. An ordinary life. She saw her own romanticism as a rotting tooth capped with gold. Her jaw ached. She looked upwards through the blossom at the blue sky in which sharply-defined white clouds moved very slowly towards the sun, like cut-outs on a stage. She became afraid, wanting to turn back: she must get the bread before the scene ended and the day became grey again. But she needed this peace so badly. She grew self-conscious as a swarthy youth in a cheap black velvet suit went by whistling to himself. With only a little effort she could have made him attractive, but she no longer had the energy. Panic made her heart beat. Charlie could go over the top any minute. He might stack all the furniture near the doors and windows, as he had done once, or decide to rewire his equipment (he was useless at practical jobs) and be throwing a fit, breaking things, blaming her because a fuse had blown. Or he might be out in the street trying to get a reaction from a neighbour, baiting them, insulting them, trying to charm them. Or he might be at the Princess

Alexandra, looking for somebody who would trust him with
the money for a gram of coke or half-a-g of smack and stay
put until closing time when he promised to return: restoring
his ego, as he sometimes did, with a con-trick. If so he
could be in real trouble. Everyone said he'd been lucky so
far. She forgot the bread and hurried back.

The children were still yelling and squealing as she
turned into the square in time to see him walking away
round the opposite corner of the building. He was dressed
in his combat beret, his flying jacket, his army-boots, his
sunglasses. He had his toy Luger and his sheath-knife on
his belt. Trembling, she went down the steps of the basement, put her key in his front door, turned it, stepped
inside. The whole of the front room was in confusion, as if
he had been searching for something. The wicker chair had
been turned over. The bamboo table was askew. As she
straightened it (for she was automatically neat) she saw a
note. He had used a model jeep as a weight. She screwed
the note up. She went into the kitchen and put the kettle
on. Waiting for the kettle to boil she flattened the paper on
the draining board:

*1400 hrs. Duty calls. Instructions from HQ to proceed at
once to battle-zone. Will contact at duration of hostilities.
Trust nobody. Hold the fort.*
– BOLTON, C-in-C, Sector Six.

Her legs shook as she crossed back to the teapot. Within
three or four days he would probably be in a police station
or a mental hospital. He would opt to become a voluntary
patient. He had surrendered.

Her whole body shook now, with relief, with a sense of her own failure. He had won, after all. He could always win. She returned to the front door and slowly secured the bolts at top and bottom. She pushed back the shutters. Carefully she made herself a cup of tea and sat at the table with her chin in her hand staring through the bars of the basement window. The tea grew cold, but she continued to sip at it. She was out of the contest. She awaited her fate.

Laura Norder

BY JOHN MORTIMER

'Little Margery's going to join the battle for Laura Norder,' Tim Oldroyd told their friends when his wife was appointed a magistrate. Law and order was one of his favourite expressions, something he had always 'stood for', but he made it sound as though what he was standing for was a curiously named woman, poor old Laura who was under constant threat from delinquent youth and the anarchist forces of the Party Opposite. When he boasted of his wife's appointment to the minor judiciary, it was as though he were announcing a singular and astonishing triumph of his own. As he told her every time the subject was mentioned, which was with embarrassing frequency, she would never have got the job if she hadn't had the good fortune to be the wife of Tim Oldroyd, Member of Parliament for Boltingly and a parliamentary secretary at the Ministry of the Family.

Tim Oldroyd had been a pallid, shy young man, until some lurking ambition, as hidden up till then as an inherited disease, led him to stand for the seat at Boltingly. A change came over him. He announced that he was now to be known as 'Tim', in the modern way of politicians. He became even paler and grew a paunch and a little sandpaper moustache. His voice, always high-pitched, now emerged as a prolonged whine of outrage. The most frequent objects of his falsetto wrath were schoolteachers, one-parent families, unemployed school leavers who went joy riding and traded soft drugs in the town's precincts, and those who slept in wigwams or up trees in protest at the new eight-lane super-highway across Boltingly Meadows. His rage was frequently directed at his wife, and then his squeals were weighted with sarcasm and interrupted by moments of light laughter. 'For God's sake, pay attention in court, Margerine!' he told her. 'You know how you tend to let your mind wander. Don't wool-gather! The clerk's there to stop you doing anything damn silly. Just get it into your head that, in this country, people don't get stood in the dock unless they've committed something fairly outrageous. Support the police, and you won't go far wrong. Who's your chairman?'

'Dr Arrowsmith.'

'Frank Arrowsmith's a wise old bird.' The Oldroyds knew all the important people in Boltingly. 'Listen carefully to what Frank's got to say. Follow his instructions to the letter, and you won't go far wrong. I'm sure he won't expect you to make a contribution of any sort. Are you listening, Jerry?'

In fact his wife was staring out of the window at her garden, the lawn she mowed to a soft green velvet and the long border, set against an old brick wall, in which the flowers were all white. The garden, more than anything else in her life, was what kept her with Tim.

'Yes, I'm listening,' she said.

'I don't suppose you've got a suitable hat?'

'I'm afraid not.'

'Pity! In the good old days, lady magistrates wore hats. Made them look imposing. That's not your line of country, is it, Margery? You couldn't look imposing, with or without a hat on you.'

From behind the coffee-pot, across the polished oval table with its Laura Ashley place-mats and Portmeirion breakfast china, Margery Oldroyd looked at her husband and wondered if he'd seem more imposing in a hat, a Princess Di straw perhaps, with an upturned brim and a long ribbon, or a more ornate affair with feathers and artificial roses. How would Tim look, crowned with bobbing cherries like his dreadful mother? This unexpected thought made her giggle.

'And do try not to giggle in court, Margerine.' Her husband issued a serious warning. 'There's a breakdown of respect for all established institutions. As things are today, we really can't afford a magistrate who giggles.' With that he left the breakfast table for the lavatory, and Bagpiper, the Scottie dog which, in the Oldroyd family, filled, inadequately, the place of a child, rose from the hearthrug and strutted off looking, in its own small way, as superior and discontented as its master.

Margery Oldroyd looked back on twenty-five years of astonishing emptiness. She and Timothy had been at Keele University together. A quarter of a century before, at a party in the JCR, when Tim was a skinny student with fairish hair falling into his eyes, she had felt moved by the resolute and purposeful manner, that doomed but bravely undertaken battle against his nonexistent sense of rhythm, in which he had tried to dance alluringly to 'I Can't Get No Satisfaction'. She was a spritely dancer, light on her feet as plump people are, a girl with large, surprised eyes who giggled a good deal. She was attracted by something in Timothy missing in herself, and took it for an infinite ambition: she couldn't guess that it would be so quickly satisfied by becoming a parliamentary secretary and the member for Boltingly. After the JCR dance she led him to her room and steered him towards the bed. When, in a remarkably short time, it was over, she smoothed back his straying lock of sandy hair and mistook his incompetence as a lover for sincerity.

Nothing, on that evening, prepared her for the stranger he was bound to become; nor for the alarming intensity with which, she found, she had grown to hate him. This hatred had been born and grew like an advanced and over-active child, even before he started calling her Margerine.

On the magistrates' training course, when they were lectured and questioned on the elements of the law and basic court procedure, Margery had found herself unexpectedly popular. She listened hard, picked up knowledge quickly, and showed no signs of giving trouble. Now her first day had come, and she was surprised at how calm she felt, far calmer than she had been at breakfast, when her hatred of Tim bubbled up from her stomach and seemed likely to choke her. Now, on the bench, she felt as though she were at a pleasant dinner party to which, she was thankful to say, her husband hadn't been invited. She sat on the chairman's left. A retired GP, Frank Arrowsmith had the confidence of a man who, throughout his life, had found it easy to charm women. He may not have been a particularly clever doctor, but he was always a popular one. Now he sat back at ease in his high-backed, leather-seated chair, listened to tales of distress with a faint smile of amusement, and imposed fines, or brief terms of imprisonment, in the soft, reasonable voice he had used to recommend a course of antibiotics or a fat-free diet. On the other side of the chairman sat Gordon Burt, a prosperous garage owner whose skin and clothes hung loosely about his body in greyish folds, giving this squat man, Margery often thought, the appearance of a baby elephant. The first time the comparison had occurred to her she had giggled.

The new Magistrates Court in Boltingly was built of glass and concrete. Inside there was a pervasive smell of furniture polish and disinfectant, and the air-conditioning hummed in a soporific fashion. During the first batch of cases, Margery's attention wandered. She thought of Tim in his office, accepting a cup of coffee from Charlotte, his inevitable researcher. Charlotte, naturally, was everything Margery wasn't, young, slender, intelligent, the possessor of a First in PPE from Lady Margaret Hall, the owner of a 'super little Lotus Elan' which she could drive with skill at speeds Margery could never manage. A girl who, as Tim frequently told her, 'knew her opera' as Margery never would, although whether the world of opera belonged to Charlotte and no one else, or whether the talented researcher had a private opera of her own, Margery had only once asked, to be met with a look of contempt. Charlotte, she knew perfectly well, was someone to whom Tim made love with greedy haste during lengthy lunch hours or late-night sittings. She would never become Charlie, or even

Lottie, although Margery had quickly been demoted to Marge or Jerry and, for some years now, to Margerine.

'If the bench pleases, may I mention the separation order made in this court?' she heard a solicitor ask in respectful tones, as though from a long way off. Why hadn't she separated from Tim, or even divorced him? He was never tired of telling her that any hint of a broken marriage in the Ministry of the Family would severely 'embarrass the government', as though she cared how embarrassed the government became. When he said this, half threateningly, half in pathetic entreaty, she nursed her ever-increasing dislike in silence. Why should she separate from him and move out of the house and away from the garden she loved, to live in a rented flat in Boltingly and haggle over her maintenance, as the couple were going to haggle now in court in front of her? The story of her marriage would, she knew, have some ending, but not that one. So far as Tim Oldroyd, MP, was concerned, she thought, separation was far too good for him.

'This is the murder,' Dr Arrowsmith smiled and whispered, calling for attention in the way a bridge player might remind her, 'Your deal, partner.' It was the big event in the Boltingly magistrates' day, R. *v.* Mustoe, a committal in a murder trial. Margery picked up her pencil and gave the case her full attention.

The man who had been led into the dock, guarded by two prison officers, looked puzzled. He wore jeans and an anorak, and he stared around the court as though he wasn't sure of its reality, or whether he was in a dream. He had brown curling hair that he wore rather long, and he had, Margery noticed, delicate hands with tapering fingers. He seemed, on the whole, to be taking little interest in the proceedings.

'Mr Mustoe and his common-law wife Louise had been separated for some six months. She was living in a mobile home up by Boltingly Meadows, and he was sleeping, as he told the officer in charge of the case, "rough". Apparently he had reason to believe she had formed a relationship with a man working on the new super-highway. Er . . . um—' The young man from the Crown Prosecution Service shuffled his papers nervously and cleared his throat. He looked hot and uncomfortable. What's he worrying about? Margery wondered. This was only a preliminary hearing. He had nothing to do but call a few witnesses to show that there was a case sufficient to send up to the Crown Court. Mr Mustoe's solicitor, a lined and yellowing old professional who spent every day in some local criminal court, closed his eyes, leant back, and offered no assistance.

'On the night of the twelfth of April,' the prosecutor resumed uncertainly, 'Mr Mustoe was seen by several witnesses approaching the mobile home. He hammered on the door and was finally let in. Witnesses later heard sounds of quarrelling. We don't know what time Mr Mustoe left, but in the morning Louise Rollins's partner, who had been away for several days, returned and found her dead. The cause of death – you will hear the doctor's evidence – was manual strangulation. Certain fingerprints—'

'Not admitted!' the old professional boomed without getting to his feet, and the young man from the Crown Prosecution Service subsided meekly.

'Yes?' Dr Arrowsmith raised his eyebrows at the old professional, who now rose, his hands clasped together on his stomach, and boomed again, 'The fingerprints are not admitted. I shall be cross-examining the officer.'

'But the manual strangulation,' the retired doctor probed gently. 'Is that admitted?'

'Oh yes, sir. We admit manual strangulation. By *somebody*.'

Gazing vaguely round the court, Mr Mustoe, the man accused, caught Margery's eye, and for no particular reason, smiled at her.

'Such amateurs, these criminals! I believe they want to be caught. Why didn't that fellow Mustoe take the precaution of learning a little basic anatomy?' At half-past four the committal proceedings had been adjourned until the following Monday. Mr Mustoe was remanded in custody, and the magistrates retired to their room to enjoy their statutory tea and biscuits before dispersing. Dr Arrowsmith stretched out his long, well-tailored legs and sipped the watery Lapsang of which he brought his own supply. 'I'm not going to ruin the lining of my stomach with the prison officers' Indian you could stand a spoon up in,' he always said.

'Anatomy?' Mr Burt preferred the local brew. 'How would that help him?'

'My dear Gordon, you might know all about second-hand cars, but you'd make a rotten murderer. The carotid sinus is the place to find. Only a slight pressure needed, it wouldn't leave any bruising you'd notice, and the victim would lose consciousness and be in deep, deep trouble.'

'Losing consciousness wouldn't be enough to kill anyone, though. This fellow Mustoe was out to kill her.' Margery watched as the baby elephant spooned sugar into the prison officers' tea.

'Whether the victim came out alive would depend on the situation she was in. Or he. A small squeeze and they'd be helpless.' The doctor had finished his chocolate biscuit and pulled out a silk handkerchief to wipe his fingers, on the backs of which Margery noticed small clusters of black hair. Hair came out from below his white, gold-linked shirt cuffs also, and encircled his wristwatch.

'Well, anyway.' Mr Burt sounded unconvinced. 'Where are these carotid whatever they are anyway?'

'Feel your neck. Gently now. Got the Adam's apple? Now on each side, little swellings . . . the carotid sinuses.'

Mr Burt stirred his tea as Dr Arrowsmith talked them through it, but Margery's fingers went to her neck, only a little creased by the years since she had been a student and met Tim. Now she had found the exact spot.

'I'm afraid this is rather a morbid sort of a conversation for teatime.' The doctor chairman was smiling at her again. 'No doubt it's a good thing for all of us that the criminal classes are so poorly educated. Now. Let's talk about something far more pleasant. How's your delightful garden, Margery? Don't I remember, when you were kind enough to have Serena and me over to dinner, your lovely white border? What was it that smelled so delicious?'

'That would have been the syringa, I think,' Margery told him. 'Thank you, yes. The garden's still beautiful.'

That night the Oldroyds were invited to a dinner given by the Boltingly Chamber of Commerce, a black tie affair at which Tim was to make a speech and Margery would look up at him admiringly as he painted a rosy picture of the economic situation.

Tim got home early so he would have plenty of time to change. He was greeted on the stairs by Bagpiper, who appeared embarrassingly affectionate and shot, like a bullet, at his flies. He did his best to calm the dog and then ran himself a bath.

He and Charlotte had enjoyed lunch in an Italian place in Horseferry Road and then retired to a small hotel near Victoria Station that offered reduced prices for an afternoon. Charlotte was an olive-skinned girl with thick, wiry hair, not as pretty as he would have liked her to be, and she left a musky smell on him that he was anxious to wash away. He cherished the illusion that Margery knew nothing of the way he spent his afternoons.

Tim always enjoyed his bath and avoided hotels that only offered a shower. He lay back gratefully and turned the tap on with his toe. As the warm water caressed him, the years seemed to drift away, and he was back in his student days; he sang, as he once had at a dance, 'I Can't Get No Satisfaction'. The noise of the taps and his singing drowned the footsteps behind him. The strong fingers that closed on his neck were like those of a lover.

Margery had been back to the house earlier. Then she waited, at the end of the garden, until she heard Tim's car. When he had gone upstairs, she stood by the back door until she heard the bath water running. He's washing off the smell of Charlotte, was what she said to herself. Then she went shopping in Waitrose, taking care to talk to as many acquaintances as possible. When she returned to the house, Bagpiper was kicking up a high-pitched yapping fuss, and water was dripping down the stairs. She turned off the tap and telephoned a Dr Helena Quinton who had taken over the practice of Dr Arrowsmith, now retired. Then she walked into the garden. The smell of the syringas was sweet and heavy and produced, in her, thoughts of love.

Margery wasn't back in court until the following Monday, for the adjourned hearing of the Mustoe committal. She parked neatly in the space marked Magistrates Only and went up to their room. Gordon Burt was always late, but Dr Arrowsmith was there in excellent time, drinking coffee and eating a digestive biscuit; the chocolate-covered ones were reserved for teatime.

'Margery, dear. I am most terribly sorry.' He stood and spoke very gently, using his best bedside manner.

'Thank you. And thank you and Serena for your note.'

'The funeral's tomorrow, isn't it? We'll be there, of course.'

'That's kind.'

'Helena Quinton said it must have been a sudden heart attack. The poor fellow was unconscious and then drowned. Of course, he'd been overworking terribly. Politics makes such terrible demands nowadays—'

'I blame myself.'

'Why on earth?' The doctor's arm was round her

shoulder. He was old, too old for work, but he had had, she knew, many mistresses and the smell of eau de cologne on his handkerchief was as strong as the smell of syringas.

'If only I hadn't gone shopping! If only I'd been there, in the house, when he came back.'

'That's ridiculous.'

'I felt something was wrong when I was in Waitrose. It must have been a kind of—'

'Telepathy?' the wise old doctor suggested.

'Yes.'

'You two were very close. I know you were.' There was a small silence, and he squeezed her shoulder. 'We must see more of you now. We mustn't let you be lonely.'

He moved away from her, it seemed reluctantly, when the pachyderm Mr Burt arrived in a hurry. He had also written a note and spoke softly to Margery, as though they were in church together.

'The Mustoe case,' Dr Arrowsmith became businesslike now that they were all assembled. 'Now, I don't know what we're going to hear today, but the evidence is already overwhelming. I suppose there's no doubt we're sending him for trial?'

'No doubt at all.' Gordon Burt's mouth was half full of digestive biscuit.

'Margery?'

'Oh, Tim always said I was to pay strict attention to what you said and follow your instructions. I must do that, he told me, for the sake of law and order.'

She ran the last syllables together so they sounded like a woman's name, 'Laura Norder'. And as she said it, she couldn't suppress a giggle.

Simon

BY PATRICK O'BRIAN

Simon, reading on the hearthrug, looked up and asked, 'What is a whoremonger?'

'I don't know, my dear,' said his mother, absently, poking the fire: and when she had the logs just so she added, 'But I believe it is pronounced hore, with no w. What is that book?'

'It is an enormous history of England, about Cromwell.' The news of the pronunciation of whore drove history from Simon's mind, for it shed a sudden and brilliant light on odd scraps of conversation he had heard in the kitchen: scraps that children are more likely to pick up than others. 'Maggie is going with Alfred now . . . Maggie is going with Mrs Gregory's William . . . Maggie is going with George . . . Maggie goes with soldiers from the camp.' 'That Maggie,' said Mrs Hamner, the bearded cook, 'is now the village whore.'

The word, formerly connected only with frost and aged heads, instantly took on a meaning more consonant with Mrs Hamner's disapproving tone, since from the context of Cromwell's remark it was clear that whore and harlot were the same creature: Simon knew all about harlots, except for what they actually did, and he was charmed to be so well acquainted with one in the flesh. It was like knowing a phoenix, or Medusa.

'I shall go and tell Joe,' he said to himself, and although the fire, the hearthrug and the after-tea comfort were wonderfully attractive he closed the book and hurried out.

Joseph was his elder brother, a heroic figure, already at the university, who spent these evenings of the vacation out with his gun, shooting the odd early rabbit along the edge of Barton Wood or the pigeons as they came in to roost. Simon sometimes went with him, to pick up birds, and he had noticed how cheerfully he could greet Maggie if they met, and she coming home from work: familiar greetings, Christian names, laughter. Joe would be delighted to know that she was the village whore, or harlot.

The question was, where would Joseph be? There were many possibilities, Barton being a fair-sized wood; but in the end he decided on the corner jutting out into Halfpenny Fields, where the path from Wansbury and its glove-factory meandered across the pasture to the village. There might be some mushrooms there, and in any case Joe would probably come back that way when it was too dark to shoot.

Simon, big with his news, reached the corner far too early: there were no mushrooms, and although two white scuts fled away into the undergrowth there were no birds coming in yet. Simon lingered for a while, wondering what harlots really did and trying to hoot like an owl through his fists, their thumbs joined tight.

Presently he heard a couple of shots far over on the left hand. Joseph must be shooting the pigeons feeding on Carr's broad stretch of kale: unless indeed it was the Carr boys themselves. No. It must be Joseph – the Carrs were at a football match far beyond Wansbury – and he must come back this way. Simon was certainly not going to walk along the wood to meet him and be cursed for putting down all the rabbits; nor would he cut across, with the likelihood of missing him in the thick stuff. He would fool about here, looking for a straight wand that would do for a bow until Joe appeared.

Simon was an enterprising, bird's-nesting little boy, and in this part of the wood he had found a wool-lined crow's nest last spring as well as many of the frail transparent rafts upon which pigeons laid, and of course the ordinary thrushes and blackbirds along the edge. He knew the place quite well. Yet fairly close to the path there was an oak he had never particularly noticed: not a promising tree for nests, but now with so many leaves already fallen, at a modest height he saw a rounded mass that might well be a squirrel's dray. With its twisted, nobbly old trunk the oak was easy enough to climb until he could reach the branches, and although the dray was too old and sodden to be of any interest, Simon, on coming back to the crown, observed with delight that the oak's trunk was hollow. And not only hollow but provided with a hole at the bottom, through which the evening light showed plainly: one could drop down inside the tree, down on to the deep bed of leaves, push them away and shoot out of the hole, terrifying or at least astonishing one and all. If only the tree were right on the path rather than some way into the wood the effect would be prodigious; but even so it would still be very great. An eldritch shriek might help, since it would make people look in the right direction.

He lowered himself carefully into the hollow, hung from

the edge at arm's length, let go and dropped, dropped much farther than he had expected, into the leaves. They too were far deeper than he had thought they would be, and much wetter. Under the top layer, brown and dry on the surface, like breakfast-food, came first a porridgy mass and then a vegetable mud, knee-deep. Already his shoes and stockings were hopelessly compromised; and he had scarcely realized the depth of this misfortune before he found that clearing the leaves did not enlarge the hole for more than the handsbreadth of dry on top. That was why the rest was like so much thick and indeed fetid soup: it was stagnant, enclosed. He scooped what could be scooped to one side, and no longer minding his shirt or jersey tried to thrust his head through the hole. Even forcing it with all his might, there was no hope.

Rubbing his excoriated ears he sat on the dry part and said 'I must climb up inside with back and feet, like mountaineers in a rock-fault.' But the mountaineers he had read of did not have to contend with slippery rotting wood nor with very short legs. There was one roughly three-cornered space where he could get a hold and gain three or four feet before slipping, but after that it was impossible – the width of the trunk was greater than his outstretched body – and the daylight at the top was of course far out of leaping reach.

When he had fallen half a dozen times he sat for a while, gasping and collecting himself. His bare knees were bleeding: this was nothing unusual with him – they were generally scarred – but it was difficult to see how they could have been barked in a glutinous hollow tree. Not that it signified: as he sat there he found he was trembling; and a new kind of fear – not worry or frustration or dread of reproof, but a cold deep unknown fear – began to stir about his heart or stomach.

The sound of a muffled shot calmed it for a while. 'Joe can't be long, and I shall roar out,' he said; and he contemplated the dingy wall, reflecting that if only he had not lost his penknife he might have cut hand-holds in the soft wood. Quite suddenly he saw that the wall was no longer clear: daylight was fading fast, the evening cloud gathering.

Another double shot. It seemed nearer – Joe was on his way back and if he could not be made to hear before he passed, there was no help, no help at all.

Simon began to shout, much too soon, 'Ooh-hoo, ooh-hoo, Joe, Joe. I'm in the tree. I can't get out. I'm in the tree. Joe, Joe, Joe—'

The noise of the shouting inside the tree and its urgency made him begin to lose his head and he leapt at the wall like a frightened indeed a frantic trapped animal, eventually falling back exhausted, sitting there and frankly weeping: great wracking sobs.

They calmed in time – there was little light now at the top opening, none at the bottom – and once again, but with dread-filled and reasonable purpose, he began his shouting. Yet the sound of his utmost efforts was now a hoarse whisper, no more; and even when he heard Joseph and Maggie walking along at no great distance, laughing and talking – 'Give over, now, do' – he could make nothing better than a high thin pipe and a faint battering on the spongy wood.

'What was that?' asked Joseph.

'It was only an old cat, or an owl. Come on.'

'It might have been Simon, playing a game.'

'Ballocks. Come on, if you want it. I can't be home late again: we'll go to the barn.'

Their voices died away. Simon tried two more strangled almost silent cries and gave up. The anguish of bitterly disappointed hope and underlying terror slowly gave way to a torpid misery: he was cold, too, and soaking wet.

There was one more revival, one more fit of wild-beast-leaping at the wall: and then of heartbroken tears: and then a deeply unhappy resignation, huddled for warmth in the least wretched corner.

Overhead it was full night now: stars in the darkest blue. And presently an edge of moon. There was some very small comfort in the moon, though the rising south-wester bellowing through the trees added still more to the pervading threat: yet as he looked the piece of moon was shut out – broad shoulders in the open crown of the tree, and Joseph's anxious voice: 'Simon? Simon?'

'Oh, Joe—' said Simon in a recognizable gasp.

'Reach me up an arm, will you, old fellow?'

Light-Boy

BY EDITH PARGETER
who also wrote as ELLIS PETERS

The boy with the name of a god was standing among the tamarinds at the edge of the clearing when they came, one shoulder hitched easily against a tree, his thin brown thumb just piercing the membrane that covered the first sweet juice-pocket of a palmyra fruit. Before him, beyond the trees, the tumbled sandy rocks were piled, the dark mouth of the cave-temple cool black in their hot redness; and beyond again was the wide waste of beach and the infinite blueness of the sea. Behind him was the narrow road, and on the other side of it the squat houses of the village. All through the day he had one ear cocked for any sound of a car approaching by that road; but this time there had been no car. The two women walked out of the trees below him, close to the temple, on the dusty path from the Mission settlement.

One of them was an Indian woman from Madras, with a green and gold sari, and jasmine flowers in her coiled black hair; but the other was an Englishwoman, tall and fair-haired and slender in a sleeveless cotton dress. True, she carried no camera, but by the winged sunglasses and the un-Indian sandals, and the very walk, aloof and a little self-conscious, the boy recognized a migrant. He put down his palmyra fruit against the bole of the tree and came running, eyes and teeth flashing in an eagerness and purpose that looked all too familiar.

'Oh God!' said Rachel. 'Even here!'

Sudha turned her head, following the blind, hooded stare of the sunglasses, and saw the boy bearing down upon them at a headlong run, beaming gleefully. She lifted an indifferent shoulder. 'Oh, well, we're fair game. Did you think you'd be immune in Anantanayam?'

'I suppose it was too much to hope for. But after all, Andrew's a resident. He's been digging and teaching and doctoring here for four years now. I hoped I might get by under his shadow, and be tolerated, anyhow – resident by courtesy.'

'How's he to know you're connected with Andrew? It doesn't show yet. Now if you'd been staying in his house—'

But that was exactly what Rachel had not wished to do. It would have committed her too far, and she was not yet sure how far she wanted to go. Andrew Cobb was a pleasant enough person, she respected and liked him, but she wasn't sure of anything beyond that.

They had met at a cocktail party in New Delhi; she couldn't even remember now how she had come to be invited to such an improbable function. She had wandered aghast among the sophisticated chatter of nylon-sari'd ladies with lacquered western faces and pointed scarlet nails; slender, languid males in dinner-jackets; expatriate English merchants and officials, thinking of the beggars in Old Delhi, and the labouring poor clinging to life by its fringes, aware that these people were insulated from that outer world with disastrous thoroughness by their cars and their servants and their calculated want of imagination.

Andrew Cobb had come as a breath of fresh air, blurting out, as they met in the crowd, exactly what she had been wondering: 'For heaven's sake, what are you doing in this shower?'

A big, energetic, blunt-jawed man of nearly forty, so she had seen him; a good, pig-headed, upright medical missionary, so her Aunt Mildred had afterwards recalled him. A doctor first and a schoolmaster second, who ran an Anglican school and clinic attached to the archaeological site of Anantanayam, far south in Madras State. Within ten minutes, heaving breaths of the spiced evening air into him as if he were stifling, he had seized Rachel by the arm and invited her urgently to get out of there with him. And since, whatever else he might be, he was undoubtedly real, she had gone with him gladly, and sat out the evening in a small restaurant uptown, listening as he talked about the sculptural school of Mahabalipuram, that ebbed to its remotest ripple just where the archaeologists of Anantanayam were digging, and his medical practice, and his colony of precarious converts, of whom he spoke as of unpredictable children. Later she had talked in her turn, telling him about her three-months' visit to her scattered relatives here, and about the tour south which she was planning in March. And something, too, of the bewilderment, disillusionment, doubt and hope with which India had presented her since the day of her arrival. This he had understood; he had been through the same throes. And did it, later, begin to fall into proportion and make some kind of sense? He still hoped it would, he said ruefully, some day.

And it was then that he had invited her to his remote and minor settlement, looking at her across the table with the first spark of calculation in his eyes. She had observed it, and been experienced enough to recognize it. He was lonely, and she was congenial; and where was the harm in inviting the acquaintance to unfold, and waiting to see what kind of growth it achieved? Their recent experience of the insulated bubble-civilization of wealthy India had shown them how to value each other.

So she had come. From Madras it was not so far. But she had come cautiously, jealous for her freedom and respectful of his. If she had come alone he would have insisted on her staying in his own household, but she had brought her friend Sudha with her, and made her the excuse for taking the travellers' bungalow at the edge of the beach. Nothing but a narrow plantation of young trees between the compound and the sands, deep, wide, honey-pale, with that incredible sea beyond, shading from aquamarine along the rim to the dark cobalt of the deep water. Southward, the Bay of Bengal opened into the Indian Ocean. The waves were too rough for good swimming, but to bathe there was a delight, and the view from the windows of the bungalow was beautiful beyond belief.

Andrew had accepted humbly that his own cramped quarters by the schoolhouse could not possibly compete, and had made no attempt to persuade her to alter her plans. With Sudha presiding over the domestic arrangements he could be easy about the comfort and propriety of her stay. And this neat and convenient distance between them gave him time to think before he did anything irretrievable; his good Scottish blood would appreciate that.

The boy arrived before them gleaming and panting, and halted with bare toes spread in the sand. He was slender and small, his head came no higher than Rachel's shoulder. He might have been eleven or twelve years old, she judged, but it was difficult to put an age to him. He stood straight and easily, embracing them both in a broad, white-toothed smile. No mendicant palm crept out wheedlingly, and no throaty whine fished for small coins. She saw that she had mistaken him. He was not ordinary, he was not a beggar. He had a rope knotted round his waist over the brief khaki shorts and tattered brown shirt, and an old-fashioned glass-sided lantern slung by a loose yard or so of cord from one hip. He held the lamp up before them by the metal ring at the top, and addressed Sudha confidently in Tamil.

'We were both wrong,' said Sudha, contemplating him with a quizzical smile, 'This one works. He wants to show us the shrine.'

'I am Subramanya,' announced the child in English in the voice of honey and gravel to which Rachel had become accustomed, but with a large dignity all his own. 'I am light-boy.'

'It seems it's quite dark inside the temple,' said Sudha. 'He says we wouldn't see anything without his lamp. All right, Subramanya, you lead the way.'

'Are there still priests here? We're allowed inside? Even me?'

'No priests,' said Subramanya, beaming. 'You come with me, I show you the god. You come this way.'

He pattered before them to the rough steps that led up

from the first outcrop into the low face of sandstone, and there paused to open his lantern and put a match to the wick. The light was feeble enough, the corners of the glass panels ingrained with smoke from long years of use; but he held it up towards the velvet black of the entrance as if he had been lighting princes to their coronation.

The façade was borne aloft on three rough pillars, with a relief of apsarases in flight over the lintel. A small temple it was, perhaps never used as a temple at all, only as a study in design and carving, like some of those at Mahabalipuram. The deep chamber within was carved out of the living rock. Three paces into it, and the day fell away behind them, and the chill of stone closed on them with the darkness. The boy held his lantern high before them at arm's-length, so that his thin little body might cast no shadow to complicate their footsteps.

Because she had thought him a beggar running to black-mail her for new pice, and felt herself recoil from him in weariness and revulsion, Rachel found herself deeply and penitently aware of him now as a person. Proud, conscientious and self-respecting, a small working man bent on earning his fee, he went before her carefully, step by step; and the deeper he led her into the cave, the brighter and taller grew the flame of his lamp.

'Subramanya!' she said. 'That's a fine name you have.'

The long lashes rolled back from his dark eyes as he looked up at her and smiled brilliantly.

'Do you know who that is – Subramanya?'

'Yes, I know. He's the same as Kartikeya, the son of Siva. The beautiful one,' she said, to distinguish him from Ganesh, who was also the son of Siva.

He laughed aloud with pleasure, and the lantern waved and danced. 'Yes, you are right!' He was delighted with her for knowing. Was it possible that tourists so rarely even took the trouble to read a little before they came here? It had seemed to her an obvious thing to do, and she was ashamed of the glow of achievement his response gave her.

'But this is a shrine of Vishnu, isn't it, not Siva?'

He said: 'Yes, of Vishnu,' but he said it with a vague smile and a lift of expressive shoulders, as if it mattered very little. 'Here, on the walls, see – all the comings of the god. Nine times he came.'

Deep within the rock and lost to the outer light, the chamber in which they stood was yet quite small, and all its centre taken up by a great recumbent mass of stone, on which, for the moment, Subramanya turned his back. First he must show the deep reliefs on the walls, four on either side. He reached a hand to lead Rachel carefully along after him, holding up the light to each panel as he came to it. Thicker, vaguer, coarser carving than the best she had seen, but with the same passionate movement and flow. The dynamic figures and haughty, superhuman faces loomed out upon her in the flickering light, every shadow gouged deep into blackness.

'This is Varaha. You see? He came as a boar, because demons had captured the earth goddess and buried her deep underground, but the Lord Vishnu dug her out with his tusks.'

For every avatar there was a reason, every strange form of divine incarnation had its own logic. He led her through them all, as ardently as if he saw the carvings and told the stories for the first time. Behind her, Sudha rustled her silks against the stone, and the scent of her jasmine flowers revived in the coolness and the dark.

'And the seventh is Rama. And the eighth is Lord Krishna. All Vishnu. All God. And he will come another time.'

He turned at last to the centre of the chamber, and laid his hand with a possessive gesture on the long curve of a great stone thigh. The lantern, held aloft over the reclining figure, showed them Vishnu sleeping. More than lifesize, the vast, graceful body filled the circle of light and jutted out beyond it. Subramanya lit it for them piecemeal beginning at the head. This was a solitary Vishnu, unattended by the heavenly beings she had seen afloat above him at Mahabalipuram, watched over no longer by his consort Lakshmi, stripped even of the cobra-hood canopy and the tall crown. An older Vishnu, perhaps, and a simpler – austere, beautiful and remote. His body was half-naked, thinly-carved draperies covered his loins. The pure, still features of the great face balanced death and sleep. Rachel was aware of a loneliness and a sorrow that reminded her of something closer to her own experience, and for a moment groped in vain for the key to her memory.

The great hewn slab of stone, the stretched body and the monumental hands laid lax and calm drew curtain after curtain for her, and showed her the image she needed. There was no instant of revelation, only the knowledge with her suddenly that these things had always been one. This noble and withdrawn figure could have been a Christian sculpture of the entombment. The face was not less lovely and lonely and sorrowful. The body contained no less surely all the doom of mortality, all the promise of immortality.

'It's strange,' said Rachel aloud, 'he makes me think of my own God.'

'Strange?' said Subramanya, puzzled. She saw the delicate brown face for the first time utterly grave, lit sharply from above as he held the lantern high. 'It is not strange. He *is* God.'

'My God, as well as yours?'

'Of course. Everybody's God. Why not? Yours, mine, everybody's.'

'If we have the same God,' she said, faintly smiling, 'why do the priests here refuse to let me into the shrines?'

The white and gleaming smile flared again, disdainful and amused. 'Oh, priests!' said Subramanya scornfully. 'But I show you everything here. I hold the light for you, and you see something that is your own as much as mine. That is not strange.'

She was silent a moment, pondering. The boy, untroubled, unable to understand what she should find here to trouble her, waited innocently, watching her.

'You have so many gods, though,' she said. 'Some that don't resemble mine at all.'

The eloquent shoulders lifted again serenely. 'Why not? God is everything.'

He felt no need of further explanation, and perhaps he could have provided none. What he knew he knew, but his dealings were not in words. Ganesh, Hanuman, Kali, Gajalakshmi – what did it matter? Even that many personages had themselves many shapes and many names. Parvati was many, Siva many, Vishnu, this sleeper in the rock, many. Many times incarnated, and still to come again. And every avatar, Varaha, Rama, Lord Krishna, everyone was still

Vishnu. And Vishnu and Lakshmi and Siva and Parvati and Hanuman and Ganesh and Subramanya, and all the others: all were God.

'But creatures seen so differently,' she said, feeling her way towards this subtlety in him which she had so dangerously mistaken for simplicity. 'So many, and so varied – and all one? Is that possible?

'Look,' said Subramanya triumphantly, 'I show you!'

He held his lantern momentarily over the majestic face, and then caught her by the hand and drew her with him, circling the long couch of stone to the distant corner of the chamber. He lifted the light high. Only a glimmer shone upon the soles of the large, calm stone feet.

'You see? Is he any less God when we see only his feet? Do you think his face is not still there?'

She was silent a long time, considering that, until Sudha sighed and yawned, and suggested that they had seen enough. She emerged into daylight again still considering it. Subramanya had already put it by and forgotten it; he had no need to remember the logic which lived and breathed in him. He was chattering gaily rather about his parents and his little sister, when he set his lantern down on the stone steps, opened the glass door and turned down the wick. He blew out the flame, and a thin curl of grey smoke spiralled upwards for an instant and was gone. Flame and smoke, light and darkness, lived together inside the cage. Was there any need for a greater diversity than that?

They gave him more money than he expected, and he was pleased.

He walked with them halfway to the settlement, and talked merrily all the way. His father, he said, was one of

Cobb Sahib's servants, he kept the garden at the school.
But their own house was at the edge of the village; he
pointed it out as they went, a low clay shape like all the
rest. His little sister was learning to be a dancer. When she
was bigger she would go to Madras. If the memsahib was
staying here, and if she liked, Shantila would dance for her.

Nothing is rarer than to make a pure human contact;
and nothing can happen so simply and naturally when it
does happen. By the time he smiled his goodbye to them
over his prayerfully-folded hands at the edge of the road,
and darted back to his post and his neglected palmyra fruit
she knew it was not with her half-rupee that she had won
him.

'I made a friend today,' she said to Andrew that evening
over coffee, on the verandah of the bungalow he was visibly
seeing now as small and inadequate. His manner towards
her was becoming, she thought, at once more relaxed and
more proprietary. He had produced her to his nurses at the
clinic and his staff at the school with the air of one displaying
something not yet possessed, but possession of which he
was certainly contemplating.

'It's a lucky person who can ever say that,' said Andrew
cautiously. 'Who is it?'

'The light-boy at the temple. He showed us round there
this morning.'

'Ah, Subramanya! He's not a bad boy. Comes of a Christian family, of course.'

She was startled chiefly by the instant and dismaying
reaction she felt at hearing this, as though her recollection
of him shrank; as though he had somehow been belittled.

'Really? I shouldn't have guessed that. Not that it arose,

actually.' But hadn't it? Was not some kind of answer to that speculation comprehended in the answers he had given to a larger question?

'His father's my gardener,' said Andrew. 'I know the family well. My predecessor here converted the grandfather. Yes, he's a nice boy, quick and reliable. As Indians go!'

Why was it, she wondered, watching him steadily in the yellowing twilight, with the sea-wind coming in cool and fresh after the heat of the day, why was it that when he dropped some such phrase as that, quite simply and without malice, she felt herself recoil in such marked revolt? He gave all his energy to his life here, and his life was helping these people. He was right not to be hypocritical about the failings he found in them. He had as much right to his own standards and attitudes as they had to theirs and certainly more control over them. He had adapted more painstakingly to their ways than they did to his. Nor had she any justification for feeling superior.

She had come here gratefully because he was a refuge to her after too much experience too suddenly swallowed. She had come baffled and irritated by the contradictions of wealth and poverty, by the venality of much that she saw, from the buyable people in high places, through the hotel clerks discreetly black-marketeering in sterling, to the malevolent gangs of children pestering for alms, the servile and insolent room-boys, the predatory priests never content even with the most generous of offerings. From all this she had turned eagerly to an English acquaintance with standards like her own, a feeling for time, a sense of responsibility, and words which meant what they said.

And yet he had only to say something like that, and she

knew that they stood on different ground. At that tone in his voice, patient and tolerant though it was, she remembered how much more congenial, on board ship, she had found the Indians than her own countrymen, and how the missionaries, in particular, had clung together in a close little clan, and mixed less than anyone aboard with their different fellow-creatures. She remembered to detach herself from her own prejudices, to distrust her own reactions; she reminded herself that she was the creature of her own upbringing and environment, however carefully she tried to stand apart from them. She saw that all that dismayed her here was at least in part her own creation. And she was willing to wait, to continue an alien, to be rejected, to be exploited, if that was the necessary reverse of all that delighted her, the occasional acceptance, the unexpected communication, the momentary belonging.

'If you want someone to take you about while I'm busy in the clinic, mornings,' said Andrew, placidly unaware of any disquiet in her, 'you might do a lot worse than Subramanya. He knows everybody in the village, and quite a lot about the dig too.'

She took him at his word; and in the few days of her stay she thought much of the light-boy, and spent a good part of her time in his company. With this child, at least, she had no doubts of her welcome, or of the reason for it. He enjoyed her as she enjoyed him. It might be only the courteous brushing of fingers, but at least they touched.

When he invited her into his home she entered with reverence. A small, bare, clean living room, one shelf with a faded wedding photograph, an asthmatic wireless set, a low mat bed covered with a threadbare rug; and behind a drab curtain, the tiny kitchen hot from brazier fumes, a stained clay oven, and two garish pictures, one on either side. Rachel put off her shoes at the doorway and made her ceremonial 'Namaste' to a thin, worn woman who was Subramanya's mother. Like the field workers of the south, she wore no blouse under her sari, and the folds kilted almost to her knee. She had nothing to offer but a glass of water. Rachel drank it and thanked her, aware of a special and undeserved happiness.

Not until she was waist-deep in the sea that afternoon, braced against the rough waves, did she realize what she had seen in the kitchen. On one side a cheap, highly-coloured paper print of Christ, soft-faced and appealing; on the other a doe-eyed, tender-mouthed Krishna, blue-tinted and womanish, with his flute at his lips.

And she had seen no discrepancy, no contradiction. They were so profoundly alike that there was no distinguishing between them except by the blueness and the beard and the flute – superficial differences by any measure. The very same too beautiful, effeminate, sentimental art, the flowery beauty that poverty and deprivation and wretchedness need. Necessarily, a distant, hampered and imperfect view, perhaps the buckle of a sandal, a little-toe nail, but still a particle of the god. Of God.

Rolled in the ultramarine shallows, refreshed and languid and at ease, she found no fault with this dual vision. All the pantheon of India had begun to fuse into a unity for her. All the pantheons of the world.

She did not realize how strong a tide was carrying her, she went with it and was content. She watched Shantila dance, and listened to Subramanya's monotonously-sung accompaniment, and learned to distinguish *abhinaya*, the mimed interpretation of ballads and songs, from the stylized movements of pure dance. Classical Indian music as yet only confused and excited her, but the popular music of weddings and folksongs she found astonishingly approachable. And how quickly, how very quickly, someone else's fairies and gods become one's own, familiar and dear. She had only to watch Shantila cross her ankles and poise her lifted fingers on the invisible flute, and Lord Krishna was there before her, in all his youth and beauty and antique innocence.

She was changing after her bathe, on the fifth afternoon of her stay, when she heard Andrew come trampling heavily up the steps to the verandah, half an hour ahead of his usual time. Sudha was still snoring delicately under her mosquito-net, for to Sudha the afternoons were made for sleeping rather than swimming. If Andrew called out, he would wake her. Rachel opened the door an inch or two and said softly: 'I'll be out in a moment. There's a fresh lime soda in that covered jug in the cooler. Get one for me, too, will you?'

He was stretched out in one of the cane chairs when she came out to him a few minutes later, still towelling her wet hair. He looked up at her with a brief, preoccupied smile that faded quickly into a grimace of discouragement; and yet she had a strange impression that somewhere at the heart of his unexplained mood there was an odd little glow of satisfaction.

'What's the matter? Has something happened?'

'Oh, nothing I shouldn't have been prepared for, I suppose. It's only too ordinary. I finished early,' he said, 'and thought I'd get the car out and run you over to the south beach or somewhere. I looked in at the village, thinking I might find you there. I didn't, but I found something else.' He was groping deep into his bush-jacket pocket. 'You won't believe it,' he said, sour enjoyment unmistakable in his voice now.

After more than a month in India there was not much she would have had difficulty in believing. She said so, but the serenity in her tone did not seem to be what he expected of her.

'I thought Subramanya's people might know where you'd be, so I called in there. This will show you what these people are really like – unreliable, two-faced, born without sincerity. You think you've got them, and it's like holding water in your hands. You'll understand now what I'm up against. For three generations these people have been professing Christians. And look what they had pinned up on the kitchen wall! Right beside a picture of Christ!'

He whipped it out on to the table and unfolded it before her eyes with a gesture of bitter triumph. She let the towel fall into her lap, and sat for a long moment with her eyes fixed upon the garishly-coloured flamboyantly-printed page, its glossy surface seamed now with sharp white folds like scars. Lord Krishna's flute was bent, his round, girlish arm broken. The delicate, effeminate, blue-tinted countenance with its fawn's eyes was deformed by a slashed cross.

She sat looking at it, and her face was thoughtful, mild and still. She said nothing at all.

'I'm sorry!' said Andrew, stretching and relaxing with a sigh. 'I don't know why I had to take it out on you, it isn't your fault. But you see how devious they are. You can't trust them an inch.'

No, from his point of view perhaps not, and certainly one could argue, she thought reasonably, that knowing what they know, they ought not to profess conversion from one creed to another. What isn't worth keeping, isn't worth giving up, and why change one illusion, one voluntary mutilation, for another? But probably the grandfather had never really understood that his own universality was coming into a head-on clash with something smaller, less enlightened, and as exclusive as it was militant. One more aspect of divinity came graciously enough to him; how could he possibly realize that he was expected to make it, from then on, the only one? Like sealing up against the sun all the windows of your house but for one small casement. Like voluntarily walling yourself into a dark tower with one narrow loophole, when you could be outside lying in the grass.

'You made them take it down?' she asked, smoothing the edge of the spoiled picture with one finger, her voice quiet.

'Well, of course!' he said, astonished, and stared at her blankly.

'Why "of course"?' She looked up. 'They have the right to believe and worship as they please.'

'Certainly,' agreed Andrew, stiffly. 'As they please, and whichever they please. But not *both*!'

Almost pleasurably, as in a half-dream, she heard her own voice saying: 'Why not?'

'*Why not?*'

He sat up rigidly in his chair, staring at her with dropped jaw and horrified eyes.

'Yes, why not?'

She turned the picture and smoothed it out before him. 'Did you look at the other one carefully? Colour the face blue, forget the beard, and make this fellow put down his flute, and you'd hardly know them apart. Two gentle, plaintive, pretty faces. People made them exactly alike because they needed exactly the same from them. True, we're looking at the likeness on one of its lowest planes, but the same holds good higher up, you know. All that is different in them is the conventions. Why not both? They're one and the same.'

He was clinging to the arms of the chair as if the world had begun to rock under him. He stared under knotted black brows, trying to grasp the magnitude of her blasphemy. His jaw worked, and he couldn't speak. He drew a convulsive breath and whispered creakingly: 'You're not serious! You don't know what you're saying!'

'I am serious. Do you mean you've never really caught a glimpse of it? In four years? Everybody who ever got as far as imagining the inevitability of God was looking at the same sun through his own particular little window. The view doesn't even vary so very much, not until the creeds become business. When the priests move in, and start cornering, and organizing, and retailing what the saints left freely about the world for everybody to enjoy, then the distortions and perversions begin. But that doesn't alter the first principle. Nothing can.'

'You're just being deliberately perverse. I don't see the slightest resemblance between this . . . this thing . . . and the church calendar they've got there on the wall beside it. That's all very facile talk about the two pretty faces. I know our almanacs aren't great art, just as well as you do. But supposing this had been Hanuman, or Ganesh, as it very well might have? What then?'

The heat with which he had begun this outburst cooled quickly, she heard the note of security steady in his voice again, and was sure in her heart that he could not be shaken. In a moment he would be sounding indulgent, reminded to his comfort that she had been in India no more than four or five weeks, and was only running true to beginners' form in knowing everything.

'It wouldn't have mattered,' she said simply. 'I thought this might have made it easier to see, just the fact that it was Krishna. But it makes no difference. They're all aspects and allegories.'

'And a beautiful monotheism embracing them all, I suppose, when one develops eyes to see!' He laughed shortly and angrily. 'Rachel, you're not really such a fool as all that.'

She looked back at him without any answering indignation, even smiled a little. 'Did you ever wonder why Tagore and Gandhi so often wrote simply "God"? Because they meant it, that's why. And long before their day Indians were leaving the evidence for us all over the place, if we cared to see it:

> *"the loving sage beholds that Mysterious Existence*
> *wherein the universe comes to have one home;*
> *Therein unites and therefrom issues the whole;*
> *The lord is warp and woof in created beings."*

384

That isn't one of the desert fathers, that's the Yajur Veda.'

'Well, now come down out of the clouds for a moment, and look around you, and see what goes on at ground level.'

'It was right down at ground level I got all this,' she said mildly. Below ground level, actually, she thought. But of course I had a lantern and a guide. 'Would you believe it,' she said, 'I ploughed my way conscientiously through most of the Vedic translations before I left home? And it never really occurred to me that they meant exactly what they said! "One All is Lord of what moves and what is fixed, of what walks and what flies, this multiform creation." That's in the Rigveda. "Our father, our creator, our disposer, Who is the only One, bearing names of different deities".'

'There's a lofty literature to every heresy and every heathenism,' said Andrew violently. 'But "If the light that is within you is darkness, how great is that darkness".'

She had been ready to continue the argument with goodwill, but that stopped her. After that there was nothing to say; she heard it as an oracle. She lifted her head and studied him with a long, thoughtful, wondering look. His darkness seemed to her impenetrable.

She relaxed with a sigh, and reached for her glass. The scarred Krishna rustled mournfully under her hand. She took it up gently. It was Subramanya who carried a lantern.

'May I have this? As a souvenir.'

'Of course, if you'd like it,' he said stiffly.

He got up, and went to lean on the verandah rail. 'Shall we go out? It's a bit late now, but we could still go down to the Point, if you feel like it?'

385

But when she agreed that it was a little too late, and remembered that she had a dress to iron before dinner, he seemed, if anything, rather relieved. The whole thing must have been a shock to him. Probably he was already reconsidering about her, drawing back a little, making sure the way of retreat was still open. Maybe it was high time to move on, and leave them both a breathing-space.

She mentioned that evening, over coffee, and in the right tone of regret and reluctance, that Sudha had to get back to Madras, and that she really ought to go with her and see about her flight to Calcutta, before it became altogether too hot to go there at all. Andrew made the right disappointed noises, and cautious feints at dissuading her, but she saw that the news was at least as welcome to him as it was to her. And Sudha, who could always be relied upon to do all things gracefully, sighed her regrets over her coffee cup, and explained sadly that her husband was coming home from New Delhi two days earlier than she had expected him, and she must be in Madras to welcome him.

So that was that. Rachel knew exactly how it would end. They would part on the best of terms; but after the first dutiful letters of thanks and valediction they would let each other drop, gently and gratefully and once and for all. No hard feelings. But it was just as well to have found out in time.

She went down in the morning towards the cave-temple. The boy with the name of a god was sitting on his heels in the sandstone portico, with a long blade of grass between his teeth. He spat it out when he saw her coming, and joined his long, brown hands beneath a dazzling smile. She sat down beside him on the steps, and opened the flat, cardboard folder she carried.

'Subramanya, this afternoon I'm going away, back to Madras.'

'I shall be sad,' he said, but so serenely that it was plain he would not remain clouded for long.

'I brought you back this.'

She opened the folder between them on the step. She had pressed the picture between the folds of a linen towel, but the thin white scars would never come out. She looked at the mutilated face, and was aware of belated anger. What right had anyone to distrain a poor man's possessions in the name of religion? What happened to courtesy and decency before a fundamentally good man could so forget himself?

'Why did you let anyone force you to take it down? It was your property, you had a right to hang it wherever you liked.'

He looked at her gravely, but without any distress, his large eyes wide open to the sun. 'It did not matter so much. It is only a picture. Cobb Sahib is like a child about pictures. You must go gently with children, when they do not understand.'

'Yes,' she said, for some reason gloriously reassured, even though Andrew would surely remain a child to the end of his self-sacrificing days in this place, and never come near understanding of the thing he had done, or the forbearance extended to him. 'Yes, I suppose so.'

'He is a good man. It would be wrong to hurt him.'

He pricked up his head alertly, looking beyond her towards the road. A car and its attendant dustcloud rounded the curve of the village, the first tourists of the day. Subramanya tightened the cord round his waist, and hitched the lantern expectantly against his hip.

'Lord Krishna is not jealous; he knows, he will wait. Some day Cobb Sahib will stop caring so much about images, and look for God.'

That was perfect, there was nothing more to be said. He had illuminated everything.

'Take my picture with you,' he said suddenly. 'I don't need it. It was mine, I bought it. I give it to you.'

The car had stopped in the arc of gravel by the road; two men were getting out, festooned with cameras. Subramanya rose to go to his duty.

'Not because it is a little spoiled,' he said, turning on her his sudden, blazing smile. 'I like it better now, because you brought it back. But I give it to you.'

'Thank you, Subramanya. I'll keep it gladly.'

'To remember me,' he said, already skipping away from her with one bright eye upon his clients; but he turned once more before he left her, and joined his hands in a last salute.

'Namaste!'

'Namaste!'

He ran away from her as he had run towards her on the first day, headlong and eager, clutching his lantern firmly by the ring at the top. As she drew back into the trees with the cardboard folder under her arm she heard him announce himself magnificently to the newcomers, astride before them at the edge of the sandstone outcrop, with the instrument of revelation uplifted proudly in his hand.

'I am Subramanya. I am light-boy.'

An Evening to Remember

BY ROSAMUNDE PILCHER

Under the dryer, with her hair rolled and skewered to her head, Alison Stockman turned down the offer of magazines to read, and instead opened her handbag, took out the notepad with its attached pencil, and went through, for perhaps the fourteenth time, her List.

She was not a natural list-maker, being a fairly haphazard sort of person, and a cheerfully lighthearted housekeeper who frequently ran out of essentials like bread and butter and washing-up liquid, but still retained the ability to manage – for a day or so at any rate – by sheer improvisation, and the deep-seated conviction that it didn't much matter anyway.

It wasn't that she didn't sometimes make lists, it was because she made them on the spur of the moment, using any small scrap of paper that came to hand. Backs of envelopes, cheque stubs, old bills. This added a certain mystery to life. *Lampshade. How much?* she would find, scrawled on a receipt for coal delivered six months previously, and would spend several engrossed moments trying to recall what on earth this missive could have meant. Which lampshade? And how much had it cost?

Ever since they had moved out of London and into the country, she had been slowly trying to furnish and decorate their new house, but there never seemed to be enough time or money to spare – two small children used up almost all of these commodities – and there were still rooms with the wrong sort of wallpaper, or no carpets, or lamps without lampshades.

This list, however, was different. This list was for tomorrow night, and so important was it that she had specially bought the little pad with pencil attached; and had written down, with the greatest concentration, every single thing that had to be bought, cooked, polished, cleaned, washed, ironed, or peeled.

Vacuum dining room, polish silver. She ticked that one off. *Lay table.* She ticked that as well. She had done it this morning while Larry was at playschool and Janey napping in her cot. 'Won't the glasses get dusty?' Henry had asked when she had told him her plans, but Alison assured him that they wouldn't, and anyway the meal would be eaten be candlelight, so if the glasses were dusty Mr and Mrs Fairhurst probably wouldn't be able to see far enough to notice. Besides, whoever had heard of a dusty wineglass?

Order fillet of beef. That got a tick as well. *Peel potatoes.* Another tick; they were in a bowl of water in the larder along with a small piece of coal. *Take prawns out of freezer.* That was tomorrow morning. *Make mayonnaise. Shred lettuce. Peel mushrooms. Make Mother's lemon soufflé. Buy cream.* She ticked off *Buy cream*, but the rest would have to wait until tomorrow.

She wrote, *Do flowers.* That meant picking the first shy daffodils that were beginning to bloom in the garden and arranging them with sprigs of flowering currant, which, hopefully, would not make the whole house smell of dirty cats.

She wrote, *Wash the best coffee cups.* These were a wedding present, and were kept in a corner cupboard in the sitting room. They would, without doubt, be dusty, even if the wineglasses weren't.

She wrote, *Have a bath.*

This was essential, even if she had it at two o'clock tomorrow afternoon. Preferably after she had brought in the coal and filled the log basket.

She wrote, *Mend chair.* This was one of the dining-room chairs, six little balloon-backs which Alison had bought at an auction sale. They had green velvet seats, edged with gold braid, but Larry's cat, called, brilliantly, Catkin, had used the chair as a useful claw-sharpener, and the braid had come unstuck and drooped, unkempt as a sagging petticoat. She would find the glue and a few tacks and put it together again. It didn't matter if it wasn't very well done. Just so that it didn't show.

She put the list back in her bag and sat and thought glumly about her dining room. The fact that they even had a dining room in this day and age was astonishing, but the truth was that it was such an unattractive, north-facing little box of a room that nobody wanted it for anything else. She had suggested it as a study for Henry, but Henry said it was too damned cold, and then she had said that Larry could keep his toy farm there, but Larry preferred to play with his toy farm on the kitchen floor. It wasn't as if they ever used it as a dining room, because they seemed to eat all their meals in the kitchen, or on the terrace in the warm weather, or even out in the garden when the summer sun was high and they could picnic, the four of them, beneath the shade of the sycamore tree.

Her thoughts, as usual, were flying off at tangents. The dining room. It was so gloomy they had decided that nothing could make it gloomier, and had papered it in dark green to match the velvet curtains that Alison's mother had produced from her copious attic. There was a gate-leg table, and the balloon-back chairs, and a Victorian sideboard that an aunt of Henry's had bequeathed to them. As well, there were two monstrous pictures. These were Henry's contribution. He had gone to an auction sale to buy a brass fender, only to find himself the possessor, as well, of these depressing paintings. One depicted a fox consuming a dead duck; the other a Highland cow standing in a pouring rainstorm.

'They'll fill the walls,' Henry had said, and hung them in the dining room. 'They'll do till I can afford to buy you an original Hockney, or a Renoir, or a Picasso, or whatever it is you happen to want.'

He came down from the top of the ladder and kissed his wife. He was in his shirt sleeves and there was a cobweb in his hair.

'I don't want those sort of things,' Alison told him.

'You should.' He kissed her again. 'I do.'

And he did. Not for himself, but for his wife and his children. For them he was ambitious. They had sold the flat in London, and bought this little house, because he wanted the children to live in the country and to know about cows and crops and trees and the seasons; and because of the mortgage they had vowed to do all the necessary painting and decorating themselves. This endless ploy took up all their weekends, and at first it had gone quite well because it was wintertime. But then the days lengthened, and the summer came, and they abandoned the inside of the house and moved out of doors to try to create some semblance of order in the overgrown and neglected garden.

In London, they had had time to spend together; to get a baby-sitter for the children and go out for dinner; to sit and listen to music on the stereo, while Henry read the paper and Alison did her *gros point*. But now Henry left home at seven-thirty every morning and did not get back until nearly twelve hours later.

'Is it really worth it?' she asked him sometimes, but Henry was never discouraged.

'It won't be like this for always,' he promised her. 'You'll see.'

His job was with Fairhurst & Hanbury, an electrical engineering business, which, since Henry had first joined as a junior executive, had grown and modestly prospered, and now had a number of interesting irons in the fire, not the least of which was the manufacture of commercial computers. Slowly, Henry had ascended the ladder of promotion, and now was possibly in line, or being considered for, the post of Export Director, the man who at present held this job having decided to retire early, move to Devon, and take up poultry farming.

In bed, which seemed to be nowadays the only place where they could find the peace and privacy to talk, Henry had assessed, for Alison, the possibilities of his getting this job. They did not seem to be very hopeful. He was, for one thing, the youngest of the candidates. His qualifications, although sound, were not brilliant, and the others were all more experienced.

'But what would you have to *do*?' Alison wanted to know.

'Well, that's it. I'd have to travel. Go to New York, Hong Kong, Japan. Rustle up new markets. I'd be away a lot. You'd be on your own even more than you are now. And then we'd have to reciprocate. I mean, if foreign buyers came to see us, we'd have to look after them, entertain . . . you know the sort of thing.'

She thought about this, lying warmly in his arms, in the dark, with the window open and the cool country air blowing in on her face. She said, 'I wouldn't like you being away a lot, but I could bear it. I wouldn't be lonely, because of having the children. And I'd know that you'd always come back to me.'

He kissed her. He said, 'Did I ever tell you I loved you?'

'Once or twice.'

He said, 'I want that job. I could do it. And I want to get this mortgage off our backs, and take the children to Brittany for their summer holidays, and maybe pay some man to dig that ruddy garden for us.'

'Don't say such things.' Alison laid her fingers against Henry's mouth. 'Don't talk about them. We mustn't count chickens.'

This nocturnal conversation had taken place a month or so before, and they hadn't talked about Henry's possible promotion again. But a week ago, Mr Fairhurst, who was Henry's chairman, had taken Henry out to lunch at his club. Henry found it hard to believe that Mr Fairhurst was standing him this excellent meal simply for the pleasure of

394

Henry's company, but they were eating delicious blue-veined Stilton and drinking a glass of port before Mr Fairhurst finally came to the point. He asked after Alison and the children. Henry told him they were very well.

'Good for children, living in the country. Does Alison like it there?'

'Yes. She's made a lot of friends in the village.'

'That's good. That's very good.' Thoughtfully, the older man helped himself to more Stilton. 'Never really met Alison.' He sounded as though he was ruminating to himself, not addressing any particular remark to Henry. 'Seen her, of course, at the office dance, but that scarcely counts. Like to see your new house—'

His voice trailed off. He looked up. Henry, across the starched tablecloth and gleaming silverware, met his eyes. He realized that Mr Fairhurst was angling for – indeed, expected – a social invitation.

He cleared his throat and said, 'Perhaps you and Mrs Fairhurst would come down and have dinner with us one evening?'

'Well,' said the chairman, looking surprised and delighted as if it had all been Henry's idea. 'How very nice. I'm sure Mrs Fairhurst would like that very much.'

'I'll . . . I'll tell Alison to give her a ring. They can fix a date.'

'We're being vetted, aren't we? For the new job,' said Alison, when he broke the news. 'For all the entertaining of those foreign clients. They want to know if I can cope, if I'm socially up to it.'

'Put like that, it sounds pretty soulless, but . . . yes, I suppose that is what it's all about.'

'Does it have to be terribly grand?'

'No.'

'But formal.'

'Well, he is the chairman.'

'Oh, dear.'

'Don't look like that. I can't bear it when you look like that.'

'Oh, Henry.' She wondered if she was going to cry, but he pulled her into his arms and hugged her and she found she wasn't going to cry after all. Over the top of her head, he said, 'Perhaps we are being vetted, but surely that's a good sign. It's better than being simply ignored.'

'Yes, I suppose so.' After a little, 'There's one good thing,' said Alison. 'At least we've got a dining room.'

The next morning she made the telephone call to Mrs Fairhurst, and, trying not to sound too nervous, duly asked Mrs Fairhurst and her husband for dinner. 'Oh, how very kind.' Mrs Fairhurst seemed genuinely surprised, as though this was the first she had heard of it.

'We . . . we thought either the sixth or the seventh of this month. Whichever suits you better.'

'Just a moment, I'll have to find my diary.' There followed a long wait. Alison's heart thumped. It was ridiculous to feel so anxious. At last Mrs Fairhurst came back on the line. 'The seventh would suit us very well.'

'About seven-thirty?'

'That would be perfect.'

'And I'll tell Henry to draw Mr Fairhurst a little map, so that you can find your way.'

'That would be an excellent idea. We have been known to get lost.'

They both laughed at this, said goodbye, and hung up. Instantly, Alison picked up the receiver again and dialled her mother's telephone number.

'Ma.'

'Darling.'

'A favour to ask. Could you have the children for the night next Friday?'

'Of course. Why?'

Alison explained. Her mother was instantly practical. 'I'll come over in the car and collect them, just after tea. And then they can spend the night. Such a good idea. Impossible to cook a dinner and put the children to bed at the same time, and if they know there's something going on they'll never go to sleep. Children are all the same. What are you going to give the Fairhursts to eat?'

Alison hadn't thought about this, but she thought about it now, and her mother made a few helpful suggestions and gave her the recipe for her own lemon soufflé. She asked after the children, imparted a few items of family news, and then rang off. Alison picked up the receiver yet again and made an appointment to have her hair done.

With all this accomplished, she felt capable and efficient, two sensations not usually familiar. Friday, the seventh. She left the telephone, went across the hall, and opened the door of the dining room. She surveyed it critically, and the dining room glowered back at her. With candles, she told herself, half-closing her eyes, and the curtains drawn, perhaps it won't look so bad.

Oh, please, God, don't let anything go wrong. Let me not let Henry down. For Henry's sake, let it be a success.

God helps those who help themselves. Alison closed the dining-room door, put on her coat, walked down to the village, and there bought the little notepad with pencil attached.

Her hair was dry. She emerged from the dryer, sat at a mirror, and was duly combed out.

'Going somewhere tonight?' asked the young hairdresser, wielding a pair of brushes as though Alison's head was a drum.

'No. Not tonight. Tomorrow night. I've got some people coming for dinner.'

'That'll be nice. Want me to spray it for you?'

'Perhaps you'd better.'

He squirted her from all directions, held up a mirror so that she could admire the back, and then undid the bow of the mauve nylon gown and helped Alison out of it.

'Thank you so much.'

'Have a good time tomorrow.'

Some hopes. She paid the bill, put on her coat, and went out into the street. It was getting dark. Next door to the hairdresser was a sweet shop, so she went in and bought two bars of chocolate for the children. She found her car and drove home, parked the car in the garage, and went into the house by the kitchen door. Here she found Evie giving the children their tea. Janey was in her high chair, they were eating fish fingers and chips, and the kitchen smelt fragrantly of baking.

'Well,' said Evie, looking at Alison's head, 'you are smart.'

Alison flopped into a chair and smiled at the three cheerful faces around the table. 'I feel all boiled. Is there any tea left in that pot?'

'I'll make a fresh brew.'

'And you've been baking.'

'Well,' said Evie, 'I had a moment to spare, so I made a cake. Thought it might come in handy.'

Evie was one of the best things that had happened to Alison since coming to live in the country. She was a spinster of middle years, stout and energetic, and kept house for her bachelor brother, who farmed the land around Alison and Henry's house. Alison had first met her in the village grocer's. Evie had introduced herself and said that if Alison wanted free-range eggs, she could buy them from Evie. Evie kept her own hens, and supplied a few chosen families in the village. Alison accepted this offer gratefully, and took to walking the children down to the farmhouse in the afternoons to pick up the eggs.

Evie loved children. After a bit, 'Any time you need a sitter, just give me a ring,' said Evie, and from time to time Alison had taken her up on this. The children liked it when Evie came to take care of them. She always brought them sweets or little presents, taught Larry card games, and was deft and loving with Janey, liking to hold the baby on her knee, with Janey's round fair head pressed against the solid bolster of her formidable bosom.

399

Now, she bustled to the stove, filled a kettle, stooped to the oven to inspect her cake. 'Nearly done.'

'You are kind, Evie. But isn't it time you went home? Jack'll be wondering what's happened to his tea.'

'Oh, Jack went off to market today. Won't be back till all hours. If you like, I'll put the children to bed for you. I have to wait for the cake, anyway.' She beamed at Larry. 'You'd like that, wouldn't you, my duck? Have Evie bathing you. And Evie will show you how to make soap bubbles with your fingers.'

Larry put the last chip in his mouth. He was a thoughtful child, and did not commit himself readily to any impulsive scheme. He said, 'Will you read me my story as well? When I'm in bed?'

'If you like.'

'I want to read *Where's Spot?* There's a tortoise in it.'

'Well, Evie shall read you that.'

When tea was finished, the three of them went upstairs. Bath water could be heard running and Alison smelt her best bubble-bath. She cleared the tea and stacked the dishwasher and turned it on. Outside, the light was fading, so before it got dark, she went out and unpegged the morning's wash from the line, brought it indoors, folded it, stacked it in the airing cupboard. On her way downstairs, she collected a red engine, an eyeless teddy bear, a squeaking ball, and a selection of bricks. She put these in the toy basket that lived in the kitchen, laid the table for their breakfast, and a tray for the supper that she and Henry would eat by the fire.

This reminded her. She went through to the sitting room, put a match to the fire, and drew the curtains. The room looked bleak without flowers, but she planned to do flowers tomorrow. As she returned to the kitchen, Catkin put in an appearance, insinuating himself through his cat door, and announcing to Alison that it was long past his dinner time and he was hungry. She opened a tin of cat food and poured him some milk, and he settled himself into a neat eating position and tidily consumed the lot.

She thought about supper for herself and Henry. In the larder was a basket of brown eggs Evie had brought with her. They would have omelettes and a salad. There were six oranges in the fruit bowl and doubtless some scraps of cheese in the cheese dish. She collected lettuce and tomatoes, half a green pepper and a couple of sticks of celery, and began to make a salad. She was stirring the French dressing when she heard Henry's car come up the lane and pull into the garage. A moment later he appeared at the back door, looking tired and crumpled, carrying his bulging briefcase and the evening paper.

'Hi.'

'Hello, darling.' They kissed. 'Had a busy day?'

'Frantic.' He looked at the salad and ate a bit of lettuce. 'Is this for supper?'

'Yes, and an omelette.'

'Frugal fare.' He leaned against the table. 'I suppose we're saving up for tomorrow night?'

'Don't talk about it. Did you see Mr Fairhurst today?'

'No, he's been out of town. Where are the children?'

'Evie's bathing them. Can't you hear? She stayed on.

She'd baked a cake for us and it's still in the oven. And Jack's at market.'

Henry yawned. 'I'll go up and tell her to leave the water in. I could do with a bath.'

Alison emptied the dishwasher and then went upstairs too. She felt, for some reason, exhausted. It was an unfamiliar treat to be able to potter around her bedroom, to feel peaceful and unhurried. She took off the clothes she had been wearing all day, opened her cupboard and reached for the velvet housecoat that Henry had given her last Christmas. It was not a garment she had worn very often, there not being many occasions in her busy life when it seemed suitable. It was lined with silk, and had a comforting and luxurious feel about it. She did up the buttons, tied the sash, slipped her feet into flat gold slippers left over from some previous summer, and went across the landing to the children's room to say goodnight. Janey was in her cot, on the verge of sleep. Evie sat on the edge of Larry's bed, and was just about to finish the bedtime book. Larry's mouth was plugged with his thumb, his eyes drooped. Alison stooped to kiss him.

'See you in the morning,' she told him. He nodded, and his eyes went back to Evie. He wanted to hear the end of the story. Alison left them and went downstairs. She picked up Henry's evening paper and took it into the sitting room to see what was on television that evening. As she did this, she heard a car come up the lane from the main road. It turned in at their gate. Headlights flashed beyond the drawn curtains. Alison lowered the paper. Gravel crunched as the car stopped outside their front door. Then the bell rang. She dropped the newspaper on to the sofa and went to open the door.

Outside, parked on the gravel, was a large black Daimler. And on the doorstep, looking both expectant and festive, stood Mr and Mrs Fairhurst.

Her first instinct was to slam the door in their faces, scream, count to ten, and then open the door and find them gone.

But they were, undoubtedly, there. Mrs Fairhurst was smiling. Alison smiled, too. She could feel the smile, creasing her cheeks, like something that had been slapped on her face.

'I'm afraid,' said Mrs Fairhurst, 'that we're a little bit early. We were so afraid of losing the way.'

'No. Not a bit.' Alison's voice came out at least two octaves higher than it usually did. She'd got the date wrong. She'd told Mrs Fairhurst the wrong day. She'd made the most appalling, most ghastly mistake. 'Not a bit early.' She stood back, opening the door. 'Do come in.'

They did so, and Alison closed the door behind them. They began to shed their coats.

I can't tell them. Henry will have to tell them. He'll have to give them a drink and tell them that there isn't anything to eat because I thought they were coming tomorrow night.

Automatically, she went to help Mrs Fairhurst with her fur.

'Did . . . did you have a good drive?'

'Yes, very good,' said Mr Fairhurst. He wore a dark suit and a splendid tie. 'Henry gave me excellent instructions.'

'And of course there wasn't too much traffic.' Mrs Fairhurst smelt of Chanel No. 5. She adjusted the chiffon collar of her dress and touched her hair which had, like Alison's, been freshly done. It was silvery and elegant, and she wore diamond earrings and a beautiful brooch at the neck of her dress.

'What a charming house. How clever of you and Henry to find it.'

'Yes, we love it.' They were ready. They stood smiling at her. 'Do come in by the fire.'

She led the way, into her warm, firelit, but flowerless sitting room, swiftly gathered up the newspaper from the sofa and pushed it beneath a pile of magazines. She moved an armchair closer to the fire. 'Do sit down, Mrs Fairhurst. I'm afraid Henry was a little late back from the office. He'll be down in just a moment.'

She should offer them a drink, but the drinks were in the kitchen cupboard and it would seem both strange and rude to go out and leave them on their own. And supposing they asked for dry martinis? Henry always did the drinks, and Alison didn't know how to make a dry martini.

Mrs Fairhurst lowered herself comfortably into the chair. She said, 'Jock had to go to Birmingham this morning, so I don't suppose he's seen Henry today – have you, dear?'

'No, I didn't get into the office.' He stood in front of the fire and looked about him appreciatively. 'What a pleasant room this is.'

'Oh, yes. Thank you.'

'Do you have a garden?'

'Yes. About an acre. It's really too big.' She looked about her frantically, and her eyes lighted upon the cigarette box.

She picked it up and opened it. There were four cigarettes inside. 'Would you like a cigarette?'

But Mrs Fairhurst did not smoke, and Mr Fairhurst said that if Alison did not mind, he would smoke one of his own cigars. Alison said that she did not mind at all, and put the box back on the table. A number of panic-stricken images flew through her mind. Henry, still lolling in his bath; the tiny salad which was all that she had made for supper; the dining room, icy cold and inhospitable.

'Do you do the garden by yourselves?'

'Oh . . . oh, yes. We're trying. It was in rather a mess when we bought the house.'

'And you have two little children?' This was Mrs Fairhurst, gallantly keeping the ball of conversation going.

'Yes. Yes, they're in bed. I have a friend – Evie. She's the farmer's sister. She put them to bed for me.'

What else could one say? Mr Fairhurst had lighted his cigar, and the room was filled with its expensive fragrance. What else could one do? Alison took a deep breath. 'I'm sure you'd both like a drink. What can I get for you?'

'Oh, how lovely.' Mrs Fairhurst glanced about her, and saw no evidence of either bottles or wineglasses, but if she was put out by this, graciously gave no sign. 'I think a glass of sherry would be nice.'

'And you, Mr Fairhurst?'

'The same for me.'

She blessed them both silently for not asking for martinis. 'We . . . we've got a bottle of Tio Pepe . . .?'

'What a treat!'

'The only thing is . . . would you mind very much if I

405

left you on your own for a moment? Henry – he didn't have time to do a drink tray.'

'Don't worry about us,' she was assured. 'We're very happy by this lovely fire.'

Alison withdrew, closing the door gently behind her. It was all more awful than anything one could possibly have imagined. And they were so nice, darling people, which only made it all the more dreadful. They were behaving quite perfectly, and she had had neither the wit nor the intelligence to remember which night she had asked them for.

But there was no time to stand doing nothing but hate herself. Something had to be done. Silently, on slippered feet, she sped upstairs. The bathroom door stood open, as did their bedroom door. Beyond this, in a chaos of abandoned bathtowels, socks, shoes, and shirts, stood Henry, dressing himself with the speed of light.

'Henry, they're here.'

'I know.' He pulled a clean shirt over his head, stuffed it into his trousers, did up the zipper, and reached for a neck-tie. 'Saw them from the bathroom window.'

'It's the wrong night. I must have made a mistake.'

'I've already gathered that.' Sagging at the knees in order to level up with the mirror, he combed his hair.

'You'll have to tell them.'

'I can't tell them.'

'You mean, we've got to give them dinner?'

'Well, we've got to give them something.'

'What am I going to *do*?'

'Have they had a drink?'

'No.'

'Well, give them a drink right away, and we'll try to sort the rest of the evening out after that.'

They were talking in whispers. He wasn't even looking at her properly.

'Henry, I'm sorry.'

He was buttoning his waistcoat. 'It can't be helped. Just go down and give them a drink.'

She flew back downstairs, paused for a moment at the closed sitting-room door, and heard from behind it the companionable murmur of married chat. She blessed them once again for being the sort of people who always had things to say to each other, and made for the kitchen. There was the cake, fresh from the oven. There was the salad. And there was Evie, her hat on, her coat buttoned, and just about off. 'You've got visitors,' she remarked, looking pleased.

'They're not visitors. It's the Fairhursts. Henry's chairman and his wife.'

Evie stopped looking pleased. 'But they're coming tomorrow.'

'I've made some ghastly mistake. They've come tonight. And there's nothing to eat, Evie.' Her voice broke. 'Nothing.'

Evie considered. She recognized a crisis when she saw one. Crises were the stuff of life to Evie. Motherless lambs, egg-bound hens, smoking chimneys, moth in the church kneelers – in her time, she had dealt with them all. Nothing gave Evie more satisfaction than rising to the occasion.

Now, she glanced at the clock, and then took off her hat.
'I'll stay,' she announced, 'and give you a hand.'

'Oh, Evie – will you *really?*'

'The children are asleep. That's one problem out of the
way.' She unbuttoned her coat. 'Does Henry know?'

'Yes, he's nearly dressed.'

'What did he say?'

'He said, give them a drink.'

'Then what are we waiting for?' asked Evie.

They found a tray, some glasses, the bottle of Tio Pepe.
Evie manhandled ice out of the icetray. Alison found nuts.

'The dining room,' said Alison. 'I'd meant to light the
fire. It's icy.'

'I'll get the little paraffin stove going. It smells a bit but
it'll warm the room quicker than anything else. And I'll
draw the curtains and switch on the hot plate.' She opened
the kitchen door. 'Quick, now, in you go.'

Alison carried the tray across the hall, fixed a smile on
her face, opened the door and made her entrance. The
Fairhursts were sitting by the fire, looking relaxed and
cheerful, but Mr Fairhurst got to his feet and came to help
Alison, pulling forward a low table and taking the tray from
her hands.

'We were just wishing,' said Mrs Fairhurst, 'that our
daughter would follow your example and move out into
the country. They've a dear little flat in the Fulham Road,
but she's having her second baby in the summer, and I'm
afraid it's going to be very cramped.'

'It's quite a step to take . . .' Alison picked up the sherry
bottle, but Mr Fairhurst said, 'Allow me,' and took it from

408

her and poured the drinks himself, handing a glass to his wife. '. . . But Henry—'

As she said his name, she heard his footsteps on the stairs, the door opened, and there he was. She had expected him to burst into the room, out of breath, thoroughly fussed, and with some button or cuff-link missing. But his appearance was neat and immaculate – as though he had spent at least half an hour in getting changed instead of the inside of two minutes. Despite the nightmare of what was happening, Alison found time to be filled with admiration for her husband. He never ceased to surprise her, and his composure was astonishing. She began to feel, herself, a little calmer. It was, after all, Henry's future, his career, that was at stake. If he could take this evening in his stride, then surely Alison could do the same. Perhaps, together, they could carry it off.

Henry was charming. He apologized for his late appearance, made sure that his guests were comfortable, poured his own glass of sherry, and settled himself, quite at ease, in the middle of the sofa. He and the Fairhursts began to talk about Birmingham. Alison laid down her glass, murmured something about seeing to dinner, and slipped out of the room.

Across the hall, she could hear Evie struggling with the old paraffin heater. She went into the kitchen and tied on an apron. There was the salad. And what else? No time to unfreeze the prawns, deal with the fillet of beef, or make Mother's lemon soufflé. But there was the deep freeze, filled as usual with the sort of food her children would eat, and not much else. Fish fingers, frozen chips, ice cream. She opened its lid and peered inside. Saw a couple of rock-hard chickens, three loaves of sliced bread, two iced lollies on sticks.

Oh, God, please let me find something, please let there be something I can give the Fairhursts to eat.

She thought of all the panic-stricken prayers which in the course of her life she had sent winging upwards. Long ago, she had decided that somewhere, up in the wild blue yonder, there simply had to be a computer, otherwise how could God keep track of the millions of billions of requests for aid and assistance that had been coming at Him through all eternity?

Please let there be something for dinner.

Tring, tring, went the computer, and there was the answer. A plastic carton of Chilli con Carne, which Alison had made and stored a couple of months ago, that wouldn't take more than fifteen minutes to unfreeze, stirred in a pot over the hot plate, and with it they could have boiled rice and the salad.

Investigation proved that there was no rice, only a half-empty packet of Tagliatelle. Chilli con Carne and Tagliatelle with a crisp green salad. Said quickly, it didn't sound so bad.

And for starters . . .? Soup. There was a single can of consommé, not enough for four people. She searched her shelves for something to go with it, and came up with a jar of kangaroo tail soup that had been given to them as a joke two Christmases ago. She filled her arms with the carton, the packet, the tin, and the jar, closed the lid of the deep freeze, and put everything on to the kitchen table. Evie appeared, carrying the paraffin can, and with a sooty smudge on her nose.

'That's going fine,' she announced. 'Warmer already, that room is. You hadn't done any flowers, and the table looked a bit bare, so I put the fruit bowl with the oranges in the middle of the table. Doesn't look like much, but it's better than nothing.' She set down the can and looked at the strange assortment of goods on the table.

'What's all this, then?'

'Dinner,' said Alison from the saucepan cupboard where she was trying to find a pot large enough for the Chilli con Carne. 'Clear soup – half of it kangaroo tail, but nobody needs to know that. Chilli con Carne and Tagliatelle. Won't that be all right?'

Evie made a face. 'Doesn't sound much to me, but some people will eat anything.' She preferred plain food herself, none of this foreign nonsense. A nice bit of mutton with caper sauce, that's what Evie would have chosen.

'And pudding? What can I do for pudding?'

'There's ice cream in the freezer.'

'I can't just give them ice cream.'

'Make a sauce then. Hot chocolate's nice.'

Hot chocolate sauce. The best hot chocolate sauce was made by simply melting bars of chocolate, and Alison had bars of chocolate, because she'd bought two for the children and forgotten to give them to them. She found her handbag and the chocolate bars.

And then, coffee.

'I'll make the coffee,' said Evie.

'I haven't had time to wash the best cups and they're in the sitting-room cupboard.'

'Never mind, we'll give them tea cups. Most people like big cups anyway. I know I do. Can't be bothered with those

411

demmy tassies.' Already she had the Chilli con Carne out of its carton and into the saucepan. She stirred it, peering at it suspiciously. 'What are these little things, then?'

'Red kidney beans.'

'Smells funny.'

'That's the Chilli. It's Mexican food.'

'Only hope they like Mexican food.'

Alison hoped so too.

When she joined the others, Henry let a decent moment or two pass, and then got to his feet and excused himself, saying that he had to see to the wine.

'You really are wonderful, you young people,' said Mrs Fairhurst when he had gone. 'I used to dread having people for dinner when we were first married, *and* I had somebody to help me.'

'Evie's helping me this evening.'

'And I was such a hopeless cook!'

'Oh, come, dear,' her husband comforted her. 'That was a long time ago.'

It seemed a good time to say it. 'I do hope you can eat Chilli con Carne. It's rather hot.'

'Is that what we're having for dinner tonight? What a treat. I haven't had it since Jock and I were in Texas. We went out there with a business convention.'

Mr Fairhurst enlarged on this. 'And when we went to India, she could eat a hotter curry than anybody else. I was in tears, and there she was, looking as cool as a cucumber.'

Henry returned to them. Alison, feeling as though they were engaged in some ludicrous game, withdrew once more. In the kitchen, Evie had everything under control, down to the last heated plate.

'Better get them in,' said Evie, 'and if the place reeks of paraffin, don't say anything. It's better to ignore these things.'

But Mrs Fairhurst said that she loved the smell of paraffin. It reminded her of country cottages when she was a child. And indeed, the dreaded dining room did not look too bad. Evie had lit the candles and left on only the small wall lights over the Victorian sideboard. They all took their places. Mr Fairhurst faced the Highland cow in the rain. 'Where on earth,' he wanted to know, as they started in on the soup, 'did you find that wonderful picture? People don't have pictures like that in their dining rooms any longer.'

Henry told him about the brass fender and the auction sale. Alison tried to decide whether the kangaroo tail soup tasted like kangaroo tails, but it didn't. It just tasted like soup.

'You've made the room like a Victorian set piece. So clever of you.'

'It wasn't really clever,' said Henry. 'It just happened.'

The decor of the dining room took them through the first course. Over the Chilli con Carne, they talked about Texas, and America, and holidays, and children. 'We always used to take the children to Cornwall,' said Mrs Fairhurst, delicately winding her Tagliatelle on to her fork.

'I'd love to take ours to Brittany,' said Henry. 'I went there once when I was fourteen, and it always seemed to me the perfect place for children.'

Mr Fairhurst said that when he was a boy, he'd been taken every summer to the Isle of Wight. He'd had his own little dinghy. Sailing then became the topic of conversation, and Alison became so interested in this that she forgot

413

about clearing the empty plates until Henry, coming to refill her wineglass, gave her a gentle kick under the table.

She gathered up the dishes and took them out to Evie. Evie said, 'How's it going?'

'All right. I think.'

Evie surveyed the empty plates. 'Well, they ate it, anyway. Come on now, get the rest in before the sauce goes solid, and I'll get on with the coffee.'

Alison said, 'I don't know what I'd have done without you, Evie. I simply don't know what I'd have done.'

'You take my advice,' said Evie, picking up the tray with the ice cream and the pudding bowls, and placing it heavily in Alison's hands. 'Buy yourself a little diary. Write everything down. Times like this are too important to leave to chance. That's what you should do. Buy yourself a little diary.'

'What I don't understand,' said Henry, 'is why you never wrote the date down.'

It was now midnight. The Fairhursts had departed at half-past eleven, full of grateful thanks, and hopes that Alison and Henry would, very soon, come and have dinner with them. They were charmed by the house, they said again, and had so enjoyed the delicious meal. It had indeed, Mrs Fairhurst reiterated, been a memorable evening.

They drove off, into the darkness. Henry closed the front door and Alison burst into tears.

It took quite a long time, and a glass of whisky, before she could be persuaded to stop. 'I'm hopeless,' she told Henry. 'I know I'm hopeless.'

'You did very well.'

'But it was such an extraordinary meal. Evie never thought they'd eat it! And the dining room wasn't warm at all, it just smelt—'

'It didn't smell bad.'

'And there weren't any flowers, just oranges, and I know you like having time to open your wine, and I was wearing a dressing-gown.'

'It looked lovely.'

She refused to be comforted. 'But it was so important. It was so important for you. And I had it all planned. The fillet of beef and everything, and the flowers I was going to do. And I had a shopping list, and I'd written everything down.'

It was then that he said, 'What I don't understand is why you never wrote the date down.'

She tried to remember. She had stopped crying by now, and they were sitting together on the sofa in front of the dying fire. 'I don't think there was anything to write it down on. I can never find a bit of paper at the right moment. And she said the seventh. I'm sure she said the seventh. But she couldn't have,' she finished hopelessly.

'I gave you a diary for Christmas,' Henry reminded her.

'I know, but Larry borrowed it for drawing in and I haven't seen it since. Oh, Henry, you won't get that job, it'll be all my fault. I know that.'

'If I don't get the job, it's because I wasn't meant to. Now, don't let's talk about it any more. It's over and finished with. Let's go to bed.'

*

The next morning it rained. Henry went to work, and Larry was picked up by a neighbour and driven to nursery school. Janey was teething, unhappy and demanding endless attention. With the baby either in her arms or whining at her feet, Alison endeavoured to make beds, wash dishes, tidy the kitchen. Later, when she was feeling stronger, she would ring her mother and tell her that there was now no need for her to come and fetch the children and keep them for the night. If she did it now, she knew that she would dissolve into tears and weep down the telephone, and she didn't want to upset her mother.

When she had finally got Janey settled down for her morning sleep, she went into the dining room. It was dark and smelt stalely of cigar smoke and the last fumes of the old paraffin heater. She drew back the velvet curtains and the grey morning light shone in on the wreckage of crumpled napkins, wine-stained glasses, brimming ashtrays. She found a tray and began to collect the glasses. The telephone rang.

She thought it was probably Evie. 'Hello?'

'Alison.' It was Mrs Fairhurst. 'My dear child. What can I say?'

Alison frowned. What, indeed, could Mrs Fairhurst have to say? 'I'm sorry'?

'It was all my fault. I've just looked at my diary to check a Save the Children Fund meeting I have to go to, and I realize that it was *tonight* you asked us for dinner. Friday. You weren't expecting us last night, because we weren't meant to be there.'

Alison took a deep breath and then let it all out again in a trembling sigh of relief. She felt as though a great weight had been taken from her shoulders. It hadn't been her mistake. It had been Mrs Fairhurst's.

'Well . . .' There was no point in telling a lie. She began to smile. 'No.'

'And you never said a word. You just behaved as though we were expected, and gave us that delicious dinner. And everything looked so pretty, and both of you so relaxed. I can't get over it. And I can't imagine how I was so stupid except that I couldn't find my glasses, and I obviously wrote it down on the wrong day. Will you ever forgive me?'

'But I was just as much to blame. I'm terribly vague on the telephone. In fact, I thought the mix-up was all my fault.'

'Well, you were so sweet. And Jock will be furious with me when I ring him up and tell him.'

'I'm sure he won't be.'

'Well, there it is, and I'm truly sorry. It must have been a nightmare opening your door and finding us there, all dressed up like Christmas trees! But you both came up trumps. Congratulations. And thank you for being so understanding to a silly old woman.'

'I don't think you're silly at all,' said Alison to her husband's chairman's wife. 'I think you're smashing.'

When Henry came home that evening, Alison was cooking the fillet of beef. It was too much for the two of them, but the children could eat the leftovers cold for lunch the next day. Henry was late. The children were in bed and asleep. The cat had been fed, the fire lighted. It was nearly a quarter-past seven when she heard his car come up the lane and park in the garage. The engine was turned off, the garage door closed. Then the back door opened and Henry appeared, looking much as usual, except, along with his briefcase and his newspaper, he carried the biggest bunch of red roses Alison had ever seen.

With his foot, he shut the door behind him.

'Well,' he said.

'Well,' said Alison.

'They came on the wrong night.'

'Yes, I know. Mrs Fairhurst rang me. She'd written it down wrong in her diary.'

'They both think you're wonderful.'

'It doesn't matter what they think of me. It's what they think of you that counts.'

Henry smiled. He came towards her, holding the roses in front of him like an offering.

'Do you know who these are for?'

Alison considered. 'Evie, I should hope. If anyone deserves red roses, it's Evie.'

'I have already arranged for roses to be delivered to Evie. Pink ones, with lots of asparagus fern and a suitable card. Try again.'

'They're for Janey?'

'Wrong.'

'Larry? The cat?'

'Still wrong.'

'Give up.'

'They are,' said Henry, trying to sound portentous, but in point of fact looking bright-eyed as an expectant school-boy, 'for the wife of the newly appointed Export Director of Fairhurst & Hanbury.'

'You got the job!'

He drew away from her and they looked at each other. Then Alison made a sound that was halfway between a sob and a shout of triumph and flung herself at him. He dropped briefcase, newspaper, and roses, and gathered her into his arms.

After a little, Catkin, disturbed by all this commotion, jumped down from his basket to inspect the roses, but when he realized that they were not edible, returned to his blanket and went back to sleep.

A Pair of Yellow Lilies

BY RUTH RENDELL

A famous designer, young still, who first became well known when she made a princess's wedding dress, was coming to speak to the women's group of which Bridget Thomas was secretary. She would be the second speaker in the autumn programme which was devoted to success and how women had achieved it. Repeated requests on Bridget's part for a biography from Annie Carter so that she could provide her members with interesting background information had met with no response. Bridget had even begun to wonder if she would remember to come and give her talk in three weeks' time. Meanwhile, obliged to do her own research, she had gone into the public library to look Annie Carter up in *Who's Who*.

Bridget had a precarious job in a small and not very prosperous bookshop. In her mid-thirties, with a rather pretty face that often looked worried and worn, she thought that she might learn something from this current series of talks. Secrets of success might be imparted, blueprints for achievement, even short cuts to prosperity. She never had enough money, never knew security, could not have dreamed of aspiring to an Annie Carter ready-to-wear even when such a garment had been twice marked down in a sale. Clothes, anyway, were hardly a priority, coming a long way down the list of essentials which was headed by rent, fares, food, in that order.

In the library she was not noticeable. She was not, in any case and anywhere, the kind of woman on whom second glances were bestowed. On this Wednesday evening, when the shop closed at its normal time and the library later than usual, she could be seen by those few who cared to look, wearing a long black skirt with a dusty appearance, a tee-shirt of a slightly different shade of black – it had been washed fifty times at least – and a waistcoat in dark striped cotton. Her shoes were black velvet Chinese slippers with instep straps and there was a hole she did not know about in her turquoise blue tights, low down on the left calf. Bridget's hair was wispy, long and fair, worn in loops. She was carrying an enormous black leather bag, capacious and heavy, and full of unnecessary things. Herself the first to admit this, she often said she meant to make changes in the matter of this bag but she never got around to it.

This evening the bag contained: a number of crumpled tissues, some pink, some white; a spray bottle of Wild Musk cologne; three ballpoint pens; a pair of nail scissors; a pair of nail clippers; a London tube pass; a British Telecom phone card; an address book; a mascara wand in a shade called After-midnight Blue; a cheque book; a notebook; a postcard from a friend on holiday in Brittany; a calculator; a paperback of Vasari's *Lives of the Artists*, which Bridget had always meant to read but was not getting on very fast with; a container of nasal spray; a bunch of keys; a book of matches; a silver ring with a green stone, probably onyx; a pheasant's feather picked up while staying for the weekend in someone's cottage in Somerset; three-quarters of a bar of milk chocolate; a pair of sunglasses; and her wallet which contained the single credit card she possessed, her bank cheque card, her library card, her never-needed driving licence and seventy pounds, give or take a little, in five- and ten-pound notes. There was also about four pounds in change.

On the previous evening Bridget had been to see her aunt. This was the reason for her carrying so much money. Bridget's Aunt Monica was an old woman who had never married and whom her brother, Bridget's father, referred to with brazen insensitivity as 'a maiden lady'. Bridget thought this outrageous and remonstrated with her father but was unable to bring him to see anything offensive in this expression. Though Monica had never had a husband, she had been successful in other areas of life, and might indeed almost have qualified to join Bridget's list of female achievers fit to speak to her women's group. Inherited money wisely invested brought her in a substantial income, and this added to the pension derived from having been quite high up the ladder in the Civil Service made her nearly rich.

Bridget did not like taking Monica Thomas's money. Or she told herself she didn't, actually meaning that she liked the money very much but felt humiliated as a young healthy woman who ought to have been able to keep herself adequately, taking money from an old one who had done so and still did. Monica, not invariably during these visits but often enough, would ask her how she was managing.

'Making ends meet, are you?' was the form this enquiry usually took.

Bridget felt a little tide of excitement rising in her at

these words because she knew they signified a coming munificence. She simultaneously felt ashamed at being excited by such a thing. This was the way, she believed, other women might feel at the prospect of love-making or discovering themselves pregnant or getting promotion. She felt excited because her old aunt, her maiden aunt tucked away in a gloomy flat in Fulham, was about to give her fifty pounds.

Characteristically, Monica prepared the ground. 'You may as well have it now instead of waiting till I'm gone.'

And Bridget would smile and look away, or if she felt brave tell her aunt not to talk about dying. Once she had gone so far as to say, 'I don't come here for the sake of what you give me, you know,' but as she put this into words she knew she did. And Monica, replying tartly, 'And I don't see my little gifts as paying you for your visits,' must have known that she did and they did, and that the two of them were involved in a commercial transaction, calculated enough, but imbrued with guilt and shame.

Bridget always felt that at her age, thirty-six, and her aunt's, seventy-two, it should be she who gave alms and her aunt who received them. That was the usual way of things. Here the order was reversed, and with a hand that she had to restrain forcibly from trembling with greed and need and excitement, she had reached out on the previous evening for the notes that were presented as a sequel to another of Monica's favourite remarks, that she would like to see Bridget better dressed. With only a vague grasp of changes in the cost of living, Monica nevertheless knew that for any major changes in her niece's wardrobe to take place, a larger than usual sum would be required. Another twenty-five had been added to the customary fifty. Five pounds or so had been spent during the course of the day. Bridget had plenty to do with the rest, which did not include buying the simple dark coat and skirt and pink twinset Monica had suggested. There was the gas bill, for instance, and the chance at last of settling the credit card account, on which interest was being paid at twenty-one per cent. Not that Bridget had no wistful thoughts of beautiful things she would like to possess and most likely never would. A chair in a shop window in Bond Street, for instance, a chair which stood alone in slender, almost arrogant, elegance, with its high-stepping legs and sweetly curved back, she imagined gracing her room as a bringer of daily-renewed happiness and pride. Only today a woman had come into the shop to order the new Salman Rushdie and she had been wearing a dress that was unmistakably Annie Carter. Bridget had gazed at that dress as at some unattainable glory, at its bizarreries of zips round the sleeves and triangles excised from armpits, uneven hemline and slashed back, for if the truth were told it was the fantastic she admired in such matters and would not have been seen dead in a pink twinset.

She had gazed and longed, just as now, fetching *Who's Who* back to her seat at the table, she had stared, in passing, at the back of a glorious jacket. Afterwards she could not have said if it was a man or woman wearing it, a person in jeans was all she could have guessed at. The person in jeans was pressed fairly close up against the science fiction shelves so that the back of the jacket, its most beautiful and striking area, was displayed to the best advantage. The jacket was made of blue denim with a design appliquéd on it. Bridget knew the work was appliqué because she had learned something of this technique herself at a handicrafts class, all part of the horizon-widening, life-enhancing programme with which she combated loneliness. Patches of satin and silk and brocade had been used in the work, and beads and sequins and gold thread as well. The design was of a flock of brilliant butterflies, purple and turquoise and vermilion and royal blue and fuchsia pink, tumbling and fluttering from the open mouths of a pair of yellow lilies. Bridget had gazed at this fantastic picture in silks and jewels and then looked quickly away, resolving to look no more, she desired so much to possess it herself.

Annie Carter's *Who's Who* entry mentioned a book she had written on fashion in the early eighties. Bridget thought it would be sensible to acquaint herself with it. It would provide her with something to talk about when she and the Committee entertained the designer to supper after her talk. Leaving *Who's Who* open on the table and her bag wedged between the table legs and the leg of her chair, Bridget went off to consult the library's computer as to whether this book was in stock.

Afterwards she recalled, though dimly, some of the people she had seen as she crossed the floor of the library to where the computer was. An old man in gravy-brown clothes reading a newspaper, two old women in fawn raincoats and pudding-basin hats, a child that ran about in defiance of its mother's threats and pleas. The mother was a woman about Bridget's own age, grossly fat, with fuzzy dark hair and swollen legs. There had been other people less memorable. The computer told her the book was in stock but out on loan. Bridget went back to her table and sat down. She read the sparse *Who's Who* entry once more, noting that Annie Carter's interests were bob-sleighing and collecting netsuke, which seemed to make her rather a daunting person, and then she reached down for her bag and the notebook it contained.

The bag was gone.

The feeling Bridget experienced is one everyone has when they lose something important or think they have lost it, the shock of loss. It was a physical sensation as of something falling through her – turning over in her chest first and then tumbling down inside her body and out through the soles of her feet. She immediately told herself she couldn't have lost the bag, she couldn't have done, it couldn't have been stolen – who would have stolen it among that company? – she must have taken it with her to the computer. Bridget went back to the computer, she ran back, and the bag wasn't there. She told the two assistant librarians and then the librarian herself and they all looked round the library for the bag. It seemed to Bridget that by this time everyone else who had been in the library had swiftly disappeared, everyone that is but the old man reading the newspaper.

The librarian was extremely kind. They were about to close and she said she would go to the police with Bridget, it was on her way. Bridget continued to feel the shock of loss, sickening overturnings in her body and sensations of panic and disbelief. Her head seemed too lightly poised on her neck, almost as if it floated.

'It can't have happened,' she kept saying to the librarian. 'I just don't believe it could have happened in those few seconds I was away.'

'I'm afraid it did,' said the librarian who was too kind to say anything about Bridget's unwisdom in leaving the bag unattended even for a few seconds. 'It's nothing to do with me, but was there much money in it?'

'Quite a lot. Yes, quite a lot.' Bridget added humbly, 'Well, a lot for me.'

The police could offer very little hope of recovering the money. The bag, they said, and some of its contents might turn up. Meanwhile Bridget had no means of getting into her room, no means even of phoning the credit card company to notify them of the theft. The librarian, whose name was Elizabeth Derwent, saw to all that. She took Bridget to her own home and led her to the telephone and then took her to a locksmith. It was the beginning of what was to be an enduring friendship. Bridget might have lost so many of the most precious of her worldly goods, but as she said afterwards to her Aunt Monica, at least she got Elizabeth's friendship out of it.

'It's an ill wind that blows nobody any good,' said Monica, pressing fifty pounds in ten-pound notes into Bridget's hand.

But all this was in the future. That first evening Bridget had to come to terms with the loss of seventy pounds, her driving licence, her credit card, her cheque book, the *Lives of the Artists* (she would never read it now), her address book and the silver ring with the stone which was probably onyx. She mourned, alone there in her room. She fretted miserably, shock and disbelief having been succeeded by the inescapable certainty that someone had deliberately stolen her bag. Several cups of strong hot tea comforted her a little. Bridget had more in common with her aunt than she would have liked to think possible, being very much a latter-day maiden lady in every respect but maidenhood.

At the end of the week a parcel came. It contained her wallet (empty but for the library card), the silver ring, her address book, her notebook, the nail scissors and the nail clippers, the mascara wand in the shade called After-midnight Blue and most of the things she had lost but for the money and the credit card and the cheque book, the driving licence, the paperback Vasari, and the bag itself. A letter accompanied the things. It said:

> *Dear Miss Thomas,*
>   *This name and address were in the notebook. I hope they are yours and that this will reach you. I found your things inside a plastic bag on top of a litter bin in Kensington Church Street. It was the wallet which made me think they were not things someone had meant to throw away. I am afraid this is absolutely all there was, though I have the feeling there was money in the wallet and perhaps other valuable things.*
> *Yours sincerely,*
> *Patrick Baker*

His address and a phone number headed the sheet of paper. Bridget, who was not usually impulsive, was so immediately brimming with amazed happiness and restored faith in human nature, that she lifted the phone at once and dialled the number. He answered. It was a pleasant voice, educated, rather slow and deliberate in its enunciation

of words, a young man's voice. She poured out her gratitude. How kind he was! What trouble he had been to! Not
only to retrieve her things but to take them home, to parcel
them up, pay the postage, stand in a queue no doubt at the
Post Office! What could she do for him? How could she
show the gratitude she felt?

Come and have a drink with him, he said. Well, of course
she would, of course. She promised to have a drink with
him and a place was arranged and a time, though she was
already getting cold feet. She consulted Elizabeth.

'Having a drink in a pub in Kensington High Street
couldn't do any harm,' said Elizabeth, smiling.

'It's not really something I do.' It wasn't something she
had done for years, at any rate. In fact it was two years since
Bridget had even been out with a man, since her sad affair
with the married accountant, which had dragged on year
after year, had finally come to an end. Drinking in pubs had
not been a feature of the relationship. Sometimes they
had made swift furtive love in the small office where clients'
VAT files were kept. 'I suppose,' she said, 'it might make a
pleasant change.'

The aspect of Patrick Baker which would have made him
particularly attractive to most women, if it did not repel
Bridget, at least put her off. He was too good-looking for
her. He was, in fact, radiantly beautiful, like an angel or a
young Swedish tennis player. This, of course, did not
specially matter that first time. But his looks registered with
her as she walked across the little garden at the back of the
pub and he rose from the table at which he was sitting. His
looks frightened her and made her shy. It would not have
been true, though, to say that she could not keep her eyes

off him. Looking at him was altogether too much for her, it was almost an embarrassment, and she tried to keep her eyes turned away.

Nor would she have known what to say to him. Fortunately, he was eager to recount in detail his discovery of her property in the litter bin in Kensington Church Street. Bridget was good at listening and she listened. He told her also how he had once lost a briefcase in a tube train and a friend of his had had his wallet stolen on a train going from New York to Philadelphia. Emboldened by these homely and not at all sophisticated anecdotes, Bridget told him about the time her Aunt Monica had burglars and lost an emerald necklace which fortunately was insured. This prompted him to ask more about her aunt and Bridget found herself being quite amusing, recounting Monica's financial adventures. She didn't see why she shouldn't tell him the origins of the stolen money and he seemed interested when she said it came from Monica who was in the habit of bestowing like sums on her.

'You see, she says I'm to have it one day – she means when she's dead, poor dear – so why not now?'

'Why not indeed?'

'It was just my luck to have my wallet stolen the day after she'd given me all that money.'

He asked her to have dinner with him. Bridget said all right but it mustn't be anywhere expensive or grand. She asked Elizabeth what she should wear. They were in a clothes mood, for it was the evening of the Annie Carter talk to the women's group which Elizabeth had been persuaded to join.

'He doesn't dress at all formally himself,' Bridget said.

'Rather the reverse.' He and she had been out for another drink in the meantime. 'He was wearing this kind of safari suit with a purple shirt. But, oh Elizabeth, he is amazing to look at. Rather too much so, if you know what I mean.'

Elizabeth didn't. She said that surely one couldn't be too good-looking? Bridget said she knew she was being silly but it embarrassed her a bit – well, being seen with him, if Elizabeth knew what she meant. It made her feel awkward.

'I'll lend you my black lace if you like,' Elizabeth said. 'It would suit you and it's suitable for absolutely everything.'

Bridget wouldn't borrow the black lace. She refused to sail in under anyone else's colours. She wouldn't borrow Aunt Monica's emerald necklace either, the one she had bought to replace the necklace the burglars took. Her black skirt and the velvet top from the secondhand shop in Hammersmith would be quite good enough. If she couldn't have an Annie Carter she would rather not compromise. Monica, who naturally had never been told anything about the married accountant or his distant predecessor, the married primary school teacher, spoke as if Patrick Baker were the first man Bridget had ever been alone with, and spoke too as if marriage were a far from remote possibility. Bridget listened to all this while thinking how awful it would be if she were to fall in love with Patrick Baker and become addicted to his beauty and suffer when separated from him.

Even as she thought in this way, so prudently and with irony, she could see his face before her, its hawk-like lineaments and its softnesses, the wonderful mouth and the large wide-set eyes, the hair that was fair and thick and the skin that was smooth and brown. She saw too his muscular figure, slender and graceful yet strong, his long

431

hands and his tapering fingers, and she felt something long-suppressed, a prickle of desire that plucked very lightly at the inside of her and made her gasp a little.

The restaurant where they had their dinner was not grand or expensive, and this was just as well since at the end of the meal Patrick found that he had left his cheque book at home and Bridget was obliged to pay for their dinner out of the money Monica had given her to buy an evening dress. He was very grateful. He kissed her on the pavement outside the restaurant, or if not quite outside it, under the archway that was the entrance to the mews. They went back to his place in a taxi.

Patrick had quite a nice flat at the top of a house in Bayswater, not exactly overlooking the park but nearly. It was interesting what was happening to Bridget. Most of the time she was able to stand outside herself and view these deliberate acts of hers with detachment. She would have the pleasure of him, he was so beautiful, she would have it and that would be that. Such men were not for her, not at any rate for more than once or twice. But if she could once in a lifetime have one of them for once or twice, why not? Why not?

The life too, the lifestyle, was not for her. On the whole she was better off at home with a pot of strong hot tea and her embroidery or the latest paperback on changing attitudes to women in Western society. Nor had she any intention of sharing Aunt Monica's money when the time came. She had recently had to be stern with herself about a tendency, venal and degrading, to dream of that distant prospect when she would live in a World's End studio with a gallery, fit setting for the arrogant Bond Street chair, and dress in a bold eccentric manner, in flowing skirts and antique pelisses and fine old lace.

Going home with Patrick, she was rather drunk. Not drunk enough not to know what she was doing but drunk enough not to care. She was drunk enough to shed her inhibitions while being sufficently sober to know she had inhibitions, to know that they would be waiting to return to her later and to return quite unchanged. She went into Patrick's arms with delight, with the reckless abandon and determination to enjoy herself of someone embarking on a world cruise that must necessarily take place but once. Being in bed with him was not in the least like being in the VAT records office with the married accountant. She had known it would not be and that was why she was there. During the night the central heating went off and failed, through some inadequacy of a fragile pilot light, to restart itself. It grew cold but Bridget, in the arms of Patrick Baker, did not feel it.

She was the first to wake up. Bridget was the kind of person who is always the first to wake up. She lay in bed a little way apart from Patrick Baker and thought about what a lovely time she had had the night before and how that was enough and she would not see him again. Seeing him again might be dangerous and she could not afford, with her unmemorable appearance, her precarious job and low wage, to put herself in peril. Presently she got up and said to Patrick, who had stirred a little and made an attempt in a kindly way to cuddle her, that she would make him a cup of tea.

Patrick put his nose out of the bedclothes and said it was freezing, the central heating had gone wrong, it was always going wrong. 'Don't get cold,' he said sleepily. 'Find something to put on in the cupboard.'

Even it they had been in the tropics Bridget would not have dreamt of walking about a man's flat with no clothes on. She dressed. While the kettle was boiling she looked with interest around Patrick's living room. There had been no opportunity to take any of it in on the previous evening. He was an untidy man, she noted, and his taste was not distinguished. You could see he bought his pictures ready-framed at Athena Art. He hadn't many books and most of what he had was science fiction, so it was rather a surprise to come upon Vasari's *Lives of the Artists* in paperback between a volume of fighting fantasy and a John Wyndham classic.

Perhaps she did after all feel cold. She was aware of a sudden unpleasant chill. It was comforting to feel the warmth of the kettle against her hands. She made the tea and took him a cup, setting it down on the bedside table, for he was fast asleep again. Shivering now, she opened the cupboard door and looked inside.

He seemed to possess a great many coats and jackets. She pushed the hangers along the rail, sliding tweed to brush against serge and linen against wild silk. His wardrobe was vast and complicated. He must have a great deal to spend on himself. The jacket with the butterflies slid into sudden brilliant view as if pushed there by some stage manager of fate. Everything conspired to make the sight of it dramatic, even the sun which came out and shed an unexpected ray into the open cupboard. Bridget gazed at the denim jacket as she had gazed with similar lust and wonder once before. She stared at the cascade of butterflies in purple and vermilion and turquoise, royal blue and fuchsia pink that tumbled and fluttered from the open mouths of a pair of yellow lilies.

She hardly hesitated before taking it off its hanger and putting it on. It was glorious. She remembered that this was the word she had thought of the first time she had seen it. How she had longed to possess it and how she had not dared look for long lest the yearning became painful and ridiculous! With her head a little on one side she stood over Patrick, wondering whether to kiss him goodbye. Perhaps not, perhaps it would be better not. After all, he would hardly notice.

She let herself out of the flat. They would not meet again. A more than fair exchange had been silently negotiated by her. Feeling happy, feeling very light of heart, she ran down the stairs and out into the morning, insulated from the cold by her coat of many colours, her butterflies, her rightful possession.

The Surprise Package

BY LESLIE THOMAS

There would be no snow, that was certain. The weather forecaster had, with an assured gloom, said that Christmas would be mild and grey, and so it was. From one side of the window to the other the ridge stretched, flat winter-green with a band of grey sky above like a flag. It was so different when it snowed; the ridge white and solid as a slice of the Alps, and bright with people on toboggans. But not this Christmas. There would be no snow.

There would, however, be Aunt Nora and Aunt Beatty and Uncle Bernard. Geoffrey sighed with no pleasure. He could imagine them arriving, as they assuredly would and did year after year, his Aunt Nora getting out of the station taxi and brusquely sending the driver away without a tip because of the bumpy ride, Susan's Uncle Bernard driving his car at twenty-three miles an hour ('Saves wear and tear on the engine. Cars are not built like they were!'), and Aunt Beatty rosy with cold and what she believed, quite genuinely, were the joys of the season.

He knew that Susan felt the same as he did but, as she said every year after they had all gone, Christmas was a duty as much as anything. For himself, he would have given anything for a different Christmas. Just once.

At least Christmas Eve was market day in Illingford and

he never failed to enjoy that. The relatives had yet to arrive and only he and the children Peter and Julia went. Aunt Nora had been with them once and had complained enthusiastically throughout the morning, even accusing the chestnut man of selling lukewarm chestnuts. Had Aunt Beatty been there her resolute cheeriness would, he knew too well, have been wearing and Uncle Bernard would have stalked around grunting and grumbling at the price of everything, and saying that he could remember the days when markets were *real* markets.

Geoffrey and the children were in Illingford by ten-thirty and they were not disappointed.

Everything was so animated and good-humoured; there was a man auctioning last-minute turkeys with the zest of a television-games presenter; pyramids of fruit glistened under the bare light bulbs of the stalls; there were vegetables scrubbed cleaner than choirboys, Christmas cards at half-price, cheap and cheerful toys, and, of course, people crowding among the goods, breath clouding the winter air. And, this year, there was Cedric. 'You should have seen him,' beamed Peter, when they got back home.

'He could do *everything*,' enthused ten-year-old Julia. 'He could play tunes on *spoons*.'

'It's a lost skill,' Uncle Bernard said lugubriously. 'Years ago lots of men could play the spoons.'

'And women,' suggested Aunt Beatty heartily.

'Never saw a woman spoon player,' muttered Bernard. 'Women aren't quick enough.'

Peter, who at twelve was old enough to know when and how to change the subject, said: 'And he sang songs and told jokes and did tricks. He should have been on television, not in the marketplace.'

'Better than most on television, I expect,' put in Aunt Nora with triumphant misery. 'I wonder what we'll have to endure this year?'

The usual, answered Uncle Bernard in his I-know-best voice.

'We'll just have to make our own fun,' said Aunt Beatty brightly.

'Like we did when we were young.'

Geoffrey began to groan inwardly, but somehow the groan escaped. Only Susan heard it and threw him a warning glance.

The visitors went upstairs to unpack which would take at least an hour, a time Geoffrey always savoured. Afterwards they had tea, and the ghosts of Christmasses past began to materialize. It was always the same. Aunt Nora would remember some, presumably far-far-off, Christmas that she had thoroughly enjoyed, and Uncle Bernard would say: 'Ah, but we knew how to enjoy ourselves in those days.' After which Auntie Beatty would sigh her terrible sad-happy sigh and say: 'Well, we didn't have much but we made the best of it.'

In the early-dark of the evening it began to rain, and at about the same time they heard the singing in the lane outside. It was loud and strong, a boisterous baritone through the night. 'Boots, boots, boots, boots. Marching up and down again.'

'I know that voice,' said Geoffrey as they all moved to the window.

'Boots, boots, boots, boots—'

'It's the man!' exclaimed Julia.

'The market man!' confirmed Peter. 'And, Dad, he's coming up the path. He's coming here!'

'Begging,' sniffed Uncle Bernard. 'Always after something, these chaps. You mark my words. I'll be right.'

'You're usually right, Bernard,' agreed Auntie Beatty loyally.

'Or worse,' grumbled Nora. 'Robbery.'

'Robbers don't usually sing and then march up to the front door,' pointed out Geoffrey. The bell rang. 'And ring the bell,' he added.

Susan reached the door first with Geoffrey close behind and the children pushing and scuffling to get a view. The visitors stayed at a discreet grumbling distance.

'Merry Christmas, madam, sir, and children. I'm sorry I wasn't rendering a carol but I've run out.'

'That's all right,' said Geoffrey. 'What can we do for you?'

'Allow me to present myself,' said the man. His face was red and as he stood beneath the porchlight, beaming, it seemed to shine and the bristles pulled out of his chin like a layer of frost. He was engulfed in a huge, wet overcoat, its bottom dripping against his serge-trousered shins. 'Cedric Johnson, itinerant. Known as "Cedric the Nearly" – Nearly Great, that is.'

'You were in the market,' said Julia excitedly.

'Doing tricks, singing and everything,' confirmed Peter. 'And playing the spoons.'

'A lost art, sir,' acknowledged Cedric. 'But it was a good audience today.' He transferred his rubicund attention to Geoffrey. 'Sir, I am progressing North, where it is my habit

439

to celebrate the New Year. As you see, I have been beset by rain.'

He shook the water from his overcoat sleeves. 'I perceive you have a barn at the end of your field, and I am seeking your permission to rest there this Christmas Eve.' He paused, as if wondering whether he was about to go too far, then continued portentously: 'As Mary and Joseph came to the stable in Bethlehem,' before rolling his eyes piously upward.

Afterwards they kept going to the window to see the light in the barn, glowing benignly through the dark and rain.

'Up to no good,' forecast Uncle Bernard. 'Plotting, that's what he's up to. Or on the run.'

'Yes,' agreed the predictable Aunt Nora. 'That's it. He's escaped from somewhere.'

'Anyone,' sighed Geoffrey, 'who is on the run does not stand, on Christmas Eve, playing the spoons in Illingford market.'

'I'll take him a pot of tea,' decided Susan.

'And some cake,' pleaded Julia. 'And I want to come.'

'Why not open a soup kitchen and ask all the down-and-outs for miles?' suggested Bernard sourly.

Peter and Julia ignored him, and helped their mother to prepare what quickly grew into a mammoth supper for Cedric. There was ham and an axe-head of pie, a dish of potatoes, another of vegetables, and a large bottle of ale.

Geoffrey said firmly that he would take it to the barn

alone; a crowd might embarrass Cedric. Itinerants were often touchy, he'd heard.

They watched through the rain-obscured window, the children close to the glass, the two old aunts and Susan in the next rank, and pipe-puffing Uncle Bernard making out he was really interested in what was on the television, but craning over everybody's heads.

'I can't understand why people can't make their plans for Christmas well in advance,' he grunted. 'I do.'

'Yes, you do,' said Susan feelingly.

Geoffrey was gone for ten minutes. Then the barn door opened, the light was extinguished, and two shadows filtered through the garden. 'He's coming in!' exclaimed Peter. 'Dad's got him to come in!'

'I'm afraid he has, Bernard,' said Aunt Nora.

'At least he might know some new jokes,' said Beatty.

Cedric did. He arrived on the threshold as becoming as Christmas itself, his pudding face aglow and stubbled chin thrust out in trenchant good humour. 'I've done full justice to the tasty supper ma'am,' he said with an exaggerated bow towards Susan. 'I thank you for it most kindly. And I wouldn't refuse another piece of that pie.'

Flustered with pleasure, she hurried to the kitchen and returned with another slice of pie.

'I made it myself,' she said.

'I could tell, ma'am,' answered Cedric fulsomely. 'No shop pie tastes like this. This is a very prince among pies.' Somehow he had become seated in the centre of the room. The fire lent a deeper ruddiness to his face and, oddly, began to burn more cheerily itself.

As he ate the pie, he described between – and often

441

through – mouthfuls, the various pies of his experience. Even Aunt Beatty, who thought she knew about pies, had never heard of some of them; the elegant egg-and-cauliflower pies of Cumberland, the fish-and-bird pies of western Wales, the artichoke pies of Jerusalem, the huge bull pies of Spain.

He then sang a passable song about pies and added, for no apparent reason, another seasonal ditty about Christmas Day in the jungle. The facts he knew about the jungle were amazing. He told them a story from the Amazon and then set a riddle on the same subject which, to everyone's astonishment, Uncle Bernard won.

'Not many people could have solved that,' approved Cedric. Nobody could ever remember seeing Uncle Bernard blush with pleasure before, but he did now before realizing it. He said with a scowl: 'The art of riddles is dead.'

'With a few exceptions,' agreed Cedric amiably, suddenly picking up his neighbour Nora's hand and reading her fortune, which turned out to be romantic. He sang another song about a girl called Nora who had shining eyes and then, to please the clamouring children, played the spoons, which was greeted with genuine and admiring applause.

Peter wanted to learn and Cedric coached him enough to enable him to accompany a South American tango which he danced with Aunt Beatty. It was the most exciting Christmas Eve they could recall.

After helping to fill the children's stockings, Cedric slept on the sofa that night, his vivid snores fanning the fire's dying flames. The following morning, he was delighted to find that everyone had found some small present for him. In return, he wrote each of them a message in a secret

442

code; which no one could work out, even by the time they went to church.

He washed and brushed himself beautifully to accompany them, and Susan ironed the bright red muffler which had been her present to him, and beat the dried mud – clouds of it – from his long overcoat.

People in the church were surprised at his appearance, in more than one sense, but grateful for the gusto of his singing. After the first lesson, the vicar asked if he would mind moving towards the front a bit because not only the choir but the organ could do with some help. Cedric, beaming, moved to the choir stalls and led them in Hark, the Herald Angels Sing.

Everyone was delighted with him now. The congregation crowded to shake hands with him after the service; some, when his talents had been described, tentatively asking if they might possibly entertain him (or vice versa) next Christmas. Good-naturedly he said that he *might* be passing that way again. Peter and Susan were worried about this, but Cedric told them they would be first on his visiting list.

He enjoyed Christmas Dinner immensely, as did they all. Uncle Bernard and Aunt Beatty said the turkey was the tenderest ever; Nora went into raptures about the plum pudding, and Julia ate all her vegetables. As Peter was allowed to pour the wine, Geoffrey and Susan exchanged smiles.

Cedric had a little smiling sleep in front of the fire as the short afternoon dwindled from the window. Uncle Bernard did likewise, and it was Aunt Beatty who noticed that Cedric even snored melodiously.

When they were all around the fire again, they looked at him expectantly and he did not fail them. But now, he encouraged each of the others to contribute something of their own. Peter and Julia sang a pop song; their parents performed a witty dialogue which they had done once at an amateur concert party.

Aunt Nora told a long, confused, and not all that funny joke about a parrot and a mouse, and Aunt Beatty told them a true story of a lady she had once known who had fifty-three cats. Uncle Bernard surprised everyone, himself not least, by remembering all the words to 'Sam, Sam, Pick Up Thy Musket'.

They went to bed very late, each one knowing that it had been the best Christmas Day ever. In the morning Cedric had gone, leaving a note saying goodbye.

The visitors drove off, the gravel positively scooting from beneath the tyres at the sudden acceleration of Uncle Bernard's car. Aunt Beatty was thrown backwards with surprise and hooted with laughter. Nora tipped the taxi driver *before* setting out for the station, and Julia and Peter climbed the ridge to see if they could see Cedric in the distance.

'The rising of the sun, and the running of the deer,' sang Geoffrey.

'Boots, boots, boots, boots,' responded Susan in a deep voice. They laughed and embraced. 'Fancy him just turning up like that,' she said, looking at her husband narrowly.

He knew she knew. 'I had the idea when I saw him in the market place,' he confessed. 'It cost me twenty-five pounds, and cheap at the price as you'll agree. He was the best Christmas present I've ever given.'

The Flowers

BY SUE TOWNSEND

The flowers arrived at eleven-thirty in the morning. Sandra
ran downstairs to answer the door. She had been cleaning
the bath and still had a cleaning rag in her hand. It was a
massive bouquet, the delivery woman looked at Sandra
curiously noting the lank hair, the unmade-up face, the
apron and the cleaning rag.

'Mrs Lovejoy?' she asked.

'Yes,' said Sandra.

'These are for you,' said the woman, and turned as
though disappointed towards her little delivery van parked
at the kerb. The flowers were extraordinarily beautiful,
Sandra was overwhelmed by their pastel extravagance, their
heady smell.

'They can't be for me,' she shouted after the woman. It
wasn't her birthday, and she hadn't done anything to
deserve congratulations. The delivery woman assured her
that she hadn't mistaken the address and so Sandra closed
the front door and took the flowers into the dark kitchen
at the back of the house. Pink roses. Spray carnations.
Gypsophila. Freesias. Daisies. All bound together with a
pink satin ribbon. There was an envelope stapled to the
ribbon and inside a card: 'I Love You Sandra,' it said. It was
typewritten and unsigned. Sandra blushed with pleasure. It

wasn't her wedding anniversary, and anyway her husband had never bought her flowers, even when the children were born. He thought flowers were a waste because they died. House plants he tolerated, could see the point of, they were, after all, a type of furniture. But flowers, by their very ephemeral nature, were not cost effective and he was against them.

Sandra was baffled. She stared at the card. 'I Love You Sandra.' But she wasn't the type of woman that people loved. She wasn't beautiful or fascinating or clever or witty. She looked at herself in Alan's shaving mirror which hung over the kitchen sink. Her face was pale and ordinary. She filled the sink with water and put the huge posy in to soak. Then she went upstairs to finish cleaning the bath. But she didn't clean it, she rinsed it and then tipped her precious bath oil into the tub, turned the taps on and watched as the bubbles frothed.

'I love you Sandra.' Who loved her?

She stayed an hour in the bath. She washed and conditioned her hair. Removed rough skin, dealt with unwanted body hair and ignored the ringing of the telephone. When she eventually went downstairs, perfumed and dressed in her second best frock, she felt less intimidated by the flowers, and more able to accept the astonishing fact that they had been sent to *her*.

When she arrived at the baker's shop where she worked part-time, her fellow workers remarked on her enhanced appearance. Behind her back they speculated about the possibility of Sandra having taken a lover. Male customers came under closer scrutiny than usual and the shop that afternoon was full of laughter. By five o'clock the women were almost hysterical; laughing at any trivial thing, like schoolgirls, though there wasn't one of them under forty-five. Sandra didn't dare to mention the flowers though she never stopped thinking about them. When she got home she found Alan at the sink shaving. The flowers were heaped high and dry on the draining board. He was in a bad mood.

'What's all this?' he asked, jabbing towards the flowers with his razor.

'*You* didn't send them then?' she checked.

'Me?' he said. 'There's fifty quid's worth there!'

Alan knew the price of everything, he was a cost analyst. He was very careful with money: Sandra was not even allowed to buy a pedal bin. 'A cardboard box lined with newspaper serves the same purpose,' Alan had pointed out, and Sandra couldn't deny that it did. But even so, she lusted after a pedal bin, a scarlet one she had seen in a hardware shop. She had gone into the shop several times and had surreptitiously pressed her foot on the pedal.

All their money was pooled, Alan paid the bills and gave Sandra housekeeping, it was never enough. Her daughter Catherine was away at college but she couldn't manage on her grant and so Sandra secretly sent her five pounds a week tucked inside the notelets she had been given for Christmas. She asked her not to acknowledge the receipt of this money. Alan wouldn't like it. Catherine was taking Women's Studies at Bristol University and on her rare visits home she quarrelled with her father and called him 'the worst kind of chauvinist'. She urged her mother to assert herself. Sandra was always ashamed of the relief she felt when this tall, confident, pretty girl packed her rucksack and strode out of the house in her big laced-up boots.

Alan finished his early evening shave and then asked about the flowers. Sandra showed him the card. He laughed when he read, 'I Love You Sandra'. He said, 'It's obviously a mistake, who would send *you* flowers?'

Sandra was hurt by this. As she prepared their evening meal tears rolled down her face, smudging the mascara she had applied so clumsily earlier in the day.

Alan was disturbed by her tears. Sandra never cried, he tried to cheer her up by talking about his work, but even this didn't snap her out of her mood of gloomy introspection. They ate in silence until Alan said, 'You're not leaving that chop, are you?'

He said it accusingly, as though Sandra had committed a crime.

'Yes, you have it if you want it,' she said.

'I don't *want* it,' he said irritably, 'but it can't be *wasted*, can it?'

Sandra had a vision of dropping the chop inside the scarlet pedal bin, but instead placed the congealing lamb on to her husband's plate. As she moved about the kitchen he watched her carefully. She looked different, almost pretty. Why was she wearing a decent frock in the house? 'Are you going out?' he asked.

'Yes,' she replied. She hadn't intended to go out, she hardly ever went out in the evening, with or without Alan.

448

'Where are you going?' He was astonished.

'To meet a friend,' she lied. 'After I've arranged the flowers.'

There weren't enough vases so Sandra filled jugs and pickle jars and milk bottles with the sweet-smelling blooms. The small house was instantly beautified; its general shabbiness temporarily disguised. Alan sat in the lounge flanked by roses and carnations, he pretended to watch television. Sandra put her best coat on and collected her handbag.

'Well, bye,' she said. *And she went.* She didn't know where to go, she felt conspicuous wearing her best clothes on a week day. She passed by the hardware shop and looked at the pedal bin and then caught the bus in to town. The town centre was full of young people. It was as though a decree had been passed forbidding the middle aged and the old the freedom of the city. Sandra felt quite daring as she walked along the pavements – as if she were breaking a curfew. She noticed a huddle of young people waiting by the clock tower – in her day, twenty-five years ago, this had been the traditional meeting-place, where you met your boyfriend before he got his courage up to be introduced to your parents. Sandra had always met Alan here. Had waited with a beating heart to see him alight from his bus. She remembered the careful preparations she had made to look nice for him. Spending hours on her hair and make-up and sometimes changing her clothes as much as three or four times. The agonies she had gone through when he was a few minutes late!

The clock struck half-past seven and she saw several of the young people glance at their watches. Then anxiously scan the pavements for their loved ones. The night was cold and a cutting north-east wind had blown up. The young people shivered in their fashionable but skimpy clothes. When did teenagers stop wearing coats? Sandra wondered. One very pretty girl was wearing a thin dress which stopped halfway down her thighs. She shivered and hopped from leg to leg, her high heels clattering on the cobbled pedestrian precinct. Sandra wanted to mother her, to remove her own coat and give it to the girl but instead she walked to the main shopping street and began to covet the goods in the shop windows. It was ten minutes past eight when she passed the clock tower again and the girl was still there. Her bare legs were blue and she clutched her handbag to her breasts as though the bag was a source of warmth.

'She's been stood up,' thought Sandra and a huge rage filled her. She decided to wait with the girl. She stood a few yards away, close enough to hear the girl's teeth chattering. Occasionally the girl shot Sandra a curious glance which said 'Forty-six-year-old women didn't wait under the clock tower for a date. They had homes of their own didn't they? Or they met in bingo halls or suburban pubs?' Their glances met and Sandra smiled. It was now twenty-past eight – the girl had been waiting for forty minutes. Her face was pinched with cold and anxiety. Sandra spoke. 'Cold, isn't it?' The girl mumbled something, agreeing, but making it clear that she didn't want conversation. It was half-past eight when Sandra spoke again.

'Looks like I've been stood up,' she said.

The girl turned to Sandra and said, 'And so have I.'

She started to weep and Sandra took a clean tissue out of her bag and handed it to her. Heads turned in the street as the pent-up tension the girl had been feeling turned to noisy sobbing.

Sandra steered the girl to a nearby pizza restaurant, where they sat in the warmth and discussed men. Her name was Kerry, she was seventeen and in love with a youth called Daniel Wainwright. He was unreliable and was on probation for criminal damage to a Belisha beacon. If Daniel had turned up they were going to a disco pub. She wasn't wearing a coat because Daniel didn't like her wearing coats. He wanted other men to admire her figure. Sandra knew better than to criticize young Mr Wainwright, but she made some unflattering observations about men in general. She surprised herself because she hadn't realized that she had these opinions, she didn't know where they'd come from. As she saw Kerry to her bus stop she heard herself saying, 'You mustn't let a man rule your life, Kerry, he mustn't be the be all and end all.'

Kerry said, 'I'll ring him up when I get home, perhaps he's poorly.' Sandra thought she ought to hurry home, she had never been late. Alan had taken it for granted that she would be always there waiting under the clock, looking nice and being pleasant, agreeing with whatever he said, and never making demands of any kind. She hadn't liked any of the furniture they had chosen as newlyweds for their first home but she hadn't liked to say so. It was the same for the carpets and the wallpaper. None of it was to her taste. She began to refurbish her home, she window-shopped and chose the most expensive chintzy three-piece suite and curtains that draped and swagged and were edged in satin ruffles. She then revolutionized her wardrobe. In her mind she threw away the sensible clothes that Alan had chosen for her from various chain stores and she redressed herself in floaty extravagant things in soft impractical colours that would show the dirt.

Alan was asleep when she returned at half-past eleven. He was on the wrong side of the bed, in her position. His back facing the door. There was a note on her pillow. 'Who is he? I'll tear his head off his shoulders.'

Alan who had trouble snapping a wishbone on Christmas Day!

The jar of freesias she had placed on the dressing-table scented the bedroom delightfully. She searched in her wardrobe for a negligée set she'd never worn. At the time she'd thought this frothy outfit silly. Had her sister gone mad, buying her this ridiculous present? she'd asked Alan.

But now!, oh now! she looked at herself and fell in love. The bows! The ribbons! 'I love you Sandra,' she said to her reflection. She flounced and posed in the frivolous nightwear. She took her old brown bedroom slippers off. She painted her toenails – scarlet. She lay awake most of the night wondering if she really loved Alan. Alan also lay awake, pretending to sleep, which was hard work. He was consumed with jealousy – an emotion new to him. Where did she go? Who did she meet? Why couldn't he broach the subject? When did they stop talking to each other and start writing notes on the sticky yellow things he brought home from the office?

'I've fed the cat.' 'We need light bulbs.' 'Your mother phoned.'

The very monotony of these remembered communications eventually sent Alan to sleep. When he woke he turned and looked at his wife, 'What was she *wearing* for God's sake?'

He dressed carefully, he splashed aftershave on his miserable face. He put on a perky tie. He went downstairs, there was a letter from Catherine . . . She'd got a job as a waitress. The tips were incredible! A drunk had given her a fifty-pound note! 'Did Sandra like the flowers? You don't mind if I call you Sandra do you, Mum? I'm not a child now. *I do love you Sandra,*' wrote their daughter.

Alan put the letter in his pocket. He would ring Catherine when he got to his office. Sandra must never know. The flowers breathed their tender scent through the house as Alan wrote his first romantic note to his wife.

'Buy that pedal bin.'

Faith

BY JOANNA TROLLOPE

When my mother died, she left me a bookstore. In England, you would call it a bookshop, but I prefer the word store. It suggests a treasure house to me, a place full of riches and surprises. 'Shop' is more pedestrian. A shop is for the purchase of kettles and bacon and birdseed.

My mother's bookstore is in a town some two hours' drive east of Seattle and a hundred miles south of the Canadian border. It was settled by Scandinavians in the last century and if it has a domestic symbol, it must be the coffee-pot. The whole town is crazy about coffee, addicted to it. There is a coffee shop, one of a national chain, opposite my mother's bookstore, and all day long people run in and out of it for pints and quarts of coffee in giant Styrofoam cups, carrying them back to their automobiles and places of work with a kind of tender greed.

Because we are so close to the Canadian border, and so far west, Alaskans come down to our town in the winter in search of warmth and work. A lot of them end up sleeping rough or in the beaten-up taxis they ply without a proper licence. Sometimes I find them sleeping in the bookstore doorway, and I give them money to go and buy coffee in the shop across the street. I'm sorry for them, but I don't want them in my doorway. The other immigrants are Asians from the Pacific Rim, mostly Vietnamese, who inhabit a dangerous and feuding underworld. They slip through our town on their way between Seattle and Spokane, eluding gang vendettas. Neither they, nor the drug-mazed Alaskans have any use in the world for a bookstore specializing in English literature.

Although she never said so directly, I believe my mother opened her bookstore to console herself for disappointment in marriage. She was English and not of a generation to abandon a bad marriage and in any case, my grandmother had been a Catholic and a pious woman and had instilled into my mother that vows were vows. My grandmother died when my mother was twenty, and left her daughter in the care of her father, a good-natured romantic man who managed a small theatre in Yorkshire, a pretty little theatre built in the time of the English Regency. My grandfather had no religion, my mother said, but he had dreams. Once, I knew, his dreams had got him into serious trouble, but of that my mother would say nothing.

Sometimes I wonder if I have taken after him. I am not a religious woman in any way but I have noticed that I have sometimes given way to dreams. My most intense dream was when I was twenty-four, and contemplating going to Boston to work in a distinguished publishing house, and I fell in love with a man in our town. He was married, with three children, and I had known him all my life, and I fell in love with a violence that quite terrified me. We had an affair, all one summer; I shall never forget it. And then quite suddenly he told me it was impossible, it was over, he was leaving. He collected up his wife and his children and, in the exaggerated way of people in this vast country of

455

ours, took off across seven states to Greensboro, North Carolina, where he vanished, like a stone thrown into a pool. I still cannot look at the daily weather charts on television with any equanimity when the weather girl's hand sweeps over the south-eastern states.

My mother took me back in, after the death of that dream. She made me a bedroom in the apartment above the store, and she gave me customers to look after and shelves to dust and arrange. My father, by then, was living in a two-room condo on the edge of Elliott Bay, in Seattle. My mother had bought the condo, and settled him there, along with his typewriter and his wardrobe of lumberjack shirts and his eloquent, empty declarations of one day being a renowned novelist, a chronicler of his time and the American North West. It was those declarations that had once made my mother fall in love with him. And I believe that it was those same declarations, after twenty years of talk and drink and quarter-finished manuscripts, that finally set her teeth on edge.

My mother determined to make a bookstore unlike any bookstore she had known in her English childhood. They were stiff, hushed places, she said, where one whispered as if in church, and was not allowed to touch books without specific intention of purchase. My mother's bookstore was in a converted dance studio – Latin American tangos were once taught there to combat the effect of our low grey winter skies – and she divided the space up with bookshelves to make a series of little rooms, and put armchairs about with worn cretonne covers, and reading lamps, and made a play area for children with toys on a rug and a rocking horse. She made friends of her customers; she encouraged them to read. They brought photographs of their grand-children to show her, and batches of cookies and problems. Sometimes, I must admit, I was jealous of her customers.

She also had festivals in the store. At Hallowe'en she filled the window with pumpkins and witches' hats and at the New Year, she dressed it up for Scottish Hogmanay with antlers and tartan ribbons. None of that I minded; indeed, I applauded her enterprise. But at Easter, and at Christmas, I cringed. I pleaded with her every year not to give way to cheap sentiment, to superstition, but she took no notice, she went ahead. Year after year, twice a year, I had to endure the spectacle, in this remarkable store that was a shrine to the glory of the English language, of a holy garden at Easter and a crib at Christmas.

My mother made the garden herself every year, with mosses and spring flowers, and a cave built of stones col-lected on Sunday walks in the woods. The crib she had bought on her honeymoon in southern France, in Provence. It was made of some kind of pottery clay, easily chipped and crudely painted. She set it up in the children's corner between two candles, in a ruff of ivy, and it caused me, her own and only child, mortification of the acutest kind.

When she died, I felt I had two choices. Either I allowed the bookstore to remain exactly the same, a shrine to her memory, or I made some changes. I decided upon the latter. I am a better businesswoman than my mother, and although I have inherited her love of literature, I am not alarmed by technology as she was, nor opposed to the commercial sense of stocking business and computer books. I cleaned up the store a little. I took away most of the armchairs because too many people had become accus-

457

tomed to lunching in them and I did not want my stock spoiled by smears of tuna mayonnaise. I changed my mother's sentimental festivals into book-orientated festivals to celebrate a prize-winning novel, a major biography, a breakthrough cookbook. I held business-book seminars at lunchtime and poetry readings at night. I started a gift-wrapping service and opened discount accounts for local schools and companies.

My mother's customers told me the store had lost its heart. I refrained from telling them that it was no longer losing money. My grief for my mother might make me resentful at any implied criticism of my treatment of her memory, but it wasn't going to make me forget my manners. The store was not as full as it had been when my mother was alive – sometimes it had resembled a bridal shower in noise and atmosphere – but I had three times the number of account customers, most of them institutions. I had to hire a boy to help with the packing.

At night, when I had finally closed the store and set the new security alarm, I would go up to the apartment above and drink a single glass of wine. Merlot was my choice usually; sometimes I drank a Cabernet Sauvignon. When I had drunk my wine, I fixed myself something quick to eat in the microwave, and then I would settle down with a mug of coffee – Costa Rica, medium roast – to my mother's papers. It was an indulgence, a nightly fix as cherished as the glass of Merlot.

It took me almost a year and a half to get through everything my mother left – diaries, letters, photographs, playbills, cuttings, reviews, notes and quotations scribbled on the backs of envelopes.

'I can't tell you everything that's happened to me,' my mother said before she died, 'I've forgotten the half of it. But you will find everything you want to know. It's all there.

I read everything. I am a methodical person, and I discarded nothing before reading it. I made scrap-books and collections of letters in labelled boxes. I put pictures into chronological order and slid them into the vinyl pockets of albums. I copied quotations into a commonplace book, and made a history of the founding of the bookstore in a green boxfile. I hoped it would be a therapy for me, but it was the reverse. Every night I longed to find something that would reconcile me to my mother's passing, and every night she rose before me, more vivid than ever, and I missed her wretchedly. I even felt – and I am aware this is unjust – that she, with her English heritage and English assumptions, had left me stranded here alone in a country which was my birthplace but to which, because of her, I could never quite belong.

I also felt estranged by her Catholic upbringing. There were several rosaries in her drawers, and a couple of prayer books, and above her bed had always hung a reproduction of a Della Robbia Madonna and Child, a blue and white porcelain plaque. I left all these things where I found them, but I would have preferred them out of the way. Just as I would have preferred my mother – so intelligent, so warm and witty, who scarcely in my lifetime even entered a church – not to have clung so blindly to these leftover trappings of a child's past. It sometimes seemed to me like a dreadful falseness in a person otherwise so transparently honest. But we didn't talk about it. It was the only thing we didn't talk about. She said that there was no point, because she could see that my mind was made up.

Early last December, we had some terrible rains. It wasn't cold, but it was wild and wet and windy and the weather kept customers away. A businessman, whom I supplied with computer books, said that I should consider relocating to the new shopping mall outside our town where there was all-weather parking. I told him I would then suffer from the proximity of a big chain bookstore, offering immense discounts, and he gave me a considering look and I could see he knew about the immense discounts already, and was turning his loyalty to me over in his mind.

When he had gone, I closed the store early and went upstairs to my apartment. It was not time yet for my ritual glass of Merlot, so instead I obeyed my mother's lifelong habit and made a pot of loose-leaf Lapsang Souchong tea. I took this with me into my living room and put on the lamps and pulled the drapes against the wet black evening. Only one drawer of my mother's papers remained to me, and I was dreading its being sorted.

It lay on the rug in front of the electric fire my mother had insisted upon as reminding her of England. I put my tea down on the floor and then I knelt down and lifted out a heap of assorted envelopes in which mail had come over the years and which my mother thriftily hoarded. One of them was large and bulky. It had come from Hatchards, the English bookstore in Piccadilly, London, and had probably contained a catalogue. Now it had a white gummed label stuck across it, not quite straight, on which my mother had written in her bold hand, 'About my father.'

I untucked the flap of the envelope and held it open

over my hearthrug. A shower of papers fell out, newspaper cuttings mostly, and a memo badly typed on sheets of thin white paper held together with a rusting clip. I unfolded some of the cuttings. They were from English newspapers, some provincial, some national, and there were disturbing headlines: 'Theatre Manager's Theft'; 'Manager Defrauds Theatre'; 'Hand in the Box Office Till'. I picked up the memo. I could see at once from the way it was typed that it had been typed by my mother. It had no heading, only a date – November 1956. In 1956 I was twelve, and my mother's bookstore was only two years old. By 1956 my English grandfather had been a widower for sixteen years.

I quickly saw that the memo had not merely been typed by my mother, but written by her too. She described my grandfather, so wedded to his theatre that he was there seven days a week, and six nights a week too, dressed in a black evening suit with a stiff-fronted white shirt and a black bow tie, welcoming theatre-goers into the foyer. She described herself, too, going to the theatre as a child with her father and standing on the empty stage listening to the seats tipping up in the empty auditorium as the temperature changed, as if a ghostly audience waited in perpetuity for the show to begin.

She said my grandfather did everything in that theatre. It belonged to the Town Council, who furnished a Board of Trustees like characters from an Arnold Bennett novel, bluff, uncompromising, respectable northern citizens. Once a month, my grandfather reported to the Board of Trustees and wrestled with their lack of imagination, their deep-seated philistinism. In the early spring of 1956, after thirty-five years of unremitting labour for the theatre, my grandfather asked for a few months' leave of absence. He gave the trustees to understand that he would be visiting his daughter and granddaughter in America. The trustees, much startled, eventually agreed, as long as he took it upon himself to find a temporary manager.

My grandfather did find a manager, but he did not come to America. Instead, he went in search of a place that my mother said had been the dream passion of his life; he went, alone, to look for the seat of King Arthur, for the site of Camelot.

It took him three months. He went from Caerleon upon Usk to Winchester, and from thence to Cadbury Camp near Queen Camel in Somerset and to Tintagel in the Camel county of Cornwall. He hired a good automobile and stayed in good hotels. He kept a comprehensive and scholarly journal which he bequeathed at his death to a northern university to assist those studying the legends of King Arthur and the works of the poet Tennyson. And while he was away the temporary manager discovered – with no difficulty since my grandfather had scarcely troubled to conceal it – that the funds used to pay for this comfortable and chimerical journey had been removed from the straitened coffers of the theatre.

My grandfather was summoned before the trustees. He was perfectly open. He had no defence beyond this longing that had built up to a craving to find the place that had so seized upon his mind. He was perfectly happy to repay the funds by working for no more than a pittance until the debt was cleared. He then stood and looked at those solid, practical northern faces, and waited for certain dismissal and probable arrest.

'And did you,' one trustee asked, 'find Camelot?'

My grandfather admitted that he had failed.

'Then we may assume that you no longer believe in the possibility of its existence?'

My grandfather was deeply shocked. 'Oh no,' he said, in gentle reproof, 'I believe as I ever did.'

The trustees let him keep his job. 'It was the only moment,' my mother wrote, 'in all his dealings with them, when he felt that their minds were in tune with his.'

I put the memo down and merely sat there on my living-room floor. My tea had grown quite cold. I sat there for perhaps half an hour and then I rose, rather stiffly, and went into the little room my mother had always called the box room, in her English way, where we kept the lumber of our lives. I hunted about among the bundles and bales until I found the cardboard box containing the little crib figures from Provence, and I carried it down to the darkened and empty store.

There was just enough light coming in from the street to illumine what I wanted to do. I cleared a space in the window in the display of Christmas cookery books I had arranged among ivy trails and decorative pyramids of clementines and walnuts, and in it I set out the Virgin Mary in her blue robe and Joseph in his brown one and the baby in his bed of stiffly painted straw. I added the shepherds to one side and the clumsy ox and ass to the other, and positioned the three Magi at a discreet distance to await the coming of Twelfth Night. Then I fetched from my kitchen one of the slow-burning nightlights my mother had liked by her bed during the last weeks of her life, and lit it, and put it below the figures in a small green saucer. It threw

463

a pool of faint light over the central figures and cast their shadows up against the books behind them. I stood and looked at the scene for a few moments, and then I went back upstairs to pour myself a glass of wine. I am not, as I have said, a religious woman and I never will be. But I knew then – and will now know for ever – the curious power of possibility.

Santa Claus' New Clothes

BY FAY WELDON

'I'm so happy we can all be together like this,' said Dr
Hetty Grainger. She sat in the antique carver chair at the
head of the Andrews' festive board. There was turkey for
the carnivores, and nut roast for the others, with a rich
plum and chestnut sauce to go with it, to prove vegetarians
can be indulgent too, not to mention sensuous, should
ritual so demand. There were crackers on the table, and
paper hats, and the scent of incense to remind everyone
that the Hindu, the Buddhist and the Christian gods (did
not the Trinity make three?) come from the same source,
were of the same oneness. The Andrews were the kind who
normally went to church once a year, to midnight service
on Christmas Eve. But not this year.

Dr Hetty Grainger's voice was sweet and low. She murmured rather than spoke, so that all the Andrew family,
usually so noisy, fell silent to hear her speak. 'I'm so happy
we can all be together like this.'

Although now in theory an Andrew herself, Dr Hetty
had retained, if not exactly her maiden name, at least the
one she'd acquired on her first marriage: Grainger. She'd
done this, she said, for her patients' sake. Troubled as they
were by one kind of stress or another, they hankered, or so
Dr Grainger said, for the tranquillity of continuity. To turn

from Dr Grainger into Dr Andrew would be to rub the salt of her own new-found happiness into the wounds of her clients' neuroses. 'Tranquillity' was one of Dr Grainger's favourite words. She used it a lot. The Sea of Tranquillity on the moon, for example, was a place with which Dr Hetty Grainger felt she had some special connection. It sent its sentient spirit out to her. Just to think of this unearthly place – so quiet, so dark, so cool, so beautifully named – lulled Dr Hetty Grainger and soothed her when she was in any way stressed.

'She's OK, I suppose, but she's ever so sort of *astral*,' said Penny, aged nineteen, on first meeting her father's therapist, soon to be her new stepmother. 'I always thought the moon was just a cold lump of rock which caught the light of the sun as it went round the earth. Or is it the other way round? But apparently no: the moon is all sentient spirit and significance and stuff. Or is she just talking crap?'

And Chris, Penny's sister Petula's boyfriend, said, 'No, it isn't crap. I think what Dr Grainger has to say is really interesting. This is the New Age, after all. Everything *means* something. And at least she makes your father happy.'

And, after that, opposition to Hetty Grainger within the Andrew family fell away. She made their father happy.

This year the Christmas Eve service on local offer seemed to the family a rather formal, old-fashioned and decidedly chilly event, in a church which had needed a new heating system for years and never got one. Hetty didn't want to go, anyway, so in the end nobody went. It would have felt impolite to leave their new stepmother behind.

Hetty Grainger was shortly built and mousily pretty, with soft natural hair which fell brownly around a pale plump face. But her hips were wide and filled the antique carver chair at the head of the table almost as amply as had those of her predecessor, Mrs Audrey Andrew. Dr Hetty didn't diet, as Audrey had. Dr Hetty knew that if you ate a healthy, wholesome diet, as additive-free as could be managed, you would be the weight and scale that nature intended, not that fashion dictated. If fate had made you pear-shaped, so be it.

Dr Hetty's husband Philip Andrew, engineer, regarded his new wife fondly from the other end of the table, carving knife poised ready to start on the turkey. His chin had doubled compliantly and happily since Hetty had replaced Audrey. Now his body was heavier but his life was agitation-free. Dr Hetty was against conventional medicine. The weighing of the body, the measuring of blood pressure, cholesterol, and so on, was just the orthodox doctors' way of adding to the stress of modern life.

Dr Hetty Grainger should know: she'd trained as an orthodox doctor. But a patient had died under her care in the hospital where she'd had her first job; not her fault: an inquest had exonerated her; but Dr Hetty had realized just how dangerous medical practice could be and had chucked the whole thing in. She'd wondered what do to with her life, had happened to meet Swami Avakandra, had been most impressed, had trained as an Avakandrist – a six-month residential course – and thereafter counselled in the Swami's name.

The Jungians looked kindly on the Avakandrists, who mixed the search for the archetype with a rich interpretation of symbols, made extensive use of dream and hypnotherapy, acknowledged a deep inherited collective unconscious,

467

whilst teaching that the knowledge of ultimate reality came through sexual love rather than through cognitive processes. A state of ill heath, whether mental or physical, would arise when a spiritually sensitive individual, consciously or otherwise, distanced himself from that ultimate reality. The task of the Avakandrist healer/therapist was to lead that individual back to appropriate paths of awareness. And thus Hetty had led Philip.

'I'm so pleased,' Dr Hetty Grainger went on, 'that after the upsets of the last year we can all come like civilized people to the Christmas ritual!' And she raised her glass of wine to all of them, the glass being one which just happened to have been Audrey's favourite. A strand of blue ran through the clear stem. Audrey had bought it at a car boot sale which she'd gone to with Philip, just a couple of years back. The goblet had turned out to be Venetian glass – what a snip! That had been one of the couple's last outings before Philip, facing possible redundancy at work, suffering from enigmatic heart pains, had become Dr Grainger's patient, or client, and had realized that the time had come to think about himself, not his family. Everyone's spiritual duty was to themselves.

'Yes, I'm so pleased we have managed to be civilized!' murmured Dr Hetty Grainger. 'Divorce and remarriage needn't be a source of grief and anger, if only they can be seen for what they are; a healthy readjustment and rearrangement of family relationships.'

And the Andrew family nodded an only slightly muted agreement. On either side of the refectory table were seated Henry, son number one, aged twenty-six, strong and handsome, and his pretty wife Angie with the little girls Sue and

Sal; Petula, twenty-two, daughter number one, with her artist boy friend Chris, and Penny, nineteen, daughter number two. And of course Martin, aged nine, Audrey and Philip's last child, the afterthought, the happy accident, the apple of everyone's eye. Child number four. Son number two.

Martin alone looked puzzled. Martin alone responded.

'What's "civilized"?' asked the child. Interesting! They all waited for Dr Hetty's reply. Dr Hetty would know. She was the one with the insights, who knew what maturity meant, who knew how peace of mind was achieved. She it was who had brought the Andrew family all together again round the Christmas table, in harmony after the previous season's dispersal and disarray. Dr Hetty who that day had stood in what was once Audrey's kitchen and was now hers, and had worked so hard to prepare the turkey, in spite of her vegetarian convictions, and made the nut roast, and the plum sauce with chestnuts, and boiled the organic pudding. Who, with Philip, the father, had strung the home with tinsel and sparkling globes, and adorned the tree with decorations taken from the cardboard boxes into which Audrey had so carefully packed them two Twelfth Nights back, before placing them in the cupboard under the stairs. Here Dr Hetty had come across them. 'So pretty!' she cried. 'In some things Audrey had such good taste.' Oh, Dr Hetty was generous.

In fact Dr Hetty Grainger was doing everything she could to repair the damage to nerves and family-togetherness perpetrated by Audrey, who had been so insanely negative, so angry, so bitter, so antagonistic to the point of insanity when her husband had fallen in love, wholly, fully, totally and for the first time, at the age of fifty-seven.

'But this marriage has been dead for years,' said Philip to Audrey. 'Why are you being like this? What are you objecting to? Surely it's better to be open about these things?'

'I didn't think it was dead,' said Audrey, 'and neither did you until you started going to see that bitch. How much does she charge you for the privilege of breaking up your marriage, your family, your life?'

'She's trying to save my life,' said Philip. 'You wouldn't understand. She believes in me, she listens to what I'm saying. She's patient, she's kind, sweet, gentle, never in a hurry.'

'You pay her to be those things,' wept Audrey. 'I'm just your wife. What chance do I have?'

None, it seemed. He had walked into her surgery, Dr Hetty Grainger had looked up from behind her desk and met his eyes and seen Osiris to her Isis. The love and compassion she felt for all her patients had blossomed at that moment into something amazingly particular. Philip Andrew was what her life was all about. Dr Hetty Grainger, his. Both had had to wait through dreary years, but now the time of decreed fruition had come. Her marriage was over; his family all but grown. Their drudge through the material world of pre-love was at last finished. Even before the sexual contact, so intrinsic a part of Avakandrist healing, both had understood that this was destiny. The initial touch, her finger stroking his cheek, had merely confirmed a love, a connection, already in existence.

Philip Andrew, engineer, nuts and bolts man, hadn't

known a thing about Isis and Osiris, but it all made sense when Dr Hetty explained it: spouse and sister both. His own previous ignorance now horrified him: why had he waited so long to start living? Yet he was fond of Audrey; he loved his children. He did not want to hurt them. He could only hope in the end wife and family would understand.

He loved the way Dr Hetty Grainger could explain and define not just the world but him to himself. She knew so much! But then she worked for a living; she wasn't idle; she got out into the world; she was open to fresh ideas. Audrey had always stayed home; she was a traditional wife. Her very existence could only be parasitical not just on her husband's maleness and income but on his mind. Audrey had docked her husband's spirituality as she tried to dock his sexuality, by owning it, withholding it, confining it. Not her fault, probably, but there it was. No wonder poor Philip had heart pains.

Hetty, for all her prim and gentle looks, would do anything Philip wanted, follow anywhere her patient's sexual fantasies led. This, too, was part of the Avakandrist teaching: the approach to ultimate reality through strange and winding paths, through unconditional yet unpossessive physical love. The Avakandrists didn't make much of this aspect of their doctrine in their public statements, didn't stress it too much in their publications; the world was a sexually nervous place, all too likely to unfairly misunderstand, to use scandal to condemn a life-enhancing and primarily spiritual movement. To put it bluntly, spouses, at the best of times the source of stress, would object too much if they knew too much.

But now it was Christmas Day; the second since the split, the first since Philip's divorce and remarriage. Hetty was now training, at Philip's expense, as a straightforward Jungian: she'd lost her dedication to the Avakandrist doctrine – her new husband did not want her showing too many male clients the way to health and happiness, selfish of him though it might be – and the family was once again gathered together under one roof and all was peace, prosperity and understanding. Tranquillity. Thanks to Hetty's strength of purpose and the lawyer she'd recommended to Philip, Audrey had failed in her attempts to take the house and disrupt the family.

Everything was fine, in fact. Except for Martin, staring at Hetty, still waiting for an answer, his big eyes narrowed in his little face. He spoilt his looks when he scowled. A pity Martin was so much Audrey's child in both looks and temperament: Martin the afterthought, the late child; the mistake, to put it bluntly. Philip had not wanted his declining years – or so he had regarded them pre-Hetty – filled with first nappies and infant protest, then school bills and teenage trouble; Philip had thought it self-willed and selfish of Audrey to go through with a late and unplanned pregnancy. Though once Martin had arrived he was of course welcome.

'What's "civilized"?' Martin asked, and Hetty publicly pondered. Everyone waited. Philip noticed that the skin of the turkey was pale, dry and stretched, not brown, wrinkled and juicy as it would have been had Audrey cooked it. As she had done for the family for how many years? Twenty-six? Well, Christmas was a tricky time for everyone, as Hetty had pointed out, now so many made sequential marriages. Meanness of spirit created a 'who goes where' syndrome.

When the point of the carving knife met the stretched skin, the flesh split and shuddered apart, and when the knife went into the meat the blade met a kind of pallid, stringy resistance. Audrey's turkeys dissolved to the touch of the blade, gave themselves up willingly to the feast. But then she basted. Hetty didn't bother. Philip shivered a little. Audrey was OK, though. She had finally gone to her parents in Edinburgh. Audrey had wanted Martin to spend Christmas up North; Philip felt that was out of the question. This was the house where Martin was accustomed to opening his presents; his elder brothers and sisters were coming for the day; the child should not be used in the parents' disputes.

'But Mum will be all alone, Dad, if I'm not there.'

'Christmas is for the children, Martin; stop worrying about the grown-ups. It's too bad of your mother to make you feel guilty.'

And in the end it had been decided through solicitors – Hetty felt it was always easier on the child to deal with such matters formally – that Audrey could not provide so domestic, peopled and cheerful a festive season as could Philip and Hetty, with their two incomes, so today Martin sat at his father's table, a little niece on either side of him – how they adored him! If only the boy wouldn't try and spoil the atmosphere: like his mother, a born wet blanket.

Dr Hetty Grainger's feeling had always been that Martin might need a little pressure to help him adjust to the new set of interpersonal relationships at home. Dr Grainger should know. She worked with children a good deal, though having none of her own. Dr Hetty was on something called the Victims of Child Abuse service register and spent an afternoon a week counselling at the Family Therapy Centre.

'What's "civilized"?' Martin repeated.

Martin rang his mother frequently, all the way to Scotland. That was understandable, that was OK, except his mother kept him talking and talking, no doubt on purpose. The telephone bill would probably amount, as Hetty observed one night to Philip, laughing her gentle laugh, tucking her short legs between his long skinny ones, to a few months' worth of her current retainer from the VCA.

'The trouble with Audrey,' Dr Hetty said, 'is that she's one of the Pall Bearers of life. I'm using an Avakandrist term here.'

'A pall bearer?'

'One of those people who blame others for difficulties they themselves have brought about. They're the hands which hold back the wheel of life, refusing ever to let go. You can tell them because they always cost you money!'

Audrey had never slipped her leg at night between Philip's. Audrey had liked to lie parallel but close, taking up whatever position her husband did: her strong, flawed, bony, cool body stretched against his. Only when Audrey was pregnant did she become warm – really warm: it was like sleeping next to a hot-water bottle. Hetty gave Philip her leg as a token but kept the rest of her body at a distance. Hetty was both intimate but remote: less familiar, less familial, more exciting, for ever a challenge to be approached with reverence and respect. Sometimes he worried about sleeping in the same bed with Hetty as he had for so many years with Audrey, but Hetty said a good bed was hard to find and had performed some kind of ceremony with candles and incense which would, she said, deconsecrate the bed, free the material object from its person-past. Hetty was spiritual, but not sentimental. Now, answering Martin's question, she took her time. Everyone waited.

'Civilized behaviour, Martin,' said Dr Hetty Grainger, finally, 'is acting, not acting out. For example, not running up telephone bills simply to spite your father and me.' She smiled as she spoke, to show she wasn't being in any way negative, merely constructive. Martin's eyes narrowed further. Audrey's eyes could look just like that, thought Philip. Martin should have been allowed to go to Edinburgh for Christmas.

'Civilized behaviour, Martin,' said Dr Hetty Grainger, 'is my understanding why you do such a selfish thing, and forgiving you for it, and helping you not to do it again. You want to hurt me, Martin, because you are angry and jealous: of course you are, you feel there is not enough love in your father for you as well as for me, but there is, I promise you there is.'

And she smiled again at Martin, brown eyes glowing. He did not smile back.

'Civilized behaviour,' said Dr Hetty Grainger to the whole table, her entire being alight, spoon poised over the Brussels sprouts – the whole serving system (Philip, turkey and nut roast; Henry, plum sauce; Hetty, vegetables) was held up – 'is coming to terms with and controlling our negative emotions, letting go. It is the manners which come from an open heart. It is sharing and caring. It is the open acknowledgement of our passions. It is moving over to let others in. It is smiling, even when we don't want to, until

475

the smile is real. We must try to be civilized, we must act civilized, otherwise we end up as the Serbs and the Croats, at each others' throats. Literally. Here in the Andrew family we've tried and we've succeeded, and, as I say, I'm proud of us all. That's my speech for today.'

She lowered her bright eyes; her face sweetly pink with emotion, vulnerable and charming. No wonder Philip loved her.

But Martin stared on, unsatisfied. Dr Grainger ignored him.

'Where's Granny?' asked Sal, who was four. 'Why is that lady in Granny's chair?'

'Granny chose not to be here,' said Philip, 'And I'm sorry about that too. She was invited, of course.'

'But she chose not to be civilized,' said Hetty.

Now Sal's eyes narrowed. Some characteristics do seem to run in the genes: or was she just copying Martin?

'Shall we pull a cracker, Sal?' asked Philip, quickly.

'No,' said Sal pushing away her plate. 'Crackers come between turkey and pudding, not now, stupid.' And neither Sal nor Sue, who was three and took her lead from Sal, ate a thing thereafter. Angie apologized for her children.

'They're so fussy about their food sometimes. And of course they're exhausted. They were so excited last night they couldn't sleep. What with Santa Claus and coming to Grandpa and Granny for Christmas Dinner—' Her voice faltered.

'Audrey preferred to be in Edinburgh,' said Philip, unnecessarily. 'You know how she loved those Scottish winters.'

'Mum isn't in the past tense for me,' said Henry. 'Not yet, at any rate.'

Martin, strangely, was holding Sal's little hand against his heart. Perhaps she gave him strength.

'Let go the past,' said Dr Hetty Grainger quietly and softly from her carver chair at the head of the table. 'I would have welcomed Audrey here today, but she refused: not even for her own children would she come. That is her decision. We must accept it, rise above the sorrow it causes us. Let us raise our glasses to a future filled with love.'

'I think you're a selfish bitch,' said Martin to Dr Hetty Grainger, clearly and stoutly. 'You've no business sitting there. That's my mother's chair. She's meant to be serving the vegetables, not you. Those are her plates you're handing round. You didn't even heat them. You talk so much everything's gone cold.'

'Little Martin,' said Hetty, 'I understand your aggression but there's more to this ritual than heated plates. Christmas is not about food, or presents, but about rebirth. It's the festival of starting over, and that's what we're trying to do. As for chairs and plates and so on, your Mummy told us she didn't want any of the material objects in this house, that your Daddy could have them all, and since your Daddy and I share everything, love and life, that includes the relevant things as well. Your mother walked away from all this of her own free will because she couldn't understand love; she was not a spiritual person. And your Daddy worked for this lovely house all his life, didn't he. Your Mummy just sat and enjoyed the fruits of his labour until one day the bough was empty and no fruit fell. Everything

477

is ripe for the time it's in; love must be worked for, earned. So here's to the future!'

How luminous her eyes were as she raised her glass.

'Bitch,' said Martin again. 'Why does nobody see she's a bitch?'

'Don't embarrass your stepmother,' said Philip. But nobody was following Hetty's example and raising their glasses. It seemed she was drinking alone.

'Is that lady sleeping in Granny's bed?' asked Sal. 'There was a nightie under the pillow which wasn't Granny's. I bet she is. Why doesn't Grandpa stop her?'

'Don't call him Grandpa any more,' said Hetty. 'Call him Philip. Grandpa is so ageing.' She was barely forty herself.

'Bitch,' said Martin again, and now he'd said it thrice it was Emperor's New Clothes time. The Andrews saw Hetty Grainger more clearly for what she was: a horror came amongst them. All except Philip, of course, so deep in his positive transference was he.

'Perhaps Martin had better go to his room,' said Philip to Dr Hetty, and Dr Hetty said that was a good idea. 'Aloneness quiets the unquiet spirit,' said Dr Hetty Grainger.

So Martin ran weeping to his room, into loneliness, except that Sal and Sue came running after him to keep him company and when Martin put his head under the pillow to bury his grief, they did the same, sharing the same breath. They ended up giggling, not crying.

The grown-ups finished their meal in silence, and that evening Martin made his phonecall to his mother longer than ever, this time on purpose.

'I told them,' said Martin proudly. 'I told them what she was. I saw her off. You can rely on me.'

LIVING WITH M.E.

THREE PERSONAL STORIES

LUKE MERCHANT

Luke is nine years old and was diagnosed as having M.E. in March 1993, although his parents suspect he has had it for longer than that – possibly since he was four years old. He was born with a pancreas problem which, while uncured, no longer creates difficulties for him.

He uses a wheelchair when he goes out of the house to help him conserve his energy. He has a home tutor for five hours and fifteen minutes a week. He has a sister, Hannah, who is three, and a foster brother, Daniel, who is sixteen. He lives in Essex.

My name is Luke and I got M.E. sixteen months ago. We went on an activity holiday and when I got home I was exhausted. Mummy and Daddy came home exhausted too but they got over it and I didn't. My mum took me to the doctor who said that I had M.E.

When I was ill it hurt everywhere. I started off seeing double, so that I would see two chairs instead of one, for example, and I would try and sit on the wrong one and fall on the floor. The double vision lasted about two months. I also got head-aches which felt like electric shocks. I still get these occasionally. My arms hurt sometimes and my heart starts going very fast, which is a bit scary. I have pins and needles in my hands and

481

sometimes in just one finger. It's not easy to explain these things and I don't think my friends really understand it, because I don't really. They know I get lots of aches and pains and that there are things I would like to do but can't. I'd really like to be able to ride a bike. Somebody broke my bike but when I get better some people are going to give me a new one. I'll ride it in the park.

I used to do horse-riding but I don't any more because of not being well. I could do massive jumps. I fell off loads of times because the horse bucked me off. I like computers; things like Game Boy and I've got a Sega Master System as well. I really like Super Mario 2 and Sonic. I read some comics but I don't read as much as I used to. I don't think I can concentrate that well. I can only read a page at a time. It's not really a problem for school work but I do need to concentrate for that. A tutor comes to my house so I don't have to go to school.

It's difficult to get up in the morning. Usually I'm tired and it depends if I've slept well that night. Once, although my tutor was there, I slept until two o'clock in the afternoon. I just thought it was about eight o'clock and I went downstairs and got quite a shock.

My tutor is nice. He understands if I'm tired out or something. He does origami with me and I like writing stories about my favourite friends, Robert and Nicky.

I'm not really worried about falling behind with my school work because I went into school with my old teacher and we'd been doing some work, sums, and I saw that my class had been doing the same things. I was quite pleased with that. It helps being taught one-to-one. I do forget things though. It makes me angry that I can't do things.

I'd like to go back to school because I enjoyed it so much.

I'm not saying I'm fed up with Mum, but I'd like to meet other friends.

My wheelchair is helpful. It's easier than walking because I get pains when I walk. My friends don't mind my wheelchair. First of all I had this very slow one and then I got a sports one which is blue. I went into class and all my friends said, 'Wow.' Some people stare at me in my wheelchair, but I don't take any notice. People ask why I'm in a wheelchair and I just say because my legs hurt.

Once I told my friend Josie that I'd got M.E. and he thought it meant a mental illness. He'd never heard of M.E. I tried to explain but it's difficult.

I get angry about not being able to walk very well because my legs are not very good. I get angry with my sister. I think it's because she's well and I'm not. I don't get angry with Mum . . . well, I get angry with her sometimes. I don't know why really. I get frustrated.

When I fell ill I felt like I wanted to die. I just wanted to get rid of my M.E. I often feel like I want to die. At Easter I didn't feel very well. I had a lot of pain and a lot of headaches and aches all over and I was tired. I told Mum and Dad I wanted to die and they were upset. I don't know if I really want to though. Probably when I die it will be even more painful. I cry a lot because I'm sad when I've got M.E. but I try and hide it from people. I do think my M.E. is going to get better. I can't have it for that long because you can't have it for your whole life, can you? I've got a little bit better. I think my pains have gone down a bit. I'm looking forward to being well. It would make me happier. I can't really remember what it was like when I was well before, it was such a long time ago. When I grow up I want to be a doctor – a GP. I want to be able to make people better.

ONDINE UPTON

*Ondine Upton is thirty-five and works part-time in charity mar-
keting. She lives in London with her partner, James Park. She
has had M.E. for seven years.*

One morning, I found myself lying flat on my back on a
London pavement, unable to move, with concerned faces peering down at me. It had happened before but never in such a
public place, and I could see the disbelief in people's faces as
I gently rejected their outstretched hands, explaining that I
needed to just lie there for ten to fifteen minutes, until the
muscles in my legs started to work again. It hit me then that
I was beginning to accept as normal what other people found
alarming.

I had been ill for over a year before I realized that I had
M.E. My image of the illness involved people lying prostrate
in bed, unable to move for months on end. Somehow I could
not connect that with the two or three days a month when my
muscles just would not work, or the fact that every evening
and weekend I could do little more than lie on the sofa and
read. And I was working. How could I have M.E.? The endless
rounds of doctors and alternative healers led nowhere. I was
told either I had nothing, or, by one naturopath, that I had a
little bit of at least six different viruses from Epstein Barr to
glandular fever.

My boss suggested it was psychosomatic. But it didn't *feel* psychosomatic when my muscles just stopped working, or my brain became so thick and cloudy that thoughts got lost and entangled. Not much use when trying to negotiate a contract or to get through the washing up without breaking something. Was it possible that I was resisting something from my past? And why, on many days, did I feel 'normal' and able to achieve a great deal, but on others wiped out by just a couple of hours' work?

In many ways it was a relief when I was eventually diagnosed as having M.E. I was told that I would be well again within the year; since I was young and generally healthy, they said that I fell into the group which recovered fast. Anyone could be ill for a year, I reckoned, and images of the novels I would read filled my mind.

It wasn't at all as I had imagined. My eyes would become tired after reading for half an hour, the words dancing on the page, and I would realize that I couldn't remember what I had just read. I found myself unable to understand long sentences, unable to connect the beginning, the middle and the end. Newspapers became deeply confusing.

I would sleep for hours and hours and then spend the rest of the day lying on my battered pink sofa. Because my muscles ached so much, I would have three long baths a day, the hot water temporarily easing the pain. Sitting up was difficult, standing was impossible; walking far more bearable, if and when I could do it. On many days, the flight of stairs to my front door seemed unconquerable: a trip to the corner shop on a good day would take two or three hours to recover from, draped over the sofa and wondering why those laconic Victorian heroines had ever seemed romantic.

I tried to just 'be' and let things happen, to do things when

485

I *could* rather than when I wanted to. My doctor's words became a mantra: rest is the only cure. The first two years were full of trying to find undemanding things to do, to fill the time and help me survive the waiting. I began to find pleasure in smaller and smaller things – like watching the raindrops run down a windowpane for an hour. Even television was too demanding, the noise and images becoming too loud and confusing after just twenty minutes.

Friends were one of the biggest challenges: how do you explain to someone longing to rush round with grapes and sympathy that actually you are too tired to see them? And how do you tell someone who eagerly rings with information about a recommended naturopath or homoeopath that you already have a list of twenty others waiting for the next time you have the energy to try yet another new treatment? You quickly discover who is easiest to have around, those who can casually make their own coffee and find the milk in the fridge, talk about simple things, and show a real interest in how you are coping.

It was frightening too that many of the friends whom I had found most exciting and stimulating were now beyond me. I needed much calmer people around me. To have an intellectual or demanding conversation was an impossibility, and just the attempt would leave me feeling desolate and aware of what I had lost, rather than warmed by the visit.

Often if I was with someone, I would find my energy unexpectedly fading away. Keeping a mechanical smile on my lips, I would nod and ask questions, but all the while I felt as if I was an actress playing the role of my former self. I could appear so vibrant, healthy and interested, that people would be surprised when I slipped up: smiling widely when someone told me a friend's mother had died, unable to connect the words and their meanings and the appropriate action. Other times I became absurdly clumsy – spilling things, knocking things off tables or piercing my cheek with a fork when aiming for my mouth.

Many friends thought that being ill meant I would have a lot of time on my hands – to do wonderful things like work out the meaning of life or read this century's major novels in chronological order. How could I explain that tiny things took hours and many of the practicalities of everyday life were beyond me? That actually I had less time than they did, even though they were working a long, hard week. Washing my hair was a major venture, only to be undertaken on a 'good' day. I hadn't realized either how difficult it is to be dependent on people for things: for someone else to have to do the shopping, washing, cleaning and to have to be grateful when actually you're longing to be able to do them for yourself.

In the first few months, I would get terribly angry or frustrated. Sometimes I would rant and rage, screaming and sobbing, some small conscious part of my mind knowing that I would only make my M.E. worse by exhausting myself. But letting the anger out did make things more bearable, if only for a while.

I felt that both my mind and my body had deserted me: Who was I? What was left? I felt hollow behind my smile, out of touch with anything that remotely resembled the me I had got to know over the past twenty-eight years. Sometimes I was aware that there was a me hovering there, waiting to come back. At other times, I felt as if I didn't exist.

Throughout all this, people kept telling me how healthy I looked. When I stumbled off a plane in Edinburgh and made a lunge for the waiting wheelchair, I could see that the stewardess thought I was shamming it. And most people never saw me when I was collapsed in a heap, hidden indoors. Nor did they know how many days' rest it took to prepare myself for a social event. Revelling in such occasions, I would push myself too far, letting my adrenalin give me an extra boost. I knew that I would pay the price but I couldn't resist the little demon inside me saying, what the hell, you're enjoying yourself, you can pretend to be a normal person occasionally.

I measured time: hitting the first anniversary of the day I stopped work was very tough. Hitting the second tougher still, but then things started to pick up slowly. I would notice I could do things that I hadn't been able to do before. Small landmarks mattered: occasionally driving a car short distances, walking a little further and a little more often, reading news-papers again or making a witty comment. At the end of the year, I started to fantasize about being able to do part-time work, and I began a one-morning-a-week counselling course. It felt like an amazing achievement.

Halfway through my fourth year, James' mother offered to take us both to Central America for Easter. How could I say no? But I almost did, terrified that my body wouldn't cope, and that I would be a terrible drag on them both as I hid in my room. I said yes, and amazed myself by not coming back to Britain for seventeen months.

I decided to stay in Guatemala and learn Spanish. The town of Antigua was flat, pretty and extraordinarily tranquil. Life was very easy for foreigners – and cheap. But it was the first time I'd been alone both emotionally and physically (no one around to just nip out and buy my toothpaste!). Some days I could do no more than lie in bed, but it didn't matter. I went on getting better. Within five months, I was up to travelling around Guatemala on beaten-up old buses, carrying one change of clothes and a book in a tiny cotton bag.

My life was beginning to feel like my own again. I worked for a short time with a Guatemalan nurse on an HIV/Aids education programme for prostitutes. Three months later, I couldn't resist the lure of South America stretched out before me. I spent another seven months travelling, building both my confidence and my health every step of the way. The more I could do, and the more I could look back and say, 'Wow, I couldn't have done that six months ago,' the more my confidence grew. It made me realize quite how much it had shrivelled, as my body and brain had ceased to do what I wanted them to.

My confidence returned as I notched up my achievements: the small ones like managing a two-hour walk or spending three hours talking without fading away. Or the larger ones like learning to scuba dive, swimming with hammerheads (sharks have been my lifelong phobia), surviving a guerrilla siege in a small Peruvian mountain town or travelling to Bolivian villages and dancing in their fiestas, the first foreigner they had seen for months.

Often I would have to spend two or three days in bed if I'd been overdoing things. I still had to cope with the isolation of being ill, viewed as the strange antisocial one, unable to join in the chatter if I was trying anything remotely energetic. After any exertion, regardless of where I was, I would lie flat on my back, eyes closed, half-meditating to cut out all noise and mental stimulation so that I could regain my energies.

London was a total shock after South America. I knew it would be, coming back to 'real' life and a mountain of things I'd left undone in my flat through years of illness. But I was extraordinarily lucky and got the first job that I applied for. Two of the interview panel knew enough about M.E. not to shy away from the risk of taking on someone like me. Working three days a week – even though the people I worked with were flexible and supportive – was extremely tough. I rapidly discovered that I only had the energy to work: the rest of my life had to be put on hold. My body became less fit again and my social life all but evaporated. But it was worth it, to be able to use my skills again, to feel that I was having a real impact, and to earn my own money again.

I'm still searching, no longer for a miracle cure, but for ways of maximizing my energy, and using it creatively. I am learning to pace myself better and am trying to find that elusive balance between activity and rest, work and friendship. I know I often overstep the limit, unable to resist the appeal of the moment, but equally realize that the more I pace myself, the more I will be able to do.

Paddy Masefield

Paddy Masefield is fifty-three and divorced with one daughter and two grandchildren. He was a theatre director, playwright and arts consultant. He has had M.E. for ten years and for that time he has been unable to work, but he sits on a number of arts, media and disability committees, while surviving on state benefits. He lives in Worcester.

Like a number of people who subsequently contract M.E., I was extremely energetic if not hyperactive up to the time I got it. I was directing a community play with two hundred and fifty actors in Carlisle. For recreation I was a marathon runner. I was also commuting over the country doing arts consultancy work, so I was leading an incredibly busy life. But it was an ideal life for me. I'd never been happier, nor in a sense freer, nor more able selfishly to do whatever I wanted to do in either work or leisure.

In the very early stages I experienced just a slowing down, although I didn't realize that this was what was happening to me. I'd stopped running, and the standard of my work as a consultant had begun to drop. I'd begun to do strange things without realizing that I couldn't account for them. For a two-hour drive, for instance, I would have to consume four bags

491

of chocolate sweets. I realized too that for about a month I'd been falling asleep in the middle of each day.

I went to the doctor saying that I had problems. 'Nothing the matter,' he said. 'What you should do is take more exercise.' As my doctor was desperately overweight and I was a marathon runner, this seemed quite amusing to me at the time. I did actually listen to him though, because I was already so confused. I started going on fifteen-mile walks because of not being able to run. Afterwards, I would pass out. Then one day I suddenly became a total allergic. This is a slightly dramatic state because if anybody walked into the house wearing aftershave, bang, I'd just pass out. Even a teaspoon of tap water, because of the chlorine, would knock me out. I got progressively worse and the assumption was that I'd got something like a brain tumour and probably didn't have much longer to live.

My family paid for brain scans, discovered that I didn't have a tumour, which left me still with the problem of not knowing what was wrong. I embarked on a series of interviews with different specialists in search of a reason for the multiple symptoms that had left me virtually unable to walk, read, think or speak. The overwhelming consensus was that I was hysterical and over-imaginative. 'After all, I did work in the theatre.'

Then Clare Francis came out about M.E. on television. At that time it was a terribly brave admission to broadcast. I was one of the thousands who saw that programme. It had an immense effect on me. I burst into tears because somebody for the first time was telling me what I had. I'd recognized myself absolutely in what she said, and was then able to discover consultants who specialize in M.E.

In retrospect, those early days of M.E. are still a bit of a haze. One of the dominant symptoms was the lack of short-term memory. While with great effort I can recall nearly all events before M.E., for quite large areas of my life since then memories are blotted out. It was extremely difficult for me at that time to write more than half a dozen lines. Focusing was a big problem. Because I couldn't read, people gave me tapes of books and radio programmes, but I found myself switching them off after five minutes, unable to remember who the characters were or follow the plot. Having no short-term memory did have its comic sides. At night you might put a pound of butter on the doorstep and try to put the cat in the fridge.

The prevailing feeling was that my body had gone bad on me, like something left in the fridge for too long. I had no facility to be objective or explain things as I can now. It would be a hard enough struggle to say, 'It's like your brain being filled with porridge,' – which wouldn't mean much to people, so I'd say, 'Well, try and imagine you've got the worst hangover you've ever had, you've got a really bad bout of flu, you've got a migraine and you've just run fifteen miles in that condition.' And that still wouldn't be a really adequate description.

So I tried another analogy. Getting my body to respond was like running a large car on a torch battery. You could sound the horn for fifteen seconds, turn on the lights for ten seconds or get the engine to run for five seconds. You certainly couldn't do all three at once. To this day, if I try to talk while I'm walking, I'm liable to fall over, and any day may bring a choice between either getting dressed *or* making two phone calls.

I lost nearly all the friends I had before M.E. either because they couldn't cope with the change in me or couldn't cope with someone so severely ill, or just because their lives took them elsewhere. At first, I was confined to a single room in a single house, so there was an immediate sense of deprivation and loss, of feeling very alone because the world didn't understand me. The inability to handle stress caused by M.E. can make you very erratic in personality. Your mood swings violently when under great pressure, and there's a tendency to have panic attacks. I remember trying to get out of the house because I thought it would be healthy to take some exercise. Within a hundred yards of hobbling along on two sticks, I was lying under a hedge curled up in a foetal position, crying in terror of the open road ahead of me.

In general, I've been slow to understand how to manage my illness. It's fairly embarrassing to me that I only realized, after seven years of illness, that if I applied to the council for a hundred per cent grant to install a stairlift in my house, it would mean I would have more mental energy as a result of not using my physical energy in trying to walk up and down my stairs twice a day. I only acquired a power wheelchair three years ago because a disabled colleague asked what on earth I was doing with a manually operated one. It just hadn't occurred to me.

Colleagues with M.E. and disabled colleagues in general have been my salvation. It has been like acquiring a whole new family, and it is they, in the main, who have become my friends in times of need, my accomplices in small shared jokes and above all mentors in my world of ignorance. It is they who have encouraged me to focus on my abilities, instead of on my impairments. Through them I have learnt that I am only 'disabled' by the world if I let it do that to me. So I no longer see myself as someone *unable* to read, or walk, or write but as someone who can and does do an immense amount. I sit on the Lottery Distribution Board of the Arts Council of England, chair theatre and editorial boards and make speeches about M.E. all over the country.

I now focus on my own management of my illness as the

key to survival. Because if you try to be super-heroic, as I did initially, and believe that you can conquer it by refusing to admit that it exists, or just walk further than you can actually safely walk, you will be disabling yourself as surely as someone with a broken leg who rips off the plaster cast and insists on playing football. The two times I've been hospitalized in an emergency, and the times I've had major relapses putting me back into bed for months, followed bad planning in my life when I tried to do too much, or got too excited. It's the hardest thing to spot, when you're about to do too much. Some are lucky and just get more tired and can't speak, but others of us are like hyperactive children. We go over the top into false energy and are briefly wonderful company, but end in tears and severe relapse.

If you can manage it, if *you* can be the boss, then you can live with M.E. and still have a full life, even though there are hours, days, months and even years when it gets the upper hand. I've just come through a year of being frequently confined to bed for weeks. Although that's a very negative experience, I know that by accepting being in bed, by being in control of my life, then I'm in control of the M.E. and that's what managing is about. It means being practical and realistic enough to recognize the extent of the M.E., the severity of the M.E. and what you might at first call the limitations imposed by it.

M.E. Factfile

Who has M.E.?

There are at least a hundred and fifty thousand people in the UK suffering from M.E. (myalgic encephalomyelitis) of all ages and backgrounds.

Twenty-six thousand of them are children. More women than men are affected.

Twenty per cent of sufferers will be permanently disabled.

Sixty per cent will recover a proportion of their former functioning, while never regaining full health.

Most were fit and active up until the time when they contracted M.E.

Teachers, doctors and other health workers are the groups most at risk. This is probably because their jobs combine continuous exposure to infection with gruelling work schedules.

What are the symptoms?

M.E. is the most severe of the various chronic fatigue syndromes.

Recent research suggests that M.E. is a neurological disease that affects the immune system. It causes extreme physical and mental exhaustion and persistent flu-like symptoms.

Sufferers are also likely to have a number of secondary symptoms, the most common of which are:

Muscle weakness and pain
Lack of concentration
Poor memory
Headaches and migraines
Blurred vision
Disturbed sleep
Panic attacks
Depression
Rapid mood change
Hypersensitivity to light and sound
Low-grade fever
Digestive problems
Food allergies
Alcohol intolerance
Abnormal sweating
Tinnitus
Poor circulation
Numbness

Symptoms tend to fluctuate considerably, becoming more or less severe within minutes or days. They are invariably aggravated by over-exertion.

What causes M.E.?

The cause is still unknown. Some researchers think M.E. is caused by a single virus which had yet to be identified. Others believe that it is multicausal, usually triggered by a prolonged viral infection evolving into M.E. when it is combined with

497

other factors affecting the immune system. These include bacterial infections, antibiotic use, nutritional deficiency, allergy, food sensitivities, vaccinations, trauma and stress.

There is no single diagnostic test to indicate that someone has M.E. All that doctors can do is to look at the patient's history and symptoms and rule out conditions that have similar symptoms, such as glandular fever and myasthenia gravis. M.E. has been recognized by the Department of Health and the World Health Organisation, but some doctors still do not take the disease seriously. As was the case some thirty years ago for those with multiple sclerosis, it is sometimes dismissed as 'all in the mind'.

What has research revealed so far?

Research into M.E. is desperately underfunded, and little is known about the causes, the effects of the disease or what treatments can aid recovery.

Research funded by Action for M.E. and carried out at the Middlesex Hospital by Dr Duvva Costa has shown a significant reduction to the blood flow in several areas of the brain, but especially in the brain stem, in M.E. patients compared to normal controls and depressed patients. This could account for the 'brain fog' experienced by so many people with M.E. In muscle biopsies of people with M.E., a large number show evidence of structural changes and indications of a persistent virus. The only treatment that has been scientifically demonstrated to have any positive effect of the majority of patients is Oil of Evening Primrose, which has been shown to alleviate some symptoms in eighty-five per cent of sufferers.

498

How is it treated?

There is as yet no cure for M.E. The earlier the illness is diagnosed and the patient gives up strenuous activity, the better the prospects of an early recovery.

Doctors with experience of M.E. normally recommend prolonged but not total rest. Patients are advised to 'pace' themselves. They are advised to use only seventy-five per cent of available energy, leaving the surplus to aid the healing process. Many find it very hard to gauge how much energy they have to spare, as it fluctuates so rapidly. This erratic nature of the illness, with alternating 'good' days and 'bad' days, makes it very difficult for sufferers to plan their lives.

A vast range of alternative treatments has helped some people, but none has ever been shown to have consistently good results. Most, though, find that they benefit from adjusting their diets, ruling out foods to which they have developed an intolerance and increasing their intake of vitamins and minerals.

Exercise is an extremely controversial area. Action for M.E. believes exercise may be of benefit as long as it is kept well within the limits of the patient's capacity. The graded exercise programmes that encourage patients to push themselves beyond their capacity, to the point of relapse, should be avoided as this leads to a reduced chance of full recovery.

Many sufferers spend a lot of time and money looking for treatments that will improve their condition. Unfortunately there is no research or proven results to guide them in their exhausting search.

Recovery prospects

Most sufferers recover gradually over a period of between two and ten years, though few experience full health again. The majority feel that their recovery is helped by learning how to manage their illness.

Many have periods of feeling well, alternating with serious relapses.

Some remain chronically ill for the rest of their lives.

Action for M.E.

Action for M.E. was set up in 1987 to provide information, support and other services to people with M.E. It funds research, and campaigns to bring about the full recognition of M.E. as a physical illness, as well as working for improved treatment, benefits and services for sufferers.

Action for M.E. believes that orthodox and complementary approaches should be combined in treatment. It sees the condition as one that has primarily organic causes, but where various forms of stress may play a role as a co-factor. It is a sufferer-led organization, with the majority of its council and patrons having either M.E. themselves or a close relative with the illness.

Members receive the organization's journal, *InterAction*, which is recognized to be one of the most informative and lively self-help journals, valued both for its broad perspective and its holistic approach. They also have access to a comprehensive series of Fact Sheets, a twenty-four-hour helpline (0891 122976) and a network of support groups. Other services include a telephone counselling service, a welfare benefits advice line and therapy information line.

In the near future, we are hoping to provide more support to parents of children with M.E. and to set up an advocacy programme which will provide a voice to sufferers who find themselves confronted by the scepticism of doctors, employers and friends.

Action for M.E. is a small but dynamic national organization, which is attracting increasing support. Membership now stands at eight thousand. It patrons are Melvyn Bragg, Clare Francis, Jimmy Hood MP and Sir David Puttnam. Its President is Lady Elizabeth Anson. It is poised, ready to develop the services it offers to everyone with M.E. and to invest in urgently needed research. Any donation you are able to contribute will make an enormous difference to all those with this as yet little understood disease.

and Chronic Fatigue

You've got flu
And a hangover
And you've just run five miles.
How do you feel?

Like someone with M.E.

❑   **YES.** I would like to help Action for M.E. with its crucial work.

I enclose a donation of: ❑ £100 ❑ £30 ❑ £15
_____Other

❑   I have M.E. and would like to know more about Action for M.E. I enclose a large SAE for more information.

Name ....

Address ....

....

.... Postcode ......

Telephone Number ....

Please make cheques payable to Action for M.E. and send to: Action for M.E., P.O. Box 1302, Wells, Somerset BA5 2WE.

✂

About the Authors

DOUGLAS ADAMS (born 1952) created *The Hitch Hiker's Guide to the Galaxy* as a radio series, and then wrote it again as a novel. He read English at Cambridge and at various times in the past has worked as a hospital porter, barn builder, chicken shed cleaner, radio producer and script editor of *Dr Who*. He has written five novels in the increasingly inaccurately named Hitch Hiker's Trilogy, and two novels about the detective Dirk Gently. He lives in London with his wife, daughter and a large collection of left-handed guitars.

JEFFREY ARCHER became Britain's youngest MP at twenty-nine, when he won the Louth by-election in 1969. On the verge of bankruptcy, he resigned five years later and wrote his first novel, *Not a Penny More, Not a Penny Less*. His novels have been published in twenty-three languages and sixty-one countries, and have sold over one hundred and twenty-five million copies worldwide. He became a life peer in 1992 and lives in Grantchester with his wife Mary and their two sons.

IAIN BANKS was born in 1954 in Dunferline, Fife. He went to Stirling University and was variously employed before giving up his day job in 1984, on the publication of *The Wasp Factory*.

He writes nominally mainstream books under the above name and – following an arguably successful bid for the World's Most Penetrable Pseudonym title – science fiction novels under that of Iain M. Banks. He lives back in Fife now, where such eccentricity is tolerated.

CHARLOTTE BINGHAM suffered from M.E. twenty-five years ago, and so has great sympathy for the condition. In partnership with her husband, Terence Brady, she has written for such series as *Upstairs, Downstairs, Take 3 Girls, No Honestly* and *Pig in the Middle*. She is also the author of fourteen novels. In 1995 she won the Romantic Novelist Award for *Change of Heart*.

CATHERINE COOKSON was the illegitimate daughter of Kate whom she believed to be her older sister. She was manageress of a workhouse laundry in Hastings. Later she had a guesthouse where she met her husband, Thomas Cookson, a grammar school master. Now in her ninetieth year, she has had ninety books published, sold over one hundred million copies worldwide and been made a Dame. She has suffered from M.E. for years.

JILLY COOPER was employed as a receptionist, copy writer and publisher's reader before becoming a columnist for the *Sunday Times*. She has written over thirty books including romances, five blockbusting novels (*Riders, Rivals, Polo, The Man Who Made Husbands Jealous* and *Appassionata*) and children's stories. She has been married to her husband Leo Cooper for thirty-four years and they have a son and a daughter. Her hobbies include music, mongrels and merrymaking.

LEN DEIGHTON's first novel, the legendary spy thriller *The Ipcress File*, was published in 1962 and made into a film starring Michael Caine. Since then, he has written more than thirty books, many of them spy thrillers (such as the *Game, Set* and *Match*, and *Hook, Line* and *Sinker* trilogies) but also several books on military history, including the recent *Blood, Tears & Folly.*

COLIN DEXTER, a former Classics master, created Inspector Morse – one of Britain's most popular and engaging detectives – in his first novel, *Last Bus to Woodstock*, which was published in 1975. A number of Inspector Morse books have been televised, starring John Thaw and Kevin Whately. Dexter has won both the Crime Writers' Association Gold and Silver Dagger Awards twice.

KEN FOLLETT was born in Wales in 1949, and is the son of a tax inspector. After studying philosophy at University College, London, he worked as a journalist in Wales and then in London. He wrote novels in his spare time, until his eleventh novel, *The Eye of the Needle*, became a bestseller. He now has over twenty books to his credit. He is a Shakespeare enthusiast and keen amateur musician, playing bass guitar in a blues band. He lives in London with his second wife, Barbara.

CLARE FRANCIS is the author of six internationally bestselling novels, *Night Sky, Red Crystal, Wolf Winter, Requiem, Deceit* and *Betrayal.* Before these, she wrote three non-fiction books about her voyages across the oceans of the world, *Come Hell or High Water, Come Wind or Weather* and *The Commanding Sea.* She first had M.E. as a teenager and then recovered until 1985 when she became ill again. She was actively involved in setting up Action for M.E. and was their President from 1988 to 1995.

DICK FRANCIS (born 1920) was a child star at horse shows all over Britain. In 1948 he became a professional National Hunt jockey. He rode for the Queen Mother and from 1953 to 1954 was Champion Jockey. After he retired from racing, he became racing correspondent for the *Sunday Express* and started to write racing thrillers. He has been awarded an OBE, as well as the Crime Writers' Association Cartier Diamond Dagger for his outstanding contribution to the crime genre. He and his wife, Mary, divide their time between England and the British West Indies.

GEORGE MACDONALD FRASER, former soldier and journalist, is the author of the internationally popular Flashman novels and of the Private McAuslan stories. His other novels include *Mr American*, *The Pyrates* and *The Candlemass Road*. He has written a history of the Anglo-Scottish Border Reivers, *The Steel Bonnets*, and his recollection of the war in Burma, *Quartered Safe Out Here*. His screenplays include *Octopussy* and *The Three Musketeers*. He describes his hobbies as snooker and talking to his wife.

STEPHEN FRY, writer, actor and comedian, is probably best known for his television roles in *Jeeves and Wooster*, *A Bit of Fry and Laurie* and *Blackadder*. As well as writing two books, *The Liar* and *The Hippopotamus*, he has also written several plays and screenplays and contributed a weekly column to the *Daily Telegraph*. His hobbies include smoking, drinking, swearing and pressing wild flowers.

PHILIPPA GREGORY trained as a journalist before joining BBC radio. She read history at Sussex University and has a PhD in eighteenth-century literature from Edinburgh University. A number of her novels are set during this period, including her most recent novel, *A Respectable Trade*. She lives with her family in West Sussex where her bestselling Wideacre trilogy was set.

JAMES HERBERT, the youngest of three brothers, was born in the East End of London. After leaving school, he studied at Hornsey Art College. His first novel, *The Rats*, was enormously successful and he is now Britain's number one horror writer. His seventeen novels include *The Magic Cottage*, *Haunted* and *Portent*. He lives with his wife and three daughters in Sussex and London.

ELIZABETH JANE HOWARD (born 1923) is the daughter of a timber merchant and a ballet dancer. After studying to be an actress, her varied career included modelling for fashion magazines and working as a continuity announcer for the BBC. At twenty-seven, she wrote her first novel, *The Beautiful Visit*, which won the John Llewellyn Rhys Memorial Prize. She has written a number of novels, short stories and plays for television and is best known for her evocations of English life during the war years in the Cazalet Chronicle.

P. D. JAMES was born in Oxford in 1920. She has worked in the National Health Service, and in the Home Office, first in the Police Department and then in the Criminal Policy Department. The majority of her thirteen crime novels feature the poet detective Adam Dalgliesh. She chaired the Booker Prize Panel of Judges in 1987 and served as a Governor of the BBC from 1988 to 1993. In 1991, she was awarded a life peerage. She is a doctor's widow and has two daughters and five grandchildren. When not writing, she enjoys exploring churches and walking by the sea.

KATHY LETTE's first novel, *Puberty Blues*, leapt straight onto the Australian bestseller list and became a major movie. After several years as a newspaper columnist in Sydney and New York, and as a TV sitcom writer in Los Angeles, she wrote *Girls' Night Out*, *The Llama Parlour* and *Foetal Attraction*. She now lives in London with her husband and two children.

MICHAEL MOORCOCK (born 1939) had his first novel published when he was twenty-three. Since then he has written more than eighty books, both fiction and non-fiction, but is best known for his fantasy writing. For a time, he wrote and performed with the rock groups Hawkwind and Blue Oyster Cult, and from 1964 to 1980 he edited the fiction magazine *New Worlds*. His novel *The Condition of Musak* won the Guardian Fiction Prize. He lives in Texas and London.

JOHN MORTIMER was born in 1923 and educated at Harrow and Brasenose College, Oxford. He is a playwright, novelist and former practising barrister. He has written many film scripts, stage, radio and television plays. Horace Rumpole is probably his best-loved character, and all the Rumpole stories have been made into television series. He won the BAFTA Writer of the Year Award in 1980. He lives in the Chilterns with his wife and daughters.

PATRICK O'BRIAN is the author of the Jack Aubrey and Stephen Maturin novels, about the British Navy during the Napoleonic Wars. As well as his seventeen novels, he has translated Simone de Beauvoir and André Maurois into English and has written a highly acclaimed biography of Picasso.

EDITH PARGETER (1913–95) worked as a chemist's assistant and dispenser for seven years before joining the WRNS. As Ellis Peters, she wrote medieval thrillers about Brother Cadfael, which were televised starring Derek Jacobi. Under her own name, she wrote historical novels and short stories. She translated classics from Czech into English and won an award for her services to Czech literature. In 1994, she was awarded an OBE for her services to literature.

ROSAMUND PILCHER was fifteen when the Second World War broke out. On leaving school, she worked in the Foreign Office and then joined the WRNS. Her first story was published in *Woman and Home* when she was just eighteen. She has written many novels, including *The Shell Seekers*. She lives near Dundee with her husband. They have four children and eight grandchildren.

RUTH RENDELL, creator of Chief Inspector Reginald Wexford, has been writing crime novels for over thirty years. She has won a number of awards for her work, including The *Sunday Times* Award for Literary Excellence in 1990 and the Crime Writers' Association Gold Dagger (four times). She is a Fellow of the Royal Society of Literature. Her novel *King Solomon's Carpet*, written under the pseudonym Barbara Vine, was shortlisted for the Whitbread Award.

LESLIE THOMAS (born 1931) lost his mother and father within six months of each other when he was only twelve. He and his younger brother, Roy, grew up in a Dr Barnado's home. After his first novel, *The Virgin Soldiers* (influenced by his time in National Service), was published Thomas gave up working for newspapers and became a full-time writer. He now has twenty-three novels, three travel books and two autobiographical accounts under his belt. His interests include antiques, classical music and islands, all of which he shares with his wife, Diana.

SUE TOWNSEND was born in Leicester and left school at fifteen. She was employed in a variety of unskilled jobs before her writing career took off in the early 1980s when she won a Thames Television Bursary competition. She is best known for her disarmingly honest but very funny portrayal of a teenage schoolboy, Adrian Mole, who first appeared in *The Secret Diary of Adrian Mole Aged 13 and ³/₄*. She is married and has four children.

JOANNA TROLLOPE was born in Gloucestershire in 1943. She worked in the Foreign Office and was a teacher for twelve years, before becoming a full-time writer. Her novels are quintessentially English and address the daily dilemmas of modern life, usually from a woman's perspective. *The Choir* and *The Rector's Wife* have been serialized for television. She has written historical novels and seven contemporary novels, of which *The Best of Friends* is her latest.

FAY WELDON studied Economics and Psychology at St Andrews University. After a decade of odd jobs and hard times, she started writing and now has over twenty novels to her name, as well as many television and radio plays. Her work is translated into most world languages. Her ninth novel, *The Life and Loves of a She Devil*, was made into a film starring Meryl Streep and Roseanne Barr. A Fellow of the Royal Society of Literature, she is married, has four sons and lives in London.

Copyright
Acknowledgements

and Chronic Fatigue

**You've got flu
And a hangover
And you've just run five miles.
How do you feel?**

Like someone with M.E.

☐ **YES.** I would like to help Action for M.E. with its crucial work.

I enclose a donation of: ☐ £100 ☐ £30 ☐ £15 _____Other

☐ I have M.E. and would like to know more about Action for M.E. I enclose a large SAE for more information.

Name ....

Address ....

....

.... Postcode ......

Telephone Number ....

Please make cheques payable to Action for M.E. and send to: Action for M.E., P.O. Box 1302, Wells, Somerset BA5 2WE.

✂

79M

3388